PAUL;
LEAP INTO THE ABYSS!

Other books by

Nik C. Colyer

Channeling Biker Bob 1 Heart of a Warrior
Channeling Biker Bob 2 Lover's Embrace
Maranther's Deception Lost in the desert
Kicking Ass and Taking Names
Poetry through the eyes of a tough guy

All books avaliable through
Singing Reed Press
228 Commercial St. #173
Nevada City, CA 95959
Bikerbob@ncws.com
530 470-8739

Acclaim from Readers

"This third one is wild. I like how Mr. Colyer led us down the path of the female experience.
> Jacklyn Katcher Billings, MT

"What a great desert journey. I loved the mystical part.
> John Dunkin St. Louis, MO

"Don't pick up this book unless you have nothing else to do, because I couldn't put it down.
> Jason Biggs Inglewood, CO

"Wow, the desert trip was fantastic. I was so there, I had to go visit the area to see if it really existed.
> Cindy Woolerman Los Angeles, CA

"I loved Nick Brown. He reminded me of myself a few years ago. I can't wait for the forth book.
> Tim Bushing Brookings, OR

"It was so exciting, I read this one without stopping."
> Ronnie Pepper Visalia, CA

"Nik Colyer's work always leaves me thinking. My husband and I have read this series to each other."
> Susan Hurshing St. George, UT

"Left me wanting more."
> Pamela Smith Boulder, CO

This book is dedicated to the

WEST

The West symbolizes shadow,
the element water and autumn.
The West brings the setting sun,
oceans, emotions and courage.
The West rules: feelings, love,
sorrow, weeping, fertility, the
unconscious mind, dryness, skin,
hair, the lakes, rivers, streams,
pools and springs. Its color is
Black. The animal is Jaguar.
I honor the West.

If modern man stands at the far edge of the age
of reason looking over into the abyss of his deeds,
what can he see?

Without a strong inner emotional life, a man of
intellect lives in an isolated, empty, ivory tower
disconnected from all the things he might love.

Channeling
Biker Bob 3

Third in a four part series Nik C. Colyer

Heart of a Warrior
Lover's Embrace
Magician's Spell
Wisdom of the King

Singing Reed Press
Nevada City, CA

Singing Reed Press trade paperback: June 2006 1st. edition

Publisher's Calaloging-in-publication Data
(Prepared By the Donohue Group)

Colyer, Nik C., 1948-
    Channeling Biker Bob. 3, Magician's spell / Nik C. Colyer. - Singing
Reed Press trade pbk. 1st ed.
    p. ; cm.

    "Third in a four part series: Heart of a warrior, Lover's embrace,
Magician's spell, Wisdom of the king [not yet published] ."
    ISBN: 13:   978-0-9708163-2-0
    ISBN: 10:   0-9708163-2-4
    LCCN 2006925885
1. Men--Psychology--fiction. 2. Women--Psychology--Fiction. 3. Men-
-Conduct of life--Fiction 4. Women--Conduct of life--Fiction. 5. Man-
woman relationship--Fiction 6. Harley Davidson Motorcycle--Fiction. 7.
Marijuana abuse--Fiction. 8. Guides (Spiritualism) --Fiction. I. Title.
II. Title: Magician's Spell

PS3603.047 C433 2006
813/.6   2006925885

Book design by Tilly Sinclair   Cover design by Zoe Alowan
Thanks to my editors, Bobbie Christmas and Melissa Marosy.

Printed on 100% post-consumer, chlorine free paper
in the United States of America
10 9 8 7 6 5 4 3 2 1

To little
JANICE MOULDS

AUTHOR'S NOTE

Since I've written about the masculine journey in the first two Biker Bob's, it is time to bring the feminine into the picture.

I am a man, and as much as I try, I cannot see the story from a female point of view. I did many hours of study, asking hundreds of questions of my wife, close women friends, and my editors to get the female perspective as right as possible.

Although this book continues with the weekly men's meetings in the desert, long rides with the One on One gang, mystical adventures in the desert, intimate conversations with Biker Bob, many of the following pages will also journey into the feminine experience.

Everything I have written about concerning men and women's issues in the Channeling Biker Bob series comes as a direct result of successfully working day to day conflicts in my marriage.

I place the inspiration for most of what I have written at the doorstep of my ever-searching wife, Barbara, for without her, I would have been content to live out my life as many men; working, going to the movies, taking vacations, without thinking much about anything beyond the next turn. In this series, as in life, she truly is my muse.

Hope you enjoy the story.

Nik.

One

Odyssey

I kick start the engine of my Indian, wave goodbye to Nick and his girlfriend, and take a long sweeping arc around the top of the hill. When I start down, I'm beginning my odyssey. Whatever is going to happen is going to happen. However far I'm destined to get is how far I'm supposed to go.

The drive through town is a little sad. I have no idea if I'll ever see Victorville again. I want to return to Stewart and my family, but starting a journey like this, I don't know where I'm going to end up. Bob has something in mind and I'm compelled to follow his lead.

Once through town, I pull out onto Highway 29 and head west toward the open desert.

In fifteen minutes, I pass through Twenty-Nine Palms, and ten minutes later, the town of Joshua Tree. At the end of town, I turn right and drive the long climb into Joshua Tree National Park, the only scenic way to get onto Interstate 10 from Victorville. Since I'm on this journey, I may as well make it scenic.

Channeling Biker Bob 3

I pull around another bend on the cute little two lane and next to the entrance kiosk of the park. A young blonde woman pokes her head out the window. Her hair is tied back in a tight bun, but it's obvious her curls reject restraints. Her blue eyes sparkle. She can't be more than twenty-five. She studies my bike and yells over the lumping of my idling engine, "Isn't that an Indian?"

Since there are no cars coming either way, I turn my bike off so we can talk. "This one was built in the fifties."

She pops back in the window, gets off her stool, and opens the door at the back of the building. She can't be any taller than me, and I'm barely five four. Over the tic-tic of my cooling engine, she takes a long, slow saunter around my bike, studies each chrome part, each spoke of the wheel, every square inch of leather. She asks, "Where are you headed?"

She runs a finger over the saddlebags I'd so painfully oiled and re-oiled last month to soften the dried leather. I turn to her. "I don't know just yet. Maybe New Mexico, but who knows? Anything can happen."

She gets around to the front of the bike and looks at me with excitement in her eyes. "I had a dream about this bike last week. I mean all the way down to the chrome studs on the saddlebags. This is the exact bike."

"You ride?"

She gets a longing look on her face. "Not a big bike like this yet, but I'm working on it. This guy Bob keeps appearing in my dreams."

A chill runs up my spine. "What's he look like?"

"Lanky with a black ponytail and a little graying goatee."

I drop the kickstand, lean the bike, kick my leg over, and sit sidesaddle while she squats on her haunches studying the pearl front fender.

She points. "God, I even dreamed about this little paint chip on the edge of the fender." She turns her face up to me. "Where do you live?"

"I'm not sure at the moment, but my husband and kids are waiting for me at Big Bear. You know, on the mountain."

She stands to her full height, steps back until her butt touches the building. Her face pales. "Did Bob send you?"

My chill turns into a full-blown shiver. "I'm never sure, when it comes to Bob. Did he send me, or did I just happen to be here?"

She asks, "you know Bob?"

I spread my arms, pointing my right fingers at the handlebars and my left hand at the saddlebags. "This was his bike."

"Oh my God." She slides to her butt on the small concrete curb next to the building. Her olive National Park pants recede enough to show pink socks with red hearts under regulation black combat boots.

A large recreational vehicle pulls up to the opposite window heading out of the park. The woman quickly stands and looks at me with a worried frown. The few lines in her face make me re-guess her age, maybe early thirties. She turns back to the RV, then to me again. "Wait right here. I have so many questions. Promise you won't leave."

"I won't leave." I think to myself that the journey has begun.

She races into the booth, takes the ticket stub from the RV, and as it pulls away, she steps out of the building. "How did you know to come here?"

3

"What do you mean?"

"Bob's been visiting me for weeks. He said who you are, but it's hard to believe you're actually here."

"Biker Bob?"

"Yes, Biker Bob. You know, the ghost."

I cross my arms in front of me, almost hugging myself. I get anxious whenever Bob's name is mentioned in our group, but this young woman has never met any of us, and she knows about Bob, too. This is weird.

She gives me a concerned look. "Are you okay?"

I shake off the fight-or-flight feeling and nod. "I'll be okay. Bob told me to go on this journey. I have no idea what I'll encounter. Really, I just want to get off on my own for a while, but maybe Bob has other ideas."

The young woman turns as a large black SUV pulls in behind me. She steps over to the window and takes the money from the older couple, goes inside the office, and puts a National Park packet together for them. When she comes out, two other cars have lined up behind the black one. She hands the Chevy a ticket and gives a short explanation about the park. When the SUV pulls off, she turns to me. "This is the busy time of day. I need to talk more about what's going on. Could you go to White Tank Campground and set up camp for the night? I get off work in three hours, and I'll meet you there." She hands me a map, takes my money, gives me a permit, and points out the direction of the campground.

I'm still in shock but I agree. I straddle my bike and slam my whole body into the kick starter. The engine fires and lumps into life. She puts her hand on my left shoulder and speaks loud in my ear. "Bob told me you were coming."

I'm in shock. It's one thing to discuss Bob among the

One-on-One bikers, but this is too much. I kick the bike into first and turn to her. "See you at the campground."

I rev the engine, slide the clutch out, and pull away from the kiosk. Although Bob is bouncing around in my head, I can't help taking in the pristine beauty of the park. The desert, in its spring splendor, comes right to the edge of the road. The long sweeping vistas of cactus, tough desert plants, and sunburned boulders contrast with a brilliant afternoon sky. It all clears my senses. The road is a meandering two lane that fits between outcroppings and slides beside long, open washes, now brilliant with color.

I ride three or four miles until I come to a single left turn. Although the desert clears my brain, Bob and his tricks still float around in my head.

I pull over and have a look at the map to see which way it is to White Tank Campground.

When I turn left and drive less than a mile, I come to the summit of a long climb I've been making since leaving Victorville. The eastern view of thirty miles of open desert is so inspiring, so overwhelming, I almost miss the White Tank Campground sign. I turn left and drive slowly a few hundred yards into a series of campites hidden among gigantic white granite boulders. As I idle along the little dirt road, passing parked RV's, tent campers, trailers, and even a converted school bus, I find an open site at the far end of the campground. It backs up to a three-story-high boulder that protrudes out of the desert sand like a giant white disk. I pull into the site and turn off my bike.

The first thing I notice, after my hearing calms from the sound of the wind and my engine, is the absolute silence of the desert. The only exceptions are some birds singing and two people talking. I look for the source of the noise. A young couple sits on a boulder a half mile into the desert behind my campsite. I can hardly see them, but the silence of the desert is so complete, I can hear their every whispered word as they slog their way through a discussion about going back to Los Angeles or staying in the desert for another day. He wants to stay, while she is intent on returning. The argument is a common one I have heard many times, but each person gives the other the room to finish his or her sentence without interruption. I wish I had binoculars, because I'm sure they're using a talking stick.

I unsnap my right saddle bag and remove my hiking shoes, three pairs of socks, my trimmed down version of a purse, two extra blouses, and finally at the bottom, the two-person tent. I practiced at least ten times at home so I wouldn't look like a fool trying to figure something new out. The tent goes up in a few minutes. I unbuckle my sleeping bag from the back seat of the bike and unroll it into the tent, then zip the door closed to keep out the little critters of the desert. I step back and admire my success.

There are still a few hours of daylight left, so I put on my hiking boots and walk a mile to the top of the hill overlooking the campground.

During the hike up, I see hundreds, maybe thousands of flowers protruding from every possible crack and crevice, some growing directly from the rock.

It's March, and the desert is alive with plants blossoming quickly before they shrivel in the blazing April and May sun.

I reach the top and look out to see splashes of color for miles. Entire sections of otherwise barren earth is alive with yellows, blues, the violets of the desert sunset, and a dozen shades of green that blanket the landscape. I kneel and look closely at my feet and realize that not one of those millions of flowers, not one of those tufts of green are individually any bigger than my thumb, and most are smaller than my fingernail.

I sit on a rock the size of a truck and study the scene until the day wanes. There are no clouds on the horizon, so I know from experience the sunset will be plain compared to the speculator view on cloudy afternoons. I hike back to the campground, set up my single burner stove, open a container of freeze-dried lentil soup, and start dinner.

Off in the distance, I hear the familiar sound of a motorcycle as it downshifts.

My single serving of soup is ready and I've poured it into a new stainless steel cup. The motorcycle has entered the campground and is working its way closer. As I take my first sip of soup, the bike pulls into my site and parks next to mine. The person takes off the solid black full-face helmet, and it's the blonde.

"Hey, how you doing?" She unstraps a small ice cooler and an even smaller cardboard box from the back seat of her older 750 Yamaha. I know only because the emblem on the tank says Yamaha 750.

I turn and sit on the table part of the picnic table, then put my feet on the seat. "I'm okay. What do you have?"

She hangs her helmet on the handlebars and snatches the cooler. "Thought we'd share dinner, so I went back into town to get some things and stopped at my favorite Asian restaurant to pick up some takeout."

I look at my meager cup of soup and abandon it. "No

kidding, I was just thinking of Kung-Pao chicken."

She steps to the park bench and sets the cooler on the table next to me. "I brought a little wood, too, in case you wanted to have a fire when it gets dark."

She sits at the far end, upon the table like me and digs into the ice chest. "Brought a couple of Saint Paulie's." She pulls out a full-size Leatherman tool and flips out the can opener part, then pops the caps of two bottles of iced beer. She hands one to me.

I take a long drink, feel the fragrant fizz of the carbonation tickle my throat and the strong flavor activate my taste buds. When I'm finished, I look at the label. "I don't usually like beer, especially those stupid grocery-store beers, but this one is different. I like it."

She reaches into the box and pulls out familiar paper containers with wire handles. At the same time, she lifts her beer and shows me the label. "Local liquor store orders it for me special. Let's see, we've got Kung-Pau chicken, shrimp fried rice, and Hunan beef. I got a couple sets of chopsticks, but didn't think to bring plates. I guess we're going to have to rough it." She smiles and hands me a set of sticks.

I take a second, much shorter swallow of beer, and open the flaps of the first container. "This is perfect. I was about to eat freeze-dried soup."

She opens the second container with fried rice. "Hey, forget that soup; we'll dine tonight."

Although I'd never do it at home or allow anyone else to, I pick up the Kung-Pau and transfer pieces of chicken and vegetables into my mouth using the chopsticks as scoops. I never could get the hang of those stick things.

We eat in silence for twenty minutes, trading containers until they're almost empty and I'm stuffed.

Although the campground has other people who are doing the same things, making fires, clinking dishes and silverware, their sound is absorbed by the silence of the desert. All I can hear is the last dusk call of birds, the slight breeze brushing my ears and hair, mixed with the sound of us slurping and shoveling Chinese takeout and drinking sips of beer.

I set the empty container of Kung-Pau on the table beside me. "I don't know your name?"

"Katherine Burns, but you can call me Kat if you want. What about you?"

"I'm Renee Chance."

She gasps. "Not the Renee Chance from a few years ago?"

"Depends on what happened a few years ago." I feel myself bristle.

"You know, when Stewart Chance and Bob took the talk-show scene by storm and you came in at the end and knocked 'em dead with your stuff about how a woman sees the world. You were fantastic. You spoke in those few minutes everything I had been trying to say for years."

I shift on the bench and look at her to see if she's giving me a hard time. "Oh really?"

"Those few sentences changed the way I look at life." She blushes slightly. "I know Biker Bob came through Stewart during those months of talk shows."

I pick up the last of the beef. "It was obvious, wasn't it?"

She puts her fried rice container on the table and shifts to face me. "It was obvious to me, but the one thing I wasn't sure of, because you seemed so inspired, did. . . I mean. . . did Biker Bob come through you too?"

I bellow a bit too loudly for my taste. "Oh my God, no, Katherine. It would be way too weird to have a guy inside my skin."

"I thought so, but you were so passionate, I mean after you got over your initial nervousness."

"Well, thanks for the compliment, but it was just me trying to find some equilibrium when it came to my new loudmouthed husband."

"You did great, and since Bob wasn't talking through you, I'm even more impressed. Where did you come up with that stuff?"

I'm on the spot. I have no idea what she's talking about. "You know how it is. I never think about what I'm going to say before I say it. It just comes out."

"I know what you mean. My boyfriend hates that about me."

"What?"

"That I say stuff before I think about it. I guess I could be a little more careful."

"I don't think you need to be more careful," I say. "We women simply speak our thoughts as we feel them. I think it's perfect for us. The only problem, as I see it, is that men need to find a way to get used to it."

"Oh God, don't tell my guy that, he'll go through the roof."

I take the last sip from my warm beer. "I think it's high time men learn how to listen to their women without trying to fix anything and without trying to rush us to the end of our thoughts."

She blushes. "There, you've done it again."

I put both arms out to my side, hands palms up, and shrug. "What?"

"Once again, you've said something that has forever

Odyssey

changed my entire outlook on life."

"Come on, you've heard that before."

"Honest, this is the first time, but I have only one question." She lets the sentence fade, like she can't quite bring herself to ask.

"What's that?"

She giggles. "How in the hell do we get those guys to listen?"

I snicker. "There's the problem, now, isn't it?"

We sit in silence as the day slowly fades to dusk.

She finally stands and walks to her bike. She removes a key from her Levi's and unlocks the left saddlebag, one of those plastic police-kind that is efficient but not too great looking. She gathers an armful of firewood. Still leaning down, she asks, "are you and Stewart still together?"

"Oh, yes. We'll always be together."

"If you don't mind my asking, why are you out here alone?"

It's my turn to blush. "I guess I'm looking for myself. Stewart and I have been together for twenty years. The last few have been the best, mostly because Biker Bob has been helping both of us, but more so because Stewart has learned how to hold his own when I feel we need to talk."

She carries the wood over to the fire pit, drops it outside of the stone circle, and goes back for more. "I wish my guy could hold his own. He gets so angry, I'm always afraid to say anything."

"Well, shit, girl, that ain't no way to live."

She bends down and reaches into the box for a second load. "Tell me about it, but I don't know what to do. He's never hit me, but someday he might, so I hold back and

11

hold back until, you know, that time of the month when I can't hold back any longer. I let him have it with both barrels. God, I hate myself when that happens."

"You're telling the truth, and as far as I can figure it, screw men if they can't handle the truth."

She stops with the arm load of wood and looks me directly in the eyes. "Is that how Stewart and you work it?"

"Stewart is the other type of man. He doesn't explode, he implodes."

"Oh, yeah, I know the kind."

"My job is to keep him talking and listening at the same time. His tendency is to glaze over and go blank."

She looks at me. "In some ways, I wish I had a man like that."

I sort my thoughts in the silence.

"No, you don't." I say. "The way Stewart used to be was much worse than an explosive man, because he would stab you in the back when you least expected it. At least you know where your guy is coming from."

She turns, puts the wood down, tears off a few splinters from three or four pieces, and stacks them in the center of the pit. She takes a single match, lights it, and holds it under the splinters until a tiny blaze dances. She adds some small sticks, a few larger ones, and in a minute a little fire casts shadows on the disk-shaped boulder behind her.

I point at the fire. "There is something impressive."

She turns toward me. "What's that?"

"Building a fire with one match and no paper."

"Oh, twern't nothin' ma'am," she says in a Texas cowboy drawl.

Once the little blaze is dancing, she sits back on the

seat part of the bench. "You can't camp without a fire."

I say, "I never had much luck with fires."

She looks at me. "Tell me how you came by this bike. It's been in my dreams so many times, but I had no idea it was connected to Bob."

"Biker Bob gave it to me."

"Yeah, I know that, but what I'm curious about is how. Him being a spirit and all."

I tell her about Stewart and me buying the house in Big Bear, and how I came upon the key to the storage unit in the town of Reseda. I talk about going to that unit and how the bike was sitting in the middle of the room with a tarp over it. How excited I felt getting on the machine for the first time, and how the note on the seat gave the contents of the storage unit over to whomever opened the door. I told her about the note from the owner of our new house, dead some five years, and who Robert Freedman was. God, it's a little spooky telling the story again. It's been months.

"So, if Robert Freedman was Biker Bob. . ."

I answer a list of questions as long as my arm about Bob. Her final question makes me look at her, though night has fallen and the fire is to her back, so I can't see her face. "How come you left your family behind?"

My defensiveness leaps to the surface. I hear a snap in my answer. "I didn't leave them, I'm just taking time off. I'll be going back in a few weeks."

There is a long silence before she says her next sentence. "I wouldn't be so sure."

"What do you mean?"

"I don't know, Bob just told me to say that. He's been in my dreams pretty regularly lately, and most of the subjects have been about you showing up. I never gave it much credence, because I thought it was just some weird dream, but when you pulled up to the kiosk today, it all came into focus."

"What do you mean?"

She drops another stick on the fire and sparks float toward the star-filled blackness. She rotates back to me. "I still wasn't sure until you mentioned Biker Bob, then I knew the whole thing wasn't a dream, but Bob was telling me something, and I'll be damned whether I liked it or not, I was going to have to follow through."

"Bob can be pretty persistent."

"I'm learning that. The amazing thing is, I had no idea how I was going to do it and still keep my job. I love working for National Parks, and I wasn't willing to trade it off for some dream, but as you said, Bob can be persistent."

"What did he want you to do?"

"Ride with you and protect you."

I snort. "What do you mean protect me? I don't need any protection." I point at her. "I don't know if you've looked at yourself lately, but you're even smaller than me. I think that both of us together couldn't beat our way out of a wet paper sack."

She laughs. "I know, but it's what Bob said to do."

I drop onto the lower seat and lean closer to the fire. Once the sun goes down, the desert turns cold. Another minute of silence goes by before I say, "So, if you're supposed to protect me from what neither of us knows and I'm going east to New Mexico, how are you going to do that and still keep your job?"

She turns her head to me. "That's the strange part. My three-week vacation started at the end of today's shift. A few more hours and I would have never met you."

"Guess Bob's got some kind of plan," I say.

"So, what do you say, can I come along?"

I smile and extend my hand to shake. She takes a second to comprehend what I'm trying to do and cautiously grasps mine. Her grip is firm.

"Who am I to go against such a well-developed plan? I don't know how you're going to protect me, but if Bob says you're coming, I guess you're coming."

"No problem my little Yamaha riding with your Indian?"

I snicker. "That bullshit of only Harleys and Indians riding together is for those idiot macho guys. As far as I'm concerned, as long as you can keep up, getting in the wind is getting in the wind."

She smiles, tosses the last of her beer down and puts the bottle back into the paper bag the Chinese food came in.

I say, "I'll wait here in the morning while you go home and get your gear."

"No need," she says. "I wasn't sure if you would have me, but Bob was so insistent, I brought everything I'll need."

"What about your boyfriend?"

"What about him? He's either waiting when I get back or he's found some twit to shack up with. He ain't too much of a keeper, anyhow."

"You bring a tent?"

She stands and walks to her bike. "Brought it all, including the most important part, my ATM card." We both laugh.

"Good idea, because I wasn't planning on sleeping on the ground the whole time."

She opens the lid of her plastic saddlebag and pulls

out a small, soft plastic tube. "That's good, because I can only take so much tent camping." She pulls the contents out of the pouch, and in less than a minute has a one-person tent assembled and resting against the rock opposite the fire from mine.

The fire eventually dies, and we settle into our sleeping bags for the night. The stars fill the sky.

I didn't get very far today, but maybe Bob really does have a plan, and just maybe I really am on a journey of discovery, not just some stupid vacation.

Two

Pottery

This time, I'm going to throw a full twenty-five-pound bag of clay. I pull out a single block from a half ton I had delivered last week. I unravel the wire tie, strip the heavy plastic bag back and plop the raw clay on the dry four-inch-thick slab of plaster. Before I get my hands muddy, I reach over and pick up what's left of yesterday's joint, strike a wooden match, and take a long pull. In a few moments the effects of the smoke, which I've held in my lungs as long as possible, radiates out from my chest, into my belly and arms, into my legs, and finally causes a noticeable relaxation in my brain. I need only one hit, but I take a second just to celebrate the twenty-five-pounds of clay. I set the joint into its little tray on the shelf and study the clay with renewed interest.

With both of my palms, I push into the edges of the clay, forcing the square corners in, rolling the mass as I go. I pull my palm back and take another swipe, rolling the clay again. I force it into a submissive ram's horn shape, wrapping the narrow ends, continuing to stretch the clay, pushing the outside surface toward the center, exposing the next inner layer, mixing the viscous material, looking for ever-present bubbles.

As air pockets present themselves, I take another swipe with my palms and push the air to the surface, crushing the pockets, removing yet another possibility of a lump, when I pull the walls of my vase toward the ceiling.

When I'm sure every possible bubble has come to the surface and been purged, I pick up the wad of chocolate clay and gently thump it on the table, turning it with each contact until I have a small soccer ball of moist, flexible clay.

The door opens, and Carolyn pokes her head in. "What do you want for lunch, Nicky?"

I turn to her, away from the moment, away from my future, and I'm pulled disappointedly into the present. I want to be nice, but my concentration has been compromised. "Give me another hour."

"But," she says, "it's one o'clock, and I don't remember you having much of a breakfast."

I look at the perfectness of the ball of clay and back at her concerned face. "I need more time."

"I'll bring you a sandwich," she says in a bit of a snit and closes the door behind her. The garage drops back into the perfect silence of concentration.

I take the clay and walk over to my electric wheel, set the ball down carefully on a side table, and grab a plaster bat; a plate of plaster an inch thick and the size and shape of a large dinner plate. I reach inside the bucket of water and dig deep into the bottom sludge until I can feel the right consistency of slippery clay. I pull out a few fingers full and spread it thick on the plate of the wheel.

"Baloney or turkey?" I hear from the kitchen next to my studio.

"I don't give a flying fuck," I want to say, but I know she is simply trying to take care of me. "Turkey," I yell, knowing that if I don't answer, I will be forever distracted by her endless questions.

I spread thick wads of the sludgy clay into three separate sections of the wheelhead and push the plaster bat onto the clay, attempting to center it on the wheel as much as possible.

I touch the control pedal with my foot and get the wheel to spin to check my centering.

The bat is in place, and I pick up the ball of clay, lift it high into the air, and slam it—

"Mustard and mayonnaise?" she asks from the other room.

The noise breaks my aim, and I end with the clay off to one side of the wheelhead. "Shut up, damnit. Leave me alone." I want to say, but I don't. Hell, we've only been together a few months, and yelling at her would not be constructive to the relationship, which I am beginning to appreciate.

"Both," I say.

It's only clay. It'll take only a few moments to remove it from the wheel head and reform it back into a ball. I peel it off the plaster, then gently pound it onto the bat at every angle, pushing the domed shape into a ball.

Once the clay is into a general sphere, I slam it hard into the bat, and this time it's reasonably centered.

"Come in and eat some lunch, Nicky."

I feel like some eight-year-old with Mom constantly dogging me to eat my vitamins, drink lots of milk, brush my teeth, and who knows what else women do in their never-ending efforts to save their men.

I'm finally at the only time in the entire process of throwing my first twenty-five-pound ball of clay that I can take a break. If not, she'll distract me during some critical part and ruin a perfectly good throw.

I stop the wheel, stand, look longingly at the ball of clay, turn, and step from my clay-spattered closet into her sparkling kitchen with every dish in its rightful place; every knickknack, and there are plenty, in a precise position to maximize usage of her space. God, I hate those cutesy little porcelain dogs with smiles, penguins of all sizes, and that idiotic mouse collection.

I step over to the sink and wash my hands of my beloved clay. I turn back to the table where a sandwich and some chips lay perfectly positioned on delicate white china.

A frosty non-alcoholic beer stands next to a bottle of stone-ground mustard, all sitting on a frilly lace tablecloth.

What happened to the days of eating next to a greasy carburetor with bike pieces scattered on a newspaper? How did the smell of gasoline get replaced with fu-fu girl smells? What happened to my white bread with a slab of meat, eaten with Harley grease?

I sit at the little round table she bought last month at a furniture outlet and stare at the meal.

"Well, eat up," she says. "The bread will get stale."

I pick up a chip and toss it into my mouth, take a swig of pretend beer, and pick up one side of the perfectly cut sandwich.

I'm about halfway through the meal when she sits across from me and looks into my eyes.

Uh-oh, I've seen that look. I know something is up.

Hell, all I want to do is get back to my vase, but something is bothering her.

I swallow the bite, take another drag from the bottle, and look into her deep blue eyes. "What's up, Carolyn?"

"Oh, nothing," she says with a melancholy sigh.

God, I hate it, when not only do I know that she's got something on her mind, but it's my job to drag it out of her.

"Something is going on, Honey," I say. "I sense it in your voice."

Her expression shifts from faraway to an intense glare. "There's nothing in my voice, Nicky Brown."

Jesus, she used my full name. Something's up, and it's big. I want to get back to my clay, but maybe it's time to be a supportive male.

"Come on Carolyn, something is on your mind. Why don't you just tell me and get it over with?"

I guess I could have used more tact, but hell, I want to get back to my clay.

There's a noticeable chill in the room. Her hackles are up and that sad melancholy look of disappointment has turned into something I've never experienced with this woman. With Melinda, yes, her hackles were up most of the time, but I thought Carolyn was different. She's so sweet and gentle.

Melinda busted my chops, even after we separated and I promised myself I'd never choose a woman like her ever again. Right now, Carolyn has that same Melinda look. I lean back and get my feet under me. I'm ready to bolt the second a dish flies or a fork sails across the room at me.

I'm relieved when Carolyn puts her face in her hands and breaks down crying. I hear some words, but they're

Channeling Biker Bob 3

muffled and make no sense.

At least she isn't going to punch me out or throw something. I sit across from her and wait for the rains to subside. My feet are still under me, and I'm ready to bolt at the slightest provocation.

After a long pause, using her paper napkin to wipe her eyes and blow her nose, she says, "you never spend time with me anymore,"

I reach across the table and take her hand. "I'm sorry, but I've got things to do."

A fresh bout of tears rolls down her cheeks and her renewed sobs match the waterworks. I can't tell if the whole display is for my benefit, or if she really is sad. Hell, I just told her the truth, and I thought the truth was what we'd agreed upon. The truth, the whole truth, and nothing but the truth. Maybe all bets are off if she's feeling upset. Maybe she wants me to lie.

I'm not sure which is worse, being left to guess what Carolyn wants or dealing with Melinda's direct line of violent outbursts. At least with Melinda, I knew exactly where she was at any given moment. There was no guessing, just ducking the next blow.

I want to get back to my ball of clay, but I don't dare.

Carolyn comes out of her crying and looks at me with big, red, puppy dog eyes. "I need you to pay more attention to me, like you did back when we were in Victorville. I hate it here in San Francisco. There's so much to distract you."

Why do I have to carry my own load and entertain her, too? Why can't she find her own interests?

"Because her interest is you, Pal."

I spin and look toward the sound that came from behind. At the door, wearing a black leather vest, riding

22

chaps, and Harley boots, his black ponytail hanging from under a classic James Dean hat stands Biker Bob.

"What are you doing here?"

"Just helping out."

"Helping out with what?"

"Shit, Nick, don't you get it? You're about to leap headlong into the real part of this relationship."

"What do you mean?"

He points toward Carolyn. "You've got a tiger by the tail, my man, and you don't even know it."

"What the hell are you talking about? Melinda was a tiger, and I couldn't handle that action. Carolyn is a whole different kind of woman." I turn and point in her direction, but she's not there. The table is still here, her chair is pushed away from the table like she got up, but I didn't see her leave. I look about the room and my first reaction is relief. I can finally get back to my clay.

"No," Bob says, "She ain't no Melinda, but don't you get it, man? No matter how hard you try, you're always going to pick the same type of woman."

"Carolyn doesn't give me black eyes."

"That may be true, but she still has similar issues as Melinda, because she's dealing with you, and you, my friend, are still the same."

Bob takes five steps across my dinky kitchen to the far side of the table and sits where Carolyn had been sitting. The scene fades, then comes back into focus.

"Carolyn may not be as physical as Melinda, but trust me, she'll be giving your manhood a black eye." Bob reaches over and grabs one of my potato chips. "Hey, just in time for lunch." He pops it into his mouth and crunches it into oblivion.

I glare at him. "How can you compare Carolyn with

crazy Melinda. Carolyn is kind and gentle through and through."

Bob stops chewing and looks at me with his, "you idiot" gaze. "Kind and gentle for now, but there's a tiger under that lamb's exterior. Your romantic stage is coming to a close and the hard part of the relationship is about to begin; that is if she's willing to stick around."

"Hard part?"

"Hey, my man, you just witnessed a preview of how she responds to conflict. Her tears are going to be real and the issues will be real. The only difference between her and Melinda is that Carolyn internalizes her conflicts and blames herself."

I pick up the sandwich and open my mouth to take a bite, then say, "Melinda never internalized one word."

Bob smiles and grabs another chip from my plate. "You pretty much got that, but be prepared, because a different kind of shit's going to hit the ol' proverbial fan. Carolyn's brand is much harder to recognize."

"What do you mean?"

"Her worries won't be as easy to read as Melinda's. You're going to have to keep your eyes wide open. You won't be protecting yourself physically with your arms; you'll be protecting your balls this time. You could cut out the smoke and it would help a lot."

I feel myself pale and my balls tighten with his words. "What do you mean?"

Bob smiles. "Sorry, I can't tell you, because even I don't know what it's going to look like. All I know is the power struggle phase sets the stage for the rest of your years together. You're about to enter into the Twilight Zone of relationship, and Man, you've got to be careful or you'll end up like Stewart was when we first met him."

Pottery

"Stewart? You're painting a pretty bleak picture."

"It isn't bleak, unless you succumb to the Sirens of Titan."

"Sirens of Titan?"

"The tears you just witnessed are the Sirens of Titan, my man. Although her sadness is real, we men must be careful not to give into the sweet melody. It would be so much easier to meet her needs and try to fix what's wrong, but trust me, you will do so by giving away your masculinity."

I take a bite of the second half of the sandwich. "What the fuck are you talking about?"

"There is nothing to fix. She is simply going through her own emotional upheaval. If you try to fix it, giving away your balls during the attempt, it will never be enough, and she'll end up resenting you."

"Okay, so what do you have in mind?"

"Simply witness her upheaval. Don't give any advice. Don't attempt to repair or change anything about you because of what she says, and most importantly, don't take what she says personally."

"What do you mean?"

"Don't get pissed because she's taking your time with her emotions."

"I wouldn't do that."

"Come on, Nick, just a minute ago you were railing against her wasting your time. You wanted to get back to that ball of clay."

"She was taking away from my creative time."

"Sure, man, and I got a bridge to sell you."

I give him an insulted glare.

"Okay, how come when I'm here, your precious ball of clay is not as much of an issue?"

25

"You've got so much to say."

He smiles, snatches another chip and looks at it. "Hold the flattery, dickhead. I'm thinking that those tears scare the fuck out of you. I know they frighten me to the core, because I'm never sure when they'll end. Our job is to not be frightened, but to hang in there and witness her all the way to the end and not take what she has to say personally. It's really all she wants."

Bob pops the chip. "Man, these things are good."

"Jesus, Bob, what is it with you and potato chips?"

He smiles. "She said you never spend time with her anymore. What was your first reaction?"

I look at him, knowing that it's some kind of trick question. "My first reaction?"

He nods.

"Hell, that's easy. All I have to do is schedule a dinner and maybe a movie, and the problem will be over, so I can get back to my clay."

He grabs another chip. "Ain't going to happen."

"What do you mean?"

"It isn't what she wants."

"Come on, Bob; she said I wasn't spending enough time with her. She loves to go to the movies, so piece of cake, I take her to the movies."

He speaks in a sing-song voice. "It isn't even close."

I drop the remains of the sandwich on my plate and pound my hand on the table a little harder than I want. "Shit, Bob, just come out with it."

Bob doesn't flinch. Not one eyelid flutters. "I already said it, but you were looking for the logical way out of this mess."

"What's wrong with logical?"

"It's a guy approach. We want to find the straightest

line from point A to point B. Am I right?

"So what's wrong with that?"

He picks up another chip. "Nothing. It's just not where a woman wants to go. Trust me, the first words out of her mouth are not what's bothering her. She has to run the gauntlet to search her way through the quagmire of her emotion before she can find her real question. The wonderful thing is, if we can hold our responses long enough and not take what she says personally, she will eventually discover her own questions and answer them herself. Shit, man, we don't have to fix a thing."

I awake in late afternoon slumped over my wheel. I remember hardly being able to hold my eyes open, wedging my first twenty-five pound bag of clay and forming it into a ball, then slamming it to the head of my wheel. It's still here waiting for my command, waiting for me to shape it into something.

I drop my clay spattered hands into the bucket of water, grab a towel, and dry. A half joint is calling me from its shelf. I grab it and a wooden match and take a long pull. Life looks much better. I set the smoldering joint in its little tray and hunt for my sponge in the bucket, wring it out, then dribble water over the clay.

When I lock my thumbs and drop my hands over the clay, at the same time, I push my foot on the control pedal and apply pressure to the side of the clay with both palms, locking my elbows against my body to steady the spinning lump. It yields to my command slowly, and I push harder, forming the ball into a round mass, smoothing the surface until the entire mound is perfectly centered on the wheel. The clay spins without the slightest wobble.

With my sponge, I sop excess water off the surface,

then with both thumbs, plunge down, down, into the center of the clay, making a funnel shape to within a half inch of the plaster bat.

I must decide what I'll make. Will it be a large vase? Twenty-five pounds could easily make a thirty-six-inch tall container.

I grab my wooden paddle and shape the interior of the cone to make a gentle arch from the center out to the edge of the clay, leaving a three-inch-thick wall. Now that the first part is complete, I wet the clay with my sponge, lock my thumbs together, and with both index fingers, take my first pull, bringing the three-inch-thick clay wall skyward to a height of six inches off the wheelhead. The next pull nets a nine-inch-tall rim and the next, twelve. A simple ten-inch-wide cylinder for now, until I have stretched the clay to my desired height and thickness.

On my next pull, the rim leaps to eighteen inches and the wall thickness of the clay reduce to one and a half inches.

Okay, everything is perfect. I wring out my sponge and dry the surface of the clay. If I want this thing to stretch to its limit, I must let it dry a while, but I'm too excited to stop. I want to see what it will look like. I've been here before. If I don't give it time to set up, the walls might collapse under their own weight.

With the surface as dry as I can get it, I open my arms, stand, and walk away from potentially the biggest piece of pottery I have yet to attempt.

Something about the smoothness of the clay excites me. Something about taking the clay out to its limit intrigues me like nothing else. Tightening the last bolt of a fully custom Harley comes close, but making pottery is immediate. Where it took months to complete building a custom bike, with clay, I can feel the rush of success many times in a single day. Not only that, but I never have to deal with some dickhead biker who thinks that he and his bike are the most important things since the dawn of time. I don't have to deal with guys and their misplaced manhood extending to their big dick motorcycles. The one percent of one percent guys aren't that way, and if I could have exclusively worked on One-on-One bikes, I probably would have been happy, but they were a small percentage of the people I was forced to deal with to stay afloat. It's a fucked-up world, and the world of bikers is no different.

The kitchen door opens, and Carolyn pokes her head around the door. "You ready for some lunch?"

I look around the room expecting that Bob is involved in a little charade again. I look at my two-foot-tall cylinder of clay, then turn back to her. "Sure, give me a minute to clean up."

She closes the door. I step over to the washbasin and turn on the water.

Having stripped my outer clay-saturated pants and shirt, I step into Carolyn's knickknack kitchen and sit at the table in front of the exact sandwich I'd eaten in my dream. I look around again for Bob, but this time it's just Carolyn and me.

Three

Being With A Woman

"I can't do it anymore," I announce while standing in front of the fire, twenty men sitting in a circle around the small blaze.

"What's that, Tazz?" one of the men asks, though I don't look up to see who spoke.

"I can't take her constant nagging. Donna hasn't let up for months, and I can't figure out what's bothering her."

Another voice leaps out of the semi-darkness. "She probably doesn't know. When my wife goes on the warpath, she seldom knows why."

I lean down, pick up another three-inch-thick log and toss it into the dying fire. As the sparks fly upward toward the star-filled sky, I say, "She's really not on the warpath, but comparatively that is much easier to deal with. It's her constant nagging, not even hard nagging, but there is a steady pressure for me to perform."

Twig's deep baritone comes out of the dark. "And

31

even if we try, whatever we do is never good enough."

I turn to him and give him a smile of relief. "It's not good enough, you're right. Why is that?"

Twig gives me one of his big-faced grins, spreads his arms, and shrugs his shoulders. "One of the mysteries of being with a woman." When he drops his arms, he gets a serious look. "The biggest question I have is are we supposed to be calm and not let that kind of thing bother us? Our women aren't able to. They get to dump all over us, but the shit hits the fan when we say one little word."

A chorus of grunts and chuffs ring out from around the circle. Has every man who is in a relationship made some kind of sound of frustration?

Twig says, "If we are living in a time where men and women are equal partners, then both people must have the room to equally vent frustrations and complaints while the other listens. I don't know about the rest of you guys, but Melinda pays lip service to us being equal. When it's time for me to bring up an issue with her, watch out, because she flies off the handle and won't let me finish my sentence."

Almost every person in the circle calls out into the darkness. Almost, I say, because Bucky is the only silent one. He finally stands, steps over to the thin slice of tree trunk, and picks up the talking stick. The moment he grabs it, the circle goes silent.

Buck paces around the fire swinging the feathered stick, finally pointing it at the sky like some extension of his forefinger. "Leslie never nags at me because I never let her. I know it's not fair, but the only way I can keep my sanity around her is to keep that yapping voice of hers away from me. Either I leave or worse yet, I yell until she's forced to shut up. So far my method has worked, but I watch her every day pull further away from me, and I don't know how to get her back."

Buck still has the stick. He's pointing it toward the stars, but his tough exterior shatters. He looks like he's on the edge of crying, though I've never, in the ten years I've known him, seen him shed a tear.

We're all holding our breath.

He turns, paces back to the south end of the circle, spins, and returns to the north. After five or six trips, he says with a choked sound, "I gotta change my approach or she'll leave."

He turns, shuffles over to the cedar round, and puts the talking stick back in its position.

When he sits, I ask, "You need some feedback, Buck?"

He holds up one of his gloved hands, the chrome spikes reflecting the fire. "Not right now," he says softly, "but maybe later in the evening."

I turn and search the crowd. I'm leader tonight, so it's my job to throw out the first subject, and when I do, we'll see where the chips fall.

Stewart stretches his long basketball-player limbs, gets up and steps over to the cedar round. He kneels and puts his hand on the stick, but doesn't pick it up. "Renee's been gone for almost a month. I thought I was going to miss her, but if we are talking about nagging women tonight, I have to say that now that I have a little space from her, she is the nagging queen, and I don't miss that part of her at all. Without her around, my kids and I get along much better. Without her constant intervention, we've been dealing with each other, and that's a good thing." Stew takes his hand off the stick and stands.

Max speaks, but he doesn't get up to retrieve the

stick. "I guess I'm the nagging one in my family."

Stewart shifts his weight onto one foot and rotates to face Max. "You? How could that be? I thought only women were naggers."

It's obvious that Max is having a hard time with his revelation, so I put my hand up for Stew to be quiet. "Let the man talk, Stewart."

Stew looks at me, steps to his tree round, and sits.

Max opens his arms and shrugs. "My girlfriend and I have been working out some crap about keeping the house clean. I kind of want it much cleaner than she does. She dumps her stuff all over the place and doesn't pick it up for weeks. I try to give her time, but she isn't aware that anything is messy. It drives me crazy."

Buck speaks up. "Leslie's the same way with her apartment. It scares me to think about living with her."

Max looks over at him and nods. "Thanks, Buck. I thought I was the only one. I thought maybe I was being too finicky, but if I don't say anything, the stuff keeps piling up until there's no place to walk. There's no room on my desk; there isn't even a place on the couch for me to sit. I try to hold back as long as possible, but usually I'm livid in three or four days. Either I pick up the whole mess myself or I nag her."

Buck rubs his eyes. Through his hands, he says, "Holy shit, is this what I have to look forward to?"

Bill interjects his usual elongated story, this time about his wife. When he's done, the subject goes around the circle. An amazing seven men, including me, have the same problem at home, and none of us knows what to do about it. When it gets back to Max, he's the most articulate about the issue. "I know she has just as much right to live in our house as I do, and if I keep at her, something is going to happen that won't be pretty."

"But shit, man," I say. "What the hell are we supposed to do, just walk over the piles of dirty laundry and try to find a clean glass in a sink full of three-day-old dishes? I can't even find anything in the refrigerator, because everything is simply pushed in. The things in the back could be months old; I'd have no idea. We feed from the front few layers."

A number of grunts come from around the circle until Stewart stands again, casually walks over to the talking stick, and picks it up. The circle goes silent and every face is trained on him. "Renee and I had the same problem, and before Bob showed up, I dealt with it by becoming her housemaid. I did that for years. She'd come in from work and toss her coat on the couch, kick her shoes across the room, drop her briefcase at my feet, and go to the fridge, then leave the butter and whatever else on the counter. I dutifully cleaned up after her; that is, until Bob came along."

Stewart turns to me, then looks at each man. "When Bob suggested I stop cleaning up after her, I tried, but my tolerance level for messiness was much lower than hers. After a day or so, I found myself straightening up just to get some walking room."

Stew walks around the fire, picks a small log, and drops it on the blaze. The sparks leap toward the inky sky. When he straightens up, as if the timing has to be perfect, he has my uninterrupted attention. "After I spent a few months trying to figure out what to do, Bob gave me a suggestion. He said that probably what I needed was to take some of my house back."

In his showman-like setting of the stage, which is why Stewart is our point man, he walks over and sets the stick back in its place next to the bowl, feather and corks.

"What the fuck, Stewart? What do you mean?"

When he sits, he looks at me and the other twenty expectant faces.

Bill screams, "how the fuck do we take some of our house back?"

Stewart smiles. "Bob told me to claim one shelf in the refrigerator that was just mine. Renee could neither put anything on that shelf nor take anything off that shelf."

"What?" Bucky yells and leaps to his feet. "Bob told you to claim a shelf? Come on man, just one shelf? What about the rest of the fucking house?"

Stewart's smug face breaks into a grin. "Bob said that one shelf in a woman's house would be battle enough to start with."

"A single shelf?" Bill says. "Hell, I can claim a single shelf later tonight when I get home."

Stewart looks over at him and his smile widens. "Yes, you can, but that's the easy part. Keeping that shelf is a whole different story."

"What do you mean?" Buck asks.

"Think about it, Buck. It's probably the very reason why you're afraid to have Leslie move in. Don't most women pretty much take over the inside of a house? They're all interior designers. They know exactly where everything must go, and things like moose heads," he looks at Twig, "belong in the garage with the other guy things. She wants frilly curtains, her pictures on the wall, only her knickknacks in the windowsills, and definitely every inch of kitchen counter space filled with juicers, toasters, and whatever other appliance she thinks she needs to run a kitchen, despite the fact that she uses the appliance only for Thanksgiving dinner."

"You're right," Buck says. "I like my kitchen counters clean of clutter so there's a place to prepare food."

Stewart's smile drops into a dark grimace. "Trust me, Buck, she ain't going to give up even one square inch to no interloping man. My single shelf in the refrigerator has been an ongoing battle for two years."

"What do you mean?" Bill asks.

Stew turns to him. "Although she agreed to gift me with a small corner in the entire house that I could call my very own, Renee constantly puts things on my uncluttered shelf. At first I thought she was consciously undermining our agreement, and maybe unconsciously she still is, but she says she just didn't have any other place in the refrigerator to put anything, and my little clean shelf is a convenient place to put something temporarily."

Bill says, "You mean I can't even have a single shelf I can call my own in the entire house?"

"You can call it whatever you like, just understand that you will have to reclaim that space every day for a year or so until she finally gets it."

Bill drops his elbows to his knees and his head into his open palms. "Can't things be easier when it comes to dealing with women?"

Stewart snickers. "Not my kick-ass woman."

The men in the circle grunt in agreement.

Bill looks up. "In reality, if we're living in a world where things are supposed to be equal between men and women, shouldn't I be able to claim half of the house to be the way I like it?"

"Good luck, Buddy," Stew says. "Renee and I have

been working this issue for two years. I've managed to claim a single shelf in the refrigerator that she violates only once a week or so. I've got one single two-foot-square corner of counter space in our huge kitchen, and a half of a shelf in the medicine cabinet."

"That ain't much," Bill says.

Stewart's smile returns. This time it's a satisfied smile, and his face looks relaxed. "That's why having her gone is such a blessing. Don't get me wrong, I miss her like the dickens, but for the first time since she and I started living together, I get to hang the pictures the way I want them." He looks at Twig. "Hell, if I had a moose head, I'd hang it in the living room."

Twig says, "I ain't got that moose head anymore. Melinda forced me to get rid of it."

Stewart throws up his hands and shrugs.

"I know where you can buy one," Twig says. His eyes are brighter.

Stewart's arms drop. "It would be a waste of money. The day Renee returns, that moose head would be in the garbage. You know it, and I know it."

Twig says, "I guess you gotta pick your battles."

After a short silence, I turn. "Hey, Buck, you want to talk more about you and Leslie?"

He takes a long inhalation and lets his breath out in a fast, single sigh. "I don't know what to do. I know she has a lot to say, but I can't let her say it. I'm afraid that once she gets started she'll never stop."

Buck's lower lip quivers. It's the most I have ever seen from him, and when this happens, I can never tell if he is about to hit someone or if he's on the verge of tears.

I look around the circle of misfits and outlaws. The scene has changed from whining and complaining about our general condition as men, especially with our women, to one of focused seriousness. Each man looks at Buck. I can tell they want to help him through his confusion.

"What would happen if she never stopped?"

Buck shakes his head slowly. "All I know is the longer her words go on, the more nervous and anxious I get."

Twig asks, "how long have you waited for her to talk so far?"

Buck looks at Twig's big face. He doesn't glare, but I can see that even speaking about this subject is hard for Buck. "Thirty seconds, I guess, maybe a minute."

Charlie, who sits across the fire, stands so he and Buck can see one another over the flame. Charlie is the psychiatrist in our group. Although he seldom gives professional advice, he does toss in a potent word or two once in a while, and tonight is no exception. "How old do you feel when she starts in?"

This question has been asked before, so we all know not to think about the answer. Usually the first word that pops up is the correct one.

Without looking at Charlie, Buck fires a fast, one-word answer, "Seven."

As if a light has turned on and the clouds opened, Buck's entire face lights up. "Holy shit, my mom used to rant for hours. She'd never let up, and hell, I was only seven. There was nothing I could do to stop her."

With his single, short question, Charlie cut through the bullshit. He sits and disappears in the sea of faces around the campfire.

Buck spins and swings his arms. "I used to have to sit through hours of her raging. It was mostly about what assholes men were. What she forgot was I was also

a male, and she was talking about me." Buck's quivering
lip worsens, and he sounds choked. He's on the edge of
something big, and I think maybe he may have put his
toe over the line.

He drops his face into his palms. Although I hear no
sobs, he's doing much more than thinking. His breath
heaves. His exhalation is broken. Through his hands
he moans, "That woman never gave me a break. She was
always on me about something, and she never let me
say anything." He turns his head up to us and tears run
down his cheeks. "She never listened to anything I said."
He speaks in a demanding tone, like he wants one of us
to do something.

I look at Bill, who is about to tell some God-awful
story and ruin any chance of Buck finding the source of
his anxiety. I spin quickly toward Bill, leap to my feet,
and point at him with a glare. Bill's first word never
leaves his lips.

"Why didn't she give me a chance to talk?" Buck
moans the question more to the billions of stars over our
heads than to any specific person. "Why didn't Jacky or
Billie or Karen give me a chance to talk? Why do they
all have to talk so much? Where do all the words come
from? Why can't I stop them? Who am I? Where do I
belong?"

There it is, the big question. "Who am I?" It's always
the big question. Maybe Buck is going to break through
after all. We all wait in silent anticipation for him to
question himself into a corner. He always blames
everyone else, when we all know it's only him doing it to
himself. We all do it to ourselves. It's the big answer. We
seldom come to the answer unless we are pointing our
finger at someone else. God, I love this circle of men.

Buck's questions ramble on into a distant obscurity until he is out of them. He sits, tears drying on his face. The quivering of his lip is gone, replaced with a huge question mark, like it's tattooed across his forehead.

We all sit for a minute or two in silence, in awe of what happened. Our hardest-assed biker got to his core question. He's confused, maybe for the first time since I've known him. Rather than his tough biker exterior, his softer side is exposed. It's the side with the seven-year-old's questions that never got answered. It's the side he put away for years. Now he gets to go back as an adult and experience those questions again, this time answering them for himself.

I love sitting in these circles. These kinds of things don't happen that often, but when they do, it makes up for all the evenings of storytelling and whining that we all fall prey to.

Buck puts up one spike-gloved hand in a halt gesture, though he needn't, because not a word has been spoken since his revelation. "I'm done for now."

I look at my watch and wonder what happened to the time. "It's nine o'clock, guys, and unless a man has something that he can't hold for another week, it's time to close for the evening."

The circle is silent, filled with expectant faces, but no one wants more time, so I say, "Let's all stand and gather closer around the fire."

Once each man is on his feet, we close the circle, coming in tight until we stand shoulder to shoulder. Each man's arms extend across the shoulders of both men on either side of him, hand resting on the man beyond. The contact is binding; the closeness confirms that we were able to break the normal bonds of masculine behavior of staying isolated from one another and not asking for help.

We stand for a minute while I release any helpful or harmful spirits, including Biker Bob, because though he was not physically present tonight, I always feel him close during moments like these.

When I've finished with my last duty as leader for the evening, I pass the baton by choosing another man for next week's leadership. Once I've chosen Bill, each man pushes a foot full of sand over the fire until it's buried.

With the chaos of many conversations at once, we walk to our bikes. The first bike to fire is Stewart's; his is always first, and the lump-lump sound drowns out any attempt to talk. In seconds all the bikes are running. Drivers and riders roll along the small ravine, back to the real world, leaving behind, as if in a dream, the magic of what happened.

In a single-file line, we wind along the bed of the gully until the well-worn trail leads up the wall and by the burnt out old farmhouse, past the hopelessly stripped and rusted automobiles, out to the steel front gate hanging askew on one twisted hinge, and onto the pavement. Some go left to Barstow, while others ride south with me.

Once the engines come up to speed and we are all in formation, we are like a snake, slithering along old Highway 66 moving in a roar of thunder and flash of chrome and leather. It is a fitting end to such an incredible evening.

In twenty minutes, north of Victorville, the first man turns off, and our pack breaks up. By the time we are at the southern end of town, only two of us are left, Stewart and I. When we reach my turn, I hold my right palm vertical as we ride side by side. Stewart does the same with his left hand and we slap fingertips. "See ya later, Tazz," he yells. His smile is the last thing I see as I turn left and roll as quietly as possible into my neighborhood. With my engine turned off, I coast up my driveway and into the garage.

Four

Billy Black

I awake to a cacophony of birds calling dawn into existence. My tent, with its screen overhead, allows me to see the huge disk of a rock we camped next to, the sky, and a large spiny cactus. Once my eyes have adjusted to staying open, I sit up and look out of my tent. My pearl colored Indian sits next to Katherine's 750 Yamaha, dwarfing it in size.

I almost never get up early, but this morning, with the birds and the silence of the desert, is different. I unzip my tent and wiggle my way out of its small opening. Once standing, I stretch, yawn, and walk over to the dead ashes of last night's fire. Two empty beer bottles sit on the picnic bench, and a few pieces of wood lay next to the fire pit.

As the sky opens from dark gray to light lavender, eventually shifting to peach and finally the blonde of day, I stand in awe of my first morning on my own in almost twenty years. For a brief moment, I wonder how Stewart is doing getting the kids ready for school without me, but my gaze catches the sight of another desert vista with a hawk circling. It's looking for breakfast.

When the sun finally breaks over the ridge twenty

miles away and casts light and shadows, defining each
stone, each plant with a crystalline clarity, Katherine
rustles in her tent and unzips the door. She backs out and
re-zips, then turns to me with a sleepy grin. "Where's
the coffee?"

I smile, but say nothing. It's been an hour or so of saying
nothing and my brain has not adjusted to conversation.

She runs fingers through her tangled blonde hair,
walks over to the bike and pulls a small hatchet from her
right saddlebag. After a few minutes of splitting one of
the pieces of wood into splinters, then striking a match
to the assembled pile, she has a small blaze and puts on
a kettle of water to boil.

"You're prepared for every situation," I say after she
pours two cups of instant and we both have taken a sip.

"I like my coffee," she says, "and I knew we might be
in places with no Starbucks."

I take another sip. "I'm glad you're prepared for tent
camping, because I don't know the first thing about
living out in the open."

"Comes second nature."

I smile. "Lucky for me."

She drags out a small frying pan and positions it in
place of the kettle. "I brought some eggs for breakfast."
She pulls out a container with a half dozen eggs and walks
over to the fire. "I forgot oil, so we'll have to eat them
scrambled, if that's okay with you."

I nod.

She cracks each egg, stirring them into the pan.

Although I would never have eaten eggs like these at
home, they taste great. We sit on our park bench eating
and sipping coffee as the sun heats the day.

Kat turns to me. "Where are we going?"

Billy Black

I look at her and nod in an eastern direction. "I was headed for New Mexico, but I'm almost certain I'll never get there."

"Why not?"

"When I started this odyssey, instead of planning out every move, I left myself open to fate. You were my first turn in this adventure, and I'm sure there will be more if I can stay open to whatever comes."

She sets her empty cup on the table and takes a last bite of eggs. "Bob told me to ride with you, so in a sense I am also staying open to possibilities. I've never done a journey like this before."

I gather the dirty dishes. "Let's break camp and get on the road."

She reaches out to take the dishes. "There's no water in this campsite, so we'll have to store the dishes dirty and wash them later."

I take a paper towel, also supplied by Katherine, and dry wipe the dishes, then she repacks them. We break down our tents, and in twenty minutes, I drop my full weight onto my kick pedal, and the twin cylinders roar into life. Although her Yamaha has a different tone, our two engines sound good together. We pull away from the campsite. I give a last look at the huge disk of a rock and the dwarfed park bench under it. We roll along the dirt road past other campers cooking breakfast and getting ready for a day in the desert. The flowers along the roadside are a sight. The desert floor looks like a lawn, it's so green and lush.

The long open pans of flowers, the blooming desert cactus in the contrast to heat-scorched rocks and sandy bottoms leave no doubt that at any other part of the year, this country is uninhabitable. I'm glad it's early spring.

Channeling Biker Bob 3

Our two engines rumble through rock canyons and over summits that look over more than twenty miles of untouched desert. We follow the winding rough two-lane until we come to the southern entrance of the park. Katherine greets one of her fellow workers and the man wishes her luck on her journey, then we ride off and down the long hill toward Highway 10.

Immediately after leaving the park, I notice empty beer cans, wheel tracks leading off into the distance over the terrain, discarded tires, and rusted car bodies alongside the road. Ah yes, humanity at its best. Without the protection of park boundaries, people are free to trash the habitat.

Once down the long hill, we cross over the freeway and turn left going east. We crank up our engines, ride tandem at seventy, pass big-rig trucks and cars with suitcase-piled roof racks. The speed is exhilarating. The open sky above my head and wind in my face make me feel alive.

By noon, before crossing the Colorado River and the Arizona border, we pull off the freeway into the town of Blythe. Stewart told me about this town from his adventures a few years ago. Although his experience was of a barren desert town, we pull in next to the lush Colorado River and feel the moist air of the water.

We park and turn our bikes off. I still feel the vibration in my body. I drop the bike on its kickstand and dismount, then stand with feet and legs almost numb from hours in the saddle.

"God, that was a long ride," I say while we walk to the water. "I'm not used to sitting so long in one position. Maybe I'm too old to be doing so much riding."

Once we're cooled, we drive into Blythe and find a

Billy Black

small café along the dusty main road. It's nothing special, but it looks better than the chain restaurant across the street.

Katherine removes her sunglasses as we enter the fake tile-floored building. We walk to the counter. A waitress pushes her way through double swinging doors and gives us a friendly grin. "Sit anywhere you like. I'll be with you in a minute."

I remove my jacket, and we find a seat next to the front window looking at our bikes.

"Hi," a wide-hipped waitress says as she places two glasses of ice water on the table and sweeps a lock of auburn hair away from her steel blue eyes. She pulls two menus from under her right arm and slides them onto the table. "I'll be back to take your orders." She spins on one heel like a drill sergeant, stomps back to the order counter, and grabs two full platters.

I take the water and down the entire contents in three long gulps. When I set the glass down, Katherine has done the same.

"Kinda thirsty," I say.

"I could drink a gallon." She giggles and crunches on a small piece of ice.

I pick up the menu and scan a list I can find in any restaurant in America. Burgers and fries, biscuits and gravy, three varieties of turkey sandwiches; all of the standard stuff, until I come to a single item at the bottom of the page: Bob's Blue Plate Special.

It doesn't say what the Bob special is, but since I'm attempting to follow signs, the Bob part of the entry catches my attention, and I tell Katherine, "If she comes while I'm gone, order the special for me." I point at the line on her menu as I get up. "I've got to wash up."

I walk across the restaurant with twenty sets of eyes giving me furtive glances, wind my way along a hall and into the smallest restroom I have ever seen. If there's room to turn around, I'll be surprised.

I pee, then squeeze my way to a sink the size of a dinner plate, wash my hands and splash water in my face, then look in the mirror. My ever-growing wrinkles stretch away from my eyes and form around my chapped lips. God, I'm getting old, and I'm sure the desert winds aren't helping.

I search my purse for some lipstick, then notice a business card lying facedown on a dirty glass shelf hung a few inches above the sink faucets.

I ignore it and find my lipstick, then apply a soothing layer. When I return the lipstick to my purse, I can't help myself. I peel the card off the glass, turn it over, and read bold gold lettering across a gloss black surface: One Percent of One Percent. The name on the bottom says Billy Black with a phone number below it. I turn the card over, then back again. What would a business card like this be doing in the women's bathroom?

I take a last check on my hair and lipstick, and with card in hand, I walk out of the bathroom.

I sit across from Katherine and lay the card in front of her face up. She glances at it and gives me a quizzical stare.

"I found it in the women's bathroom."

She looks back at the card, then at me. "And?"

"It's the same group my husband belongs to."

"No kidding," she says. "Do you know this guy?"

"Never heard of him, but I think it's a sign, just like meeting you yesterday. I don't know what you want to do, but I have to find this guy." I can't believe it, I'm starting to sound like Stewart.

She looks at the card again. "He lives here in Blythe."

She hands the card back to me. I take it. "The strange thing is that I thought the One Percent of One Percent Club was local for the Barstow area. Here we are a few hundred miles east, and this card shows up."

A new waitress steps to our table with two platters. "Two Bob's Blue Plate Specials." She sets them down and starts to turn, but I ask, "Is Bob the owner of the restaurant?"

She turns toward me, rolls her eyes, and gets a sarcastic smirk on her long, narrow face. She puts one hand on her wide hip. "Mike's the owner. He's my husband. He thinks he has these dreams about this guy Bob, who once in a while tells him what to cook. I think Mike's gone off his rocker." She turns and rushes back to the order counter.

All of the blood drains out of my face.

Katherine looks at me. "Are you okay, Renee? You look like you saw a ghost."

I take my glass of water and down the contents, open my paper napkin, pour some ice in, and close it. I put it to my forehead.

Katherine asks, "What's going on, Renee?"

I look at her with the ice held to my temple. "It's the same Bob, I'm sure of it."

"Biker Bob?"

"Yep, the one and only."

"Maybe you better eat something." She points at my platter of food.

I look down at a turkey pastrami on light rye. I pick up the sandwich and study its contents. A slice of provolone cheese with minced black olives mixed with Dijon mustard. "It's my dream sandwich," I say. "If I was at home and had all of the right ingredients, I would make this exact sandwich."

Katherine looks at hers and blanches. "Thin-sliced salmon with dill pickles," she says. "Romaine lettuce and a thin layer of mayonnaise on a sourdough French roll. My god, I couldn't ask for a more perfect combination."

I wave to the waitress. With a coffee pot in her hand, she walks over to our table and asks, "is everything okay?"

"Everything is fine," I say, "but how did your husband know exactly what we wanted?"

She looks around and leans closer to the table. "To tell the truth, I have no idea how he does it, but he's right on the button every time. You'd think the Blue Plate Special was a dish for the day, but not with my weird husband. He says he dreams about it, but I don't know. The guy's always been a bit wacko. Lately, things have been getting more than a little odd."

I flip the card over and extend it to her. "Do you know this guy?"

She lifts her glasses hanging from her chest and studies the glossy black surface. "Oh, sure. I've never met him, but he and Mike are in some kind of club together. I try to stay away from all of that mumbo-jumbo stuff as much as I can. I've got too much work to do around here."

I ask, "can I speak to Mike for a moment?"

She sizes me up and gives me a suspicious glare. "Why do you want to talk to my husband?"

Her hackles are up, so I put my hand in the air to expose my wedding ring. "I live in Big Bear, and my husband belongs to the same biker club as the guy in this card. I just want to ask some questions about the club."

Her face relaxes. "He's pretty busy with lunch right now, but in about a half hour he'll have some time." She looks around at the crowd. "I've got to get back to work. I'll tell him." She spins on her heels, races to the order counter, and grabs another set of platters.

I take my first bite of the sandwich, and it's heavenly. I taste a touch of some herb I don't expect.

By the time I've finished my last bite, a big guy with a cue-ball head steps over to our table. "Martha said you wanted to talk to me." He has a gravely voice. He wipes his hands on a dirty apron wrapped around his waist. Three large tattoos on each arm cover most of the skin and wrap under his skimpy tank-top tie-dyed shirt.

I hold the black card for him to see. "Your wife said you might know this man."

He takes the card and studies it, squinting to read the name. "Well, hell, I don't have my glasses." He hands the card back to me. "What am I reading here?"

"The name's Billy Black."

His eyes get large. "You two are looking for Billy Black? What the hell for?"

I look him square in the eyes. "Biker Bob sent me."

He leans closer and drops to a whisper. "Bob sent you?" He takes a quick glance around and looks at me again. "The Biker Bob?"

I smile but don't say a word.

He turns to Katherine. "Scooch over, because we've got some shit to talk about."

Katherine moves along the seat toward the window and the big guy sits across the table from me. "You two aren't from around here, are you?"

Katherine says, "I'm from Twenty-nine Palms and she's from Big Bear."

I say, "we both have had dealings with Bob, and my husband belongs to the One Percent of One Percent Club."

He wrings his hands. "No shit. There's a chapter in Big Bear?"

"Barstow, but they're close to each other."

"Hell," he says, "I thought we were the only ones. Bob came to me and a few local guys two years ago, and our group formed out of his visits."

I say, "Stew and the guys thought they were the only ones."

"Man, this is big stuff." He turns to me. "Billy Black is kind of our leader, in a loose sense of the word. He was the first one in these parts who was visited by Bob."

"Is he around today?"

"Kinda. The funny thing is, he's been asking for you too."

"Us?"

"Not by name, but he mentioned that pearl Indian." He points out the window. "That's your bike out there, isn't it?"

I nod. "Bob gave me that bike."

"No shit."

There is a moment of silence, then I say, "You know how to find Billy?"

"Sure, kinda." He pulls a felt-tip pen from his apron, grabs the card and turns it over. In a half minute, he's sketched out a reasonably simple map along the levy. "Billy's in a houseboat on the river. It takes a bit to find him, if he wants to be found."

I lean forward as he turns the map to face me. "Just

follow these turns. You might think you'll never find the place, but the road takes you right to his doorstep." He draws a deep breath and lets it out. "If he's there."

I take the card, reach over to my leather jacket in the corner of the booth and put it in the top pocket. I look at Mike. "How did you know what to prepare for us when we ordered Bob's Special?"

He gets a big grin that reminds me of Twig's goofy smile. "Hell, I have no idea. I take a break and let Bob take over. He's the one who made your sandwiches. I just went along for the ride."

Katherine says, "It was the best sandwich I'd ever eaten."

He looks around in a furtive glance. "Don't say that too loud, because everyone would order the special, and Bob'd be taking over most of the time."

I ask in a quiet tone. "You mean not many people order the special?"

He gets a sheepish smile. "I only add it to the menu when Bob tells me to."

Katherine points at herself and me. "Today's special was just for us?"

Mike turns to her. "I had no idea who was going to order it, but here you are, One on One members from Barstow. Bob knows what he's doing."

The front door opens and three couples walk in. Mike stands and looks down at us. He puts out his monstrous paw and I swipe my fingers across his, like I've seen Stewart and the boys do with one another so many times. He smiles. "I've got to get back to work. It was good meeting you two." He turns to Katherine and swipes fingertips with her. "Good luck with Billy Black; he's a handful." He rotates on his heels and walks to the kitchen.

Katherine and I stare at one another, barely a word between us, as Mike's wife comes over with a scowl. While she clears our dishes, she says, "Mike said your sandwiches are on the house."

"Well, thank you," Katherine says.

"Don't thank me; it wasn't my idea."

Katherine turns to me as we get up, gives me a secret glance, and looks at Mike's wife. "Well, thank Mike for us, will you?"

The woman huffs and stomps off to the kitchen with our plates. Although I hate waitresses with an attitude, I drop a twenty on the table, and we walk outside to our bikes. I kick mine into life and Katherine hits her starter. We roll away from the curb and pull into traffic, what little traffic there is.

Once out of town, we stop. I pull a map from my saddlebag and look for the crossroad, Mulberry Street. The map indicates a mile or so before the turn off. I gun my engine and crank up to fifty. Katherine pulls in beside me in a tandem roar of engines, weaving along below the levy, knowing that on the other side is the Colorado River, but not seeing one sign of water in the barren landscape.

I almost miss the bleached Mulberry Street sign hidden behind a huge pampas grass. At the last possible second the sign appears. We turn left and drive a block on a dirt road toward the levy, then up a driveway to the top of the embankment where I kill my engine. Katherine follows suit, and we sit overlooking a lush, green landscape next to a meandering river maybe a hundred feet wide. A wooden house rests on three huge metal pontoons moored against a rotting wood-beam dock.

I drop my bike onto its kickstand, dismount, and lean to swipe at some of the desert dust that's accumulated on my leather pants. It all came from driving the single block of Mulberry Street, which looked as though it had not seen any road work in a decade.

A footpath leads down toward the dock. A yellow chopped Harley with a moderately extended front end and skinny spoke front wheel sits on the worn dock timbers.

I remove my cap-style helmet and lace it onto the throttle side of the handlebars, shake my hair out, and drag my fingers through it.

Katherine removes her full-face helmet and looks at me. "This place feels strange. You sure you want to go down there?"

I pull the black business card from my top pocket and look at it. "We're here, so we might as well see what's waiting for us."

She shrugs, and I walk ahead down the path. The second I put one foot on the dock with its gray planks and rusted steel turnbuckles, a medium tenor yells from the shadows. "Don't move a step closer. What the hell do you want?"

Both Katherine and I freeze. I search the shadows, but see no one. I hold up the card as if it has some kind of magical protection. "I found your card at the restaurant and Mike gave us directions to your place."

"Why the fuck would Mike do something like that?"

I've still got my hand high in the air with the card extended. "Bob sent us."

"Bob who?"

"Biker Bob," Katherine says a little too loud.

"Which Biker Bob?" he asks.

"You know, the dead one."

After a protracted silence, he says in a less demanding

tone, "Okay, you can come aboard. Go around to the front deck."

I stand and walk over to the deck of the houseboat. When I step aboard, the boat dips slightly in the water with my weight. Katherine follows close behind without saying a word.

We walk the length of the craft, come to a weather-worn deck and face a slightly built man who can't be an inch over my height. He holds a large military weapon pointed downward. He doesn't greet us or step closer, but stands at a kind of attention.

I shade my eyes to see him. "I'm Renee Chance," I say as friendly as I can muster. I step forward with my hand extended, but he doesn't move except to shift his weapon slightly from pointing at the deck to pointing at my feet.

He makes a quick gesture with the barrel of his gun, motioning for us to move to the right, facing the harsh glare of the sun. "State your business," he barks in a military command.

Shading my eyes, and unable to get a clear view of him other than his Jimi Hendrix shock of hair, I say, "We really don't have any business. I found your card in the women's bathroom of the Shady Rest Restaurant, and Mike told us where to find you. We thought maybe you might know our next move."

"Your next move?" he asks in a higher pitch than before. "Your next move. What, do I look like some kind of psychic?"

"No," I say. "We thought the card was a sign from Bob."

"How do you know Bob?"

I point back to the top of the levy. "That's Bob's old

Billy Black

bike that he rode before he died."

There is a moment of silence. "Bob didn't ride no rice-burner Yamaha."

Something inside of me snaps. I've been insulted and ordered around one too many times in the last five minutes. "No, you idiot, not the fucking Yamaha. Don't you see another bike up there? Can't you maybe figure it out on your own, or do you need a road map?"

I watch the barrel of his gun rise. I scream, "Don't you even pretend to point that fucking gun at me unless you plan on using it."

The barrel drops.

"And, what, aren't you going to invite us in out of the sun, or do you have the social skills of a turnip?" I'm on a roll, so I keep going. "Mike trusted us enough to give us your address. Shit, Billy, you're looking at two unarmed women here, not some military operation. Either you put that gun down and invite us in, or we're leaving your sorry-excuse-for-a-human-being this minute."

I put both hands on my hips and glare at him for five seconds, but he still doesn't move. I turn to Katherine and almost scream, "Let's get the fuck out of here. This uncouth bastard has no idea how to act." I rotate away from the dock and take my first step toward the bikes before I hear the click of steel. Is this guy going to shoot us? I look back and see that he's put the gun on the metal table beside him, barrel facing away from us.

"Okay," he says in a timid voice.

I stop, turn to him and speak in a softer voice. "That's better. Gees, Billy, you don't get many visitors, do you?"

"I'm not used to people," he says, "and I guess I don't know how to act."

"Do you want to invite us in and maybe offer us a cup

59

of tea and a muffin or something?"

"Oh, yes, please," he says quietly as he opens the sliding glass door and stands back to usher us in.

The inside of his house looks like it belongs on the cover of Good Housekeeping or better yet, Architectural Digest. It looks as though he was expecting us all along. Low counters, made of finely polished dark wood, separate the one-person kitchen from the living area. Exquisite paintings of desert and river landscapes cover the walls. Some are stacked one above another. The painter's style is the same in each piece; a surrealistic quality, while adhering to realistic content.

I turn to him. "These are beautiful. Who painted them?"

He blushes through the scraggly beard that hangs to his chest. "I did. It's just a hobby."

I turn and admire a six-foot-wide canvas of a long, open desert scene with deep shadows and a violet and crimson sky at dawn or after sunset. The cactus and scrub brush are so real it feels like I'll get stuck by spines if I touch them.

"How do you do it?" I turn to a mid-day piece of a roadrunner. The bird looks like it's going to jump from the canvas, run out the door and disappear into the desert.

"Hell," he says. "I don't know how, I just do it. I start in with an undercoat and fill in the blank spaces in my head."

I turn and sit on a kitchen chair carved from mesquite branches. Katherine sits next to me and asks, "Who was your teacher?"

Billy walks into the tiny kitchen and lights the stove. He draws water into a kettle and puts it on the flame. "I never had any teachers. I just bought some paints when I got back and started painting. For years it was the only thing that kept me sane."

"Got back?" Katherine asks.

"From Nam."

"Viet Nam?"

"Oh yeah." He smiles. "I don't get much news, and I keep thinking Nam was the last war. Guess there's been a few since."

Katherine grimaces. "A few too many."

After a moment of awkward silence, he says, "I was in Special Forces for eighteen months before I was wounded and came back to the States. Once I got back, the contrast of what I'd been through and the ridiculous sheltered life everyone else was living drove me here, where I don't have to look at it."

He drops onto a chair and puts his fist under his chin. "And to think, all Nam was about was oil. I sacrificed my youth and killed so many because my government told me to. I'm haunted by the ghosts of the people I murdered."

I see the deep wound in his face. It's been thirty years, and he's never come to terms with it. The man is hollow. I ask, "Have you been living here all this time?"

He nods. "After some years in Phoenix, I landed right here on this boat. It's my island of sanity. This boat and the One on One guys have been my only life raft."

"And painting," Katherine says.

"Yes, and my painting. Without it, I would have killed myself years ago." Billy points around the room. "These are more recent canvases. My early ones were much darker."

"Do you have any of those?" I ask.

He turns and looks at me, probably to see if I'm serious.

"I have a few in my bedroom," he says. "I could bring them out."

"Are they hung?"

He nods.

"If you don't mind, I'd like to see them where they are."

He stands and walks around the counter, then strides across the small living area. He reaches the carved wooden door, turns, and motions us over. "I'm not going to be able to show you from there."

Both Katherine and I are on our feet and move quickly toward him, as if at any given second he might change his mind and we'll miss the opportunity.

He opens the door and waves us in before him. We step inside his immaculate room with a stiff military single bed, military hiking boots neatly positioned at the foot of the bed, pictures of Army buddies behind glass hanging on the wall and another military-green rifle resting against the nightstand.

He steps in and points at the right wall. A dark painting of distant bombs and blood-filthy men, all helping one another through a swamp, hangs alone. The painting hangs slightly askew on the wall. "This was the first one I painted."

Although it lacks the surrealistic quality of his newer work, technically, the painting is uncanny.

"This was your first painting ever?" I ask.

"Other than finger paints as a kid."

"What about this one?" I point at a wide canvas of a gray military gunship. Two soldiers are standing on the forward deck pointing at a deep burgundy sunset with a dark violet jungle in the foreground.

"That was one of the early ones, too. I keep it around

to remind me of a quiet morning on the Mekong River. It was the morning before all hell broke loose."

He drops into a memory, and it doesn't look like a good one, so I change the subject. "Billy, where did you get this talent?"

He looks at me with a surprised face. "The war brought it out of me. I had to put that anger somewhere. Those military assholes fucked up my life forever, and I was only eighteen. Instead of going off the deep end, I funneled my anger into paint. It worked then, and though I'm not as angry these days, painting still calms me."

I reach over and pat his shoulder, but he leaps back, slamming hard against the wall. The painting behind him rotates a few more degrees to the right. "Don't touch me," he screams in a hysterical, high-pitch. "Don't touch me." He hugs himself. "Don't touch me," he whimpers. Although his lower lip and chin quiver, he doesn't cry. He slides down the wall. "Don't touch me." I can barely hear him as he sits on the bare floor, tucks his head into his knees, and pulls himself into a tight ball.

I motion to Katherine, and we leave the room.

She closes the bedroom door behind her and mouths, "Wow."

The teapot screams.

I rush to the stove and turn off the flame. The kettle settles into an ever-quieter moan covering the sounds coming from the bedroom.

We've finished our cup of tea before Billy opens the door. With an embarrassed look, he walks past Katherine and me sitting on his little couch. He positions himself at the small, round table in his kitchen. Once he's taken a sip of tea, he looks into the living area at us. "Sorry, I have a condition I picked up in that dirty little war."

"There's nothing to be sorry for," I say.

Katherine is quick to change the subject. "Can you tell us how many paintings you've completed?"

He brightens. "I couldn't say for sure, because in the early days I didn't have much money, so I painted one over the top of another. It's only in the last ten years or so, since the government paid off the vets who were exposed to Agent Orange and all of those other stupid chemicals, that I've had money to buy new canvas and good paints. I guess I finish a canvas every week or two, depending on my energy."

I say, "I see only a few finished canvases on the walls here. Do you have your other stuff stored?"

He points above our heads. "The more current work is upstairs, but I ran out of room years ago, so I have a storage unit in town with a bunch of pieces."

"Can we see them?" Katherine asks.

"It's all old business," he says. "No point in seeing that crap."

"I'd love to," I say, but he shakes his head and I realize he's embarrassed to have so much attention. I want to see what he's done, but his erratic behavior fifteen minutes ago cautions me not to press the point.

He enters the living area and sits on the recliner across from us. I'm careful not to extend my feet and accidentally touch him. I don't want a replay of what happened.

"Do you display your stuff in a gallery?" I ask.

He shakes his head. "I'm not that good yet. Maybe once I get a better handle on color, but I'm not ready."

I can't believe he's saying this. "Billy, you're the best painter I have ever met. Your work should be out in the world."

He brushes me off with an unbelieving grimace.

Billy Black

We sit in silence while I take a sip of my tea. I ask, "How did you meet Bob?"

Billy's glare shifts and he smiles. "Biker Bob helped me work out some color problems I was having maybe five years ago. He came to me in a series of dreams and gave me hints of other ways to approach color mixing. He's really the driving force behind the new kind of painting I've been doing."

"Bob came to me two years ago," I say, "and helped my husband and me get through a difficult spot in our relationship."

Billy shifts uncomfortably in his chair.

"Maybe you heard of Stewart Chance?"

He looks at me with an incredulous stare. "You're The Renee Chance?"

I nod.

"No kidding," he says. "I saw the two of you that afternoon on the TV in Mikes Café. All of us had been following Stewart whenever he appeared on those talk shows, but when you came on, the restaurant was full of people waiting to see what was going to happen next. Man, you two were great together. It gave real meaning to the word 'relationship'."

It's my turn to feel embarrassed. "I guess it was a day to remember, but I didn't think so many people were watching."

"Are you kidding? Everyone I know was watching. Stewart had been wowing us for a month before you showed up, and the two of you together was icing on the cake." He gets a suspicious glare and puts one finger up as an explanation point. "Was that really Biker Bob inside Stewart?"

I smile. "Oh, it was Bob, all right. He turned our sedate

65

little world inside out. Stewart could have never come up with that kind of stuff on his own. Back then, my Stewart was. . . well. . . he was a wimp. The new Stewart often infuriates me, but I wouldn't go back for a second."

Billy says, "Bob visits me once in a while in my dreams. Me and Mike are the only ones Bob comes to in our group so far."

I change the subject. "Bob sent me on this journey, and directed me to your front door, maybe to see your paintings, but knowing Bob, there is much more to this. I just don't know what it is yet."

Billy picks up his cup and takes another sip, then gives me and Katherine a strange look. "I know."

"You know?" I ask with excitement.

"Bob told me this afternoon while I was napping. It couldn't have been twenty minutes before you two rode up. He didn't exactly say that you would be driving on the levy, but he told me to keep an eye out."

There's silence for a moment. It looks like Billy is contemplating whether to say the next sentence.

"Come on, Billy," Katherine says. "You've got to tell us."

He turns to her. "It's a secret spot out on the desert only a handful of people know about. Bob told me to take you there."

I turn to Katherine. "See, I told you that card meant something."

"Holy shit," she says. "When do we go?"

Billy stands and looks as though he's ready to get on his bike this second, but he goes back into the kitchen.

I have to turn to see what he's doing. "Well?"

"We could leave now, but it's a ways, and I don't think we'd make it before dark. Do you have camping gear?"

Billy Black

"Yes," Katherine says, "We're all set. All you got to do is get us to a store for food, and we're ready to go." She looks at me. "Well, at least I'm ready."

I smile at Billy. "I'm following Bob on this journey. Wherever he leads, I'll go."

Billy gets an excited look. "I'm ready now, but we better wait until morning to get a fresh start. It'll take most of tomorrow to get there as it is, and I'd hate setting up tents with headlights."

I stand and look across the counter at Billy. "Okay, I guess we'll see you in the morning."

He frowns. "You don't have to go. I have an extra bedroom and an extra cot. It'll just take me a minute to straighten it out."

I look at Katherine as she says, "I wouldn't mind staying here on the river rather than some crappy motel next to the freeway."

I look at Billy. "If you don't mind?"

He gets an embarrassed look. "I haven't had many visitors these last few years. Mike and the men from the One on One drop by from time to time, but I've never had two women visit, especially two as handsome as you."

Katherine laughs. "Get outta here."

"No, I'm serious. If you two don't mind sitting still while I lay in come color on a canvas or two, I'd love to use you as models."

It's Katherine's turn to blush. "Are you serious? I can't sit in one place for more than two minutes at a time."

"You don't have to strike a pose or anything. Just sit around like you are and keep talking." He gives her an excited little boy look.

Katherine looks at me and nods. "I'd be honored. Maybe we could sit out on the deck and drop a line in the water. I love fishing, especially for bass."

He grins. "Hell, yes, I've got some gear on the back deck of the boat. I'll get you all set up, and you could sit in the shade while I do some sketches."

I ask, "What kind of fish do you catch around here?"

"Lots of bass for sure, some rainbow, and once in a blue moon, I'll pull out a German brown. They're the best to eat if they're wild."

I stand and look over the rail at the lazy Colorado River. It's the same river that roars through the Grand Canyon and the same one that empties into Mexico's Sea of Cortez. I have my back to Billy and Katherine. "Do they stock this river?"

"Not the river, but stockers swim down from the dams. It usually takes them a few years to get down this far, and by then they have reverted to tasting wild."

Kat says, "get me a pole and a cold soda, and I'll be happy for hours."

Billy opens the refrigerator and brings two cans of soda to the table, then disappears down the hall. The next I see, he's carrying two poles and a tackle box along the railing to the front deck. I take my first sip and unwind myself from the kitchen chair. Katherine gets up, and we both step out onto the deck.

By the time we sit on the plastic lounge chairs, Billy has the hooks wormed and he's dropping the lines over the rail. He hands one to me and one to Katherine. "Okay, you two stay right here, and I'll get my canvas set up." He rushes back into the houseboat.

***

During lunch, all I can think about is the clay cylinder

in the garage. I see that inch and a half thick wall going skyward for three feet, maybe more, until it can't squeeze any thinner.

"Nicky, what are you thinking?" she asks, and I bring my eyes back into focus to see her sitting across the table.

"Oh, nothing," I say.

"Come on, you were thinking something."

I'd better answer, but I already know the clay vase isn't exactly what she wants me to talk about. I think fast to come up with the right answer. "Maybe we could go to a movie later this afternoon?"

She gives me a sly look and twists her face in the way she does when I've given the wrong answer. "That would be nice, but it's not what you were thinking."

"What's the big deal about what I'm thinking?"

"What's the big deal about not wanting to tell me?"

Shit, she's pretty much got me there, so I say, "I was thinking about the twenty-five pounds of clay I started to throw before lunch. It'll be my first—"

"Is that all you can think of is clay?"

Although I can't help it, my face scrunches into an exasperated grimace. "You asked."

"Men," she says. "All they think about is work."

"Hey, at least I'm not a sports junkie."

She looks at me and smiles. "If you were, I'd never be with you. Can't you think about us once in a while?"

"I thought about us going to the movies," I say in my defense, but I already know the answer will not be good enough. Nothing is ever good enough for this woman.

She looks me directly in the eyes. God, I hate when she stares me down, trying to get right inside my brain. Is it a woman thing, because every woman I have ever been with can't help but do it.

I grab my plate and glass, get up, and take three steps over to the sink, mostly to get away from her staring. After scrubbing my dishes and putting them in the rack, I turn toward her again, and sure enough, she's still looking at me. "Sorry, Honey, I think about what has my attention at the moment. Maybe it is a guy thing, I don't know. Right now clay has my attention."

For a moment, she has a Rock of Gibraltar expression. I think I'm home free. I said exactly what I felt, and she heard me without taking it personally. The expression lasts long enough for me to think these thoughts and let my guard down, but with the suddenness of a desert storm, her face prunes and her lower lip quivers. When a gasp bursts forth, I know I'll never be able to get back to my clay. The damn cylinder will dry up and wither away to a pile of dust before this woman will let me go.

Her tears roll down her cheeks. A long sob leaks from her as she drops her face into her hands.

I glance at last month's calendar on the fridge, and sure enough, that little red dot I secretly put on Wednesday of last month was exactly twenty-eight days ago. Must I follow her down into this rabbit hole of self-pity and slither with her in the mire of female hormonal expression?

Like a foghorn off in the distance, quiet but distinct, a voice goes off in my head. It's not my inner speech, but a separate one that I've grown accustomed to. "If you love this woman and you want to keep her love, you must leap into her hormonal chaos with your whole body and soul."

"I just want to throw some pots, Bob." I think back to the voice inside of my head.

Billy Black

"You've got the rest of your life to throw pots, dickhead. Right now, and every twenty eight-days for years to come, your woman needs you."

"She always needs me. When do my needs get met?" I hear a snicker, then the words, "That, my man, is a whole other ball game. Right now she doesn't even realize that you have needs. She thinks you just want to get away from her to throw another pot."

In my mind, I say, "Well, in a sense, she's right."

"Think very carefully about what you need from her, other than sex, that is."

My mind is blank.

After a moment Bob says, "It's okay, you don't need to come up with anything right this second. Just think about it. For now, your woman needs you to witness her going through her emotional journey. Walk over there and put your arms around her. Tell her you love her, but whatever you do, don't try to have sex with her."

I turn my head as if I could catch him off to the right of my shoulder. I scream in my head. "Sex will fix it for her. She'll calm down if I can get her to come."

"At this moment, sex is just a band-aid, and it's her last choice. She'll take it because she thinks that it's the only way to connect with you, but what she really wants is kindness, compassion, and mostly understanding."

I shake my head. "What can I do to fix her?"

"There is nothing to fix, Nick. Just get on the roller coaster with her and ride it out. She needs you right now, and if you want to be closer to her during the next twenty-odd days, roll up your sleeves and get to it."

Although it rubs against every fiber of my being, I walk over, pull up a chair, and sit next to her. When I put my arms around her and touch my forehead to hers, she bursts into another long bout of tears, but something else happens. She leans against me, and I wrap my arms around her even more, encircling her tighter.

For five minutes we sit. I'm in an awkward position as she pushes against my chest, crying harder, until I feel the intensity wane. After another minute, the waterworks relax. When we're left with sniffles, I reach across the table for the box of tissues. I slide two between the indistinguishable line that separates her from me.

She pulls back slightly, puts the tissues to her nose, and blows, then puts one arm out into the air and drops the tissue on the floor like a discarded kernel of popcorn in the movies.

She wraps her arms back around me and snuggles her face into my clay-spattered chest.

"Thanks, Bob," I say inside my head.

Five

Medicine Bag

My engine thunders under me as I float past open country with broken fences and abandoned farm houses where years ago people tried to make a living on the barren landscape of sand and salt brush. Thinking about me and Melinda, I drive past a few remaining rusted-out cars and trucks left in the 1930's by those desperate souls drawn to California in bankrupt vehicles. They made it past the state line, but blew a piston, a rod or the last spare tire with no money to buy another. Travelers pushed the hulk off the side of the road and maybe whole families put out their thumbs to get to Los Angeles. The abandoned cars became parts vehicles. Over the years, the cars were stripped of anything remotely usable, slowly rusted in the dry desert air and decomposed until they became part of the landscape. Mature cactus and full-size mesquite bush grow next to them, a testament to how long they've been parked. The overall expanse, the distant mountains, and open sky above easily compensate for the automotive litter.

This road isn't as smooth as the Highway 66 it runs parallel to, but it's much more authentic. When I have time, and today I do, I weave past the ruts in the pavement, over derelict bridges above nonexistent creeks, and under the occasional cottonwood, the only large tree that will grow unassisted in this bone-dry landscape.

I reach down and feel my engine; it's cool enough on this burner of a spring morning.

Melinda continues in my thoughts and how well we have been doing these last months since the men and women have been getting together weekly. Maybe there is something to being listened to by someone other than one's mate. I know I feel supported when I meet with the One on One guys every Thursday, but the meeting seems so much more colorful when the women are present.

A jack rabbit leaps out from under a greasewood bush and sprints alongside me for a hundred yards. I look at my speedometer. I'm doing fifty, but the little guy is pulling away from me. When he turns left and darts across the road, I release my throttle and slow, so I don't hit him.

The road makes another of those long banking turns. I lean into the turn and feel the shift in gravity as the bike wheels grip the pavement, holding me in an upright position. Once I'm back out on the straightaway, I let my mind drift with the sound of the steady beat of my Harley.

My new bike business is starting to build momentum, and I'm getting jobs more interesting than brake repair and throttle replacement. Last week a guy from Apple Valley brought in a load of boxes and a totally stock ridged frame. He said money was no object. He wants a custom chopper to ride to next year's Reno Street Vibrations run. It's a 1947 Knucklehead his dad rode when he was young.

Now, this is a project I can sink my teeth into. I've already removed all of the extra tabs and kicked the neck out five degrees to allow for an eight-inch extended front end.

I make another turn and the side road ends onto the highway. I stop at the sign, turn right and crank my engine through every gear, pushing eighty for a half mile before I drop back down to the more reasonable speed limit of fifty-five.

It's always an exhilarating half-minute when I feel the raw power, the rush, then roar, and finally the howl of the wind.

First, the ever-familiar railroad tracks, then as the steel rails cut through the hills, Victorville comes into view. I pull through three sets of lights, turn right, then a quick right again and left into old Glen's driveway. I wave at him sitting on his porch swing, roll past Melinda's car and into the garage Glen and I share.

When I turn my engine off, my legs vibrate long after I unfurl the kickstand, lean the bike, get off and step around to the front of the house. "Hi, Glen, how are things today?"

He holds up one gnarled hand, each knuckle swollen to twice its normal size. "Oh, things are pretty good, considering my arthritis is acting up again."

I reach into my pocket and pull out a roll of twenties that came from the custom basket case I got in yesterday. "Sorry, Glen, I'm a couple of days late on the rent."

I peel bills from the stack and step over the two-foot high picket fence that surrounds his postage stamp of a yard. I hand the bills through the rose bush that climbs up the porch railing to the roof.

Glen takes the money with a twisted, old-man smile and rubs it across his five-day-old gray beard. "The root of all evil."

"What?"

"What, boy, you never went to Sunday school? The love of money is the root of all evil."

I snicker. "The only Sunday school I ever went to was the race track with Dad, but I pretty much learned the same thing there. Dad chased after it like nothing else mattered. He was sure in love with the stuff."

Old Glen's eyes brighten. "Well, you get your lessons where you can. As long as you learned it, I guess it doesn't really matter where."

"Hey, these days I'm just paying bills, but I'm happy with life."

"That's what it's all about."

I turn, wave at Glen and climb back over his little fence. "I got a girlfriend to tend to, Glen. I'll talk to you later."

Just before I step out of sight, old Glen says, "When you going to make her an honest woman?"

I stop and look at him. "What do you mean?"

"Married, buddy. Ain't you never heard of getting married?"

Although I never flinch, my insides take a leap. My guts twist. The only indicator to Glen that the "M" word affects me in the slightest is a stutter of the first word of my reply. "I. . . I can't afford it."

"Hellfire, son, don't you know?"

I cross my arms on my chest. "What am I supposed to know?"

"You'll never be able to afford it. How pregnant can

76

one woman get before you decide to marry her?"

Oh God, weren't things complicated enough? Now I have to worry about marrying Melinda. I unwrap one arm from my chest and wave Glen away, turn, and start up the rickety steps. As I step on number three, the wood gives a noticeable crack but doesn't break. I make a mental note to step lightly on number three in the future.

When I open the door, there she is in her shining womanly beauty. Her belly looks no larger than normal, but her face has the healthy flush of a woman acting out her destiny.

"Hi, Honey, I'm home from the salt mines."

She steps over and kisses me on the cheek. "Can you get me a can of tomatoes on the top shelf? I can't reach it."

I step over to the cupboard and stretch for a can. When I get it, I open the silverware drawer and grab the opener. "Want me to open it?"

"Sure," she says. "Pour it into the sauce. We're having spaghetti tonight."

"Hey, my favorite."

Hell, I don't know what happens. I never know what happens, but in thirty seconds we're into it. She's yelling at me for some perceived negative comment about the spaghetti, and I'm trying to protect myself from her feminine upheaval.

In my men's group I've been working with getting angry without being physical. The only way I'm able not to cross the line into violence is to remove myself from the verbal abuse Melinda piles on so easily. I'm about three minutes into her getting more and more insistent with her reasons why I am such a jerk, when I feel my anger coming up the express elevator. My fist clenches, a sure sign of going over the top. The toaster oven will be the next victim of my enraged psyche. I'm ready to pick it up and send it on its last journey across the room before it lands in the garbage forever, but I bought this one last week, and I'll be damned if I'm going to succumb to her badgering.

I turn, walk out the front door, slam it behind me, and stomp down the steps, almost forgetting to step lightly on the weak third step.

I walk to my bike ready to get the fuck out of here, ride off into the sunset, and forever leave that razor blade of a mouth behind. Jesus, I didn't do a thing.

I don't leave, though. I don't even start the bike. For a while, until I've calmed, I simply sit on the saddle holding the grips extra tight. In a minute or so, bored with sitting, I stand, go to the workbench, grab my polish and a clean rag. I start on the handlebars, squeezing the rag between the cables to polish sections of the bars I usually overlook when getting ready for a ride. I concentrate on the little corners and crannies for five minutes before my hands stop shaking and my body calms enough to take a full breath.

Old Glen comes hobbling around the corner. He walks up to me, puts one gnarly hand on the handlebars, and leans on the bike. "She kinda blindsided you on that one, heh?"

"What?"

He gives me a wry smile. "The spaghetti thing."

"How do you know?"

"I may almost be blind in my old age, but my hearing's sharp as a tack."

I pull the rag out and feed it into another hard-to-get-to area. "You heard what she said?"

"Most of the time, yes, but most of the time I pretty much ignore you two. This time, I thought you could use a word or two."

When I'm done, I lay the cloth across the handlebars, grab my beard, and pull on it nervously. "What words do you have that could help in this situation?"

"I wasn't always a cranky old man, you know. There was a time that I had a beautiful and sparky young wife like you. There were times when she blindsided me with every issue under the sun."

"Even all those years ago?"

He nods. "It's universal and the issues cut across time."

"So what the hell did you do?"

He drops his hand from the handlebars, reaches to his neck, and tugs at a thin leather string hidden under his plaid shirt. When he pulls at the end of the string, a small worn leather bag slides from between the shirt and his chicken-bone of a chest. Without taking it off, he lets it drop to the middle of his chest, exposed maybe for the first time in years.

"What the hell is that?"

His cataract eyes take on a gleam I've never seen. He looks directly at me. "It's protection. When I was married, oh hell, it must have been forty years ago, an old sage Indian gave this to me. He said it had big medicine inside and that I was never to open it."

I lean back on my seat. "What's it do?"

"Keeps the female spirit from attacking."

I bend down and have a closer look. "No shit. Does it work?"

"It worked with me and LuLu."

"That bag kept you from fighting with your wife?"

"Not exactly, but it gave me the choice as to when I was ready to go into relationship battle with my LuLu. It certainly kept me from being blindsided by her."

"Man, that thing must have some big mojo to be able to do that."

Glen grabs the little bag and lifts it between us. "We all make our own mojo, Thomas. The magic is in the agreement."

"Agreement?"

He smiles and wiggles the bag from its string. "There is no magic in this world. You have to make conscious agreements with your woman, and both of you have to learn to honor them. Therein lies the magic."

I point at his chest. "What possible agreement could I make with a bag like yours that would help?"

"Each couple makes their own. LuLu and I agreed that whenever this bag was hidden under my shirt, she was free to bring up issues. It was like I was saying to her that I felt strong enough to field any subject that she was ready to talk about. But when the bag was showing, like it is now, she couldn't talk about issues."

"Shit, man," I say. "I'd have the bag out all the time."

"That was my first response, too, but you got to be fair. Remember, discussing issues for a woman is their doorway to intimacy. They do it with their women friends, and they long to with their men, so we have to be open to doing it their way at least fifty percent of the time."

"I can bring it out whenever things get dicey, can't I?"

"Sure, you can do anything, but if you want a woman who is happy with her relationship, you got to engage with her and work it all the way to the end, too. This is simply a safety valve to keep things from getting violent.

Medicine Bag

You drag it out when you are on the edge, and it will keep you from going berserk, but you better damn well be on the edge, because, remember, women are very intuitive. She'll know if you're trying to ignore her."

I stand and tower over him, the little gray-haired man with his deep-set wrinkles and his almost nonexistent vision. "Thanks, Glen," I say. "Guess I'm going to have to get one of those bags."

He takes a deep breath, exhales slowly, grabs the bag, and slips it over his head. "This thing has been with me for decades. It's saved me many times from getting trampled by my wife." With a tear in his eye, he hands the bag to me. "Since my LuLu died three years ago, I don't have much use for it these days. You take it and use it in good health."

I take the worn leather pouch and study it closely. "You said there was something inside?"

He shrugs. "Don't know; I never opened it. I was told not to. I do know there's something outside, though, and that's what I'm giving you."

I open the string and slip it over my big head. It almost doesn't fit, but I manage to get it on, and it falls to the middle of my sternum. I grab the bag and yank on it to center the string, and it drops an inch lower.

His smile widens. "There is one thing I forgot," he says. "When you have the bag out and you don't want to field any of her stuff at the moment, you must give her a time in the near future when you'll be willing to hide the bag again and leap into the fire of conflict with her."

My face drops into a frown. "I do?"

"Sorry, Twig, but you got to be fair with her, and you got to do it within hours, not days."

"Hours?"

"The bag is a tool to give you time to prepare."

"I really don't want to prepare for anything. I'd much rather send her to her girlfriend's to work it out. They understand one another so much better. They can wallow in feminine chaos together; they do it so well. I'd much rather polish my bike here alone in the garage while she goes through her bullshit."

Glen's smile turns to a grimace. He draws one of his gnarled old-man hands over his face as if to clear the cobwebs. "Sure, you could do that, and I'd understand. All of your biker buddies would understand. None of us want to go through that with any woman, but you got to remember, you can't just take her to dinner and a movie once in a while and expect that to be enough intimacy for her. Some women need conflict and the working through it as a way of getting close to their men. It's hard wired into a woman. She needs to test the waters of her relationship on a regular basis to feel connected."

My face blanches. "You can't be serious?"

"'Fraid so." He drags the single high stool out from under the workbench and seats himself.

I turn to face him. "Why does she have to do her testing on me?" I cross my arms over the top of my ever-expanding belly.

Glen swings a doubled fist at my shoulder and clips me gently. "Because she loves you, and her love is what opens those doors in your heart and keeps them open. Otherwise you'll shrivel up and turn into an old man like me much too quickly."

"It's so much hassle."

He gets tears in his eyes and looks at me with an intense glare. "That may be true, but you must consider the alternative."

"What's that?"

"Being like me, so lonely without my LuLu that I really don't care to live much longer. Like Melinda, she was constantly wanting more from me. At the time, I thought she was more hassle than she was worth, but now that I have a little perspective, she was the one single light in my otherwise bleak life. Now that she's gone, there's little left to care about."

I pull my leg over the gas tank and sit sidesaddle on my seat. "You paint a dark picture, Glen."

"It's not so dark when you're young, because there's so much to do in life, but when you're older, things like companionship count a lot. Look, kid, go up there and get back into it with her. Work it until you get to the end. Use that talking stick of yours. It looks like it helps. I wish I'd had something like that when LuLu was around."

I stand and tower over him sitting on his stool.

He says, "Go get her, Tiger."

I take a deep breath, hold the pouch around my neck for good luck, and stride across the garage. As I reach the first step of the stairs, from behind me Glen says, "Thomas."

My hand on the splintering railing, I turn.

"Don't present her with the pouch concept right now. Wait until things are back to normal. When the two of you are doing well again and she is more receptive, talk to her about it."

"Normal? Glen, I don't think things will ever be normal with this woman."

He grins, and with an upward flip of his hand he waves me up the stairs.

On the third step, I hear it crack again.

***

The next morning, Katherine awakes early and pokes me into consciousness. "Look at the sunrise, Renee."

I open one eye, but my focus isn't active, so all I see is a pink blur.

"What time is it?" I grumble and pull the single thin cover over my head.

"Who cares what time it is? You really have to see the sky."

As I attempt to return to my nest of sleep, Katherine dresses, leaves our little floating room, and steps out onto the deck of the houseboat. It feels like seconds later, but once I open my eyes, the day is in full swing. Kat shakes me to awareness. "I think we better get on the road," she says. "Billy's ready to go. All we got to do is get you going."

After a quick shower, an even quicker cup of coffee, and some toast, Billy and Kat herd me outside and onto the weathered dock. Coffee cup, and the remains of the piece of toast in hand, we start up the short incline to our motorcycles.

Katherine is first to reach the bikes. She turns. I'm still struggling to climb the dirt path. Billy starts his and rides past me to the top of the levy. When I get to the top, I yell at Billy over the sound of his engine, "I know it's a Harley, but it looks different from the bikes I've seen. What kind is it?"

He turns off his engine and holds up one hand and bends over to catch his breath.

"Jesus, Billy," I say. "What's wrong?"

His finger pops up and points toward the sky. "A minute," he says, still breathing hard. His color is gray and he doesn't look that good.

While I wait, I check my oil and gas, then throw a pressure gauge on the tire that's been leaking. It's low three pounds.

"I. . . breathed something. . . in Nam," he puffs, still panting, but able to speak. "Never was the same. . . since. It's worse as I. . . get older."

"You should get that checked out," I say. "Stuff like that could get serious."

He leans against his bike seat and looks at me. "Oh, I've had it checked and rechecked, but the Veterans Administration says there's nothing they can do. The bastards know what happened to me, but they won't diagnose it properly, because they're afraid they might have to pay me a little more disability."

"Maybe you need to sue them to get some answers," Kat says.

"Tried that. They have a whole chorus line of lawyers that show up in court that'll rip anyone to shreds. I had to live in Phoenix for five years to fight them, while they opened and inspected every facet of my life. I finally got tired of the hustle of city life and gave up. They weren't going to budge, and I was running out of time and money. I settled for pennies and ended with enough to put a small down payment on my houseboat. I've been here ever since."

Billy straddles his saddle. He pulls the bike off its kickstand, leans to rotate his distributor, and engages the choke like I do. Before he leaps into the air, Katherine asks, "What kind of bike is it?"

Billy looks at her, then puts one hand on the chrome knobs atop the engine. "They call it a knucklehead. This one was built in 1948 and I rebuilt it fifteen years ago, with a lot of help from some renegade Harley mechanic."

"Nick Brown?" I ask.

Billy turns to me. "How'd you know?"

"Lucky guess."

"You know Nick?"

"You could say that. He's part of the One on One group in Barstow."

Billy's face lights. "No kidding. That guy built the best bikes. You know where I can get a hold of him? I need a tune-up, and the dicks around here haven't got a clue when it comes to these older bikes."

I lean down, set my empty coffee cup on the dirt, and rotate my distributor. While I engage my choke, without looking at Billy, I say, "He quit working on bikes. He's throwing pottery in San Francisco these days."

Billy puts one hand to his scraggly salt-and-pepper beard and pulls on it thoughtfully. "I don't get it. He was the best there was. Why'd he quit?"

I rotate the starter kick-pedal and look at him. "Guess he got tired of bikes."

"No shit." He continues to stroke his beard. "Man, will wonders ever cease?"

I leap into the air and slam my full weight into the starter pedal. The engine catches on the second try. While feathering the throttle, I lean down and rotate the distributor back to its running position.

Billy's Harley takes four or five kicks and a lot of coaxing once it starts, but he finally sits in the saddle and pulls the bike up to a balance position. He raises one hand high in the air and circles his single extended finger.

As usual, Kat's bike starts without a hitch, and we roll off the levy and down the path called Mulberry Street.

Medicine Bag

On the main road, Billy's bike leaps forward and we follow him through town to a gas station. At the pumps Billy keeps his engine idling while he fills his little two-gallon peanut gas tank. Both Katherine and I filled ours yesterday, so I put a pound or two of air in my leaking tire as we wait for him to pay for the gas.

Back on his bike, Billy leads us through the remaining part of town and up a ramp to Interstate 10. We head east into the vastness of the Arizona desert.

The morning is cool, and riding is easy while the sun rises into the sky. In a half hour we reach a short mountain range and climb, arrow straight, into the hills, then overlook the next part of the highway again as straight as a beam of light. It stretches down into a long bowl and up the next set of barren hills some fifty miles away. At the bottom of the bowl, in blazoned contrast to the miles of open desert we've passed, stands a series of gas stations; a couple of Ma and Pa markets; and what looks like ten square miles of crushed desert made into a huge hodge-podge parking lot. Two overpasses mark the beginning and end of the so-called town. The place looks deserted.

Billy pulls off the freeway at the second off-ramp and winds his way to a side road that leads northeast. The road is not as well maintained as Highway 10, and I find myself dodging small potholes and road bumps.

I pull next to Billy. "What was that?" I point at the so called town behind us.

"Quartzite."

In the distance ahead of us, a single tree stands beside the road. I gun my engine and shoot out ahead of Billy and Katherine. As I get close to a huge Joshua tree, I pull into the shade. Billy and Kat follow.

I unfurl my kickstand and turn my engine off, then let the bike drop its weight all in one movement, like I've seen Stew and the boys do a hundred times. Everything is timed perfectly and the bike falls into position in one smooth drop without me touching a foot to the hard-packed sand. Yes, I did it.

In a moment, Billy and Kat have followed my lead. Other than the sound of our cooling engines, the silence of the desert drops in around us like an invisible blanket. I remove my helmet and take in a deep breath of warm air.

Billy is off his bike. I turn to him. "Quartzite is an odd name for a town, and what was all of that about, anyhow?"

"This time of the year less than fifty people live there, but last month, in February, it's hard to imagine, but over a million people hunkered down in those dusty parking lots with their RV's and trailers. It happens every year."

"What the hell were they doing there?" Katherine asks.

"The annual gem and mineral show." Billy stretches by bending at the hip and touching his toes. "For a month, starting February first, everybody and his brother lines up in row after row selling everything from amethyst to automotive polish. Man, it's a real zoo."

I twist at my hip to stretch. "No kidding? For a whole month, you say?"

"They hang out in their RV's and sell mostly gems for the jewelry trade. It's famous for people coming out of the desert with whatever they found during the year. Most of it is garbage, but once in a while some old geezer will come across something interesting, and he'll have a pickup truck full of it. The stone nuts from around the world show up and try to find guys like that."

Kat bends at the hip. "Where do they put all the RV's?"

He turns toward the town and sweeps his arms. "They spread out into the desert. For a month the place is crazy with snowbirds getting away from the weather up north."

I try to imagine a million people in that dinky town, but the enormity of the vision evades me.

The morning has warmed and the shade of the Joshua tree is a nice break from the intense March sun.

"How far are we driving?" Kat kicks at a star thistle growing next to the broken barbed-wire fence. The wood posts are rotted. Only a few post snags remain and two rusted strands mostly lay on the sandy earth. The decomposing wire stretches for miles along the highway.

Billy points up the road. "Once we get to the last outpost we'll have an eighty-mile ride to Lake Alamo."

Katherine gives him a suspicious look. "Where in hell would you find a lake in this barren stretch of desert?"

He grins and his small teeth show for the first time. "Oh, it's there, all right, in the most unlikely place you would expect." The grin disappears as quickly as it appeared, replaced with his more common tight-lipped smile. "Once at the lake, you'll have to walk a few miles."

"That's good," I say. "We've been sitting in these saddles for a few days. I could use some exercise."

Billy rotates his distributor and flicks a hidden switch under his seat. "We still got thirty miles to the last outpost."

I retard my distributor and throw my weight into the kick pedal. My engine fires on the first try. Billy's takes a few kicks, but it finally comes to life, and we are once again driving along the broken highway, dodging potholes and the occasional jack rabbit.

The sky is azure blue. The range of mountains in the distance keeps getting closer, but as usual, we're much farther away than I guess. An hour later we come to the base of the ragged mountains. The road breaks away from its arrow straightness and weaves into the foothills. Before we begin the serious climb, a settlement the size of a postage stamp appears along the highway. Billy pulls in for gas and kills his engine.

The corroded gas pumps have the ridged squareness of the 1950's, with the amount pumped metered on tumblers, like old slot machines. Each number is so faded that someone has rewritten them with a felt tip pin and it looks like more than once.

After I fill my tank, I walk to the little store to pay. The rusted screen door squeals when I pull it toward me and step inside. It slams behind me as I walk on the painfully dry wooden floor. An old golden retriever, lying on a dusty green blanket next to the door, raises its head enough to see who's entered. It gives a deep sigh, a snort, then drops back into its original sleeping position.

A short man in his forties stands behind the cash register. He has unusually wide weight lifter shoulders, massive arms, and a chest as thick as a small car. From first glance, his bronze skin looks like he carries not one extra ounce of fat on his whole body. His face is round, like an Eskimo or maybe Seminole Indian, with beady all-black eyes. When he smiles, three front teeth are missing. "Don't get too many pretty women in here." He's either paying me a compliment or hitting on me; I'm not sure which.

His unusual stature demands my complete attention.

I can't turn my eyes away from his long, black ponytail, the silver hoop in his right ear, and the huge turquoise ring attached to his sausage-shaped index finger. The ring looks like a new addition.

I'd better say something soon, before I embarrass myself. "Do you have gum?" I ask in a last-ditch effort to make some kind of reasonable sound, though I never chew gum.

He lifts a meaty arm and points toward the third aisle. "About halfway back, eye level."

I turn and get a first glance at the store. It's a shambles. The cans and jars of food scatter along the shelves; a single can of beans here; a jar of mustard there. Two jars of Skippy peanut butter are the only thing that there are two of on the entire length of the shelf. Desert dust coats everything.

I walk slowly along the aisle until I reach three choices of gum. Each looks like it has been sitting for years in the same position without being touched. I grab the first pack that catches my eye, turning it to one side and tamping it on the shelf. A layer of dust slakes off the yellow packaging, brightening the colors.

When I rotate back to the attendant, his gaze has shifted to the small television that murmurs in the background. I turn toward the rear of the store and the cold storage, then walk to the four glass doors, mostly filled with beer and cold bottles of wine. From the looks of things, beer and wine are much faster movers than anything else in the store. The bottles and cardboard holders they rest in are fresh.

In a small corner at the bottom, under four gallons of milk that look outdated by a month, a short row of bottled water lines one shelf. I open the door and grab two of the bottles as Billy steps in.

"Hey, Billy," the wide-shouldered cashier says. "What you doing in these parts?"

Billy smiles wide-toothed for the second time since I've met him and lifts one hand, fist closed, with his thumb pointing over his shoulder toward the front door. "Going to the spot."

Katherine opens the screen door, walks in, and stands behind Billy.

"You taking these two?" the attendant asks.

"Yep." Billy's a man of few words.

The attendant's round face drops into a scowl. "Well, shit, Billy, it ain't no vacation spot, you know. You just can't take anyone there, especially these two women." He says "women" with an air of disgust, like we're going to foul the spot.

"Look here, asshole." I stomp toward the counter, ready to ream the guy out, but Billy interrupts.

He holds a hand toward me. I stop forward movement, while Billy speaks. "It ain't no vacation, Ed. We got business there."

The attendant puts both hands on the counter. "What kind of business you got with two good lookin' women?"

I'm ready to lob the bottle of water across the room at him. I want to scratch his eyes out. The way he's built, all muscle and not much flexibility, I can easily leap across the counter and crack him one across the nose before he can begin to flinch. Suddenly, I understand how violence gets the best of Melinda.

Although I want to lay the man out, I hold myself back, open the bottle of water, and take a long, slow drink.

Billy's answer surprises me. "Bob sent us."

The guy's squared shoulders sag, as if someone let air

out of them. "Bob, are you sure?"

Billy turns to me and rotates his hand to beckon me toward him. "Ed, this here's Renee Chance."

I stand my ground. I'm not budging an inch toward this Ed guy, except to attack his sorry ass.

Ed's disapproving gaze doesn't waver from Billy's eyes. "What's that supposed to mean?"

"Stewart Chance," Billy says, like the guy's supposed to understand.

He looks at me, back at Billy, then me again. He speaks with surprise. "You're The Renee Chance?"

I don't move or speak.

"The one on the talk show?" Ed is awed. "Stewart's wife?"

"I am nobody's wife," I say with my chin set and fists clinched.

Ed turns to Billy. His eyebrows rise.

Billy says, "Bob sent us, and we need you and Cherry's help getting to the spot."

Ed's demeanor changes. He looks excited and jubilant. "You want us to take you there?"

Billy nods.

Ed turns away from the counter, walks from behind then over to me, holding out one of his sausage-fingered hands to shake. "It's good to meet you."

He advances much too quickly for my liking. I take three quick steps back and hold both arms up as if I'm protecting myself from attack.

He stops in the middle of his advance and gets a hurt expression. His eyes glass up, and he looks as if he is about to cry. The guy looks like a five-year-old who got reprimanded by his mother. He drops his outstretched hand. "I just wanted. . ." the remainder of his sentence floats off into the ether, unspoken.

We stand for what seems like a millennium in awkward silence, no one moving, before Billy speaks. "Will you and Cherry take us, Ed?"

Mister body builder turns away from me with his hurt face. "Billy, you know only Cherry can take women there."

"Bob wants both of you. I don't know why, but he specified both of you."

"You'll have to wait until after five when the store's closed. We don't have anyone to fill in."

"Sure, man. After five is probably better. How about we wait out at the lake? We'll get settled in and they can start up the canyon in the morning."

Ed, with his no-nonsense weight lifter body; his thick, calloused hands; and piercing beady eyes, flushes and stammers. "All this depends on if Cherry wants to go to the lake. I gotta talk to her first."

"Sure, Ed," Billy says. "Go talk to her. We'll keep an eye on the store for you."

"She's in town getting supplies. She should be back by four or five."

Billy says, "Well, hell, man, I don't want to wait around for no woman to make up her mind."

I snap my head away from the freight train of a man and glare at Billy. He doesn't look my way, but continues speaking in a sarcastic tone. "How about we wait at the lake? If your wife decides she wants to come along, we'll see both of you there. If she doesn't, well, if she lets you, maybe we'll just see you. Otherwise we'll find the canyon with or without your damn sorry-ass Indian blessing."

"Canyon?" I ask. "What canyon?"

Ed takes in a breath and holds it for a moment. It looks

94

as though he's going to explode, but he lets it out and smiles. "No wonder you never got a woman in your life, Billy Black. You are one cranky son of a bitch."

The two men smile. Ed steps forward as if he's going to hug Billy, but Billy backs up almost to the door. "Don't touch me," he says three times. Each repeat gets more plaintive and desperate.

Ed stops his advance, again with a hurt face. "Sorry, man, I forgot."

Billy looks as though he's going to turn and bolt out the door, but he stays, and with a choked voice says, "I just can't."

Ed backs up a step to give Billy room. "It's okay, man; ain't no one gonna to touch you. I forgot is all."

Although Billy's body stands rigid, he looks as though his psyche has crumpled to the wood slat floor.

Ed turns to me, giving Billy time to regroup. "You want me to ring you up for that stuff?"

I'm still stunned and have a hard time responding. It takes a second, but I finally lift the two bottles of water and the gum, then hand them to Ed. He walks around to the back of the counter and the cash register's clicking sounds breaks the unbearable silence. "Did you get gas?" Ed asks.

"Nine dollars and thirty-three cents."

The register goes through a half dozen noisy cycles and comes to a rest spitting out the short ribbon of tape. "That's fourteen twelve."

I pull a twenty from my Levi's and hand it to him. He counts the change, but I don't hear him. I put the money in my pocket as Katherine quietly goes back to the cold storage and removes four bottles of water. On the way to the counter she grabs a Snickers candy bar.

While Ed rings her up, Billy comes around. He steps back to the beer case and pulls three bottles of water.

When Ed finishes ringing us up, he says, "we may be a while getting to the lake. Maybe you three might want some steaks out of my freezer. They'll be thawed by the time you get to the campground and set up."

"Sure," Billy says. "These from one of the cows in your herd?"

Ed laughs. "Hell, yes; only the best for me, my wife, and my friends."

I look at Kat.

"You guys wait here," Ed says. "I gotta go in the house freezer for the steaks." He exits through a door behind the counter.

I turn. "You going to be okay, Billy?"

"I guess. I just wished I. . ." his sentence fades as his face reverts to one of resignation.

When Ed returns, he holds out a frost-covered package carefully wrapped in butcher paper. "I put a couple extra in there for Cher and I when we get there." He hands me a small grocery bag. "Here's some vegetables from our garden and a bunch of potatoes. That should be enough to have a good meal tonight."

I take the bag and look at a handful of carrots, three gigantic tomatoes, a half-dozen small zucchinis and a small plastic bag of something that appears to be mushrooms.

I close the bag. "Thanks, Ed."

He nods. "You better get going, so you'll have enough light to gather firewood."

We step outside and in a moment our engines roar to life. We leave the rundown gas station with Ed and his massive shoulders standing next to the rusted pumps.

The ride into the hills is filled with long banking turns on smooth pavement. Most of the time there's enough room that we ride three abreast, spilling over into the oncoming lane. The entire eighty miles into the desert, except for the road itself, is void of any sign of humans. We pass not one car, nor see any airplanes, only the occasional speed-limit sign and the long ribbon of dark, gray pavement.

Since we're in no hurry, we drive at a leisurely forty-five or fifty miles an hour, slowing for skittering jack rabbits, a herd of wild mules, and a single desert tortoise the size of a spare tire. It moves slowly along the side of the road.

After passing over the second range of mountains, we drop into a long, open valley. Before I see the water, I smell moistness in the air.

We take a last turn facing the setting sun and crest a small hill, then face a ten-mile-long lake. It can't be more than a mile wide.

Fifteen minutes later, Billy indicates a right turn, and we pull into an abandoned campground of two hundred well-developed campsites. Each site is paved, has a picnic bench and a steel ring designating the location of the campfire. Not one automobile is parked in the campground, so Billy leads us to the far edge of the pavement overlooking the calm lake. He parks out on a point, turns his engine off, and unfurls his kickstand. He leans his bike and dismounts. Kat and I follow suit.

The bikes engines have turned their last revolution and the vastness of the desert lake surrounds us like a heavy blanket of snow in midwinter. It's so silent that the buzz of a fly can be heard from fifty yards.

The few clouds off in the distance are golden with

the final setting of the sun. Content sounds of wintering ducks and geese float up to our ledge some fifty feet above the water's surface.

I stretch vibrating and tired muscles, lean over, and touch my toes, holding that position to relieve my sore back.

Kat extends her arms and leans back. "That was one long ride out into the middle of nowhere."

Billy bends sideways. "To top it off, we gotta scrounge around for firewood before it gets dark."

"Firewood?" I say. "Where do you suppose we'll find firewood in this barren landscape? All I've seen is cactus and an occasional greasewood bush."

Billy stretches the opposite direction. "I'll scavenge along the lake for driftwood. There is usually a fair amount this time of year."

Kat points back the way we came. "I saw a few pieces in one of the campsites when we came in." She looks at me. "Maybe you'll ride with me and we could scour the campground for abandoned chunks of wood."

I look in the direction she's pointing. "With all of these sites, there must be some left over firewood."

"All we need is enough for the night." Billy nods toward the setting sun. "Tomorrow, you'll hike up the canyon."

Kat sits on her bike and indicates that I should join her. When she starts and drives off with me on the back, Billy disappears down the embankment.

We cruise slowly, weaving in and out of the endless small cul-de-sacs that lead off of the main road. I grab a split piece of cedar, a round of driftwood with one end charcoaled, some wrist-thick sticks, three hardwood logs stacked neatly next to the fire pit of campsite seventeen, and we have enough to return our booty to the camp.

Medicine Bag

Once I unload the lapful of wood, Kat and I continue our slow, winding approach, systematically searching each site. We come back to our bivouac three times with a lapful of wood. After the third load, Kat turns her engine off, and we dismount.

As we carry the wood to our fire ring, Billy climbs out of the ravine with an arm load of bleached sticks the size of his fingers and four logs as thick as Ed's forearms. He drops his load atop our pile and studies the knee-high stack. "That's enough to get us dinner and through the night. What do you think?"

I nod and smile but don't speak. I put one hand on my hip and kick a loose log onto the top of the pile.

Billy drags out cooking utensils from his right saddlebag. "I've been thinking about those steaks ever since we saw that turtle. I think it's time to eat."

"It was a desert tortoise," Kat says while snapping some of the smaller sticks Billy brought up from the beach.

He shrugs. "Tortoise, turtle, what's the difference? I'm still hungry."

Dusk colors turn to twilight and the first star shines overhead. Kat gets the fire started and puts on a large pot of rice. During the forty-five minutes it takes for the rice to cook, the three of us relax, sitting in a line on the side of the park bench closest to the fire. Kat and I hug our end of the bench, careful not to touch Billy.

Although the sun was hot during the day, March still brings chilly evening air. I'm finally forced to put on my leather riding jacket for warmth.

Katherine checks the rice every five minutes until all of the water has disappeared.

A light strikes the hills from the way we came, and a distant roar of a single engine echoes across the terrain.

Billy slips another of his bleached logs into the fire and points. "There's Ed and Cherry."

Sparks leap into the air and race one another high into the night sky before they extinguish themselves one at a time in a death dance of heat waves.

Kat and I say nothing, just look in the direction of the approaching noise through the flicker of the muted light.

In less than a minute, a single headlight leaps over the hill. The sound of the engine triples, and the bike thunders toward our little campsite.

"Jesus," I say, still looking off in the distance. "Doesn't he have any mufflers on that bike?"

Billy wiggles a stick into the coals. "Don't think he believes in 'em. Out here, there's really no need, anyhow. The last cop is in Quartzite, and he's only part-time."

I say, "What about the people he passes and hearing loss from exposure?"

"What about his hearing?" Kat pulls the blackened pot from the fire and replaces it with a ten-inch stainless steel skillet she had in her saddlebag. I think she brought the entire kitchen, the things she comes up with.

She splashes olive oil in the pan and tosses on two almost thawed steaks. The sizzle covers the distant sound of Ed's Harley for a moment, but when the bike finds the last small hill, the engine gives a final roar and relaxes into the long downhill grade before turning into the campground.

He idles the five hundred yards to our site, pulls his bike next to Billy's, turns his obnoxious engine off, and the silence of the night returns as does the dull yellow of the campfire instead of the glare of his headlight.

A woman, the size of a Buick, dismounts from the back of the bike. She's almost six feet, has heavy shoulders, thick arms and wide hips. From first glance I can only guess that, like Ed, she has zero extra body fat.

When she pulls off her helmet, long, straight onyx hair cascades down her back, spilling over her right shoulder. She drops the helmet onto the clutch side of the handlebars and turns to us. "Hey," she says with a husky voice. "Is the food ready? I'm starved."

Kat breaks her gaze, slides the spatula under one of the steaks, and inspects the cooked meat with a flashlight. "It's getting there." She doesn't look up at the woman.

Ed has his helmet off and is waddling around his bike stiff-backed all the way to his waist. He moves toward the fire and his entire body rotates to accommodate the step. He grabs the woman's hand as he approaches. "This is my wife, Cherry." Ed introduces each one of us, then he and Cherry go to the next campsite and drag a picnic table to the opposite side of the fire from us and sit with their hands warming over the small blaze.

As the two steaks are cooked, Kat spatulas them out onto plates, then spoons some rice and the squash. She hands the two plates over to Ed and Cherry. The dish looks and smells great.

Kat slips three more steaks into the pan and maneuvers them around until they fit.

I watch Ed cut a slice of steak with his Leatherman tool, then hand the knife to Cherry. I ask, "Where exactly is this secret spot?"

Chewing the bite, he lifts his hand and points over my shoulder with one of his sausage fingers. When he finishes chewing, he says, "About five miles. We'll give you a ride partway, but you have to walk into the canyon."

"What's this 'you' stuff?" I say. "I thought you three were going to lead us in there."

He takes the knife back from Cherry and points it at her. "This is a woman thing. Cherry's taking you. We'll keep an eye on the bikes."

Kat bends over the fire, slips her spatula under the steaks, and turns on the flashlight. "How do you like your steak, Billy?"

"Well done," he says.

"What kind of well done?"

"Turn it into a hockey puck, and I'll be happy. You got any steak sauce?"

She looks at him. "We're not in a restaurant."

"How about a little salt," Ed asks as he forks some rice into his mouth.

Kat turns to her little cooking kit and tosses the salt shaker across the fire to him. He snatches it out of the air like a Frisbee and shakes a liberal amount over his entire dish.

I look at Cherry. "What's this special place like?"

She swallows and takes a sip of water. "It's different for each woman."

"What do you mean for each woman?"

She takes Ed's Leatherman tool and works on another piece of meat while she speaks. "The canyon we're walking to has been a woman place from before my great-great grandmother was born. We'll walk it without food or water, so eat up, because this may be your last meal for a while."

***

I climb the steps and open the front door. Melinda turns from washing dishes and looks at me.

I say, "maybe we could try again."

Medicine Bag

Her face, which had a familiar grimace, relaxes. She grabs the dish towel and dries her hands while fully turning toward me. "We could try." She steps closer to me.

I open my arms and fold them around her as she stands in front of me. "Sorry, Twig, I don't know what comes over me sometimes. I just want to make you the bad guy, and yet I know you're the best thing that's ever happened to me."

"Can I get that in writing?" I ask as we hug. I feel her belly push against mine.

By noon, after a long lingering in a Saturday bed, we get up, shower, and dress. I want her to go for a ride with me, but the doc says no motorcycles, so we take the car and go to, of all places, the library.

She digs through childbirth books and drags them one at a time over to me, points out relevant sections, and reads passages about the birthing process. I linger in the novel section awaiting the next barrage of tidbits brought to me by the feminine. I feign interest, but truth be told, I'm deep into a mystery novel by Randy Wayne White.

I keep marking my page when she brings me a new piece of information, then return to the story after she disappears into the halls of childbirth.

After an hour, with Melinda carrying a stack of books and me with my one novel that will take me a month to complete, we check out the books and go back to the car.

I start the engine. "Where to now?"

She places her books in the back seat. "We could take a drive up to Stewart's and see how he's getting along."

"It's a long drive. Maybe we'll call to see if he's there."

She gives me a tired smile. "Good idea. There was a phone in the library, back by the bathrooms. Why don't you make the call? I'm feeling exhausted so I'll stay here."

I turn off the engine, get out, and dig for some change as I walk into the building. I step across the long, high-ceiling hall to the back of the room where the signs point out the restrooms. In the middle of the two bathrooms an ancient dial pay phone is solidly bolted to the wall. I lift my two quarters to the coin slot and see a small sign embedded in the metal that says ten cents. Without thinking much about how cheap the call is, I dig for a dime and drop it in the slot, then dial Stewart.

The receiver makes a funny clicking sound and rings. On the third ring the phone is picked up and a strong tenor comes over the line. It's not Stew.

"Hey, Twig, how you doing?"

"Bob?" I barely get out the single word.

"Bingo," he says. "How are things going with your soon-to-be bride?"

I look to make sure no one is around. The old library building looks new. "Bride?" I say. "Melinda and I don't believe in marriage."

I step as far away from the phone as the cord will allow and peek around the corner. The building looks the same, but not the same. Something has shifted. Is the paint different?

"Melinda may say she doesn't believe in marriage, but if you pop the question, I'll give you dimes to dollars she'll say yes."

"I don't think so. She and I talked about it a lot when she first got pregnant."

"Okay, if you are so damn sure about it, then it won't

hurt to go over there right now, get on your knees, and pop the question."

"Is this why you're calling me?"

"You called me, my man. Go outside and ask her, then get on with your life. Trust me, it's easier on the kid if you're married."

I feel a bead of sweat trickle down my temple and bury itself in my beard. My hand holding the phone trembles slightly. "It's no big deal either way."

The line is dead for ten seconds, then Bob speaks in a mocking voice. "If it ain't no big deal, why are you sweating?"

Another trickle slides down my face. I reach up with my other hand and wipe before it reaches my nose. I realize there's no air conditioning in the building.

When my attention returns to the phone, it's dead, and a second later the dial tone returns. I close my eyes for a second, dig into my pocket for more change, and notice the phone is no longer the ancient dial type, but a push button that costs fifty-cents for a call. I add quarters and dial again.

"Stewart?" I say.

"Hi ya, Twig," he answers with a surprise tone. "You know, it's time to marry Melinda."

"Jesus, Stew, you too? Is there, some kind of conspiracy to get me married?"

The line is silent for a moment. I'm almost ready to ask if he is still there, when he says, "I just woke up from a nap."

"Don't tell me," I say, but don't finish the sentence.

"Bob came to me not two minutes ago. He said you would call, and he told me to tell you to marry her."

I hold the phone away from my ear and look at it like

I can see Stew. "Holy shit, there is a conspiracy."

When I put it back to my ear, Stew says, "Bob's behind it, so I'd suggest you listen carefully. He wants you to go outside the library right now and ask her."

"Okay, okay. Jesus, I can't believe how insistent he is. Melinda and I thought we'd take a drive and come visit."

"You going to ask her?"

"Maybe."

"Do it, Twig, then come on over. The kids are at a friend's house for the day. I'm dinking around the property."

"We'll see you in an hour."

"Sounds good."

I'm still a little shaken from talking to Bob and hearing his suggestion, no, more like command. I walk outside to Melinda pouring through a Lamaze birthing book. She looks up when I get in the car. "Twig, there's so much to learn."

I take her freckled little hand. She gives me a curious expression. "What's up, big boy?"

I open my mouth, but nothing comes out. I feel my insides turn to jelly. My breath comes in shallow gasps. The single bead of sweat from earlier has reproduced and feels like a river pouring over my brow and down my face.

"Are you okay, Twig?"

I try to answer, but succeed only in nodding.

I want the words to come out. It's a great moment, but nothing comes. I want to tell her how much I love her and how I want to be with her the rest of my life, but all I can do is make some unintelligible mumbling sound.

She squeezes my hand and searches my eyes. "Twig, what's going on?"

"I. . . I. . ." is all I can say, then give up and take a deep

Medicine Bag

breath. It's my first in what seems like an hour. In a last-ditch effort, like a drowning man grabbing for straws, I blurt out two words, but they're good words, and I see her face flush after I say them. "Marry me?" She scrunches her face. "What?" The second set of words are easier. "Will you marry me, Melinda?" "But you... I..." she stammers, which makes me feel less alone in my awkwardness.

I press on while squeezing her hand, maybe a little too hard. "Marry me, Melinda, because I love you." Her face is flush and her breathing is shallow like mine a few moments before.

Each time I say the words, it gets easier. I get out of the car, drop down to one knee on the pavement, and look across the front seats. I want the world to know, so I say it loud into the parking lot. "Marry me, Melinda, because I love you and I want to be with you the rest of my life. I want us to grow old together."

Melinda takes a breath and holds it. She shakes her head. I'm not sure if it is to clear the cobwebs or if she's refusing.

"Marry me, Melinda, because I want us to be married when we have our baby."

Her head is still shaking.

***

I look at the cylinder I threw an hour ago. Now I have a chance to get back to it. I sit at my clay-spattered chair, grab a sponge, and dribble chocolate-colored liquid over the walls of the clay to moisten the surface.

My foot pushes on the drive pedal, and the twelve-inch-tall, one-and-a-half-inch-thick cylinder spins.

I stand, and with a wet sponge the size of my thumb, reach my hand to the bottom of the tube, being careful that my arm doesn't touch the inside wall. When I reach the bottom, I search the base of the wall with my forefinger, then pull ever so slightly sideways toward me, while pushing in with the forefinger of my other hand on the outside to support the wall. The wheel head spins maybe sixty revolutions a minute. Slowly, as if my fingers are a stylus on a record player, I work my way up the cylinder, coaxing the clay to rise as the wall thins to three quarters inch. I reach the top and feel the clay pull, so I stop the pressure and squeeze a little more water from the sponge, adding enough lubrication that my inside finger again slides freely along the clay.

Again at the top, I lighten up on the pressure and complete the pull by squaring the top edge. The cylinder is eighteen inches tall and still running true; no wobbles, and bless the clay gods, no lumps so far.

The second and third pull brings the clay up to a towering two feet, but the top wobbles slightly. I hate wobbles, and I spend time cinching the upper edge by pushing down as the wheel head continues to spin slowly. Although the wall at the bottom is still an inch thick, the top edge has thinned. I still don't have enough control to keep the cylinder even.

Once the top is running true again, I plunge my hand down into the center, right up to the pit of my arm. I know this pull will be my last on the cylinder, because I won't be able to reach the bottom any longer. This being the case, I push my fingers together, building a deep groove in the clay, drawing it to a half inch thick, and begin the long tedious journey to the top of the cylinder. Three quarters up, and the cylinder has risen to a whopping three feet. My fingers dry off, and I am forced to soak the sponge, being careful not to get the fragile wall too wet, for fear that it will collapse.

When I take up where I left off, I pull less material, knowing I can come back to that spot for a second pull later.

The tube of clay is three and a half feet tall by the time I reach the top, and I still have another quarter inch of clay to pull. My God, this thing is taller than I've ever imagined.

The very last pull brings the clay up to almost four feet. I have to stand on the chair to work on the top few inches. Miracle of miracles, the clay is still centered and running true while the wheel head continues to slowly spin, showcasing my work in a glistening tube of wet chocolate.

I take my sponge, squeeze out the water, and proceed to softly stroke the outside surface, drawing off extra water. It takes a stick with my sponge attached to the end to remove excess water from the inside of the cylinder.

When the clay body looks drier and less glossy, I slowly bring the wheel head to a stop. It's time to let the clay set up for an hour or so to strengthen the walls before attempting to shape the tube into what, I'm not sure yet. It's not going to be the platter I thought I was making.

I rinse and dry my hands, reach to the upper shelf, and grab the half joint I'd puffed on an hour before. I lean back and fire up the roach, pulling a long draw on the smoke and taking it into my lungs. My body tries to cough the smoke up, but I force myself to hold it down while my lungs spasm.

Once I've let out the air, my entire view of everything

in my immediate environment crystallizes into a clarity I can never experience any other way.

I put my hands behind my head, and study the body of the clay, imagining a Greek-style urn with huge handles or a long tapered vase. The possibilities are endless.

My concentration is broken when the garage door opens and Carolyn pokes her head in. First she looks at me, but the cylinder catches her eye. "Nicky, that one's taller than you've ever done."

She steps into the room and closes the door behind her. "What's it going to be?"

"I don't know yet. I have to let it set up a little."

I grab a stick match and strike it on one of the rusted legs of the pottery wheel. When it lights, I draw the match to the joint that has yet to leave my lips and pull in another lungful of the sweet smoke. With breath held in, my voice higher pitched, I speak, sucking in fresh air. "Maybe a vase."

Carolyn looks at me and shakes her head. "That smoke will be the death of you, Nicky."

I pull the roach from my lips and hand it toward her. "You want some?" I say, still holding the lungful.

She gives the little bullet of paper a grimace and looks at me. "You got to ease up on that stuff, Nicky. It's clouding your head."

I look at her disapproving stare and point at the cylinder. "That might be true, but look what it produces."

She turns toward the door, walks four strides, grabs the handle and spins toward me. "Don't you think you could do just as well without smoking so much?"

"Probably not."

She shakes her head and returns to the house.

I fired up the joint on purpose to get her out of the

110

garage. I really didn't want her here in the first place. Having dismissed her disgusted glare and her sharp-pointed words, I take another drag then set the joint down. I turn back to the cylinder and imagine its possibilities.

***

"Hello, Donna," I say after digging through Nicky's nightstand, finding his personal phone book and looking up the number of Tazz and Donna.

"Yes, who is this?"

"This is Carolyn, Nick Brown's girlfriend."

"Carolyn, oh sure."

I hear surprise, also an unsure demeanor.

"How have you been?" she asks.

"Okay, I guess, but I have a problem, and I really. . . don't. . ." It's as far as I can get before I start crying. I try to finish, saying that I really don't know who to turn to, but the words don't come out.

Donna is silent on the other end of the line. I twirl the phone cord around my forefinger with tears rolling down my cheeks.

After a minute or two, I calm, and with broken sentences explain the reason for my call. "Nicky and I are living here in San Francisco, but he's frozen me out."

Donna is still silent, but she makes little deep-throated hum sounds.

"I knew when I met him that he smoked pot, but lately he's smoking so much I have no one to talk to. He just wants to make pottery and inhale those horrid joints. I swear, there is no one home when he's stoned."

I shift from my right leg to left, turn and drop to a

sitting position onto the bed. I feel my tears again and blurt out a last sentence before I start crying. "I. . . I. . . feel so alone."

Except for the little hum sounds at the end of each of my sentences, Donna continues to be silent.

When I've finally cried out the second bout, I ask, "I'm completely at a loss. Do you have any ideas?"

When she speaks, it's with a deep, soothing voice. "Tazz used to smoke a lot, and I always gave him a hard time for it, but it never worked. One day I realized that it really was his choice to do the things he did, and with the support of the One-on-One women, I completely backed off and let him do what he had to do."

"I guess I give Nick a hard time," I say, "but when he's stoned he's in la-la land and I can't reach him."

Donna lets me finish my sentence, then says, "I didn't just let him off the hook, though. I told him that he could continue to smoke like he did, and I wasn't going to say another word, but I was giving him notice that someday within the next six months I was going to pack my bags, and the kids and I would leave him to his pot. If he loved the pot more than me, he deserved to have it all to himself."

"What happened?" I ask, feeling a lightness with the finality of her statement.

She gives me a short snort then laughs. "The bastard forced my bluff. He smoked for another four months, until one day, and it was through a lot of help with Al Anon and the One-on-One girls, I packed my stuff, and the kids and I moved in with Bill and Paula for a few weeks.

"I guess he quit?"

"Oh yes, he quit all right, but it was a long drawn-out

battle he had with that addiction."

"It's an addiction?" I switch the phone from my right to my left ear during the second or two before she answers.

"Oh, yes; it is definitely an addiction."

"But it's so innocuous. How could goofy marijuana be an addiction?"

"Hell, Carolyn, almost everything can become an addiction. Look at sugar. It's probably one of the biggest addictions there is, it's just so accepted that no one thinks of it as such."

"I smoke pot once in a while," I say in my defense. "I never feel addicted."

There is a short silence, then Donna says, "You can probably drink a few beers once in a while, too. If I remember correctly you still have your girlish figure. You probably don't have any problem with sweets, either."

I feel a bit nervous, because she is getting close, so I interrupt. "No problem with any of that stuff; you're right, but what's that got to do with Nicky smoking pot all of the time?"

"He's addicted."

There, she said it. In the back of my mind I already knew it, but Donna's confirmation locks in the reality. Nicky is addicted to marijuana.

"Oh, God," I pull a finger through a lock of my hair. "What can I do? I can't leave him." I feel a ball of tears well up in my throat, but they don't break the surface.

"I know," Donna says. "Like most of us women, your addiction is Nicky."

The tears burst forward like a river. I bawl so hard I'm afraid Nicky will hear all the way out in the garage, but I can't help myself. She's so right. I'm addicted to Nicky and the relationship. "I. . . I. . . can't leave him." I say in broken speech, "I just can't."

The line is silent until I've once again calmed. I take a deep breath and sigh with an exhale.

Donna speaks. "The kids are just getting off the bus, so I have to go. Give me your number so I can call back and check in once in a while, but for now think about what I said. You don't have to do anything, just think about it."

I give her our phone number and hang up, then drop my face into the pillow and bawl my eyes out, making my screams into the pillow so neither Nicky or the neighbors can hear.

Six

Drill Sergeant

It's long before dawn when someone shakes me awake. The quarter moon gives me enough light to see Cherry standing over me. She speaks, as though everyone but me is already awake, "Come on, Renee, it's time."

I look about and see rustling sleeping bags. Billy stands over the rekindled fire, his hands outstretched to get warm.

Without saying a word, I drag my Levi's from the bottom of the sleeping bag, wrestle them over both legs, and pull them up to my waist. Katherine stands, rolls up her sleeping bag, and stuffs it into her tote sack.

I finally buckle my belt, slip into yesterday's shirt and climb out of the bag.

I ask Cherry, "why so early?"

She puts the last touches on some hobo coffee. "We have a long way to go before nightfall. It's best that we get an early start."

After I stow my sleeping bag, I step over to the small

fire, stand across from Billy and warm my hands. "You ever been up this canyon, Billy?"

"Can't say that I have, but I've been to the mouth of it many times. It's a woman canyon, you know."

"Yes, I know, I just thought. . ." I let the sentence fade and stand for the next minute or so in silence until everyone has gathered around the fire.

Cherry points to me. "Billy and Ed will drive you and me to the mouth of the canyon, then come back for Katherine. That way there will always be someone here to keep an eye on the bikes."

I look around. "I don't think there is a soul for fifty miles in any direction. I'm not really worried about my bike."

"It's Friday," Billy says. "In an hour or so, the weekend warriors will be here in droves. This place is a zoo on the weekends."

"What are you guys going to do while we're gone?" Katherine asks.

"Hell," Ed says with a snicker. He looks at Billy. "We'll get in a little fishing and join in with the nightly festivities."

Billy grins.

Cherry gives Ed a dirty look. "I don't care what you do as long as you keep that little dick of yours in your pants where it belongs."

"Jesus, Cherry," Ed says. "You don't have to get so graphic."

Billy speaks in a serious tone. "I'll keep an eye on him for you, Cherry."

"Jesus H. Christ." Ed raises both arms shoulder high in a questioning stance. "No one has to keep an eye on me, Cherry. When have I ever been unfaithful to you?"

"How about five years ago?"

"What, am I never going to live that one down? I just kissed her."

Cherry glares at him. "No telling what you would have done had I not come home."

"Come on, kids," Billy says. "No point in getting in a fight right before you go up that canyon. It's not good for the spirits."

"Spirits?" I say, anything to change the subject.

Cherry and Ed stand across the fire glaring at one another. Kat and I glance at Billy, who says, "Really, Cherry, you know as well as I do there ain't no one out here but a bunch of old crusty drunk fishermen, but if some knock-dead gorgeous blonde happens to make the wrong turn and drives out into this god-forsaken country, then I'll make sure ol' Ed here steers a wide path around her. That sound pretty good to you?"

Cherry's hackles drop. She turns away from glaring at Ed and points her fierce intent at Billy. "You promise?"

Billy lifts his hand, points one finger at his face, licks the end, and crosses his heart over his leather jacket.

"Okay, then," Cherry says, "Let's go."

We walk over to the bikes. Ed and Billy start theirs. Cherry and I climb on the back. So I don't have to touch Billy, as he clearly reminds me before he starts the bike, I lean against his substantial sissy bar that stands a foot over my head. His bike is right out of the Jurassic period.

We roll to the highway. I hope the ride to the canyon won't be long, because the minuscule pad of leather Billy calls a seat on the fender of an old style rigid frame without shocks, is sure to shake all my female parts loose before we get there.

The boys turn right and continue along the road we came in on. They drive in tandem parallel to the lake, then once over the dam, the road turns to rough washboard dirt, and I'm certain my entire digestive system is going to rattle apart.

After an interminable four or five miles, the bikes make a right onto a small dirt trail. I thought the dirt road was rough, but this one is hell.

For a mile, the bikes buck and weave to miss the bigger holes then turn again onto a footpath and stop. When the engines are off, Cherry and I dismount. I say to Billy, "You can ride my bike, Billy, when you come get us."

His smile turns to a hurt pout. "You don't like riding my bike?"

"It's not that, Billy; the road is too rough."

His pout turns back to a smile. "We're not coming back to get you, Renee. You girls will get back on your own."

Cherry looks hard at Ed. "Katherine rides on the back of Billy's bike. You got that?"

"Jesus," Ed says. "Cherry, you are one jealous. . ." he lets the sentence drop.

"Billy," I say. "If that's the case, I'm going to save Kat's body parts and ask that you ride my Indian when you bring her."

"Okay," he says, "but I still don't see the big deal."

Cherry slips in, "You obviously never rode on the back of that freaking knucklehead, Billy Black."

The bikes crank up and roll out of the canyon. In the silence of the desert, their sound slowly fades, but never quite disappears.

After a moment, I turn to Cherry and point into the mouth of a gorge. "Is this the canyon?"

She doesn't turn to me, but continues to look in the direction of the disappearing sound of the motorcycles.

Drill Sergeant

With a distracted voice, she says, "It's the start of your journey, but the real canyon is about a mile in."

The entire time the sound of the bikes fade off into the distance, then the roar of a single bike builds in intensity again, Cherry stands sentinel overlooking the path. I try to engage her in conversation, but all I get is short answers. She never once turns away from the direction of the approaching bike.

When the noise of the engine gets so loud that I think a freight train is rolling through the canyon, Ed's bike reappears. Only then does Cherry turn away and act like she is preparing something on the gravel. As Ed pulls in, Cherry looks up as if she is surprised by his arrival.

Once the bike is off and quiet is restored, Katherine gets off and turns to Ed. "Billy's bike looks uncomfortable, can I ride back with you?"

While looking at Cherry, he says, "You women will be returning on your own."

Katherine looks first at me, then at Cherry. "Is that true?"

Cherry, still acting like it was no big deal that Ed left her side unchaperoned, says, "So true you won't believe it. So, how about it Ed. You get the fuck out of here, and we'll get on with this little adventure."

Ed steps over and tries to peck Cherry on her cheek, but she turns away. "I told you not to drive her."

Ed gets a hurt look. "Billy's hip was bothering him."

She glares at him.

Ed throws up his hands, walks over to his bike, starts it, and disappears around the first bend.

The sound of the bike is far off as Cherry still stands looking in the direction of its disappearance.

Kat elbows me and nods toward Cherry.

I whisper, "She's got it bad."

"You got that," Kat says.

Cherry breaks herself away from her stance, turns toward us, and says, "I ain't got nothing bad. I just don't trust the bastard." She hoists her light daypack and turns toward the canyon. With her back to us, she says with a drill-sergeant snap, "Once in this canyon there will be no talking."

I realize that neither Kat nor I have our packs, our sleeping bags, or anything for camping.

"Where you are going," Cherry says out of the blue, like she read my thoughts, "you won't need any backpack or sleeping bags."

Continuing in the drill-sergeant mode, she stomps up the foot-wide trail, with us moving along in her wake. Her long legs make it hard for Kat and I to keep up.

The moment I step within the walls of the ancient canyon, with its dry creek bed of fine sand that snakes up the center of tapered walls some hundred feet tall, the flora shifts from little dots of cactus budding out of the rough terrain to giant, majestic, two-hundred-year-old saguaros packed arm to arm, standing at least thirty feet tall. I've never seen so many grandfather saguaros, each with dozens of arms.

The coolness of the morning air makes the march bearable, but Cherry is certainly pulling us along in her wake. She is a no-nonsense hiker, and normally that would be okay, but in this canyon, I want to slow down and enjoy the view.

Since she has an attitude about talking, I stay silent and attempt to keep up. It's not easy, though. She trots on the gravel and leaps over small boulders.

A quarter of a mile into our march along the winding

creek bed, the terrain shifts from gentle slope gravel and flat sun-baked stone to larger and larger, then even larger decomposing granite boulders. Our gentle walk through the canyon changes into scrambling between, over, and under rocks, some the size of a house. Although the rocks are easy to climb because the granite is rough, like coarse sandpaper, I bang my elbow and a knee on the unforgiving surface and scrape off a few layers of skin. To keep up, I can't take the time to look at the wounds, much less tend to them. I simply keep climbing, snaking under and over huge rounded boulders, climbing higher into an ever-deeper and narrower canyon.

I want to say something to the macho Cherry as she climbs rocks like they are kiddie jungle gyms. We come out onto an opening with a single vertical wall fifty stories from where I stand, to a distant top I cannot fully see.

Cherry stops, turns toward Kat and me who are still climbing the last few boulders, puts her hands on her hips, and glares at us until we're standing at the base of the slab of granite cantilevered over our heads by fifteen feet.

"We'll take a break here," she says in a whisper and leans her entire body flat against the wall. "We can talk while we are not walking, but only in whispers."

She has hardly broken a sweat, while both Kat and I are soaked from the effort. I point to the top of the ledge high over our heads. "We aren't going to climb that, are we?" I say with my voice low.

She nods and points out past me. I turn and look over the canyon we came up, out onto a wide mesa some hundreds of feet below us. Forty or fifty miles to the east, three ragged mountain peaks poke out from an almost flat basin. The morning sun bounces off a string of vague cirrus clouds reflecting a golden burgundy and violet mauve, with a background of the turquoise sky. The sun is minutes from breaking over the distant peaks, and it casts long tendrils of golden beams of light. There is more color and spectacular spires then I've ever seen in a sunrise.

Kat, Cherry and I stand motionless and wordless for five minutes as the sun leaps from behind the distant peaks, bringing on a day I already think could easily be over, I'm so pooped.

The rays strike our little bivouac outcropping. Cherry turns toward the cliff. She points up. "We're climbing that."

"I don't know about you," Kat whispers, "but I'm afraid of heights. What we just climbed was frightening enough. I'll wait here for your return."

Cherry swings her hand and stops just before she touches Kat's cheek. I don't know if I'm imagining it, but it looks like little bolts of lightning flash from each of her fingertips. "Wake up, Katherine. This is no stupid little hike in a safe national park. This is life or death. You wait here, and tonight, because you are not up there," Cherry points high above our heads again, "the canyon spirits will chase you down and force you to dive head first off that boulder." Cherry takes five steps to the edge of our flat rock. Her finger rotates to her right in a downward position. I step over to her and look down some thirty feet into a crevice and see two bleached skeletons crumpled on top of one another.

Cherry says in a whisper, but loud enough for Kat to hear, "Those two stayed behind; one five years ago and one last year."

"What is it?" Kat asks with a nervous shutter.

Drill Sergeant

"Dead people," I say.

"Oh, my God," Kat moans. "What have I gotten myself into?"

Cherry steps back to Kat. She says in a more gentle voice. "If you follow my every move, you can make it, but you have to pay attention. Always keep three parts of your body in contact with the face of the rock, and you'll be fine. If you have a vertigo problem, don't look down. Keep looking at me. I'll be right above you.

Kat's, voice quavers. "But. . . but. . ."

"There are no buts in life," Cherry says. "You make this wall, and nothing will ever stop you again."

Cherry bends, then removes her shoes and socks. "We have to do this shoeless, because there are ledges you must feel with your toes and fingernails."

"My feet aren't that strong," I say. I can hear myself whine. "Can't I keep my shoes on? I'll be careful."

Cherry gives me a harsh glare. "Keep your shoes on, and you won't make the climb."

"I'm going back," I say with a resolve that calms my shaky nerves.

"There is no going back," Cherry says. "Since I can remember, no one has ever made it back from here. They have all disappeared, lost somewhere out there." She points across the mesa. "There is only going forward, and you must make a choice here. Are you willing to give up your life because you are afraid to climb this rock, or are you ready to live life to its fullest, with only a small chance that you will fall to your death?"

"Small chance?" Kat asks. "It looks like that ledge up there leaves little chance that we will make it."

Cherry, for the first time since her confrontation with Ed about his errant sexual desires, relaxes her face. She

123

reaches out slowly and places her open palms on each of our shoulders. "There is a way, and I will show you, but you must trust that you can do such a feat, or you are already lost."

She grips our shoulders and pulls both of us in toward her. Me, in my five-four height and Kat not much taller; we're drawn in nose level with Cherry's muscular chest, her breast the only softness. She hugs both of us for a long enough time that both Kat and I cry. Cherry pulls us in closer and holds us for five more minutes until both of us have expressed our fears and tears. When the last sniffle is complete, Cherry releases us and grips our hands. I grab Kat's, making a complete circle. Cherry leans down to our eye level. "You are both powerful warrior women. You have the spirit to complete this. I would have not brought you here had I not known that you have a good chance to make it." She holds our hands up into the air and starts in on a long, slow chant. "Hey, ya,ya,ya. Hey, ya,ya, hey ya,ya." I join in, then Kat. "Hey, ya,ya," we sing in quiet harmony. Ten minutes go by while we chant, twenty, then I feel an inner strength from my womb, up into my chest, to my arms, and my head. The moment I feel the extraordinary energy, Cherry stops chanting, breaks the circle, puts her finger to her lips to silence us, and starts the first step up the face of the cliff.

I remove my shoes, tie the laces together on my belt like Cherry, and take the second position without looking back. I know Kat is two steps behind me, but I focus on the last step Cherry has taken. I concentrate on my first fingernail grip, holding onto the face of the cliff with only my will. I move ever-up, ever-forward, belly pressed to the warming rock, sun to my back, Cherry over my head, Kat below. We are a single unit, spidering up the face of the rock, ever-rising, inch by incredible inch. Other than a grunt or groan once in a while, I hear nothing but the silent breeze and a distant pair of crows.

We climb. My entire being is climbing. I am a creature bred for climbing. Each small ledge, every bump in the living rock, is a purchase for me to hold onto, a resting place for my tired limbs. My fingers are raw, fingernails long ago worn away to the quick, bleeding. I continue to look up until we are under the ledge. On a small outcropping maybe six inches wide, we settle and rest.

I want to speak, but Cherry has anticipated my words and puts her finger to her full lips.

The breeze cools my sweaty body. I look at my bleeding toes. My nail polish, the same color as my blood, seems frivolous, unnecessary, stupid even.

We sit side by side until our breath calms, until the sweat dries. Cherry points above us to the cantilevered ledge sticking some fifteen feet into open space. She grabs my hand and Kat's and we regroup our strength from one another, becoming again a single unit ready to slither along the nothingness of the rock, under the ledge, and out toward the precipice, with some five hundred feet below us. Cherry, Kat, and I take a deep breath together. Cherry releases my hand and stands. I watch carefully as she walks with her fingers over her head until she finds a natural hand grip that allows her weight to swing free of any thing other than her single hold on a three-inch-wide, one-inch-deep fracture in the rock. As she swings, her left hand extends and finds a crevice I would have never seen. She grabs on and waits for her body to stop swinging.

A piece of me is so frightened, so fundamentally bone-chillingly scared that I'm frozen to my little ledge. I've decided to stay here forever. If I had a cell phone, I would call air rescue.

The other part of me looks at the climbing problem, Cherry's longer arms, her extra weight. Can I reach that far out and grab the second hand grip?

Cherry pulls her body up, her thigh and arm muscles bulging with the strain, and hooks one foot into another hidden ledge. She lets go of her first grip and hangs almost upside down. When her body swings out toward eternity, she clasps yet another small crease in the rock and pulls herself out of my line of vision up toward the top of the outcropping.

The part of me that wants a cell phone and air rescue has to be put away for the moment, and the part of me who is one with the rock and one with my fellow climbers comes forward. I finger my way out to the first hand grip. It's a better grip than it looks. I feel like I can grab on and hang indefinitely, if I choose. I let go of the safe six-inch ledge I stood on and allow my body to swing freely. I hear a gasp from Kat as I reach for the second grip and don't find it. My body swings back toward Kat. I kick hard and force my arm to extend farther than I have ever asked it to reach. The second grip is there. I barely hold it. I let go with two fingers and walk farther onto the grip. It takes only seconds, but it seems like ten minutes. I'm finally able to get a firm grasp on the rock. My sore, bloody fingers hold on as I let go of the first position. I swing my short little leg high over my head like Cherry, trusting that there is something to latch onto. To my relief, it's there. I pull with everything I have with my one leg. I grip the rock with my thighs and let go of position number two. I swing my body up and beyond the ledge. When I look back at Kat's gray face of fear, her grimace of death, I grin at her. Her fearful eyes bore a hole in mine, then I swing free and pull myself onto the upper part of the flat, thank-the-gods-I'm-safe outcropping.

I lie on the rock. My legs bounce hard. My whole body shakes. My breath gasps. I look at the sky, and the world is a crystalline blue. My back lies against mother earth. My life is clear and unencumbered. Cherry is lying on her back next to me. She turns her head with a worried look. "It doesn't look like your friend is going to make it."

"I know," I say with a clarity and trust that even I can't believe. "Can we help her?"

"Even if we can, her life will be a hollow cavern if we do. She will never be able to live past this moment. This is her work and hers alone. If she survives, she will be stronger than both of us put together."

Seven

Cliffhanger

When I see the face of the white stone wall, my entire body cringes. I look from the five hundred feet of sheer terror, to Renee, then at Cherry, that sadistic bitch. She says we'll climb the wall, without experience, equipment, backup, or even our shoes, and I tell her in no uncertain terms that I will not go up that face.

I did a little rock scrambling in the park last winter when Jill and her friends came through for a week. With ropes and harnesses; no chance of getting little more than a cut or bruise, we were less than thirty feet in the air, and I was still scared shitless. I got off that rock and announced that my climbing career was over.

I look up a face a hundred times harder than the stupid little boulder that I couldn't get off fast enough, and I'm supposed to climb this? No way!

Cherry, that horrible excuse for a human being, tells me that I can't stay and proves it with two skeletons. She also says I can't return. She knew she was trapping us, and that psychotic bitch did it anyway.

Barefoot, she starts up the face of the cliff like a spider. Renee follows, then me. For the first hundred feet, though I have no idea for sure, because I can't look down, the grips and crevices are pretty apparent and the face is easy to ascend, though my legs are jumpy from the strain. It gets harder, though, and first Cherry, then Renee, actually leap a five-foot gap to a six-inch ledge on the far side of a sheered section of granite. I'm not about to look down, because I'll be stuck, unable to move forward or back. I'm almost in that condition as it is.

When I make the leap, it's out of pure rage toward that ape-shouldered woman who suckered us into this mess. I make it, but one foot slips and I open a gash in my ankle. I take one of my socks and wrap my ankle to keep the bleeding from affecting the rest of the climb. I do this alone, because those two abandon me on the ledge and continue their climb. God, I'm pissed.

I'm forced to continue without a rest, without even a second breath. If I don't follow close on Renee's tail, I'll have no idea where the microscopic ledges and cracks are. It's obvious those two won't come back for me. Hell, they'll probably leave me for dead.

I wish I could slip and fall to my death, just to get the nightmare over with. I keep looking at the overhanging ledge at the top and know I'm not going to make it, so why not save myself the trouble?

I don't, though, and for some ungodly reason, I keep climbing, following Renee's hand and toe holds, mostly sliding on my belly along a sheer face. The only thing keeping me from falling is the roughness of the rock. Its coarse sandpaper texture is great for climbing, but it's not doing my fingers or the tips of my toes much good.

After what seems like most of the day has gone, Cherry

motions us to stop and sit on a minuscule ledge wide enough for my butt, though it's the widest and safest place during our climb so far. I look up and see it, only a few feet over us. The living rock cantilevers out over our heads by fifteen feet. There is no way I'm going to climb into open space with five hundred feet to the rocks. After a short rest, and my legs have been jumping like a sewing machine for the last hundred feet of the assent, Cherry— and the more I hate her, the more fantastic feats she performs, the more respect I have for her—reaches out, fingers her way along the underside of the overhang, and grabs something I can't see. It's nothing new. She's done the same incredible feats since we started this hell-hole of a climb.

She leaps out into the open air. Like swinging on a trapeze, she grabs a second hidden handhold.

She hangs there some five feet from us and the safety of the ledge, then takes the next swing and kicks her leg up onto a part of the rock I can't see, then lets go with her one hand and hangs upside down like she's working out on the rings in a gym. My next intake of air turns to a gasp.

Cherry pulls herself out of sight. I look at Renee. I want to say I can't do it. I'll die here, but I say nothing, as prescribed by that bitch. I watch Renee stretch out and follow Cherry's maneuvers. When she is out of sight and I'm alone, knowing I can't attempt what they just did, I flatten my back against the wall, with my bloody feet dangling over the edge of my fate, and for the first time, I look down. The flat bolder we stood on what seems like four hours ago at the beginning of this climb, looks like a stone I can pick up and skim across a silent pond.

I'm frightened beyond belief. I'm never going to make

it. I lean my head against the rock and attempt to breathe, but my intakes and exhales come in short huffs. I need oxygen if I'm going to even attempt a single handhold, so I sit silently and breathe deeply until I find, once again, my center. My hands and legs stop shaking and my head clears.

If I'm going to die, I may as well do it attempting this final few feet to my eternity rather than die of starvation, or as Cherry says, some spirits forcing me off this ledge during the middle of the night.

I stand and put my hands against the wall behind me. With my right, I reach above my head, then inch out. I feel the grip Renee found a few moments before. It's remarkably well fitted for a human hand. I test the hold and think maybe I can't let go of my fear. I'd better not even go there, or I'll never take my butt from the face of this cliff.

I lean out and put my full weight on the one handhold. From that moment, my entire psyche shifts into slow motion. I see each problem like it is mapped out on a piece of paper. Each move is logical and easily attainable. My body shifts and pulls itself, because I am no longer in control. I swing to the next handhold and my leg kicks up. I grip the ledge with my thigh, just as Cherry and Renee did. I let go in a purity of trusting my body. I hang for a long second or two, then I grab, but don't make the next grip. My leg slips. I swing free. Only my altered state keeps me from falling. My body swings a second time. My leg slips once again. I try for the last hand grip, but it's too far away. I remember Cherry saying we can't go back, but I've slipped again. My last attempt to go forward fails and I'm too far from the grip to reach it. My raw fingers scrape along looking for something to stop my insane slide toward death. I'm falling. I look up. Renee and Cherry are sitting, Renee with a gray face, watching me, but not getting up to help.

"Help," I squeak as my body slides another inch.

***

Okay, I asked her, and she said yes, then we're back in the car driving to Stewart's for a visit. Why am I so nervous?

She looks happy, so maybe I can broach the question.

"Melinda," I say as I turn right and start up the hill toward Stewart's.

She rotates her whole body toward me with a Mona Lisa smile. I can't tell if she is happy or pensive. "You look like you have something to say, Twig."

"I kinda do." We round the first turn of a long series of turns.

"Well, spit it out," she says, that Mona Lisa look shifts to Lucille Ball; kind of goofy.

"I was talking to Glen before we left, and he gave me this pouch." I struggle to pull the pouch to the surface. When it's finally free, I grab the leather strap and wiggle it for her to see.

She says, "looks kinda worn out and ugly, but I'm listening."

"Glen said he used it with his wife when she was alive."

"I hope so. It would be kind of hard to use it when she's dead."

She's being playful. I know she's in a good mood, but I'm still so nervous I can hardly talk. "He said it helped him prepare to have an argument with her."

Melinda's expression changes to a frown. "Yes, Twig?"

133

She's overly cautious. "Go on."

"I need to be able to get ready when we start into a fight, or I can fly off the handle and we both know what happens when I do that."

"Yes," she says.

I feel the tension. "Well, I need a warning."

This time she says nothing. I look away from the road, and her face has turned a shade darker. Her freckles stand out like hundreds of little stop signs.

"Glen said that when he wore it outside his shirt, his wife couldn't approach him with any relationship issues."

"Old Glen said that, did he?"

I know I'm stepping into hot water, but damnit, I want to finish and get it over with. "He said it worked pretty well."

"Do I get one of those pouches?" she asks.

"Sure, I guess so, but would you ever need it? I don't think I've ever blind sided you."

"If you look carefully, you fucking son of a bitch, you just blind sided me, as you have so aptly called it, with this dip-shit pouch idea."

I put the pouch into my shirt, take another quick glance at her, then pay attention to the road as we go into three sharp turns.

While still watching the road, I ask, "So the pouch idea doesn't work for you?"

"You're fucking damn right it doesn't work for me. How dare you even bring up the subject? If anyone blind-sides anyone, it is mostly you doing it to me."

I must be on today, because my mind moves much faster than usual. "The pouch idea should work well to keep me from doing it to you, too."

"Hello," she says loud and in a sarcastic tone. "Is

134

Cliffhanger

anybody home over there? Didn't I just say that it didn't work for me?"

I really don't want to get into a second fight today, so I let the subject drop and turn left onto Stewart's gravel road. The half mile of slow driving on the dirt calms things a little, but I can still cut the tension with a knife. We pull up to Stewart's driveway and park. I sigh a deep breath of relief when she doesn't want to continue the conversation.

We get out and walk across the lawn, then down side stairs to the back deck. I yell, "Hey, Stew, where the hell are you?"

He hollers from the lower deck. "Down here."

I walk to the edge and look down. Stew is dragging branches from under the deck out to a slash pile beyond the trees. "Give me a minute, I'm almost done."

"Okay," I say and walk to the lower level with Melinda. We sit in the lawn chairs by the pool.

She's still steaming, but I'm not paying attention.

"When do you want to do it?" I ask, anything to change the subject.

She turns to me with a snort. "Do what?"

"Get married."

"Never would be a good time."

"Come on Melinda, I only suggested the damn thing. If you don't like the idea, we don't have to use it."

"It's your implication that I blind-side you enough that you have to use some silly pouch to stop me."

I feel a trap. I don't catch them often, but I got this one, and I don't respond. Instead, I say, "I'd like to get married in May, before it gets unbearably hot. It'll be perfect."

"And why would you want to marry some woman

135

who is so much trouble that you must wear some pouch to stop her from talking?"

"It's not talking that I'm worried about," I say, then realize she's drawn me in, and damn it, I got suckered once again.

"What?"

"It's not being prepared to do battle with you and feeling off center from the get go. If I could have a little time to prepare, I could come at the discussions in a more positive way."

Her red face drops back to a hot pink. There is reason in her eyes. She speaks with a more normal tone. "So this pouch of yours is not to shut me up? I've been shut up by men most of my life, and I won't have it with the man I marry."

"It's not to shut you up, Melinda. It's more to put the issue on hold for a few minutes so I can prepare."

"So when do I know the few minutes are up?"

I smile. God, she's reasonable again. What a relief.

"Glen said that one of my responsibilities when I bring the bag out is to tell you when I will be ready to deal with the issue."

"You mean like you'll deal with it next week?"

"No, Melinda, not next week, but maybe within an hour or so."

"What about me, during the time you're supposedly preparing?"

"You don't trust me much, do you?"

She looks away from the vista view of all of creation and glares directly into my eyes, I wince. "Don't you get it, Thomas? I don't trust men, period. They say one thing, but mean something else. It's always been that way."

"Well," I say. "Don't feel so alone, because I really don't

136

trust women, either. Their razor tongues are always a sentence away, ready to leap at my throat in a second's notice."

"I don't have a razor tongue, you bastard."

"Oh really? If what you just said isn't razor blade sharp, I don't know what is."

"I'm expressing myself."

"At my expense."

She turns away, huffs, and leans back on the chair. After a moment of blessed silence, Stewart walks up with a pitcher of lemonade and three empty glasses. "Heard you two. If you want to be left alone, I'll leave the drinks."

I look at Melinda. "It's up to you. If you don't trust men, I wouldn't want you to feel ganged up on."

"I'll make my own decisions, you. . ." She doesn't finish.

"I don't trust women, either," Stewart says. "I think it's inherent in the human condition. We've all been wounded by the opposite sex. I mean, hell, it's so easy to shame or be shamed by Renee, I can't believe it. It's amazing that men and women are able to get together at all."

Melinda laughs. "Maybe you're right, Stew. I know that sometimes a single word he says will set me off. I know he doesn't mean to piss me off, but he does."

"Same with Renee and me," Stew says.

Melinda sets her glass on the table. "So what do we do about it?"

I listen to the two of them have a normal conversation and inwardly I breathe a sigh of relief.

Stew pulls up a lawn chair across from Melinda and says, "It's the biggest piece of work a couple can do."

"What's that?"

"To find a way to trust one another."

"It ain't easy," I say, hoping Melinda lets me into the conversation.

She glares at me.

Since Stew is here, I feel safe to continue. I'm not going to get my throat ripped out while he's around. I look at Melinda. "I really need this pouch." I pull it free and swing it from its worn leather strap.

"You can take that controlling male pouch and shove it up. . ." She looks at Stew and doesn't finish the sentence.

"I need it, Melinda, so I can prepare."

"Tough," she snaps, gets out of her chair, stomps up the two flights of stairs, and disappears into the house.

Stewart turns to me. "What the hell is the pouch thing all about?"

I explain its use and what I proposed to Melinda.

"Give her some time on this one, man. She's an intelligent woman; I think she'll come around."

"I ain't got time, Stew. Her pregnancy has put both of us on pins and needles. I need some protection, and that's all there is to it."

Stew leans forward on his chair like he's going to whisper some dark secret. He puts his elbows on his knees. "You have to get it into your thick skull that both of you are pregnant. She's the one physically carrying the child, but it's your issue, too."

"Now, how do I do that, Stew, when she's so pissed all of the time?"

"By not taking it personally."

"Not taking it personally?" I say. "Man, how can I do that when that razor tongue of hers slashes at me?"

Cliffhanger

"Remember, Twig, she's going through a ton of changes in her body. When she strikes out, it's really not about you."

I take a drink of lemonade, and put the glass down. "When she uses my name and points at me, it sure looks like it's about me."

Stew takes a deep breath, then sighs as he lets it out. "Hey, don't get me wrong. It's all pointed at you, but remember, you're the only one she trusts enough to let it all hang out. If you can hold off defending yourself while she's going through her upheaval, I promise you she'll eventually come up with her own answer. Nine times out of ten, the final answer will not be about you. If you decide to defend yourself somewhere along the way, the subject changes, and suddenly the two of you are off on some sidetrack, dealing with your defense. Two things happen; she doesn't get to finish where she was going, and you end up taking the brunt end of the drama."

I look at Stewart with a suspicious glare. "Look at me, Stew, and tell me you can do this with Renee when she's on the warpath."

He grins. "Hey, I'm only a man. I ain't Biker Bob. I'm successful about ten percent of the time these days. It's as good as it gets for me."

"Just what I thought. Theory is great, but try to put that kind of thing into action, and we all fail miserably."

"Gees, Twig, I don't see it as failure. I see myself succeeding ten percent of the time. Hell, when it comes to Renee, you got to admit that's pretty damn good."

I smile. "You got a point."

Stew picks up his glass, finishes the last gulp, and chews on a piece of ice while he speaks. "Hey, Twig, you give it a try sometime. You'll be surprised."

"I'll keep it in mind."

I hear the creak of the deck behind me, turn to see Melinda, and I'm in love again. "Hi, Honey, I missed you. How's it going?"

She gives me a suspicious glare. "You guys get it figured out?"

"Another piece for sure," Stew says.

She steps over to her chair and takes her time sitting. Stew picks up the pitcher. "Want more lemonade?"

She snaps her head toward him as if she heard a rattlesnake. "I've got something to say first. Maybe after I'm done."

Both Stew and I tighten a little, preparing for the onslaught.

She leans forward and looks at me. "Maybe your pouch idea has some merit."

I want to say something, but I stay silent.

"Maybe I do blind-side you sometimes, and maybe it's not fair to surprise you like that."

Now I really want to say something, but Stew slides his foot over and kicks my boot. I look at his contorted face and remember not to speak.

"I'm willing to give your pouch idea a try for the moment," she says. "Let's see if it might help, but you have to promise that if you use the pouch on me, you have to give me a reasonable time when you'll be willing to talk."

I raise my right hand like I'm being sworn in at court. "I promise."

She points at my chest. "Unless you want that thing out right now, I suggest you put it back in your shirt."

I look at her and grin. "Hell, Melinda, what are you talking about, I want this thing out twenty-four seven."

Cliffhanger

She also grins. "Well, fuck you, too."

I slide the pouch in under my shirt and pat it.

"Hey," Stewart says, "I want one of those."

"You make your own deals with Renee," I say. "How's she doing, anyhow? You heard from her lately?"

Stew gets a worried look. "I haven't heard from her since she left. She told me Bob suggested she not check in, but hell, a call once in a while wouldn't be too bad. Not my I-got-to-be-on-my-own wife. I've heard nothing, and what's it been, a month?"

"Hey, man, that's gotta be hard."

Melinda picks up her glass and drains the last of the lemonade. "She's out doing her own thing. She's been putting you and the kids first her entire marriage, and it's about time she put herself at the head of the line."

"I called her when I was gone a few years back. Why can't she call once a week or something?"

Melinda reaches over and pats Stewart's knee. "It's okay, Stew, she's trying to find out what her life looks like, and I completely understand not calling."

Stew gets a suspicious look. "So it's a woman thing, is that what I'm hearing?"

Melinda nods.

"I don't like it. She could at least send a postcard or something."

I put my hands behind my head. "It's a clean break. Maybe she can't do it any other way."

"For once, I think Twig's right." Melinda removes her hand from his knee and stands. "Hey, I'll get more lemonade. Is it in the fridge?"

Stew nods and drops into a pensive expression.

Melinda walks the length of the deck. Stew murmurs, and I almost can't hear. "If she'd just call. I'm worried."

I reach over and pat his shoulder. "It'll be okay, man. I'm sure she's tearing up the asphalt as we speak."

***

I never thought she'd make it, but when her head pops over the ledge, I want to leap to help her. Cherry grabs my arm. "You can't help her, Renee, or she'll never live it down."

I turn to Cherry, "But—"

"This is her work," Cherry says with a finality that glues me to my position. I pull my knees up and wrap my arms tight around my legs, rocking forward and back as I watch Kat reach for the handhold I grabbed only a few minutes ago.

When she misses by an inch, I gasp. When she slips, I leap forward, but Cherry's muscular arm grabs and holds me in place. "It's her work," Cherry growls. "Let her do it."

Still wanting to get free and help, I struggle, but Cherry's grip is much too strong, and I'm held in place.

Kat takes another attempt at the handhold, but she's slipped too far, and she can't reach it. The next slip is only an inch, but it's a critical, never-return inch, and I'm forced to watch as my friend slides off the ledge toward her death.

"Hold on with your will," Cherry yells. "Climb with your belly."

Kat moans, but after Cherry yells, I watch Kat gather strength. She stops sliding. A dark grimace comes over her face. A deep grunt from within emanates from her mouth. Her hands relax, and her fingers stop clawing for a last-straw finger-hold. She does not slip.

Cliffhanger

"Climb with your belly," Cherry says. Without any grip or perceived effort, other than a strained face, Kat's body, amoeba like, slides toward us. Her legs have released their hold and hang free, but she still moves forward inch by incredible inch toward us. The second her body is fully on the rock and her safety is secure, her face relaxes, her eyes close, and she falls asleep.

Cherry stands, steps over to Kat, grabs both of her bloody hands, and pulls her farther onto the rock. She looks at me. "She's going to have to rest a while."

"No kidding." We smile, tears in our eyes.

For twenty minutes we sit looking over the mesa, watching the distant clouds, listening to Kat's soft snoring. When she awakens, she sits up, looks at the two of us and with tears in her eyes says, "I made it."

Both Cherry and I slide over to her and throw our arms around each other and cry.

When the tears subside, Cherry pulls herself away and looks deep into our eyes, one at a time. "You have passed the first test. There is much more to come, but this," she points over the ledge, "was the hardest."

"No shit," I say. "But what I can't figure is how we get back."

Cherry gives me a secret smile, "It's a one-way journey. I've never attempted to descend that cliff. It would be impossible."

"How will we get back?" Kat asks, nursing her raw fingertips.

Cherry digs in her backpack and finds a salve. "There is no going back." She hands it to Kat. "As it is in life, there is only going forward."

"Okay." Kat has a sarcastic tone while she opens the

little glass jar. "How do we go forward and return to our motorcycles?"

Cherry smiles but does not answer.

Cuts and scratches attended, Cherry pulls on her socks, and boots, then stands. "We must get going. The sun will be setting in an hour, and we need to be far away from this cliff when it does."

I look up at her. "I'm reluctant to move, my feet are so sore."

She gets a worried look. "There are certain night spirits that exist by this cliff, and we don't want to be around when they come out to play."

Kat pulls her socks over raw toes and carefully slips her first boot on. "I'm not going to be able to walk far with my feet in this condition."

Cherry looks out toward the setting sun, then back at Kat. "I know, but maybe a mile or so to get clear of this rock."

Cherry sets out ahead of us, as usual, but not quite as fast as earlier. I notice she's favoring her right leg.

We walk for forty-five minutes in silence until Cherry stops and turns to us. "Watch for your power spot as you walk. When it calls to you, go to it and set up your campsite. I want this site without fire."

"No fire, no sleeping bag," Kat says, again in her rebellious mood. "What the fuck do you expect us to camp with?"

Cherry turns to her, a patient look on her face. "I expect you to sleep in the desert, with all the desert creatures, with the spirits, without water or food, and I expect you to do this for two nights. On the third morning, you will continue up the canyon until you find me. Is that clear?"

"Hey, fuck you and your camping instructions," Kat says. "I've had just about enough of you."

Cherry's patient expression shifts to that of a drill sergeant again. "Look, Burns, you're the one who asked to do this. You can continue or return the way you came; either one is fine by me."

Kat puts one hand on her hip. "I could continue on and find my own way out of this mess. I really don't think I need you to show me."

Cherry lifts her arms, palms up, and shrugs. "Either way is fine by me, but remember, you have no water. We humans don't last long without water. Are you willing to take the chance of getting lost out there?" Cherry points toward the mesa. It can't be seen because we're below the walls of the canyon, but I know it's out there.

Kat turns, stomps up the grade some twenty feet to the rim and looks out toward the east. "Hah," she shouts. "There's the fucking lake. All I have to do is walk that way, and I'll hit the lake."

"Fine," Cherry says, "but without a compass you'll never keep a line on that lake. All you have to do is veer a degree or two and you'll miss it altogether."

Cherry points at Kat. "It looks like you've found your spot to camp, though."

Kat looks around in surprise, then back at Cherry and me. "Maybe you're right."

Cherry says, "Dig a trough in the gravel low enough that you're below the surface, then lay a few dead branches from the greasewood tree over it. You don't have to cover every inch, just a few branches will do. Sleep in the hole, and you'll be protected."

Kat looks about. "Protected from what?"

Cherry doesn't answer, but looks at me and motions

for us to continue. She stops at the last minute before we go around the bend. "After two nights in your spot, continue up the canyon. I'll be waiting."

Kat waves us on.

During the next half mile or so, we march in silence, only the sound of our boots in the various grades of sand. When we come around a bend, the canyon widens, and halfway up the right side stands a flowering prickly pear cactus. It looks inviting, so I walk toward it and stop next to its spreading branches. It has no scent, but I study the violet pods that cover the plant, and I know I've found my spot.

Cherry looks at me. "Same thing, dig a hole and cover it with branches. No fire. See you after two nights.

***

Okay, the body of the clay has set up for an hour. The walls are stiff enough to take this one even higher. I can't believe I've actually been able to bring the cylinder up this far and not have it crash back to the wheelhead, but here it is, standing close to four feet, and there's still enough wall thickness to open it and create a design.

I need to steady my hands and concentrate. I need a hit. Before I get my hands mucky with clay slurry, I reach up to the little shelf, search in my ritual tray under dried-clay-spattered tools. I find the little roach. I put it to my mouth and light a match. I lift the match high, raise my face to the open rafter ceiling of the garage, and bring the match down to the half-inch long joint, then draw in the heat and smoke. The second hit doesn't need a match, and the third finishes off any possibility of a forth, but it's okay; I'm stoned and happy.

Cliffhanger

I rise off the chair, reach high on an upper shelf and drop what's left of the joint into a small green jar with a wide mouth I especially built to house discarded roaches saved for a rainy day.

By the time I sit back in the chair, I'm almost cross eyed by the third hit. I lean against one of the open-walled studs for a moment to enjoy the buzz.

I'm ready to lean forward and begin to open the cylinder, when the garage door opens and Carolyn pokes her head through.

Her expression shifts from smile to suspicious glare as she sniffs the air. "God, Nicky, are you ever going to stop smoking that shit? It's not good to smoke so much."

I want to ignore her and get to my clay. I want to tell her to leave me alone. I want to do a lot of things, but I'm not about to ruin a perfectly good buzz dealing with some demanding female. Instead, I smile and don't say a word.

She steps through the door and closes it behind her. "Nicky?" There's a worried look on her face. She comes over, grabs a piece of newspaper, folds it, places it on the dusty chair across from me, and sits. She looks me square in the eye. "I don't know if I can take this much longer. I need a man who is sober enough to talk to."

"Jesus, Carolyn, it's just pot."

"It's maybe just pot to you, Nicky Brown, but the fact is your mind is getting pickled, and I'm lonely."

I shrug. "Hey, you're talking to me now. What's the problem?"

"I might be talking to you, Nicky, but I'm not getting much back. You're too stoned to respond. What's going on that you need to smoke this crap so much these days? You didn't when we first met."

I look at my clay tube. I want to be left alone. I want to work on it, but this woman is obviously not going to leave me alone, so I respond. "I was smoking when we met. I've smoked most of my life. You liked me then, so who has changed?"

She leans forward. "Nicky, I get the feeling more and more that no one is home. When are you going to come out of your cloud?"

I take in a deep breath and let it out slowly, my lips pursed to whistle, but I don't. When the breath is released, I say with a stubborn growl, "I'm the same person I was when you met me, and you liked me then. All I ask is who has changed here and why do you think you can control my life?"

She looks at me with tears in her eyes. Oh God, here come the waterworks. This time she surprises me and doesn't break down. She glares at me. "I can't take this isolation much longer. You obviously need some help, and I can't be the one to help you. You've got one month to get a handle on this smoking thing or I'm leaving and going back to the desert."

I look at my clay cylinder, mostly because I can't look her in the eyes for as long as she wants.

She continues, but with a less demanding tone. Her voice is soft, like she is ready to cry. "Tell me if you heard me."

I look at her. "I heard you."

"Tell me what you heard, so I know you've got it straight."

In slow, carefully timed words, I repeat. "You're. . . going. . . to. . . leave. . . if. . . I. . . don't. . . stop. . . smoking."

Her face scrunches up. She raises one hand and puts

it over her mouth. I hear a whimper escape. She leaps to her feet and bolts from the garage, slamming the door behind her.

I take a breath, glad she's gone, glad to have my time again. I look at the clay and breathe a sigh of relief. The first pass is a light one with a soaked sponge, just to get the clay wet. The second time I pull up, I tug outward and watch the walls expand as I climb the four-foot tower, then push inward as I reach the top, drawing the mouth smaller than the original cylinder.

The third pull, upward toward the sky and all of creation, I pull the clay to what I think is its maximum. I feel the wall in the center stretch, so I let up the pressure and allow it to relax. As my fingers get to the top, I put on a little more pressure and maneuver the clay into a wide mouth with a rolled lip.

With a scraper tool, I shape the outside wall until it has a smooth, water-free surface. A slight push here and there, then an outward push with my finger from the inside straightens any ridges in the clay.

The final ten minutes of the throwing part of the project, I work carefully on the top, slowing the wheel to a crawl, giving the lip lots of attention.

When I'm done, I stop the wheel and look at my creation. It's a Roman-looking wine urn that needs a pour spout. With my thumbnail, I draw an edge at the very tip of the spout, sharpening the lip so that liquid won't dribble while it's poured.

I stand, put my hands high in the air, and look at thirty-eight inches of vase, the highest yet. I step away from my chair and back to the far end of the garage to look at the masterpiece. It's beautiful.

Because it is so big and the walls are so thin and

fragile, I decide to stop for the day and give the vase a chance to set up where it stands. I don't know how many times I've ruined a great piece by trying to take it off the wheelhead while it was wet and had it crumple.

I step over to the sink and wash my chapped hands, pick up the salve, and rub it in between my fingers with an extra dose on my cuticles.

I pull my smock over my head and hang it on a nail at the door that leads into the house. I remove my shoes, dust my pants, and walk into the kitchen.

Carolyn sits at the kitchen table with a pen in her hand, writing on a full sheet of paper. I pass on the way to the refrigerator and I see that it's a letter, but I can't tell to whom. I'm not that interested, so I get a beer, walk into the living room, and sit on the old avocado-green leather recliner, careful not to stretch the single two-inch rip on the arm. I keep meaning to get that repaired before it gets worse.

From the small table next to the chair, I pick up my half-finished John D. McDonald novel, open it to the dog ear, and scan down to the mark I put at the edge of the page with my thumbnail. In a minute, I'm into the story once again.

The next morning, I awake late with the vase on my mind. When I climb out of bed and stumble to the bathroom for a pee and a shower, I notice the three-day-old stubble on my face, but I don't want to take the time to shave.

From the bathroom, I walk through the kitchen, open the garage door, and look at my drying vase, an inch shorter, now that it has dried to leather hard.

"I'll be there in a minute," I murmur, then turn back to the kitchen and some breakfast before I get lost again in my studio.

As I'm cooking two eggs and a piece of toast, I happen to notice a letter neatly positioned between the salt and pepper shakers on the kitchen table. There is no stamp or address, just my name scrawled across the face in the neat script of Carolyn's handwriting.

The envelope is sealed tightly all the way to the edge of the glue, which forces me to tear one end and slide the letter out sideways.

I open the three folds, and a small blue piece of ribbon falls to the table. I pick it up, study it for detail, but find it lacking any special characteristics.

My breakfast needs attention, so I set the letter on the table, flip the eggs, and put the toast down a second time. I like my toast almost burnt.

Once the eggs are on my plate, butter and jam on the table, with a glass of peach juice, I take a bite of toast and pick up the letter again. In her neat script, every word on the blank page precisely lined up with the squareness of the page and with the line above and below it, I read:

Dear Nicky:

I can't live alone with you any longer. Since we moved to San Francisco, I've felt you have not been emotionally or even verbally available, and that's not the way I want to have a relationship with you or anyone.

I'm moving back to the desert for now. If you ever decide that you want to give up smoking pot, I might consider giving this relationship another try, but I can't compete with marijuana.

You can leave a message for me through Tazz and Donna, but there is no use in wasting your time until you have committed to not smoking that stupid herb.

I love you very much, and it breaks my heart to see you doing this to yourself. You have so much to offer, but you keep yourself anesthetized to the point that I feel the real Nicky Brown is not home.

I hope very much that you love me enough to give that stuff up.

Carolyn

I try to think if I even care that she's left and find a twinge of remorse for treating her so cavalierly for the past month. She's probably the best woman I've ever been with. She deserved better treatment, but I've been preoccupied lately. It's not the pot. I've been distracted with my work, and okay, maybe pottery is an obsession.

I finish breakfast, and without washing my dishes or even putting away the jam or peach-juice bottle, I step through the magic garage door and back into my fantasy world of clay and glazes.

The vase stands sentinel in the garage. I step over to it and test the surface at the bottom with my fingernail. The clay is perfect, not too hard, just right for trimming.

For a single second my mind leaps back to Carolyn's letter and how wrong I think she is. I can put the smoke down anytime I want. I look at the fresh joint I rolled yesterday afternoon in preparation for this morning, pick it up, and roll the pinched-end cigarette in my fingers. I put it in my mouth and bite off the end like one would a good cigar. Sure, I can put this smoke down anytime I want. I grab a stick match and strike it to life. I just don't want to put it down right now. When I fire up the joint and take my first deep draft, my mind relaxes and I see clearly the direction my vase wants me to take it this morning.

After a second hit, my head spinning, I put the cold joint on the shelf, take a trimming tool, slide my foot on the control pedal, and bring the wheelhead to half speed.

The top of the vase is perfect. It needs no work, but because the clay was wet yesterday, the bottom had to remain thicker than I wanted to hold up the weight of the rest of the shape. My job, now that the clay is leather hard, is to trim off the excess on the bottom, continue the sensual shape, then put a foot on it for the entire container to stand on.

The trimming tool peels off long strips of half-wet clay like I'm peeling an apple or potato. The strips spin off the vase, quickly piling up a substantial mound of scrap on my lap and spilling over to the floor.

In twenty minutes, with a careful, slowed approach to prevent any mishaps, I've continued the shape of the vase to the bottom.

I take a piece of thin piano wire, wrap it around the base of the vase, and with the wheel turning at its slowest speed, drag the wire through the thick clay base, separating it from the plaster bat.

I set the vase, still sitting on the bat, on the shelf and clean off the wheelhead.

Carolyn's disappearance hits me.

Eight

Elk Pee

I walk up the side of the ravine to a spot I picked out, turn, and watch as Cherry tromps her way around the next bend, heading farther up the canyon. I hear her footfalls in the gravel for another three or four minutes, fading, but still distinct in the absolute silence of the desert.

The sun, though still in the late afternoon sky, is on the last leg of its journey, and nightfall will be upon me too quickly. I search the hillside for sticks long enough to bridge the gap across my soon-to-be gravel bed. On the far side of the small canyon, a hundred feet from my spot, I find a rotting greasewood tree. After three armload trips back to my site, I begin the process of hand digging out a trench deep and long enough for my body. It's a slow process with bare hands, especially since the tips of my fingers are raw from climbing that impossible cliff. The gravel is soft, and I run into few rocks as I work my way down a foot, building a mound of sand on each side of the pit. When I think it's deep enough, I crawl in and lie on my back, adjusting the pit to fit my body, cupped for my butt, a small mound for the backs of my knees. When the bed's as comfortable as it's going to get, I lay the sticks over the top of the hole. Seventeen sticks certainly doesn't cover my body enough for any kind of protection, but Cherry said they didn't need to hide me.

When done, I test the hole by climbing in and lying on my back to see how uncomfortable the whole arrangement is. I wiggle my way out and sit at the top of the canyon wall some fifty feet from my camp looking west at the setting sun reflecting its final strikes of rays on the upper atmosphere, turning the world into deep burgundy, cinnamon, then sienna.

When the last bird makes its final chirp and settles for the night, when the nocturnal desert creatures scamper around, rabbit, kangaroo rat, a small snake, stink bugs, an ant or two, I muster my courage, climb into the pit, and settle in with full knowledge that I will never go to sleep. How can I, there is so much activity on the desert floor?

I don't remember much more than five minutes of those "I'll-never-get-to-sleep" thoughts, before I'm awake with the sound of something big moving close to my right shoulder.

The night is so silent, the sound can easily be a hundred feet away scuffling along at the bottom of the canyon.

I lie, heart thumping, trying to guess the time, maybe three, still a few hours till dawn.

In a sudden rush, with a freight train swiftness, the scuffling sound makes a mad dash in my direction. Has it found me? Does it smell me? Are my piddling little sticks going to protect me? What was I thinking.

Elk Pee

When the rush of the animal is on top of me, I close my eyes so I won't have to see a huge hoof of an elk or paw of a bear or cougar crash through my pathetic protection. I wait, but nothing happens. I feel it pass over a dozen times, snorting and sniffing the air. I smell the breath of the animal when it's directly above me, searching, but not finding. Although the stars give me only a slight ability to see anything other than the checkerboard patterns my eyes always make, I stare hard through the sticks hoping to catch a glimpse of the creature about to eat me. I see nothing. I hear it leap over my little indent in the sand, but I see nothing, not even a shadow obscuring the blanket of the Milky Way high over my head.

The night air is chilly, but my little indent in the gravel maintains a reasonable temperature.

I'm sure the creature will find me because I'm not only sweating, my entire body is vibrating so much that I hear small rocks sliding down the incline of my pit.

It continues to search for an hour without success and finally shuffles over the top of the canyon. I am so filled with adrenaline, that dawn breaks before I can stop shaking. It's the longest night I've ever spent.

In the morning, the whole frightening experience is like a dream. I climb out of my shelter and look around for prints to see what kind of animal it was. In the desert, unless disturbed, the surface of the floor always looks like it has not moved for a hundred years. If the sand is fine enough, one can trace the tracks of an ant, but I find no tracks or sign of scuffling. It's like the night's activities did not exist, and I'd lost all that sleep for nothing.

I'm hungry and there is no food, but my most insistent need is water. I'm so dry my tongue feels swollen, my lips

157

are chapped, and all I can think about is water.

The sun reaches my little campsite. I step to the far side of the canyon a hundred yards away, and sit under a ragged granite boulder the size of a semi truck. There is nothing to do, so I simply watch the turquoise sky, the distant playa, a hawk drawing circles in the morning breeze, and an occasional rabbit scampering up the center of the ravine.

When the sun peeks over my rock and blasts me in the eyes, I look around. Nothing has changed, though I don't expect anything different in the desert.

My thirst is more insistent, but Cherry has the only possibility of water, if she brought some, which I don't believe she did. Who knows how far up the canyon she walked, or if she is even up there? I wouldn't put it past her to simply keep walking and leave Kat and me out here on our own. I won't give her the satisfaction of going to find her before tomorrow. I'd probably never live it down if I do.

I sit, waiting out the longest day I've ever experienced, getting through a place in my mind that screams for water, grumbles for something to eat, gets angry at myself for being here, then gets angry at Cherry for setting us up like this, at Billy Black for even bringing us here, at Stewart for being such a wimp for all those years, at Biker Bob for sending me off on a wild toad ride. God, I'm angry at everyone for everything.

I spend hours ruminating about my awful predicament, wallowing in despair, falling in and out of sleep, when I realize the day is over, and darkness again has descended.

Since I napped for hours midday, I'm certain this night I'll lie awake. My body is sore, especially once I slip back into my little self-made cave and lie on the same little stones that bit into my backside the previous night.

Elk Pee

To my surprise, I go to sleep almost before I get settled, and sleep soundly until the same noise awakes me again a few hours before dawn.

I hear shuffling, sniffing, and the close crunching of gravel only something big can make. I freeze.

The creature moves around my little indent inspecting the sticks and the mounds of gravel, sniffing at the air above me. Something happens that shocks me enough to almost make me leap to my feet and run into the ink black night. I stay, but I don't know how.

The night creature, my impression of a massive deer, speaks in a clear female voice with a New England accent. "Does the Renee woman attempt to hide herself from me?"

I can't speak.

"Will the Renee woman open her eyes so we can talk?"

It really doesn't matter; eyes open or closed, I know I can see nothing. As requested, I open my right eye, expecting the creature to have its nose almost pressed against my cheek. Although all I can see is its outline against the stars, it stands to the left of me, with its big head hanging almost touching the sand. "Does the Renee woman fear me still?"

"No," I say aloud, and I truly don't. There is a gentle grace to its words, and though its mass is larger than anything I've ever seen, I don't feel threatened.

"Why are you here?" I ask.

The beast raises its stately head and sniffs the night air. Its inhale is so loud I can hear the echo off the far wall of the canyon. "This is my home. You have come to me."

My mind wraps around the statement easily as my

response is made without thinking. "I'm searching for my womaness."

"Yes, you are," the creature says. "What you don't know is that you have already found it. You will look back on these days as the beginning of your new life. In the morning, go to the great medicine woman who calls herself Cherry. When you find her, she will have a gift for you. Cherish that gift, for it represents this night and all that follows."

Suddenly, though I've never seen one, I know my magic talking creature is an elk.

It stomps one huge front hoof inches from my head, raising dust and sand around me enough that I am forced to cough. In doing so, I awake and look up at the same creature, its leg sprouts out of the gravel inches from my right cheek.

Without looking down, but simply continuing its meandering movement through the first crack of dawn, it straddles my little bivouac, spreads its back legs slightly, and I can't believe it, the damn thing takes a pee right on me, soaking my Levi's and the lower part of my shirt. I don't dare move, for this is not the magical talking creature of a few moments before. This is a twelve-hundred-pound wild elk, ready to bolt at the slightest sound, possibly placing one of those razor-sharp hooves in my stomach as it does.

Oh yuck, it's still peeing on me, and not a little dribble; Jesus, gallons of pee.

When it's done, it drops its head as if to say, "You're welcome." In the ever-gaining light, I look directly into one of its intelligent eyes before it moves on. It climbs the side of the canyon and leaps over the rim.

I'm not crushed by its hoof, but I am soaked to the

Elk Pee

bone, and I stink. God, I stink.

I climb out of my little hole and, though it's chilly, I strip my Levi's and shirt and attempt to wring them out. Urine spreads all over my hands and arms. It's a mess.

I'd build a fire if I had matches, but they'd probably be wet by now.

I stand, half-naked, freezing, waiting for day to begin as the eastern sky yawns in its slow desert awakening. An hour later, the sun finally peeks over the distant horizon, and I feel the first warming rays on my goose-bumped skin. I stretch out on a cool boulder and soak up as much warmth as possible. I think about the elk dream and what she told me. I think about Stewart and how much our lives have changed since Biker Bob came on the scene. I think about our kids and changes I want to make when I get home; that is, if I make it home.

My thirst and hunger have passed beyond grinding need to a distant consideration; not thought about much, but still there tapping on my shoulder, reminding me that something is wrong. My thoughts leap from subject to subject with a clarity I've never experienced. The answers to long-confusing questions come clear. I'm not going to have my children home much longer. What comes next? Do I want another baby? If Stewart is getting stronger and more independent, where does that leave me? What about that streak of creativity I had when I was young, the one I put aside to be a mother? Can I pick it back up?

The questions keep coming in rapid-fire succession. The answers follow so quickly I have a hard time keeping up. I need paper and a pencil or something to write with, so I don't forget.

I turn my pants and blouse over in a hopeless attempt to dry them on the rock, but at least I'm getting warmer.

I see my strengths and weaknesses. I see where I must shift certain things to clear some space for the next phase of my life; Renee the person. It's frightening, yet exciting. There are so many choices, so many variables. I must be careful with my options, because if I don't choose, as I did not do for the first part of my life, choices will be made for me. I'd been living a default life. I never chose Stewart; he just came along. I never chose to live in Sacramento or Seattle, for that matter, we just happened to land there because Stewart's job moved us there. I never even chose to have my three children; they accidentally arrived, and did I choose for little Bobbie to die? Not that I don't love my children dearly, but none of them were planned.

I didn't even plan to have sex with that hunk at work. I just fell into it on a night when my resolve was at an all-time low.

The house in Big Bear was the first thing I chose in my entire life. Going on this journey was also out of choice. Even landing here on this rock, having climbed a cliff I would never have attempted was out of choice. Cherry was very persuasive, but I chose which path I wanted to take. I'm not sure that getting peed on by that extremely oversized deer was in my realm of choices, but the message she gave me, though it was no message at all, opens a part of my mind that has been locked for most of my life.

"I'm choosing from now on," I say aloud into the silence of the desert. "I'm choosing from now on." I say louder, the sound echoing off the far side of the canyon. I scream, "I'm choosing! I'm choosing! I'm choosing!" I continue screaming, "I'm choosing!" In a surprised frightening second, I hear not an echo, because it's in

Elk Pee

a different tone. Is it in my head? I stop and allow my voice to trail off.

"I'm choosing!" I hear in the distance. "I'm choosing." The sound keeps getting closer, and I continue to listen like I can't believe that there is anyone else at all on this planet besides myself. I realize it's Katherine's words echoing off the walls and rocks the size of houses.

I look at my half-dried clothes and flip them over once again. Katherine or no Katherine, I'm not putting on wet clothes. I sit naked, soaking up the sun and listening to her make a final yell, then the silence of the desert envelopes me once again.

Five minutes later, I hear the crunching of gravel from far off and it takes another two minutes before she steps around a bend and comes into my line of view. She doesn't see me, and I sit high on my mound overlooking her as she makes her way up the ravine. When she gets under me, I take a handful of small pebbles and toss them into the air over her head. They hit and she jumps aside like she sees a rattlesnake, then looks up. "I'm choosing," she says in a normal tone.

"Me too," I say.

She climbs up to me and sits at my shoulder looking out at the warming day. We say nothing. Not that I don't want to, because I'm bursting with revelations and stories of my two nights, but the desert and the moment dictate silence.

For a half hour we look out, then I stand and put on my almost-dry, rank-smelling clothes. Kat gives me a sniff and grimaces, but still says nothing. When I'm dressed, I step back to my little indent in the sand and scatter the sticks, then fill the hole using my boot until it looks like no one has been here. I turn and reach for her hand. She takes mine, and I pull her to a standing position. In silence, we descend to the sandy bottom, then continue up the ravine.

After a mile, we come around a bend and Cherry stands half way up the side of the canyon, some thirty feet over our heads. She's completely naked basking in the morning sun. With her weight lifter shoulders, tight muscular legs, outstretched arms, her head is back, and she's looking straight up. Her small, almost muscular breasts point due east where the sun rose two hours ago. She looks as though she's been standing in that position since dawn.

Kat and I stop without a word, take a seat on a flat rock the size of a car, and look up at her. She's glowing with the golden reflection of the sun.

I lie back on the rock and put my hands behind my head. In less than a minute, I'm in a deep sleep, dreaming about the elk again. This time it's on top of the canyon some hundred feet over my head. I want to ask it more questions. I stand to yell, but my voice won't work. My clothes are gone, and I'm glad. I attempt to scramble up to the elk, but I can't find the right footing. I keep sliding back to my original position. I look to my side, and there is Kat with her clothes gone, too. Her bountiful breasts, lazily swing as she also makes repeated attempts at the crest of the canyon.

My elk finally, without ever acknowledging that I exist, turns away from the sun and takes two bounding leaps along the edge, then disappears behind the wall of the canyon. I feel a deep sense of sadness. I want to thank it for giving me so much.

I turn toward Katherine with tears in my eyes. She has tears also streaming down her face. We melt into each other's arms, hug and weep.

I awake still sobbing, and I know what I'm supposed to do. Without even looking at Katherine, I remove every piece of clothing, stand, and reach my arms high above my head. My sobs turn to a banshee wail as the sun crests the high canyon wall and shines on both Katherine and me facing the east, bare-assed naked. I feel ancient and strong and alive.

When our wailing turns back to sobs, then whimpers, and finally the tears dry on my face, I turn to her, and we fall into each other's arms, hugging for support, in recognition of the transformation we've gone through. We hug and weep again, though this time it's a joyous emotion. We hold one another in a pact of sisterhood I've never felt.

After a long while, we pull apart, sweaty from the heat of the sun and our bodies, look one another deeply in the eyes, then sit back on the rock. The moment we settle, Cherry is next to us. I don't hear her climb off the hill, and I'd have heard gravel, but she is next to us, with a hand on each of our shoulders. Not a word spoken, we leave our clothes sitting on the rock and continue up the canyon in a slow careful shoeless pace, following the sand at the bottom of the ravine.

We walk for most of the day as the canyon lessens in height and grandeur until it is a small trickle where water runs when it rains. The walls of the canyon reduce to a three-inch drop in the sand some two feet wide. The playa of an old lake bed stretches for miles in front of us with saw-toothed mountains in the far distance.

We reach a wide sandy bog in what's left of the ravine. Cherry stops and rotates her muscular body into a sitting position. She motions us to sit in the two remaining positions of a small, intimate circle.

When she speaks, it's so foreign that she sounds like a spirit. "Here is the only place we speak of our experience." Her tone is soft and inviting, but intense. It sounds like a command from a strike of lightning.

I have a hard time finding my voice. I clear my throat. "I'm choosing from now on."

Katherine repeats my mantra in an unused scratchy voice like mine.

"This is good," Cherry says. I see tears in her eyes. "I also choose from now on." She breaks down, though continues to speak through the sobs and tears. "I choose to trust Ed." Her tears flow over, and she can't speak.

Katherine, with a quaver to her voice, says, "I choose to let my man go, because he's abusive. I deserve better." Katherine, though I have no idea how, holds her tears back and drops into a dark, angry place.

Tears filling her eyes, Cherry reaches out one of her factory-worker hands and gently grabs Katherine's fingertips. "This is a safe place to let out the pain."

Just the touch of Cherry sends Katherine into a flood of tears, a dive deep into the sadness. She tries to speak, but the words don't find their way to the surface.

After five minutes, Katherine's flood of emotion subsides. "He beat me when he got drunk, and I never said a word." She draws in a deep breath then lets it all out. At the end of her exhale, she speaks. "I don't deserve that."

I reach over and slip my fingers into Kat's other hand, and we all let loose with another salvo of an emotional outburst.

The sun is dropping deep into the West when the three of us transpose ourselves from weeping to anger, to rage,

Elk Pee

to acceptance, and finally to a soft place where our living has meaning.

I look up from our small circle of nakedness in the middle of miles of nothingness, with the temperature dropping, and say to Cherry, "We don't have time to get back to our clothes."

She gives me an all-knowing smile. "Where we are going tonight, we don't need clothes."

Katherine shivers. "I'm getting cold."

Cherry looks at her. "It'll get colder before the night is out, but we'll survive and be stronger women for it."

I put my arms around my midsection and look at Cherry.

She opens her arms as if she is inviting the cold in. "Be the cold. Hold the cold in your womb. Accept the cold, and it will be nothing."

I start to complain, like I always do. I want to get angry at her and myself for being in such a predicament. I want to wrap myself in a blanket. Instead, like Cherry, I open my arms slowly, letting the dropping temperature into my belly. I lay my head back and howl like a coyote.

***

For two days I'm glad Carolyn is gone. No one to pop her head out of the kitchen and remind me about the handful of vitamins she wants me to take at every meal. No one to hound me about smoking. No one to want my attention in the way that women want attention; to talk about nonsensical things when there is so much to be done. I need to pull a handle for the biggest vase I've ever made. I take a double-fist-size piece of fresh clay and squeeze a small knot at one end as a hand hold, then stretch the clay, getting my hand wet for each pull, extending the clay, elongating it, squeezing it into a long snake. When I have the length I want, I set it on a soft cloth to dry a bit, then take a needle tool and scrape crisscross patterns into the leather-hard vase where I want to attach the handle.

I need to wait for an hour or so to allow the handle to stiffen so it can stand the thirty-inch length of the vase without collapsing. At a rest point, it's time for an attitude adjustment, so I reach for my ritual dish that holds my rolled joints. There is nothing. I remember, I smoked the last of that roach a few hours ago. No problem. I turn toward a clay-spattered desk I got at a garage sale for a dollar and open the top right drawer. Ah, yes, there is my baggie of weed. I snatch it out of the desk and unfurl it, but all I see is a spattering of crumbs in one corner; not enough for even one good hit, much less a full joint.

I search the drawer more carefully, because I'm sure I have a few roaches somewhere. I find another baggie, but it's also empty. I shake both bags out onto my ritual plate, but combined, it's little more than a pile of stems.

I'm nervous. I'm sure I have a little stash for a rainy day, but I look in every hiding place I can possibly remember and find nothing. My emergency miniscule roaches are in the jar above my ritual plate, but those are for a dire emergency. The smoke of recycled roaches is harsh and tastes like asphalt. I pick up the phone and call Hank, my favorite connection.

Hank is a dealer, so we must speak in code. "Hey, Hank," I say after fifteen rings and the answering machine kicks in. He never picks up the phone without screening calls.

Elk Pee

"Hank, I know you're there. This is Nick. Pick up, Hank. Hank." I hear a nervousness in my tone. I hang up and sit back, rubbing my face with both hands, then reach the jar and pull it down. There must be twenty small roaches I can unravel and re-roll. There will be at least a joint's worth in the jar. I lean the jar toward me and see that the single miniscule leak in the roof of this shitty-assed garage was right over the shelf. It dripped only a few drops an hour, so I slipped something in under the drip and went on about my work. That was a month ago and I'd forgotten about it. I look at the rotting gelatinous mess with green algae growing on each precious little roach.

Hell, what am I getting so nervous about? It's only pot. It's not like I'm shooting heroin or smoking opium. It's just pot, for God's sake. The stuff is harmless.

I think maybe I'll quit and give Carolyn what she's been hounding me to do for a while. Hell, yeah, I'll quit so she'll be happy. This is a no-brainer. I'll give it up, then call her in a day or so. I miss her a little.

With renewed resolve, after an hour of pacing, I turn back to my pulled handle, take the needle tool, slice a flat on the thick side, and etch crosshatches on the end of the slice. From deep inside my water bucket, down in the bottom where the most slippery clay lies, I pull out two fingers full. I dab some slippery clay at the crosshatching on the vase, then do the same to the handle. I reach inside the vase and support the drying clay wall, then push the handle, wiggling it as I push, onto the vase. The length of clay sticks out from the wall, then I shape it into a sensual curve to the bottom. I let it rest on the table while I scratch crosshatching into the bottom. A glob of slippery clay gets applied and the two are joined.

I turn the clay at different angles to make sure the handle has a smooth arch. With a sharp trimming tool, I remove the little bits of excess from each connection joint. Suddenly, the word joint reminds me of a joint and I reach for the ritual dish without even thinking. When nothing is there, my mind races through all of the other hiding places I can think of, but I already know there is nothing to be found.

I sit back and take a deep breath. Something inside is screaming, but I don't recognize it. Maybe I'm hungry, so I get up, walk to the garage sink and wash my hands. I look for the clock as I enter the kitchen, then realize Carolyn owned the clock, and she's taken it with her. I open the fridge and though it's only been two days, nothing edible exists other than peanut butter and a heel of an old loaf of bread. She did all the shopping.

I pop the heel in the toaster and bring the jar of peanut butter onto the cluttered counter. It was never this way when Carolyn was here. She's a neat-freak, and it always bugged me, but now that I'm running out of counter space, maybe her neatness wasn't such a bad thing.

The toast gets stuck in the toaster. I take a knife and dig it out, breaking off a section.

Peanut butter is on the bread. I take a bite and try to swallow with no luck, so I draw a glass of water, the only thing left to drink in the house, and wash the wad of glue down.

Once I finish the so-called peanut butter sandwich, I still have a nagging emptiness in my stomach. I dig around in the cupboards and find a can of black olives and a small jar of capers. I've got to go shopping.

The olives are gone instantly, and I'm working on the capers, but my stomach turns after the third handful.

Elk Pee

I open the phone book and call for take out. Pizza will curb any appetite. The kid on the other end of the line says it'll be twenty minutes. For no reason at all, I yell at him and slam the phone on its hook hard enough to chip the almost indestructible plastic.

I go into the bathroom and throw some water on my face, then dry it with the towel I left on the sink the night before. It's musty from being bunched up.

I want to hang it back up so it can dry, but I'm too distracted and simply toss it back on the sink, then walk into the kitchen. If I must wait an hour, I'll get into the novel I've been reading, but the increasing emptiness in my stomach is distracting enough that I finally put the book away and decide that maybe I can throw another pot.

I go to the studio and carefully remove the largest vase I've ever made. With shaking hands, and my hands never shake, I carefully lift it up to the third shelf above my head. At the last possible second, the vase slips, and a corner of the foot bangs against the shelf. I grip it in time, but I see a dent the size of a dime creased into the clay.

I ignite, enraged with myself for being clumsy. In an uncharacteristic outburst, I slam the vase as hard as I can against the wheelhead. It doesn't shatter because the body of the clay is still pliable. Instead, it collapses, with the wet handle wrapping around it. I look at the clay conformed to the wheelhead, half off of the disk, then look at my hands, which are shaking. The doorbell rings.

A pimply faced, towheaded kid in his late teens stands at the door, pizza held like a waiter in a restaurant, above his head with one hand, fingers splayed. "Brick Oven,"

171

he says, as I open the door.

"What the fuck took you so long?" I yell. I can't believe I'm using this tone with a total stranger.

The kid's face drops from a happy exuberance, to a glowering sourpuss before I finish my sentence. He opens his mouth to say something, but no words come out.

"Sorry," I say. "It's been a bad day."

His face brightens a little. "It's okay, mister. That'll be fourteen ninety-five."

He hands the pizza box to me and I give him a twenty. "Keep the change, kid." ·

His face lights up like it was when I opened the door. "Hey, thanks, mister." The kid races for his older fire-engine-red Volkswagen, leaps in, and speeds off.

I take the pizza inside and drop it on the kitchen table. Some dick-head put pineapple on my pizza. I fucking hate pineapple. Before I even take a bite, and I'm hungry as hell, I'm at the phone dialing the number on the box. I'm going to ream those idiots at the pizza parlor for not paying attention.

I've dialed the last number and the phone is ringing, but I slam it on its hanger. God, what's wrong with me? Why am I so edgy? Hell, I can easily pick off the pineapples, and I'll still have a perfectly good pizza. What, am I going to wait for a replacement?

I get ready to pull off a slice, and the idiot who cut the pizza must have used a spoon. The usual crisp-cut lines are crooked and not even close to cut all the way through. I'm on my feet and almost to the phone once again, before I stop myself. What's happening to me? Maybe I'm hungry.

I get a sharp knife from the knife block and cut the pizza, pick off the pineapple, and take my first bite. It's

Elk Pee

good, better than I remember. In five minutes, I've eaten five wedges and I'm full, but the emptiness in my stomach hasn't gone away. In fact, it's gotten worse. Maybe I'm coming down with a flu or something. If I'm getting sick, I should get provisions, and I'd better do it now.

I put on clean clothes, pull a brush through my hair, walk out to my car, and drive away in the time it took Carolyn to apply her lipstick. I turn right, then a quick left. Man, I love not having to wait for a woman. I love not being constantly late to almost everything. I'm free!

A smile comes to my lips and I truly feel free. . . for about five minutes. I get to the grocery store. I haven't shopped for myself since Carolyn came on the scene. I forgot, I don't have the patience for shopping.

I walk each aisle, grab and toss into the basket articles I think I may need for the next few days. I want out of here, and I want out fast. The aisles are crowded, and I have to maneuver around more than a few women who have their shopping carts blocking the aisle. A middle aged woman in a pink jogging suit is not able to decide if she wants canned pears or canned peaches. God, the unconsciousness of this culture infuriates me.

I'm forced to backtrack, then go to the next and back down the first aisle to find what I'm looking for, and she's still standing there comparing pears and peaches.

I happen to get in the line where the cashier can't possibly go slower. I'll be waiting for the second coming, and it's too late to change lanes. All of the others have filled. I wait, fingers tapping, for fifteen minutes while she counts every little penny, every single receipt, each soda pop can, until I almost yell at the top of my lungs, throw those cans of peaches and pears, jump on the conveyor,

173

get close to her face and scream with everything I have. I'm almost ready. Almost! The only thing that stops me is how much of a jerk I'll look like. It's not a pretty world.

I'm finally out of that god-awful place, in my car, then I stop and pick up five videos for five days for five dollars and beat feet for home before I kill someone. Man, I'm on edge, and I can't figure out why.

The cold groceries are in the fridge. Everything else stays in the bag on the table. I walk straight out to my studio, give a fleeting glance at the drying smashed vase lying across my wheelhead and reach for the jar with the moldy roaches. I don't care; I need to get straight with God, and rolling a fatty is going to be my only way.

I go back into the kitchen, pour the ten little half-dried roaches out onto the table and tear them apart one by one, emptying out their contents, which isn't enough for two good hits, so I tear up the resin-soaked rolling papers until I come up with enough to roll a fresh joint. Not a very big fresh one, but a joint nonetheless.

I strike a kitchen match and pull the smoke into my lungs, then cough my guts out, the smoke is so harsh. I try to take a second hit, but my body refuses.

"Hank, where are you, man?" I say after getting his answering machine again. "I need you, Hank. I need you, man. Call me the minute you get in."

I hang up, then the whole ball of wax hits me like a ton of kiln bricks. I look at the little pinroll joint I rolled out of old rotting roach paper. I look at the mess of blackened goo I left on the table from my frantic seizure of the very last of my stash and the recycling of that mess. I look at my shaking hand and feel my frayed nerves. I get up and walk over to her mirror, the only thing Carolyn left behind. I gander into the reflection and see a dark face. I see circles under my eyes, though Carolyn fed me handfuls of vitamins daily until she left two days ago. I look at my shaking hands. The tips of my index finger and thumb are stained with the black tint of pot resin from smoking joints so close to my fingers.

I take in a breath and can't pull in a lung full of air without coughing, and I never smoked cigarettes.

God, I'm a mess, and maybe Carolyn is right. Maybe I do have a pot-smoking problem. Maybe there's something to this addiction thing after all. I'd never have thought it, but maybe marijuana does have a dark side, like opium, speed, or heroin; not as bad, but a dark side just the same.

I take my last pin-rolled recycled joint and scoop up the split roaches and the little black crumbs, walk over to the sink, and drop everything in the garbage disposal. I turn the water on and flip the switch. The disposal doesn't even consider the pittance of material I fed it. Its motor whirs without question until I flip off the switch.

I'm done with smoking. I want to see what my life looks like without smoking pot. How long has it been; ten years, maybe fifteen?

Not two hours after I smoked the one hit of spent roaches and tarred paper, a headache begins at my temples and spreads into the crown of my skull. It's the same headache I get when I stop drinking coffee.

After I take two aspirin, I wander around the house attempting to find a comfortable spot on the couch, reclining chair, on my unmade bed. I draw a hot tub and take a cold shower. In the next hours before I attempt to go to bed and sleep, I try them all, finally ending up flat on the floor on my back in the living room, with a small pillow for my head. It's the only position that's reasonably comfortable, until my stomach cramps so much that I'm doubled over.

I feel like I'm starving, but I'm not able to eat anything more than a single bite of melon or quarter piece of banana before my entire digestive system screams like I've eaten a teaspoon of Drain-O.

God, I must be coming down with a mother of a flu.

By ten at night, the time I usually go to bed, I'm so bound up with cramps and the damn headache, there's no possible way I'm getting any sleep.

I try to read, but my arms aren't strong enough to hold the book, so I simply lie on the floor, tossing and turning, listening to a classical radio station, the only music that soothes my frayed nerves.

Somewhere during the night, but not the early part, I doze. It feels like only twenty minutes before my overly active brain attempts to leap out of my shaken body, but I guess twenty minutes is all the sleep I'm going to get.

In desperation, though I never watch television, I tune in a late-night movie channel, but I get irritated after the first commercial and almost throw my shoe through the screen.

I remember the videos and plug one in to get through the night and the weirdest flu I've ever had.

Although the movie is some rowdy shoot-em-up-bang-bang, the action soothes my raw stomach and numbs my throbbing head.

By dawn, I have gone through an old Clint Eastwood western and the first Terminator movie, my all-time favorite Sci-fi flick. I've seen it a hundred times, but never on the big screen.

As dawn arrives, then midmorning, I finish another full-length film, and my shaking hands are worse. My resolve shatters when the phone rings and Hank is on the line. "Hey, Nick, how's it hanging?" he asks in his gruff speech. The connection is scratchy, like he's on his cell phone.

"Hank," I say. "Man, it's good to hear from you. Hey, where can I meet you?" I try to act casual, but the flu has me.

Hank laughs his normal taunting mule bray, then says, "Hey, man, you got to slow down on that shit. It's going to be the death of you."

I'm ready to reach into the line and tear his throat out with my bare hands. "Don't give me any of your crap, Hank," I say, though I've never said one cross word to him; a pussycat of a man if I've ever seen one.

"Okay, Nick, okay, just hold on there, Buddy." He drops out of his friendly banter to the take-care-of-business tone. "I'll be over by University of San Francisco in an hour. That's pretty close to your house. How about I meet you at the corner of Nineteenth and Holloway in front of the university sign." He pauses, and I imagine him pulling his sleeve back to look at his gold Rolex. "Let's say noon sharp."

"Noon," I say. "I'll be there."

"See you then, Buddy." The line goes dead.

I find a split in my thoughts. Half of me is saying that last night I resolved not to smoke again for a while, to see what life looks like. The other half of me lists all of the reasons why smoking is a good idea, no, a great idea. I almost call Hank and cancel, but I never pick up the phone. The battle rages for the entire hour. How, if I have the flu, am I going to be able to drive the mile over to Nineteenth? How can I even consider meeting Hank after the promise I made myself less than twenty-four hours ago? Promises are made to be broken. As long as a broken promise harms no one, what's the problem?

Maybe I want to see what being free of pot feels like. It's been since I was a kid. Oh, hell, what's the point? Pot is so much fun.

By 11:30 it's obvious that the going-to-see-Hank part of me wins, because without even taking a shower, I'm in my car and fight the never-ending traffic to our meeting place.

I eventually find a parking place and walk out to the far southeastern corner of the college property. I stand in front of the concrete wall with its huge embossed lettering, University of San Francisco. I've got my hands in my pockets, slightly chilled. Pretty young women walk by in sleeveless blouses, but my constant roaming eye is not exactly on the opposite sex. I'm searching for Hank's black Volvo sedan.

Three times a similar black Volvo drives by, and I leap forward through the throng of people going to and from school. I stand at the edge of the pavement.

When Hank finally shows, I've been standing in frozen concentration for a half hour. He pulls to the curb, and his door locks snap open. I grab the handle and climb into the dark gray leather seat. He's dressed in a thin black leather jacket with a mauve turtleneck. His dark Mid-eastern right hand sports two gigantic gold rings with single huge diamonds. He smiles, and his gold eyetooth has a small diamond embedded in it. The blue-black color of his face complements the turtleneck sweater. "Hey, Nick, you look like shit."

I sniff from a runny nose standing out in the cold and drag my cotton long-sleeve shirt under my dripping nostrils. "I think I got a cold. You got the shit?"

"Sure, man, but you better get down and have your girlfriend take care of you. Your color isn't looking that good."

I want to tell him to fuck off. I want to scream at him to mind his own business. I want to slam my fist in his face, but I don't. I sit there while he turns right and drives down Holloway.

"What do you have?" I ask.

His tone shifts from concerned friend to Mr. Business. He lifts the console between the two front seats and pulls out a small olive jar, about an inch and a half across and five inches tall. "I got two varieties today. This is the government strain called G-4. This shit will knock you on your ass with one hit, but it ain't cheap."

He comes to a stop sign and pokes through, following congested traffic while I open the jar and take a whiff. "Man, this stuff smells good." I reach in to squeeze a single bud. The body of the bud is fat and moist, just right for a pipe.

"Sure, that's the good shit, man, but check out this other one. It ain't no slouch when it comes to knocking your socks off."

I replace the lid, and the aromatic smell continues to waft around the small space of his car. He takes the jar back, and while turning right onto a crowded boulevard, he hands me the second jar. "This one," he says, "is Afgooey, a strain that came directly from the growing fields in Afghanistan before we went in and bombed the whole place to smithereens that is. This particular plant was grown in Humboldt. Fact is, it's the deal of the day, and no slouch in its own right."

I open the lid and sniff. "I like the smell of this one." I squeeze a single bud and find it drier, just right for my favorite way to smoke, a rolled joint. "I'll take it."

"No problem, man. Give me a bill, and it's yours." He makes another right and climbs a gradual hill toward the back of a shopping mall.

I lift the jar, not high enough so anyone can see it, but enough to be able to inspect the volume of its contents. There are two nice buds the size of my thumb and a number of smaller ones the size of thumbnails. "Not much in here."

He gets a hurt look. "Hey, man, it ain't the local grocery. I got expenses, you know. In that jar is a full weighed eighth ounce, seven full grams with a little extra for good measure."

I dig in my pocket and pull out the hundred. As he turns right again back onto the busy Nineteenth Avenue, I hand over the money, drag my shirt sleeve under my drippy nose, and slide the jar into my pocket.

"Good working with you," he says and slips the money in the console with the other jar.

"How much was the other stuff?" I ask.

He gives me a horsey laugh, pulls over to the corner where he picked me up, puts his right hand on my shoulder, and pats me. "Sheeit, man, don't even ask." The door locks snap open. "Hey, you take care of that cold of yours."

I get out into the chill and noise feeling a warmth in my pocket, much better than the hundred dollar bill that was there a few moments ago.

I walk three blocks to my car and fight my way home. When I step in the door, my stomach ache comes back to my awareness. The headache redoubles, and I dive for the couch with the worst flu I've ever experienced.

After a few moments of rest, I stagger out to the garage, look at the crumpled clay that was the biggest vase I'd ever made. It's lying flat against the wheelhead, dry as a bone. I lean high over it to the upper shelf and snag the pack of papers and a book of matches.

I can hardly make it back to the couch where I'm forced to rest. I blow my nose on a tissue from a box Carolyn left.

After ten minutes, I have enough energy to take my cramped stomach, my splitting headache, and find my way to the kitchen table.

I pull the jar from my pocket and open the lid. The room fills with a sweet smell and my taste buds leap for joy.

I remove a small bud, close the lid, and crush the flower into miniscule particles. I remove one sheet, scoop up the greenery with the flap of the papers container, and pour it into the single paper. After a bit of maneuvering the little crumbles into position, I roll the joint into a tight tube, sealing the ends with a twist, and bite off the end that I stick into my mouth. I move to the couch and lie down. My stomach is still twisted and my head pounds. I hope that after I smoke this joint, maybe I'll be able to eat something, and in turn be able to take a few more aspirin without eating a hole in my stomach. I blow my nose once again before I light the match and pull in the sweet smoke for the first time in almost twenty-four hours.

Ah yes, my head relaxes, my tight jaw releases. I feel my entire body let go. Hank was right, the stuff really knocks my dick in the dirt. I sigh the smoke out in a satisfying exhale and lay my head back. Man, this is really good.

By the time I'm taking my second hit, I realize that my aching body, my splitting head, my knotted stomach are all gone. I'm normal again.

I look at the joint, and for the first time since the whole nightmare began yesterday, I realize my flu never existed. Oh, God, was I coming down?

***

I don't know, maybe I said or did something when we were at Stewart's, but when we leave his house, Twig starts in with some subject I don't understand. As always, I'm his mate and guilty of not giving the guy a chance to finish his thoughts, but damn it, he's so slow at it. I already know what he's going to say long before he finishes his first sentence. I guess I get impatient, so I slip in and complete his sentence. It's not my fault the guy's so slow.

We're cruising along, him trying to get to his point, me doing my typical helping him thing, and in a single moment I watch Twig's face lock; his jaw sets. We haven't even turned off of the twists and turns of Stewart's road and onto the main highway, when heaven's sake, Twig freezes. He's got some burr up his butt, and I can't get him to tell me what's bothering him. For the rest of the way home, every few minutes, I prod him to let it out, but he's not budging and he's not saying a word. After five miles of me prodding him, he pulls out that damn leather pouch and wiggles it at me. Finally, we pull into our driveway, and there's old Glen sitting in his regular spot on the porch swing. He waves and I wave, but Twig doesn't take his hands off of the steering wheel. He doesn't look in any direction other than up the driveway.

"Come on, Twig, you've got to wave to Old Glen."

I get no response, other than a tightening of the steering wheel and a determined focus through the windshield.

Elk Pee

Twig parks, pulls the emergency brake, swings the door wide, climbs out of my car that's always been too small for him, and stomps up the stairs. I haven't even unbuckled my belt before he disappears into our apartment.

I roll my eyes, knowing that once I go inside, there is going to be some shit to pay. Twig is hardly ever the first one. He's usually angry after I've provoked him, but today he's enraged, and for what, I have no idea.

Anything to keep from climbing those stairs and facing that sourpuss, I walk out to the front of the house and lean on Glen's fence. "Hi, ya, Glen, everything okay today?"

He turns his head away from looking at the middle of the street and grins with his tobacco-stained teeth. "Everything's okay with me, Sweetie-Pie. I'm wondering how things are going with you and that man of yours."

I give him a broken smile. "Everything'll be okay. We're having a bad day at the moment. We can't find a place where anything fits."

He snickers, leans forward away from me, picks up his filthy old coffee can, and spits out blackened goo. Heaven's sake it's gross.

"I'm sure the two of you'll get through it." He puts the can down and turns back toward me. "Did he pop the question yet?"

I blush and turn to see if Twig is standing there, then lean closer and nod. I whisper, "Couple of hours ago, but we've been scrapping ever since."

Glen's head bobs. I wouldn't call it a nod, because his last stroke left him weak in his neck muscles, and a single nod might repeat itself ten or fifteen times before he can arrest the movement.

He says, "Hey, that he asked at all is amazing to me.

The guy seemed dead set against it."

I toss up both hands and shrug. "Miracles do exist."

He giggles and with his scratchy old-man voice, says, "by the looks of him when you drove in, I'd say you got some work to do upstairs. Standing around here jawing with an old man is just making things worse."

I take a deep breath and sigh. "See you later, Glen."

"See ya, Sweetie-Pie. Good luck."

I turn, walk back to the car, get the few groceries we picked up on the way home, and take them toward the lion's den. I open the door. When I look in, Twig is sitting in his favorite chair watching, of all things, football.

I speak as I walk past to put the groceries on the kitchen counter. "You don't even like football."

He says nothing.

I take my time putting away the pasta, a loaf of bread, two cans of chili, a pound of butter, a jar of sweet pickles, and a pint of Ben and Jerry's Chunky Monkey. When everything is away and I've carefully folded the bag while on the boob-tube some overly testosteroned ape makes a run for the end of the grassy part and gets piled on by almost everyone in the game, and still Twig has not made a move, not one peep, no screaming for his favorite team, no jumping up and down like I've seen a hundred guys do before, nothing. I know he's not watching.

I put the bag between the counter and the refrigerator then walk into the living room, not that it's more than three steps. I put one hand on the arched opening between the two rooms and look at him, while the commentator drones out his impressions of another of those stupid macho moves they're so enamored with.

Twig doesn't glance at me, but he's still not watching.

"We going to talk?" I ask.

Elk Pee

He looks up with such venom in his eyes, I'm sure he'll throw the TV at me.

Finally, and I've been waiting ever since we turned onto the main highway, about an hour ago, he says, "You going to listen without interrupting me?"

He's ready to talk. That in itself is a relief. I step over to the couch and sit while the television is blaring. "Can we turn the television down?"

"No!" he snaps. "If you want to listen, just listen. It shouldn't matter that the television is running or not."

I toss up my hands. I'm ready to get up and walk out, but there is really nowhere to go. I'd better work it out with this guy, so I huff once and settle back on the couch. Heaven's sake, he is a total pain in the ass.

"Okay, I'll listen," I say as I fold my hands in my lap and give him my full attention, though the television is distracting.

He reaches into the middle of the coffee table and picks up the talking stick we made out of a mesquite branch after Bob's tools disappeared.

In my imagination, I zip my lips closed, take a key and lock them, then put the key on the table. He sees none of this goofball stuff or I'd never get another word out of him.

He glares at me and says, "When you get angry, I've heard you say over and over that all you want is for me to witness you. Nod if that's right."

I nod with my eyes wide.

I feel a softening in him. It's not something I can put my finger on, because his rigid, kick-ass, posture hasn't changed. His narrow, angry eyes haven't shifted. Maybe it's his voice, slightly more responsive.

"I've been angry all the way home. . ."

What he's saying is not rocket science. I want to say something, but he has the stick and my lips are sealed.

"Why I'm angry, I have no idea, I'm just angry."

I want to say, "now there is a revelation," but I'm silent.

He continues, "I don't know for sure, but I think I need to go through my emotion without your input. When you interject, it pisses me off, and I lose my train of thought. If you're always interrupting, and forever finishing my sentences, I'll never get to the core of my anger."

Wow, now he's saying something.

"Like you always ask from me, when I'm angry like this and it's not for any apparent reason, I just need you to witness me. I don't want your input, and I certainly don't want your wisecracks. I only want you to listen." He holds up the talking stick, obviously to remind me that I'm not supposed to say anything, like he has to remind me. Heaven's sakes though, I really have a lot to say at this point. I want to talk about my needs and what about—.

His words interrupt my internal monologue. "Nod if you think that makes sense."

Although it goes against every female pore in my entire body, my entire universe, I don't say one word and I give him a single nod. I hate being controlled by this man; hell, by any man for that matter.

He holds the stick in the air like some king lording over his lowly subject. "Even if I don't say a word, I need you to witness me without interrupting."

What the hell does he mean, even if he doesn't say a word? Does he want me to be totally silent in his stupid male vacuum?

As if he's reading my mind, he says, "I want you to give me enough time to think about what I want to say,

Elk Pee

because what I feel is buried so deep it takes a long time for it to reach the surface."

He still has that fucking male symbol of the ever-controlling dick; that talking stick. I hate every little part of it. He still holds it in the air between us in silence. After what seems like a billion years, he speaks again. "I need you to witness me without defending yourself, without any excuses, even if I start to get mad. I need to get mad. I need it more than anything."

After another long blank space in the monologue, another controlling male blank space, with great reluctance, Twig puts the stick on the table.

I pick it up to let out these miles of sentences I've been saving since we sat down, but for some reason, I restrain myself. He's saying something here, and though I still have no idea what it is, it's important. I say, "You're so frightening when you get mad. Even if you simply raise your voice a single decibel, I feel like you'll destroy me. My only response, my only protection is to match your intensity."

Against all of my instinct to continue talking, to unload everything I'm feeling, I put the stick down and look at him, expecting him to defend himself as usual. His face turns three shades darker. He looks like he is about ready to stand up and stomp the coffee table into smithereens. In a way I want him to. His hands clench and relax too many times. He's on the edge, and I don't even know what I said.

He speaks in an even tone, timed out in metronome accuracy. "I need you to witness my rage without reacting to it."

His words loosen something inside, as if saying that first sentence set into action some long-forgotten backwash of

187

emotion. "If intimacy for you is to talk until things are worked through and we are back to loving one another again, intimacy for me is to have someone who will not shrink or try to match my emotion, but hold the space so I can find my way through the quagmire to the next layer. I need someone to be with me, to experience my going down. I get that with my men's group, but I need my woman to trust that I can go there, and for her to be silent long enough for me to find that part of myself without her help."

I'm dumbfounded. If I don't meet his intensity, he'll feel more connected to me? Hell, he's a man. I don't pretend to have a clue to a thing a man really needs. I know many things that he doesn't need, like too much mothering. I know he doesn't need a hard time or to be shamed by a woman, which apparently I do easily. What about this giving him the time to explore his own emotion? How can that possibly be intimacy? What part do I play in his intimacy when I can't engage him? I don't get it.

My thoughts are running wild as a renegade desert wind, yet Twig leans back as if he's said it all, and he's finished for the rest of his life.

For a moment, I sit not knowing where to begin. I want to say so much. When I do speak, neither the words nor my subdued tone is familiar to me. "Maybe I need to get used to simply experiencing your emotion, but I don't know how."

He smiles for the first time since we left Stewart's.

Nine

Harnessing the Ape

After revealing a part of myself who's frightened that my killer ape will surface once again and smash the coffee table that I replaced just last month, I must have articulated my message, because she simply sits there and listens for the first time since I can remember. Sure, it starts with the talking stick, which opens up enough space for me to think carefully about what I'm going to say before I say it, but also room to speak the words without getting interrupted.

This time she actually heard me and didn't run off at the mouth the second I put the stick down, but held the space of silence between us.

I asked for her to witness my anger, but I sense from her expression, that not only does she not know how to do it, she doesn't know what I'm talking about.

I hear a buzz in my ears, like the sound of crickets at night or the desert cicada on a hot day. It's an electric sound I know, but can't remember its meaning until I hear from inside my body under the layers of consciousness.

It's a deep voice. At first, I don't understand the words because they're spoken so slowly, like a tape played on the lowest speed, but it quickly speeds up, and I recognize Bob's tenor.

I look at my soon-to-be wife and the expectant mother of my first child, as the voice carves a path through the ice sheets of my consciousness, breaking up huge chunks of thought as it goes through. "Get her used to your anger, Dickhead."

"What?" I ask from within. Melinda sees or hears nothing, but I think she notices that something is going on, because she studies my face.

Bob says, "Slowly and methodically, adjust the volume of your emotion over a long period, to get her used to the idea that you're not going to hit her."

"What's a long period?" I think it'll be slow hours of ever-increasing the volume before she can actually not shrink or respond in kind to my anger, because for now, the thing I need to get out is my rage in an appropriate setting where no one or nothing gets hurt.

I hear a roar of laughter inside my head, and I open my eyes a crack to see if she hears. She's sitting with her hands folded, her head cocked to one side like that dog on the old RCA logo. Is she listening?

When the laughter stops, Bob says, "Not hours, you idiot, years."

I scream with surprise inside my head. "Years?"

"It's a long, slow process getting someone used to your anger, Dickbrain. As big and threatening as you can be, I can see why."

"Years?"

"You have to consciously bring your anger to the table to the point where you see her react. Some women shrink and try to hide, but you're lucky; Melinda's reaction is apparent."

"What do you mean?"

"Think about it. You simply amp your anger up until she gets ready to meet you with her anger, then you stop."

All of this is going on in my head, but I get the feeling Melinda is listening. I open my eyes again, and there she sits, hands folded, with her curious RCA-dog look.

"What if I can't stop?"

"If you can't stop, you're experiencing your anger for the wrong reason. If you want to bring her into this part of your life and share it, you must consciously control it, so you can stop, because if you go off the deep end, you'll have to go back to step one all over again. If you want to beat her up with your rage, you're on your own."

"I want her to be in the chaos with me, to witness my confusion without her razor words."

"You must meter this anger of yours for a few years until she gets used to it."

"Oh, God," I say, "One more place where I have to put a cap on my emotion. Haven't I had a whole lifetime of holding back?"

Bob yells in my ear, "Stop whining. This is what you want and this is big stuff. Once you get her used to you, both of you can feel safe enough to be truly intimate."

Inside, I'm silent.

Bob continues as expected. The guy never stops talking. "Each time you amp up your anger until she reacts, then you stop. You sit down with her and talk about it. You share your feelings and allow her to share hers in a dispassionate, matter-of-fact manner. This technique brings her into your realm. The next time it comes up and both of you can successfully hold this anger of yours in a respectful way, then the second she starts to take it personally and react, you must stop, calm yourself, and talk about it once again."

"I have to do this for two years?"

"Or more," Bob says. "Each time it comes up, each time you're able to successfully approach, amp up, then talk about it afterwards, you will find she is able to go another step closer to experience your full-on, uninhibited rage. Isn't that what you want?"

I put my hands behind my head. "Isn't it what every man wants?"

"Not every man, Twig. A guy like Stewart certainly needs to do something like this, but he is so far from even wanting it, he'll probably have to die and come back into his next life to get to even being conscious of it."

"I thought this was inside every guy."

"It is, my man, and every woman, but we all come into our physical bodies to work on different things. Yours is rage, and a good one it is."

Bob's voice disappears, and I find myself looking at Melinda.

"What?" she says.

I shrug. Has the entire conversation with Bob lasted only long enough for Melinda to form the word "What," which she'll normally do in the first ten seconds?

Ten

Cold to Warm

Renee opens her arms to the cold, throws back her head and howls like a wild animal. Cherry is already exposed to the freezing temperatures. I can't keep from shivering. My teeth rattle. My toes are numb. I bury my fingertips in my stomach for warmth. They hurt, they're so cold.

Cherry turns to me with a military sneer, arms exposed to the plummeting temperature, and says, not in her normal commanding style, but in an inviting tone, "Open yourself to the possibilities, Katherine."

Shaky from the cold, my arms and hands wrapped around me, I say, "I can't; it's too cold."

"Remember how you pulled yourself up on that rock at the ledge of the cliff."

"No, I don't remember." My brain is too cold to think. "I don't remember anything."

Cherry's voice is motherly and filled with compassion. She drops her hands and points at her mid-section. "Do it with your belly, Katherine."

I look down at my belly and feel nothing but cold. "Open to the possibility that your belly button will warm you. Open your hands and trust, Katherine."

My whiny tone takes a leap to another octave, the same level I remember when I was a kid. "I can't."

There is a moment of silence with me chattering and shivering. In a surprise shift, Cherry, in her military bark, screams at me. "Get your hands in the air, Burns!"

Something shifts. With a puppy-dog whimper, my hands, of their own accord, leap into the air, exposing my frozen belly button, my pruned breasts, my entire core. I leap to my feet. Although I'm still frozen and shaking like the leaves of an autumn tree in the wind, I feel a small ball of warmth glowing in my midsection. It's not big, maybe the size of a peanut, but it's there.

Cherry reaches over and touches her forefinger to the exact spot where the warmth resides. Her voice is again gentle. "Now, expand that fire."

"How?" I say, my hands still held up in the air like I'm under arrest.

"Don't ask how, just do it. Trust your body, trust your womb. You have everything you need inside yourself."

The power of suggestion in play, I feel the burning heat of the ball double itself, double itself again, and again until my entire stomach area radiates with heat.

Cherry pulls her hand back and leans on her haunches.

The last of the sunlight dives behind the distant western mountains, and our little circle drops into blackness. All I see is the outline of my two companions, but I feel enveloped by the warmth. I stop shivering. I'm calm.

I drop back to my butt and we sit, knees touching, while the warmth spreads not only inside my body, but like a small campfire also within the airspace between us. No one speaks; no one moves; we simply sit in a meditative silence, warming the space around us.

A crescent moon rises in the East, giving us a small amount of light while we sit in the middle of the desert with no clothes.

A large brown bear saunters up. At first, I lose my concentration and feel the cold slip back into my little protected bubble. I realize what I'm doing and return to the focus of generating warmth. Although this same bear came to me the last two nights, I try to ignore it.

It sniffs the air around us, nuzzles up to me for a moment, playfully pushes its big nose against my back, shoving me forward a few inches, and pushing our little circle tighter. The bear lets out a deep-throated mewing, like a small kitten who wants to play, turns and meanders off into the semidarkness.

How much time has gone by, I don't know, but out of the night sky, a large bird swoops, breaks at the last second, and lands gently on the top of Cherry's head. The bird is big enough to force Cherry to stiffen her neck to hold her head up. The bird settles, preening its wing feathers. It gives a haunting dozen deep-throated hoots, then takes to the night air again, disappearing into the blackness.

I am certain that magic is in the air when the elk Renee talked about carefully crunches its way through the desert hardpan, obviously dropping through the crust like someone would pierce through ice over a snowfall. With each step, it sinks three or four inches. When it reaches us, the tops of our heads aren't higher than its knees, it lowers its head to Renee's ear, then whispers loud enough that I can hear, "You're perfect as you are."

In a fast set of moves, it raises its huge head, rotates as

if on a pivot, then gallops off going north on the playa. For five minutes, I hear its hoofs crunch through the hardpan, hear it breathing hard as it races for the other end of the dry lake bed. Gradually the sound fades until it completely disappears.

Maybe an hour has gone by, I can't tell. The eastern sky brightens, stars fade, a distant coyote howls. In a speeded-up version of dawn, the sun breaks the black of night. The distant mountains turn from a deep plum to violet, then mauve, until finally the sun peeks over the horizon.

Cherry is the first to break the circle of concentration by speaking. "I've always hated that I am tall and that I so easily go to fat."

I want to assure her how stunningly beautiful I find her, but she puts her hand out and silences me. I glance at Renee, who has a puzzled look.

"I don't like that my breasts are odd." Cherry lifts one of her small pear-shaped breasts as if she is presenting it to us. She drops her breast, but it continues to perk out into space like gravity doesn't exist. I look at her almost perfect breast and don't understand how she could feel such a way.

"I don't like my clodhopper feet," she says wiggling her toes with their unpainted and unclipped toenails. Her feet are a little big, but otherwise, I find no flaw in her muscle-rippled body.

"My face looks like Elmer Fudd," she says in an ever-constant monologue about how she feels about herself. "And look at this ski jump of a nose. My beady eyes are set too narrow. She smiles, showing strong white teeth. One incisor is pushing against an eye tooth that is turned to meet its neighbor. "My teeth are a mess, too."

Cold to Warm

Cherry holds out her farm-worker hands, calloused, short-nailed, with thick blue veins on the backs. "My hands are a disaster." She studies her splayed fingers while rotating them in the air in front of us.

In a final defacing moment, she breaks down and cries. Her hands cover her face, and she lets loose with a deep-seated wail. Tears find their way past her hands and slide down her salt-caked arms. "No wonder Ed doesn't want me," she repeats at least five times while her crying reaches a crescendo, crests, then subsides during the ten minutes we witness her grief.

When she's done and her tears dry, her face drops back to the stone-faced Cherry I have grown to love, especially after this display of vulnerability. "I'm done for now," she says.

She nods at Renee. Once the revelation sinks in, I understand at some point it will be my turn, and I'm already nervous.

Renee hates her sagging breasts, her spreading hips, her knobby knees, and a cute birthmark on her right hip. She doesn't like the stretch marks and subsequent extra rolls of loose skin on her belly, her skinny legs, her height, and her squeaky voice. The only thing I can agree with is her voice, which grates on me at times. The rest of her defacing statements are so untrue my mouth drops open in surprise and wonder about how these two women, almost perfect in their physical bodies, see themselves as flawed and imperfect.

Renee, in her stoic nature, doesn't break down and cry, but drops into a silent depression, going inward. Cherry and I witness her withdraw for ten minutes before Renee's eyes brighten once again, and she says, "I'm complete."

She and Cherry turn to me, and I'm frozen. When I

197

can speak, I wash my hands in front of my entire body and say, "I hate it all. I can't think of one part of me that is normal or even possibly acceptable."

Cherry gives me an odd smile and uncurls her fingers three times as if to say without speaking, "Go on."

"My hair is straw, my skull is odd shaped, my face is like the wicked witch of the West, and I've got crooked teeth. My little stubby neck doesn't attach to my head right. My shoulders are too narrow." I point at each of my body parts as I speak. "And look at these." I point at my large, pendulous breasts. "My tits are stupid looking, with nipples that are flat and lifeless, though it's cold out, and they should be standing up like little mountains. They've always failed me. By the time I'm forty, the damn things will be hanging to my bellybutton. Speaking of bellybuttons, have you ever seen one that looks so ridiculous? And what about the roll of fat that surrounds my waist?" I point at Renee's belly. "I would be so lucky to have a little dinky roll like yours. No matter what I do, the fat remains."

I turn to one side and point at my stupid cellulite hips and butt. "Would you look at these? Have you ever seen something so grotesque? Look at these hips; are they the most ridiculous things you've ever seen?

"I've got knock knees, chicken legs, thin ankles and geisha-girl feet." I lift one of my feet and point at my nails. "And to top it off, look at this. I have two grossly ingrown toenails."

***

I can't believe it. Unlike me with my straw-like, black, gray-streaked hair and my baby-stretched body, my wreck of collapsed tits, Katherine is a stunning blonde bombshell, even once she has her clothes off, with her slightly wide hips and those beautiful breasts that I would die for. I'm sure men line up to have a scrap of her attention, and she thinks she is ugly. She is probably one of the more beautiful women I've ever known, and I can't get over it; she hasn't mentioned one redeeming feature.

When she is finished defacing her every part, leaving not one piece of her unmentioned, I begin to understand what Cherry is up to.

When Cherry speaks, I already know what she's going to say. "All of us, even the fashion models in New York, deep down, feel flawed." Cherry points at her almost-perfect breasts once again. "Not one woman I have ever met has been happy with her breasts. I've done this ritual hundreds of times, and not one woman has ever had one positive thing to say about her body. Can you see what kind of position this culture has put us women in? Can you see that we've been ridiculed and shamed into feeling that our bodies are flawed and undesirable?"

"I like my smile," I say in defense, trying to find some piece of me that is acceptable.

Cherry looks at me. When she speaks it's with authority. "You, Renee, are one of the most beautiful women I have ever met. Childbirth and your age have shifted some parts of you, but from my point of view, still, you are a raving beauty, and the amazing thing is, you don't even know it."

I blush, because I know she is either lying or kidding.

Cherry turns to Katherine, and while still pointing at me, she asks, "What do you think about our companion?"

Katherine turns to me. With eyes that are glassed with

tears, she says, "You could use a bath, but otherwise your body is extremely sensuous and feminine, especially with your clothes off."

Leave it to Katherine to crack a joke.

Cherry turns to me. "Did you hear her?"

"Sure," I say.

"What did she say?"

I feel butterflies in my empty stomach. "I need a bath."

Cherry gives me a stern look. "Did you hear anything else?"

I'm confused. I think this is a trick question, but I can't punch a hole through it, so I answer. "A bath. She said I need a bath."

I look at Katherine, whose mouth hangs open.

"Tell her again," Cherry says.

Kat looks at me with a serious face. "Your body is extremely sensuous and feminine, especially with your clothes off."

"Oh, god." I feel tears well up in my eyes.

Cherry says, "Say it again, Katherine."

She repeats her statement, as I throw my hands in front of my face to hold back the tears. When they finally spill over, I find myself in deep-wracking sobs, blubbering about how ugly I feel and how unacceptable my body is, though I'm sure no one can hear. It's all for me, anyhow.

I cry for the longest time, end with a series of sniffles, wipe my nose with the back of my hand, then look back at two of the most beautiful women I've ever seen. They're like angels. I swear I see white wings sprouting from their shoulders.

I reach out and pull them toward me, pull them into my life, my arms, and I go into another long bout of tears, though this time they are tears of joy and support.

Eventually, I look up into those angelic eyes filled also with tears. "Am I really more acceptable than I think?"

"Yes, you are," Cherry says, "and so are we."

Cherry turns to Kat and asks me to comment. In an amazing display of disassociated feelings, Kat, though she already knows where Cherry is going, breaks down after the third time I repeat my confirmation about her beauty. She runs the same gauntlet of self-loathing disgust about herself, eventually pulling both Cherry and me into her arms. When she is done, she kisses both of us on the cheeks.

The sun is high in the morning sky when we finish. Cherry stands, lifts her hands high in the air, and stretches. Both Katherine and I follow suit, and at the same time I look for the elk hoof prints in the crunchy hardpan.

Only bare human footprints reach our little overnight place with nothing else for miles around.

"What happened to the animal prints?" I ask with my back to Cherry and Kat.

Cherry puts her hand on my shoulder. "They were dreamtime animals, Renee. Your elk will guide you in your dreams from now on. When she comes, you will be wise to listen carefully to what she says. She's your personal guide for the rest of your life."

I look back as Cherry turns to Kat. "It would be appropriate that yours would be the bear, because they are such playful creatures; a perfect match for you."

She points to the crown of her own head. "Great horned owl has been my animal for many years now, and she has helped me through many difficult decisions. These are not animals you talk about with anyone. They are very personal and lose their power the more you share them with others. The three of us are bonded in this way for the rest of our lives. Our animals can communicate with one another, which keeps us connected through good and bad times."

I speak to Cherry. "I don't remember falling asleep last night."

Cherry gives me one of her secret smiles. "It is time to find our clothes." Without another word, she turns and marches back, following the triple footprint path made by us what seems a lifetime ago.

Kat and I take each other's hand and follow, snaking along the sandy bottom of the almost unnoticeable drainage that builds to a small creek bed, to an ever-larger ravine, eventually with hundred-foot walls and boulders the size of houses.

We round the turn where Cherry's clothes are, and a small folding table with tablecloth, three full settings, fork, knife, spoon, wineglass, a large carafe of ice water, and a Thanksgiving-looking dinner awaits us complete with turkey, dressing, mashed potatoes, and gravy, all steaming hot, with iced cranberry sauce and apple pie.

Our clothes had been gathered, washed, and folded. They hang and sit on each of the three chairs.

Kat and I burst into tears at the same time. I'm overwhelmed at this kindness, the generosity, but then I see the water. I run to the table, pour a wineglass with water and gulp it down, then pour two more. Cherry, Kat, and I finish the pitcher of water in seconds, then Cherry opens the ice chest next to the table and breaks into a gallon jug. We almost finish it before we're satiated.

Once the water situation is taken care of, Kat points at the table. "Would you look at this spread?" She turns to Cherry. "How did you do this?"

Cherry gives us a Cheshire Cat smile as she dresses.

"There are no answers to some questions. Let's stay in the mystery by not asking questions, but simply enjoy our bounty and be thankful."

I follow her lead and slip on panties, a clean bra, blouse, and Levi's, all freshly washed and pressed.

I assume that the boys delivered the table, dinner and clothes, but how could they have ironed everything?

Once dressed, we sit for the meal. I keep looking at the crest of the ravine, expecting to see Billy and Ed. They've got to be close, because the meal was hot when we arrived. During the five minutes it takes for us to settle, it has cooled. How could they possibly cook the turkey and mash the potatoes, much less keep them warm?

It's all a mystery, but I put the question aside and slice the golden-brown turkey, then dish myself and my two companions thick slices while they serve potatoes, snow peas, cranberry sauce, and dressing.

The meal is the best I've ever had. The ravine fills with oh's and ah's, laughter, giggles, and an occasional burp of satisfaction.

When the meal is over, including a slice of apple pie, we all sit around picking our teeth with the individual toothpicks left next to the silverware. I look at Cherry, "Thank you so much, Cherry. How did you do this?"

She gives me one of her smiles. "I really had nothing to do with this."

I point toward what I think is the direction of the lake. "I'll have to thank the men when we get back."

Cherry gives me another kind of look. "You may be surprised."

"What does that mean?"

She says nothing else.

We sit in blissful silence for a half hour before I start

to pile the empty dishes and scrape the plates clean. Cherry puts her hands out in a halt gesture. "No need to clean up. It isn't ours to do today. Our job is to find our way back to the campground before nightfall. It'll be a hard journey, over rough terrain, but if we focus with intent, I think we can make it.

Kat points at the table. "What do we do with the mess?"

"Leave it."

"But—" Kat isn't able to get another word out before Cherry's sergeant voice returns.

"Leave it, and that's an order. It'll be enough to find our way out of this canyon. We have to start this journey now."

I burp and rub my stomach. "God, I'm stuffed."

Cherry rises, pushes her chair back in the sand, turns, and marches down the ravine.

Both Kat and I follow, leaving the best meal I've ever had. Before we round the first bend, I look back at the table and nothing is there. I stop, but Cherry anticipates my move. She is next to me and shoves me along the sandy bottom of the ravine.

I stumble on, knowing the meal actually happened, because my stomach is so full.

We wind our way along the dry creek bed, and I worry about the cliff we climbed. It was almost impossible to scale that cliff, and I know it will be impossible to descend.

Within the hour, we stand high over the edge of the cliff, look at a five-hundred-foot drop, miles of open country beyond, and the long narrow lake in the far distance.

The sun crested hours ago and is continuing on its

long journey to the western horizon.

I turn to Cherry as we rest on the edge of the precipice. "How do we get down?"

Cherry raises one hand and sweeps the landscape. "There are many things at play here, more than you can imagine." She removes two colorful bandanas from her back pocket and hands them to Kat and me. "Put these over your eyes and tie them tight so you can see nothing."

I wrap the cloth around my face and knot the ends behind my head. Cherry gently grabs both Kat's and my hands, helps us stand and back-walks us to the edge of the cliff. I can tell because the hanging boulder tapers as it reaches the edge. I'm on the tip. Cherry grips my hand tight. Kat's shoulder is pressed against mine. My breath catches. "What are you doing?"

Cherry speaks in an odd tone, like she's far away and has to yell. "This is your ultimate test to trust that you will not be harmed."

I grip her hand tighter. "We're standing on the edge of the cliff?"

"Yes, we are, and you're going to lean back as far as possible."

"Oh God, I'm going to die." My breath is shallow and fast. My heart races. My legs tremble.

Cherry, who still holds my hands, leans me back until I'm at the limit, ready to fall to my death. Maybe that's why those bones were at the bottom of the cliff. Maybe the people had fallen from here.

She says, "When you're ready, I want you to let go."

"What?" I scream. "I'm not letting go."

"Trust, Renee. Breathe into your womb and trust."

Kat mewls the same sound when we climbed this cliff.

Channeling Biker Bob 3

I hold on to Cherry's hand and try to catch my breath. "Please, Cherry, don't do this."

In a gentle tone, she says, "I'm not letting go. You'll release your grip when you're ready."

"No, no, no," I repeat.

Kat whines a similar refrain.

"When you're ready."

"I can't."

"You'll have to let go."

I cry now. "I can't. I can't."

***

Okay, I realize the entire flu episode is withdrawal from almost fifteen years of pot smoking, and most of that time it was all day every day. I never thought of pot as addictive, but maybe it is, and maybe Carolyn is right.

After lighting the one joint and having every symptom disappear instantly, what else could it be?

Although I spent a hundred dollars on the little jar of smoke, I know what I must do, and I must do it before I lose my resolve. I walk to the kitchen sink, open the jar, and take a long draw of the aromatic odor. Before I can think about it, I pour the contents into the garbage disposal and flick the switch. The motor whirs, and I turn on the water. The second I turn the disposal off, I regret my impetuous move. I want to call Hank again, but I don't. I sit quietly at the kitchen table waiting for the return of the worst flu I've ever had.

Two hours later, I'm doubled up once again, headache, sweats, chills. My entire body is screaming.

I mark the calendar, and it's the last coherent thought I have for the rest of the day.

206

Cold to Warm

I can't sleep or eat, so I find myself in front of television watching an endless list of videos to get through the day.

The next morning, it's worse, and I can't get off the couch. The videos I watched yesterday I watch again; anything to get through the pain.

Day three: my headache lessens slightly and I can eat a few sips of canned of chicken soup before my stomach locks up and I almost puke. All my joints ache. My teeth hurt. My chill-sweat repetition redoubles as I lie flat on the couch watching for the third time the same videos, attempting to keep my mind off the pain and discomfort. I sleep in fitful thirty-minute intervals; once midday, later that evening, and once at three in the morning.

Day four: I walk to the video store and get a new batch of movies but run out of energy halfway home. I sit on someone's lawn for a half hour to gain enough strength to finish the three-block journey home. I leave when an old woman in the house threatens to call the cops. I don't blame her, I must look like shit.

For the first time in days, I'm able to sleep. I don't know if it's because I am completely exhausted, but I have no choice. It feels good to wake up in the morning having slept most of the night.

Day five: For the first time since the whole mess began, I am able to go out into the garage and look at the bone-dry vase I destroyed. I clean it off the wheelhead and put some tools away, but I expend all the energy I have. I'm back on the couch watching another movie. At noon, I eat a single fried egg and a bite of cottage cheese.

Surprise, rather than wanting to throw up, my stomach feels better. I have a little more energy, and I go outside for a walk around the block. I make it back. I'm on the couch reading a book. My teeth stop hurting and my headache has drawn back to a dull afterthought above my eyes. Maybe, just maybe, I'm feeling better.

Day six: I have a bit more energy, enough to wedge up a ball of clay and slam it on the wheelhead, but not enough to throw a pot. The interesting thing is I have no interest in throwing pots. Maybe it's a constant gnawing feeling that pottery isn't enough. I never felt this before, but I never felt a lot before.

I take a pen and write some of my impressions of the last few days and find myself completely immersed in writing about my experience. Page after page, I write without thinking, without stopping. I've never written so much. The sun sets, and I don't look up to witness its passing. As night falls, I find myself spinning off of my self-exploration and writing a fictional story about the end of the world and what would happen if. . .

Since I can't sleep anyhow, at three in the morning, I've finished the thirty-page story, which has spawned three others. I feel an excitement about writing I haven't experienced in a long time.

Day seven: It's pretty good. I have a fair amount of energy, though my stamina is weak. I write all morning, take a nap in the afternoon, and my headache and stomach cramps return. I eat a hard boiled egg with a piece of bread, and I feel better.

I'm doing so well, I pick up the phone and call Donna and Tazz. The phone rings six times before Donna picks up. With her two boys in the background screaming at one another, she says in an irritated tone, "Hello."

"Donna, this is Nick Brown."

Her voice changes to a happy-to-hear-from-you tone. "Nicky, how the heck have you been?"

"Okay, I guess. Have you heard from Carolyn?"

"Sure, Nick. She's staying with us while she gets settled. She's not here right now, though. I think she's out looking for a job. They're not easy to find around here."

"Can you tell her I called?"

"Sure will, Nicky."

I can't think of anything else to say. "Have her call me, will you?"

Donna speaks with a cautious voice. "It's really up to her if she wants to call or not."

"I know, but tell her I quit smoking eight days ago."

"No kidding. That's great news. How's it going?"

"Oh, pretty good, I guess. My head is starting to clear."

The kids yell in the background and she screams at them. "I got to go before someone here gets killed. I'll tell Carolyn."

"Thanks." The phone clicks. I hold it to my ear until the busy tone starts, then absently, I set the receiver on the cradle and pick up my pen.

It's long after dark, and my hand is so cramped I'm forced to put the pen down. There must be a better way to write.

Later that night, late into the morning hours, I finish a fifteen page story about a bear who lives in the San Francisco sewers.

The phone rings. I'm startled. I pick it up and say, "Hello."

"Nicky?" Carolyn sounds tentative.

"Hi," I can't find any other words.

"Donna said you called."

"I miss you, Carolyn."

The line is silent for a moment, until she says, "Donna told me you quit smoking."

"I guess I did," I don't want to make the hell I've been going through seem like any big deal.

"You guess? Either you quit or you didn't."

"I quit eight days ago. I didn't realize how that stuff drove my life."

She sighs but doesn't say anything else. Maybe she's waiting for me to say more. I really don't have much to say.

The line is silent for a half minute before she finally speaks. "I'm staying down here, Nicky. I never liked the city much. It's too busy."

"I know what you mean. I got to stay here for a while, but I was thinking about going back, too. Would you see me if I did?"

"Only if you stay clean."

"That's fair."

The line is dead for another long period. I always feel so awkward talking to her, even at the best of times. She's usually the one to carry the conversation and I just listen, but today not much comes from her.

I break the silence. "I guess I'll go for now. When I get free here, I'll come visit. Is that all right?"

"Sure, Nicky, but don't wait too long."

***

"Damn him," I say to Donna after he hangs up. We're sitting at the kitchen table. "I can't ever get more than two-word sentences out of him."

"Don't feel too alone in that one, Carolyn. If I get more than three sentences in a row out of Tazz, I feel lucky. I don't think most guys like to talk much."

"I don't think they like to talk at all. I think Nicky talks to me because he feels pressured to do so, and that's the only reason."

"It's just how it is, Sweetie. They don't do it on purpose to fuck with us. It's just the way they're hard wired."

"Mommy," Donna's oldest, Jake says. "You said the 'F' word. You owe me a quarter."

Donna looks at him. She digs into skin-tight Levi's. When she drags out a quarter and flips it to Jakey, he grins, turns, and runs into the living room to tell little four-year old Stevey. An argument ensues, but that's how it is here at Tazz and Donna's.

Eleven

Hanging On

We back to the edge of the damn cliff. Cherry's hand is our only link from a five-hundred-foot drop to certain death, and she wants us to let go. I don't know about Renee, but I'm not letting go for anything.

"This is a place you must trust you're not going to get hurt," Cherry says.

"I know what's behind me, Cherry," I say. "How could you pretend that nothing is going to happen?"

"Trust. This is the place where you must trust."

Renee's voice goes three octaves higher than normal. "I can't. I can't."

"I'm holding you as long as you want to be held, but you must trust and let go of everything you know about this world. You will not be harmed."

"I can't, I can't," Renee whines, and I feel her trembling through the one connection I have as our shoulders press against one another.

Cherry's words break my focus on Renee's shoulder. "This is the biggest thing you're going to do in your life, but you must trust that you will not be harmed."

My breath is shallow. I can no longer speak. I know about the cliff. I also know that Cherry would not lie to us. I'm being pulled from both directions. I'm almost ready to scream. I want to scramble up Cherry's arm to safety. I feel my knees shaking, like when we climbed this fucking cliff a few days ago. How did I get myself into this situation? What is it about me that draws this experience? Why did I ever listen to some dead biker?

"Let go when you are ready," she says. There is a rare gentleness in her tone.

"I can't," I whine. "I can't."

"I'll be here as long as you need me."

Renee cries. Mixed with her tears is our mantra, "I can't."

After ten minutes, she stops crying like a sudden turning off of a spigot. One second she's trembling and mewling about how she can't, and the next she's relaxed.

At the very same second, as if on cue, I also calm. Like a branch on a dead tree, something inside snaps. I hear the noise in my ears. I relax my grip on Cherry's hand as Renee decides to let go, too. Our shoulders don't lose contact. I feel the last touch of Cherry's fingertips. I feel her short forefinger nail, then I am free to fall five hundred feet with the promise that I will not be harmed. I'm disconnecting from my body. I am certain my life has ended. Why did I let go? Why did Cherry do this to me?

My body is in free fall. My feet lose contact with the edge of the cliff. It's my final connection with earth and all I know. I reach with my left hand and find Renee. We grasp hands and tumble backwards head over heels. I let out a scream. Renee does the same. As we drop, our screams echo off the granite wall.

I thought Cherry said we wouldn't get hurt. I hear the whistle of air. Our momentum increases. I feel the rocks coming. I can visualize the two skeletons lying at the base of the cliff, wedged between the boulders. I see myself landing on top of them.

Renee's hand grips mine. My awareness switches from the fall to her hand. I find comfort in her touch. It may be the last thing I feel. I'm connected to something other than the whistle of the increasing roar of air past my ears. Our screams echo off something else. Is it the bottom of our fall? Are we getting close? The echo reflects back to us quicker as the micro-seconds tick by. Time stretches. Tumbling, we are gobbled up by the abyss. I can't stand it any longer. We should have hit bottom. I reach up and pull the blindfold off, then look at my spinning world. The cliff. Rocks. The blue sky. Back to cliffs, rocks, blue sky.

In a double view of my life, I tumble through space, and at the same time I see the first vestiges of dawn reflecting off Renee's steer horn handlebars and her white throttle grip.

My fall to certain death is overlaid with the second vision of chrome handlebars. God, it's too weird. I close my eyes. The rocks are coming. I have Renee's hand as we scream. I open my eyes, and there are handlebars. Everything is silent.

Seconds before we hit the rocks, I decide to keep my eyes open. I turn my head, and lying in her sleeping bag next to me, Renee removes her bandana and rotates her head to look at me. Fear is in her face, recognition, then delight. Without saying a word or making a sound of any kind, Renee and I roll close and throw our arms around

215

each other. We lay hugging and shivering, not from the cold, but simply from relief until we calm down and fall back asleep.

Cherry is the next thing I see. She kicks my feet in a hurried attempt to wake us up. The day is bright, though the sun has yet to crest the horizon. She speaks in a staccato chop. "Get your gear together. We gotta get out of here now."

I want to protest because I'm exhausted, but dutifully, I get out of my bag and start the process of packing. I'm half asleep. Renee, also groggy, stumbles through packing, simply stuffing things into her saddlebags at random, with little thought for what it will look like when we remove them.

In fifteen minutes, Renee rotates her distributor, flips the choke, and cranks her scooter twice before it comes to life. Billy is next, then Ed, and finally me. We drive out of the campsite. I notice all the wood we gathered is gone.

Renee pulls over, unfurls her kickstand, and leans her bike. She looks at her tire as we turn off our engines.

"My tire is flat."

Ed dismounts and steps over to Renee's Indian. He kicks the tire. "Shit, this is no place to have a flat."

Cherry's nervous.

Renee says, "I've got a hand pump, but it's going to take a while."

"Well, let's hurry it up," Cherry says.

She gets out the pump, assembles it, and connects it to the valve stem. While she pumps, she says, "The tire has a slow leak, but it never lost all its air in two days."

Billy and Ed look at one another then back at her.

"What?" she asks as she pumps.

Billy starts into a sentence, but Cherry chuffs and gives him a dirty look. He stops mid sentence.

Cherry says, "let's get some air in this fucking tire and get out of here."

After five minutes, Renee looks pooped, so Ed takes over, pushing air into the tire like a piston.

In ten minutes the tire is filled again, and we hustle out of the campground.

When we reach the top of the hill, the sun pops over the distant horizon and glares in my eyes. I motion for everyone to pull over. With idling engines we all dig for our sunglasses.

"How come we left so early?" I ask Cherry, thinking that some particularly aggressive canyon spirit was about to pounce on us and turn us all into mincemeat.

She looks over her glasses directly into my eyes and says loud over the sound of four idling engines, "The rangers come early on Sunday mornings, and I refuse to pay their stupid camping fee, so we always leave before they arrive."

***

"What?" Katherine screams much louder than it is necessary over the sound of the engines. I'm quiet, as Cherry turns toward her and Kat continues. "You mean to tell me that after all of that magical crap, after being an impeccable leader taking us through hell and back, you wake us up out of a dead sleep to sleaze out of paying twelve bucks? "I work for the Park Service, and my fucking wages come out of that ten or twelve bucks. I can't believe you."

Kat turns off her engine, leans her bike onto its

217

kickstand, and walks away from the coarse asphalt road into the desert.

Ed turns to Billy and me. "Cherry and I have to get back to the store. Come by when you're finished here."

As he kicks his bike into gear, Billy says, "Wait up, I'll come with you two."

The motorcycles roll onto the pavement. The thunder of engines quickly fade as they shrink into the long ribbon of asphalt.

I turn my engine off, then drop the bike onto the kickstand. Other than the distant roar of Ed's and Billy's bikes, our engines' tick-ticking and a slight breeze are the only sounds remaining in the golden color of early morning.

I follow Katherine's path for a hundred yards. She is sitting on a rock, elbows on knees, weeping onto a pure white blossoming jimson flower.

I walk up, drop to my knees, and put a hand on her shoulder. She raises her head, enfolds me into her arms, then bursts into more sobs, talking through her tears. "After she took us through all of that. . . She's just a. . . sleaze."

I don't say a word, but hold her until she calms. She lets go of me and drags her handkerchief across her nose.

I say, "It was a dream, Katherine. Just a very weird dream."

Katherine pulls back, then glares at me. "It wasn't a dream."

I start to argue with her as she flips her handkerchief open. "If it was a dream, how the hell did we get these?" She points at my forehead, and I reach up to find my red kerchief still tied around my head.

"How did I get cuts on my hands and feet, and why

am I burping turkey and potatoes?"

I look at my fingertips, worn and raw from the climb three days before.

My heart catches and misses a beat or two. "It was real?"

"God damn right it was real; now what are we going to do about it?" We both look out toward the last echoing sound of Ed's and Billy's engines. The two bike specks in the highway disappear over a rise taking the final sound of the engines with them.

"Where does Cherry fit into this?" Katherine asks. "Now that I hate her for being a sleaze?"

I sit on my butt next to Kat, and we look out over the silent desert.

***

Maybe it's time to put Bob's theory to practice. I turn to Melinda, and my burning anger grows a little. She looks at me with her curious expression again. I raise my voice a single level. I have not yelled, not started cussing, just slightly louder volume, but I see a shift in her attitude. I watch her little right hand drop and grab her right hip. She leans forward.

I continue to gradually get louder, still not resorting to cussing, until I see her face redden, then I know it's time to stop. I know she is on the edge of coming undone, all over me.

When I stop, I smile. Her entire body is ready for battle. She'll leap to her feet with that doubled hammer of a right fist. I've stopped at the exact right moment. With the introduction of my smile, her stance drops back to that RCA dog look; a twist to her head, listening.

"How was that?" I ask.

"What?"

"My anger."

"That wasn't your anger, was it?"

"A little bit. How did it affect you?"

She takes a deep breath and lets it out before she says, "My dad used to get angry slowly like that. Mom and I would cringe, knowing what was about to happen. When he lost it, someone always had to get hurt before it was over."

"Really?" I say. "You never told me."

"I learned to protect myself, I guess, but this is the first time nothing's ever happened. She holds out her hands, fingers splayed. "Heaven's sakes, Twig, I'm shaking."

"I see." I want to grab her hands to help calm her, but something tells me not to.

She watches her trembling fingertips. "It's like when you stopped, for the first time I was able to see where my violent response comes from. When Dad came undone, I got in the way to protect Mom. When I was young, I would end up getting beat up, but later, I did some damage myself. I guess it's where I learned all this."

Both her hands cover her mouth, and she cries. "The bastard never gave me a chance to love him," she says through a flood of tears. "He never gave me a chance."

After crying for two minutes, taking another five to taper down to a few sniffles, with a honk into a tissue, she reaches over and takes my index finger in her little hands. It's all she can hold comfortably. She looks me in the eye. Her nose is red and her eyes are tear soaked. "I sure do love you, Twig."

I smile and give her hand a squeeze with my thumb.

She squeezes back. "Why did you stop?"

Hanging On

I raise my eyebrows. "Stop getting angry in the middle?"

She nods.

I smile. "Bob."

"Damn that Bob." she says. "How does he get everything so right?"

I not only thank Bob, but file away the fact that she actually liked what I did. It would have been the last thing I could have ever guessed, but come to think of it, how many times have my guesses with women been right? In fact, I'm so used to being wrong most of the time, I use my guess as a yardstick and take the exact opposite action.

Melinda leans forward and gives me a kiss. At first it's just a regular peck, and she starts to withdraw, but then she pulls me forward toward her and plants a lip-locking kiss on my mouth.

She purrs like a cat. "You feel like having sex?"

"What about the baby?"

"The doctor says sex is good." She gropes my hairy chest under my shirt.

"Isn't our baby old enough to know what's going on? I'd feel kind of embarrassed having another person in the room."

"The doctor says the baby will feel love between us. She needs that feeling to be fully rounded.

"Yeah, but sex with another person present?"

"We're not going to have rodeo sex."

Then it hits me. Melinda said, "she".

"How do you know it's a girl? I thought we weren't getting a ultrasound."

Melinda draws back from attacking my chest and looks at me. "It's just a guess, big boy. Just a guess."

"It could be a boy, right?"

She slides her hands back into my unbuttoned shirt and pulls me to her. She kisses my fur repeatedly and says, "It could be a boy, but I don't feel boy energy."

I give into her persistence, though I do feel a little embarrassed that someone else is a part of our coupling. In five minutes, Melinda is on top of me while I lie on my back on the floor. She moves in her amazing way, only this time more carefully. Her breasts move together as she rotates her hips.

Before long, I forget about someone watching. I forget about much of anything except that amazing contact point between my woman and me, moving, coming closer to our moment in a gentle expression of love. I miss those fierce explosions that were so common for us in the beginning before she got pregnant, but this is good.

When she finds her moment, and it's not so hard for her these days, her throbbing slipperiness, her heavy breathing, and her loss of control takes me over the edge at the same time. As usual, we finish with her dropping to my chest, legs splayed, belly and breast flat on my body, feeling our hearts pounding in rhythm.

There is that long delicious period after, when our bodies are still connected, where she continues to rotate, though only slightly, attempting to hold me erect, to keep me inside, but finally I fail her, and slip into my normal flaccid condition, being pulled by gravity, nothing rigid to hold me in her any longer.

In a dreamy whisper, her head on my chest, she draws out a word like it might be the last one she's going to express for the rest of her life. "Gooodbyyye."

I smile, drop my arms to the floor, and fall into a deep sleep without dreams, without the normal tossing and turning I usually do before sleep. I drop off into the abyss of love, of being wanted by the most exciting woman I can think of.

My sleep doesn't last long; it never does, but I sleep so deep, so fundamentally complete, that five or fifteen minutes later, when I awake, I feel like I slept for two days.

The second I awake, as usual, Melinda is looking me in the eyes.

Twelve

Moving On

Katherine and I stand in the silence of the desert and look out to the south, the direction Billy, Ed and that damn Cherry went. We both stretch. I bring my hands in and look at the tips of my fingers, which are raw with a few scabs. I show them to Kat. "I guess the whole thing was real."

Kat brings her hands up and inspects the tips. "I told you." She leans down and pulls the right leg of her riding pants halfway up her calf and points. "There's that nasty scratch I got from climbing that freaking cliff, but it's almost healed. How can that happen so fast?"

I'm feeling confused as I inspect the scrapped skin along my left hip and the one elbow that got cracked as I was attempting to get over the ledge. They're almost healed. "It's all here," I say. "But I don't understand how Cherry dropped us over the ledge and we ended up in camp."

"For that matter," Kat says, "I don't understand a bunch of things, but maybe that's the point."

225

"What?"

"We're not supposed to understand. We're supposed to accept what happened and move into our new life."

I smack my palms together then dust the seat of my pants. "Other than the bruises and a clear memory of the last few days, I really don't feel any different."

Kat brushes her pants and saunters over to the bikes. "You got to admit it was an experience of a lifetime."

"God yes." I swing my leg over the saddle of my Indian, rotate the distributor, turn the ignition on, and throw my body on the start pedal. The engine fires at the last second, but not enough to start. I'm ready to take a second kick, when it comes to me as a single flash of inspiration. Standing tall on the starter pedal, my hip high in the air, I look at Kat. "What if Cherry sleazed out on the camp fee to keep us from admiring her too much?"

Kat scrunches her face. "Could that be true?"

I sit back on the seat of my bike. "I know I was starting to see her as some sort of god, especially after she dropped us off that cliff."

Kat puts one finger up. "You keep saying she dropped us, but in fact, if you remember, we let go on our own."

"You know what I mean."

Kat says, "I do know what you mean, but think about it. If we'd been dropped, we'd be victims of Cherry doing it to us. The fact that we both chose to trust that we were going to be okay means that we took possession of our own fate."

I get ready to lay into the starter pedal again. "I see, but what's it all mean?"

"God," Kat says, "We're so close to the experience we can't see its implications. I'm sure as time passes, we'll find meaning for these last few days."

I look at her. "All I can think about right now is a shower, a meal out, and maybe a nice soft bed for a couple of days."

Katherine smiles. "I'm with you."

I lift into the air and lay into the starter. When the engine fires, I rotate the distributor to the run position and my bike drops into a familiar lump-lumping. Kat's bike starts, and we pull onto the pavement, then follow in the same direction as Ed, Cherry, and Billy. We reach cruising speed, the sky is bright, the sun peeks over the hills, and the day is already warming.

Eighty miles and two hours later, I pull over at a rusted, bullet riddled road sign. It has two lines of green type on a white background. The top line reads Phoenix 192 miles, with an arrow pointing east. Below, with an arrow pointing the opposite direction, the sign reads, Blythe forty-four miles.

With our engines idling, I toss up my hands. "Which way?" I say loud so she can hear me.

Kat digs in her pocket and pulls out a quarter. "Heads East, tails West."

I nod. She tosses the coin in the air. It spins wildly, then she catches it on top of the back of her hand.

I lean over to look as she uncovers the results, and it shows the bust of George Washington. "East it is," Kat says.

I nod, kick my bike into first, and we roar toward the east, winding our way through a long low valley with slow rising hills on either side.

The hills last for another hour, then we drop into a flatness that goes forever. Some sixty or eighty miles later, we connect with a main highway and go south past a big modern sign that says Phoenix, sixty miles.

Windblown and exhausted from the vibration and constant movement, we pull into downtown Phoenix, with its traffic and noise, and up into a parking garage of a ten-story Howard Johnson. It's as if neither of us has to make a decision; the road simply leads to the driveway, and the logical way to go is into the parking structure.

We park on the fifth level and walk to the elevator. For the first time in hours, we speak to one another. "God, I'm beat," Kat says.

"I want a bath and a nice meal." I push a button, and the elevator door opens. We step in and go down to the lobby, then walk onto carpet in our weather-beaten leathers and riding gear, with my leather saddlebags over my shoulder. We walk to the main desk.

A thin-faced young man makes us wait while he types in an entry. "Yes?" His focus is still on the computer as I speak. "We want a room with two doubles."

His eyes flash up for a second. He gives us a once over and darts back to the screen. "Sorry," he says, like he doesn't have the time for us. "Only two queens."

"That's okay," I say, turning to Kat and seeing her nod. "Does it have a tub?"

"No, sorry, only a shower."

This little weasel of a man is getting to me, but I hold back, knowing the exchange will only last another few moments and we will be forever rid of him.

"Okay," I say, hearing testiness in my voice. The next few words I say with metronome precision. "Maybe you can find something with a bath and two queens."

Without even looking, he says a short, "Nothing."

It's not that he can't find a room, but the fact that he doesn't have the courtesy to attempt. In a sudden flash of anger, I stand on my toes, because I can hardly reach over the counter I'm so short. I grab the little fuck by the collar and drag him close to my nose. The color drains out of his face. I growl. "Look here, you son of a bitch, I'm tired and I want a room with a bath. I don't much give a shit how much you hate women, and I care even less what a fucked up life you have chosen for yourself. You get me a room this instant, or I'll kick your ass all over this lobby. And I want one that's not next to the elevator or overlooking the street and, oh, yes, a non-smoking room. Nod if you got that."

He nods quickly and goes back to his computer. After typing for a moment, he turns without another word, grabs a key, and hands it to me.

I smile and drop my credit card on the counter. He picks it up and runs it, then slides the check-in form for me to fill out and sign.

I look at Kat, as she stands straight-faced, hand on one hip.

I sign my credit card slip and the hotel registry, turn to the pale young man, and drop a five in front of him. "Thank you," I say. "You've been very helpful."

He says nothing and doesn't even reach for the money.

Kat and I strut across the lobby not saying a word until we are in the elevator and the door closes. Kat bursts out with a howl. "What did you do?"

"God, I have no idea. I would have never done that in a million years. No self-respecting woman would have ever done something like that."

"Renee, that was great."

I look at my hands. "I don't know what's gotten into me."

On the third floor, the elevator stops and picks up

an extremely overweight woman with her emaciated husband. They ride three floors up with us in silence. When they get out, a businessman in a blue suit gets on and rides to the ninth floor, then gets out with us without saying a word.

We walk behind him until he disappears into his room. We continue down the hall to 908. I unlock the door and we walk in. I say, "I've got the first bath," then walk into the bathroom and turn on the water to fill the tub. I notice two fluffy bathrobes folded on the counter.

"Hey, this is a nice room," Kat says, as she opens the sliding glass door to the small deck.

I walk over to a window and look at the Phoenix skyline. I pull off my leather jacket, sit on the bed, and unbuckle my riding boots.

Kat turns to me. "How about I order dinner in the room?"

I look at her. "Sounds like the best plan I've heard all day. I'm starved."

Although the tub is one of those silly straight sided uncomfortable types, the hot water is luscious, and I lounge in the warmth until it cools. I towel off, and inspect the endless number of almost healed bruises and scratches over my body. As I slip my bathrobe on, I hear a knock at the door. When I answer, the waiter pushes in a cart with delectable treats, including chocolate mousse for dessert.

We tip the waiter and sit down to the first real meal we've had in who knows how many days. Maybe the turkey dinner was real, maybe not. During the ride we snacked on nuts and raisins, but a real meal is what we needed.

After eating, Kat takes a bath as I lounge on my bed watching the evening news. It's odd, after all the changes we've gone through, the world is still embroiled in horrible wars, and people are still brutal to each other. At one moment during the news, something reminds me that I have a life back in Big Bear. I pick up the phone next to the bed and dial home.

"Stewart," I say when he answers.

"Renee?" There is surprise in his voice.

"Is everyone all right?"

"Oh sure, I've just been worried about you. Where have you been?"

Why must he put me immediately on the defensive? "Jesus, Stewart, I've been gone less than a week. What, do you want me to check in every day?"

"Renee, I don't know where you've been, but maybe you better check your calendar. I haven't heard from you in a month."

"Stewart Chance, how could you say something like that? I've been on the road for a week, if that." I remember Kat has one of those watches with the date, and I roll over to the far side of my bed and reach into her pile of clothes. The watch sits on top of her bra. I pick it up and study the miniscule numbers.

"How are the kids?" I ask while looking for my reading glasses. My eyes aren't what they were just a few years ago.

His voice relaxes. "They're fine. Sheila got all A's in school. She's at a movie with her girlfriend."

"What about Mel?"

He's started basketball, and he hasn't come home from school yet."

I look at the watch. "Jesus, Stewart, it's almost seven-thirty. Shouldn't he be home by now?"

His voice changes. "When you come home, you can

regulate the kids' movements to your little heart's content. Since I'm doing this while you're out there, I'll do it my way if that's okay with you?"

I'm silent.

He takes a deep breath and his manner softens. "Where are you, anyhow?"

"We just spent the weekend out in the desert, but we're in a Phoenix hotel, now."

"We?"

"Katherine and I." I tell him about meeting and traveling with Kat and fill him in on some of the more harrowing details of the last three days. I don't say anything about my animal. It's a friendly conversation, until I find my glasses in my jacket pocket and put them on to study the watch.

"God, Stewart." I interrupt his story about Mel's new basketball interest. "You were right; we've been gone twenty-eight days, but I only remember five."

I walk to the bathroom and knock on the door. Kat opens the door with a towel wrapped around her. The steam billows out. I point at the watch. "We've been gone twenty-eight days."

She's drying her hair. "Get out of here."

I hold the watch closer to her as Stewart says, "What'd I tell you."

"Yes," I say, while Kat studies the watch. "Where have we been might be the better question." I speak to Stewart while watching Kat's face flush.

"Stew, I've got to get used to this. I'll call you tomorrow after work, is that okay?"

"Tomorrow's Thursday, Renee. I have my men's group."

"Okay, I'll call you Friday morning. I've got to go."

He sounds reluctant. "Sure. Friday morning."

I hang up the phone and look at Katherine. "Where did we go?"

"I don't know," she shakes the watch, then looks again. "I only remember a week."

"Me too."

***

"After not hearing from her for almost a month, Renee called last night."

I've got the talking stick so no one responds, but every man in this circle is looking at me. "She told me some cock-and-bull story about not remembering the time. That's so lame."

The flame of the small fire flickers off each man's face. I pace the open space between the fire and circle of twenty-three men.

"She's been riding with some woman, and I don't know what to think about that. Maybe Renee's turned lesbian."

I need to rant a little without interruption or advice, so I continue to hold the stick. "Maybe my wife's run off with some bull dyke."

I look at Tazz. He has a serious expression.

I speak for another five minutes, mostly repeating my fears in my annoying, even to myself, anxious tone. When I set the stick down and find my seat on the one empty cedar round, Tazz speaks, slow at first, like he must wind up for the pitch. "Come on, Stew, you and Renee have been together too long for her to just abandon you. It's not her style."

Buck, Bill, and three other men grunt in agreement.

I turn back toward Tazz. "I would have never guessed

233

she was going to go off on some stupid journey with that motorcycle either, but she did. She's done a lot of unexpected things lately, and this could be another in a long line."

Tazz shakes his head. "Shit, man, I don't know her like you do, but I'm sure if she was going to pull some stunt like that, she would give you plenty of warning. I don't see her up and splitting."

I gaze at him. "You would think I know my wife, but after this last year, I wouldn't put it past her."

Buck joins in with his squeaky nasal voice. "Shit, Stew, you got to give her a chance here, man. Even if she's done the things you think, you can't accuse her of any of it until she wants to tell you. If you do, you'll push her away."

I look over at Buck. "Tell me more."

Buck waves one hand. "If you start accusing her, she just might go out and do it out of spite. What I know of Renee, she would, too."

"I'm not accusing her to her face, I'm only venting my fears here, where it's safe and I know none of you guys will tell your wives or girlfriends."

"Hell, yes," Twig says. "One of our women gets even a hint of anything we say in the circle and all of them will know it in a few hours. Nothing said here goes beyond this circle. You know that's the rule, right, Stew?"

"I know, but I just wanted to confirm it, is all. I got to accuse her somewhere, damn it, and this is the only place I know where I can totally be myself, without having to think about how Renee feels or is going to react. This is my only sanctuary."

A number of grunts and moans rise up from the fire.

I turn, look at all the men, then wave one hand. "I'm

done for now." The meeting goes on, but I really don't hear much, I'm so embroiled in my own drama of losing Renee to some motorcycle-riding bull dyke.

Close to the end of the evening, Twig gets my attention. "Hey, Stew, how you doing?"

I stare into his face, and for the first time in a while, I realize there are other men. "Not very well, I guess."

"You want to talk some more about it?"

I glance at my watch, hoping that it's nine o'clock so I don't have to go further into my twisted world of rejection. The watch says ten of. "I don't think we have time."

"Look, Stew," Twig says, "I'm leader for the night, and we've got the time, if you're having a problem. Isn't this why we meet every week?"

I rub my forehead with both hands. "I guess, but I don't want to take up what's left of our time with my stupid fears."

Twig stands, walks around the fire, and puts his hand on my shoulder. He scans the men. "Show of hands. How many men have the time to help out our brother here?"

Every hand goes high in the air. I burst into tears knowing that each man is willing to support me. Through sniffing and snorting, I try to articulate my appreciation, but I don't think I can get the words out.

Twig's hand stays on my shoulder, but when I look up, he's on his knees in front of me. He doesn't say a word, just sits with me.

"I'm so scared she's going to leave," I say in my worst whine. I look up at Twig. "I know I'm not good enough for her. She's such an amazing woman, and I'm just some boring computer geek."

I break into a fresh bout of tears, and Twig, takes me in his arms and holds me close until I'm into a wail.

I collapse as Twig holds me, supporting me; maybe the first support I've felt since I was a kid, and certainly the first male support I ever felt.

My homophobic stuff comes to the surface. I want to pull away. My embarrassment crap comes up, too. What will the other men think? How will I explain this? What ridicule will I have to face? Will I ever live down the shame? My stupid, crappy anxieties are in my throat, and the only thing that keeps me from breaking free and bolting into the night is for the first time in my life I feel truly supported by a group of men.

While Twig continues to hold me, I open my eyes, expecting to see them pointing, jeering, whispering comments to one another, but what I see is men, my men, with tears in their eyes, with compassionate faces, looking at me make a spectacle of myself. I can't stand so much compassion, so I close my eyes again.

After a minute or so, I calm, and Twig loosens his grip. In a tearful disengagement, Twig draws back, his hands still on my shoulders. His big eyes look directly into mine. "Good work, Stew."

I break down once again, though this time the tears have mostly been exorcized, and I only whimper a little.

Twig lets go of my shoulders, stands, walks back to his cedar round, and sits. He speaks to the circle. "I know how Stew feels right now. I've been there, and I felt embarrassed. Can each of you men tell him what you experienced?"

Buck stands and points at me. He's got tears in his eyes. He says, with a choked sound. "Man, I wished I had your kind of guts, Stew. You inspire me."

Buck sits, and Tazz, who's across the circle from Buck, speaks, though he doesn't stand. "Shit, Stew, you break my heart, but I know just how you feel. I've been there, man, and you did an awesome piece of work tonight."

Bill is next. I'm expecting him to tell some elongated story, but he simply says, "No wonder you're our point man. You're pointing the way for us all."

One by one, the other men add supportive comments, and it's hard to take it all in, because I was so sure I was making a fool of myself.

Finally, it gets back to Twig and he says, "I feel honored to know you, Stew. You are a man among men."

My lower lip quivers, but the tears have emptied from my body. My entire being feels light and airy. I want to leap to the moon. I want to howl like a coyote. I feel like the freest man in the universe.

All my fears about Renee, though they are still in the background, have no power. I feel strong enough that I know she's coming back, bull dyke motorcycle riding bitch or not.

I leap to my feet and scream, nothing intelligible, just an expression of delight.

My feet feel like they're floating a foot off of the ground as all the men stand, pull the circle in close and wrap arms shoulder to shoulder, stretching across the back of the next man and grasping the third man along the circle, making as much contact as possible.

We stand for thirty seconds looking at the bond created in another amazing night. Twig, the leader for the evening, speaks. "I release all the spirits we have brought into this circle tonight."

Twig looks around the circle and stops at Tazz. "You haven't led in a while, Tazz; how about you take it next week?"

Tazz nods, but doesn't speak.

Twig's last duty for the night is to lead us into a long slow buildup of a yell, with a scream at the end. The moment the scream ends, everyone slaps the hands of the man next to him.

We kick sand over the fire until it's buried, gather bottles of water, backpacks, the talking stick, and other implements of the evening.

Twig's bike is the first to start. Bill's is next, then I get my machine running, while the other fifteen or so bikes roar to life.

I'm ready to pull away and follow the first wave of bikes back out the little ravine, up the embankment to the old burnt-out farmhouse, and past the rusted hulk of a Buick. I look back and Buck is furiously kicking his bike. It's not starting.

Twig sits next to him, engine lumping at an idle.

I drive the ten yards closer and yell, "You okay, Buck?"

"Sure, man. It'll start eventually. It's been a little stubborn lately."

After the tenth or fifteenth kick, Buck collapses into his seat. He slams his open palm on his yellow peanut tank. "This fucking thing is a piece of shit."

Twig turns off his engine and I follow suit. The sound of the bikes in the distance rev up on the highway.

Twig turns to me, "Hey, Stew, you got a flashlight?"

I pull out my kickstand, lean the bike on the hardpan, get off, and look in my right saddlebag. At the bottom, among old candy wrappers, crumpled papers from work, an extra can of oil, my warm-weather jacket, and a spare pair of socks, I find my MagLite; one of those smaller versions the size of a cigar.

I hand it to Twig as he squats next to Buck's bike.

I'm always curious how mechanic types do their

magic, so I lean in and look over his shoulder. He pulls the little retainer wire off the distributor cap and removes the chrome cover. With the flashlight, he looks in close and clicks his tongue. "Jesus, Buck, I'm surprised this thing runs at all. How long has it been since you've had a tune up?"

After a long silence, Twig turns his head to Buck who is sitting on the front wheel. Buck says, "I don't know, maybe a year... or two."

"Shit, Buck, you don't have electronic ignition like Stew here. You've got to change out these points at least once a year, and you should readjust them every six months."

"I haven't had the money."

Twig flips the flashlight over to Buck's chrome exhaust pipes. He reaches out with his big meat hooks and points at the pipes. "See this blue? When your points are out, the timing is off, and the engine runs hotter than it should. It'll make your nice chrome pipes turn blue and fucks up your valves."

Bucks voice turns to a mousy squeak. "No shit?"

"Okay, man, I'm going to give you a quick fix here, but you got to get this thing tuned up."

Twig pulls out a book of matches, tears off the striker, and slides it between the two opposing point faces. He drags the sandpaper part back and forth a dozen times, then pulls his T-shirt out and slides one corner between the points.

"What's that for?" I ask.

"I just sanded the points with what I had, and there are some filings still hanging around to muck up the works. Just those small pieces of sandpaper could keep the points from contacting one another. I'm cleaning the surface." He looks close at the points. "What surface there is. Jesus,

Buck, it looks like these points have been in here since the bike was built in forty-seven."

Buck snorts in a playful way. "I know I had them changed sometime after I bought the bike back in Vegas."

Twig takes the cover of the matches and tears off a strip. He removes his Swiss army knife and loosens one of the screws in the distributor. He reaches back and pushes on the kick starter, nudging the engine to rotate a little at a time.

"What're you doing now?" I ask.

Twig points at the center of the distributor. "Look carefully, and you'll see the distributor and a high spot on the shaft. It's called the cam. When I rotate the shaft until the point contact reaches the top of the cam lobe, the points will be open as wide as they can be." He turns the engine slowly, and the points open.

"Look at that." I say.

"Once the points are all the way open, I'll slide this matchbook cover in and adjust them down until they rub on the paper which is about twenty thousandths thick. It'll get us back to town." Twig closes the points and locks down the screw again. "Buck, you gotta bring this in and get it tuned up. This is just temporary."

"Sorry, Twig, I don't have any money."

"Just bring it in, you dick, and I'll get the thing right for you. Maybe you can help me at the shop to pay me." Twig returns the cap and snaps the wire holding clip into place.

Buck slaps him on the shoulder. "Twig, you're a stand-up guy."

The silence of the night is broken when Twig turns the distributor to start position, then looks up at Buck and says, "Okay, man, start it."

Moving On

Buck swings his leg over the saddle of the bike, lays into the kick-starter, and the engine purrs to life. It settles into a lump-lump idle as Buck rotates the distributor back to running position. The prior roughness smooths out into the classic Harley Davidson sound, though Buck's bike is a '47 Knucklehead.

"Bring it in soon, Buck," Twig yells, walks over to his own bike and kicks it into life.

I start mine, and the three of us roll away from the circle of cedar rounds, along the nine or ten turns in the little dry creek bed, past the rusted and smashed shopping cart lying on its side that I keep meaning to drag out of here. We ride past a few dead and rotting tires half buried in the sand, up a small embankment, past the farmhouse, past the old hulk of a car, and finally out through the iron gate hanging half off of its hinges onto the pavement.

We turn right and back toward Victorville, driving the curvy strip of pavement with its banks and two bridges. I smell the desert sage and the change of crisp air as we pass over each bridge. Stars hang above in a huge open sky, and the melodic sound of our three engines thunders into the night.

Twig turns off first, then Buck, and I'm left with another half hour of rolling alone with my thoughts, the memories of what happened tonight, and the support I felt from the men.

By the time I get home it's almost eleven. The kids are asleep. I sit on the deck with only the sound of the pool motor humming as I look out over all of creation. I feel how lucky I am to have a wife so full of life that she's willing to go out into the unknown and find her own way, bull dyke or not. I settle into the fact that she does

241

love me, as geeky as I am, and that she will come home to her family when the time is right.

I go to bed with a feeling of support and acceptance.

Thirteen

Lighter

Day nine and I feel lighter, more able to deal with life. I take out the garbage and clean the kitchen for the first time since I quit smoking weed. It feels better when the kitchen is neat again. My stomach is still a little queasy, but I'm able to take myself to the local café and find a table. Amid the chaos of teenagers and young adults released from the bondage of the classroom, I order a steak sandwich with fries and get half of it down before I feel full. I have the remains wrapped to go and I walk back to the house, sit in front of my computer, and continue writing my fifth story, mostly to keep my mind occupied.

I find myself nodding, but I'm so interested in where the story is going, I fight the feeling and continue typing.

"So, what's keeping you?"

"What?" Bob stands to the right of my computer.

He's dressed in full leathers, his black do-rag strapped to his head, his pony tail dropping halfway down his back. "What's keeping you from going to Victorville and seeing if Carolyn will take you back?"

"I got unfinished business here."

He lays one gloved hand on the monitor and taps his bare fingertips on the screen. "Hell, Nick, you've already trashed the biggest vase you ever made. Is pottery-making so important that you'll let that woman cool off?"

"I got a month's rent already paid," I say in the weakest defense I've ever heard.

Bob's fingernails clink on the upper edge of the glass screen. "Come on, you dick, get your ass down there. You got yourself clean, but how long do you think you'll last sitting here by yourself without your people around?"

He crosses his arms in front of his chest. "Ah zay bouquet."

"What's that?"

"It's Swahili, and it means, 'The people around me are my strength.'"

I lean back in my little steel folding chair, put my hands behind my head, and give him a big grin. "I'm pretty much done with that part of my life. I'm making a new start, away from Harleys. I want to do pottery."

Bob pulls his hand away from the screen and points toward the garage. He speaks in a sarcastic tone. "Oh sure, man, you want to do pottery, but you haven't been out there since you quit smoking."

"I'm taking a break."

"Is it a break, or was pottery an extension of your pot smoking? Wasn't it easy to pour your creative talent into something that took no brain power?"

"It took brains."

"You know what I mean, no clear thought, because you've got to admit that you haven't had a clear thought in fifteen years. Tell me I'm not right."

He leans over and puts his elbows on the monitor.

I want to counter his statement, but I know he's right, so I simply sit, hands behind my head, leaning back in the chair.

"You can't let Carolyn cool off too much, Nick. Love doesn't work that way. The longer the two of you are not together, the more the love fades." He gets a fatherly look. "Button this place up, take your computer and the story you're working on, and get your ass down there before she moves on."

"Now?" I ask.

"Now, you dickhead. It may already be too late."

I want to give him a bunch of buts, but I can't come up with one good reason why it is so important for me to stay. "I'll go back when I'm good and ready. Shit, Bob, that woman dumped me."

"Oh, you poor little hurt bastard. So, it's the first time in your life that some woman was a little quicker on the draw than you. How does it feel?"

"I don't like it, and I didn't deserve it."

Bob smiles, lifts off his elbows, and paces the room. His boots land on the wooden floor like horse hoofs. He reaches the wall, turns, his hand raised and points at me. "Think about it, man. Maybe this is the first woman you even half-care about, and certainly this is the first time since you were a kid that your thoughts are clear enough to think about it. Don't let this one slip away. You know she's a good woman, so go get her." Bob walks over to me and pushes on my shoulder, throwing me off balance. My tipped chair falls backwards, me in it. I put my arms out behind me, but the fall is inevitable. The chair and I clatter to the floor, but instead of lying sprawled on my back, I'm slumped on the floor next to my desk. The chair lays sideways. I look around, and no Bob. I fell asleep and toppled from my desk.

Once back in the chair, I look at the monitor. Huge block letters almost fill the screen across the center of my page of typing. "Go Now."

I click the keyboard, and the words disappear, leaving behind the story I was working on. I try to continue, but no matter which letter I type, the words "go now" repeat themselves in a long string, each with its own exclamation point.

"Stop it, Bob," I yell.

It's dark outside and the traffic has lessened. I look at the little clock in the lower corner of my screen and it's 2:30. I go to bed and lie awake thinking about what Bob said. I try to punch holes in his suggestion, but I can't.

Fourteen

Missing Days

I awake early in the morning. My mind immediately attempts to work out where the missing twenty some odd days went, but as hard as I try, I can only remember seven of them. I look at Renee a few feet away in her bed. "What happened to the extra time?"

She turns from looking at the ceiling. "I was just thinking about the same thing, and I can recall just seven. You get any further back than that?"

"Seven is all I count. I wish Cherry was around."

"Maybe Ed and Cherry have a listed phone." Renee raises on one elbow. The first rays of the sun streak through our window. She lifts the phone and drags the crisp-edged telephone book out from under the night table. "What was their last name?"

I shrug. "I never asked. Things moved so fast the whole time they were around, I never thought about it."

"I know what you mean." Renee tosses the book back on the table. "I don't remember the name of the town."

Renee lies back on her pillow and looks toward the

ceiling. "I guess we're going to have to ride back to the store when we're through."

"Holy shit." I grab for the phone. "If we've been gone a month, I'm overdue at work."

Renee asks, "Will you lose your job?"

I click the last digit and look at her. "No, but I'm sure everyone's worried. I've never been late to anything."

My attention turns to the phone when I hear Bridgette's husky voice on the other end of the line. "Bridgette?"

"Katherine, is that you?"

"It's me."

"Where have you been? We were about to call in the SWAT team."

"I don't have time to explain now, but I got stuck out in the desert away from a phone. I'm in Phoenix and I'll be back at work in the next few days. Can you hold down the fort that long?"

She laughs the braying, mule laughter I've become so fond of the last five years. "Hell yes, sister. We'll keep them motor homes at bay long enough for you to bring on the calvary."

I smile and look at Renee who's getting out of bed and heading for the bathroom.

"I'll fill you in when I get back."

"Okay, Kat," Bridgette says. "I've got to go. There's another wagon train of motor homes coming up the gulch."

The phone goes dead and I replace the receiver.

I lie back on my pillow. I imagine Bridgette taking her time registering each RV, asking a million questions and driving the people in them crazy.

I sit up on the side of my bed and inspect the healing bruises and cuts of the last few days, or was it weeks?

Renee steps into the room. "Jesus, Kat, you've got a

huge scratch on your back." She walks over, sits on the bed next to me, then runs her finger along my shoulder blade. "How did you get it?"

"How did we get any of these? That maniac Cherry drove us to exhaustion, that's how."

Renee reaches for her daypack and pulls out a small blue tube. "Let me put some disinfectant on it." She squeezes white cream onto her fingertip.

I turn and lay on the bed to allow her to dab the cream along a stinging stretch of my back. "I think it was when we dropped off the cliff. I caught a branch on the way down."

She dabs the salve. "You certainly gashed yourself, and it's showing signs of infection." She lightly touches the cut, adding more salve to her finger as she goes. "Oh, God, look at that one." She applies more salve and touches another scratch below my waist. "Jesus, girl, you got chewed up."

I lean forward allowing her to draw a long line of disinfectant on a scratch that leads along the cheek of my butt. "That one happened at the same time."

"Really?" Renee has a distant tone. She stops and sits rigid.

I rise to a sitting position and look at her.

Her face is flushed, like she's embarrassed. "I'm sorry."

She gets off the bed and steps to the curtains and window overlooking Phoenix. Her back is to me.

"Sorry for what?" I ask.

Her words are flustered. "Just. . . just sorry."

I'm nervous and I don't know why. I just spent a month with this woman going through all kinds of hell, and suddenly I feel shy.

"Thanks for attending to my cuts," I say.

Renee turns toward me for a second, then back to the window. "You're welcome."

"Is there something wrong?" I ask, but get a long silence. I know what it is, but I can't speak the words.

I get up and walk to her. In her glorious nakedness, I notice her healing scratches and cuts from our ordeal. A few have the angry redness of infection. When I'm close, I take the salve from her hand. She lets go, but reluctantly. I dab a little on my finger and apply it to a scratch on her shoulder. The moment I touch her cut, she shudders. A second scratch on her right hip gets more salve. I turn her around to follow the scratch.

With a nervous titter, she says, "I, I, can't," but she doesn't move. Instead, she leans against the curtains and sighs.

I drop to one knee and squeeze out more goo, then apply it to a small scrape an inch above her bellybutton. She takes in a deep breath and holds it. Her held breath relaxes with a sigh and she says, "I can't."

I look up and see conflict in her face. Although there are more cuts, the last thing I want to do is drive a wedge between us. I turn away, walk to my bed and back-fall on the soft mattress. I don't know how to approach the discomfort I'm feeling so I look at the ceiling for a silent five minutes before another word is spoken.

With Renee still standing in her nakedness, me sprawled on the bed, I cut through the pea soup tension and say, "I'm sorry, Renee. I wish we could touch each other without it meaning. . ."

She turns and looks at me. "There's nothing for you to be sorry about. It's my hang-up."

I lift on one elbow. "I hate this. We went through so much together, I don't want us to be awkward."

She laughs a nervous titter. "I'll be okay in a minute, Kat. I guess I have a hard time separating touch from sex. God, sometimes I hate this culture."

"I know what you mean." I lie back on the bed looking up at the ceiling.

Another long silence builds a stone wall between us. I'm wrestling with my thoughts, my own demons, and I'm sure she is with hers.

Neither of us moves until Renee steps over to my bed and sits on the far edge. "It's just so stupid. I mean, why can't we be physically nurturing without the overlay of sex?"

I lift to a sitting position, grab a pillow, and lean it against the headboard. With my eyes glassy, I speak. "I don't know, but whatever happens, I don't want to lose your friendship." My chin quivers and I start to cry. I'm in my lonely grief, sobbing with the possible loss of the one person I have so much respect for. She's my first woman friend.

There's none of that cat-scratch competition that so often surfaces between me and other women. I don't know if it's from surviving whatever we went through in the desert together or just that she's the strongest person I know. Cherry is strong maybe to the extreme, but I feel her distance. She's more of a teacher than an equal.

Renee wraps her arms around me. I allow her to embrace me. I relax and drop my head over her shoulder, then cry harder. She pats my back and holds me tight, allowing me to cry. I've never had anyone hold me while I cry as long as I need. The men in my life always run as soon I get emotional.

I don't really know how long she holds me; five minutes, maybe ten, but eventually my tears dry and my sniffles calm, my chin relaxes, and Renee releases her tight, nurturing grip. She leans forward, stands, then extends her hands to help me off the bed. I already miss the closeness. She slides her hands up to my bare shoulders and pushes me away a foot or so, then looks directly into my blurry eyes. Tears are streaming down her face as she presses her forehead against mine and closes her eyes.

When she speaks, it surprises me. "Kat, nothing you could ever do would loosen the bond between us. You are my sister in this initiation into our feminine strength and nothing will ever change that."

I'm crying again, back to my body shaking, feeling her forehead against mine and feeling the undying support. "Thanks, Renee," I say between sobs. I open my eyes when she pulls her forehead away.

She leans forward and kisses both my eyelids. I know her kisses are from compassion and understanding and I drink them in like I'm quenching a long forgotten thirst.

My eyes are closed when she moves away. I open them to see her reach for a small brown glass bottle that sits on the night stand by my bed. I've never seen it before. I give her a quizzical look, not wanting to break the spell with words. She brings the bottle and stands in front of me. When she unscrews the shiny black cap, a deep, musky fragrance wafts past my nose. She turns the bottle over and shakes droplets of oil into her palm. She closes her eyes, inhales the scent and lets out a sigh. An extended tone reverberates inside my bones.

When Renee opens her eyes, I swear there is an iridescence that surrounds her. I start to speak, but she motions me to remain quiet. Her left palm holds the few drops of liquid. She covers it with her right palm, then raises her hands to her face in some kind of prayer. After a moment, she brings her hands back between us, and with her right index finger, begins to stir the mixture in a clockwise motion. She stops, raises her fingertip toward my forehead and touches a point above and between my eyebrows. She traces the outline of a spiral and another wave of tears cascade down my face. A cold shiver cycles through my body, a common occurrence when I'm in emotion. She matches her breathing to mine, and I feel heat radiate from my belly, just like when we were in the desert circle with Cherry.

Renee brings her fingertip to my throat and I release an uncontrollable wail, then cough, feeling myself choke on something. From somewhere in my periphery, I hear, "You can let it out now." A scream that I don't recognize at first as mine, turns into a deep guttural tone as I exhale and inhale to some unknown rhythm. I know it's just the two of us in this stupid hotel room, but I hear dozens of voices mixing with mine and with my eyes still closed, I'm inside a cavern. It's dark. Light flickers from candles, and there are shadows and shapes that I don't recognize, but I'm not afraid.

There are spirals drawn and carved into the stone walls and floors. I open my eyes and Renee moves her finger to a point between my breasts and over my heart. Her voice is clear and strong, yet nurturing. "Breathe into the back of your heart. Remember, it's a muscle, so give it room to expand."

I take a deep breath and stretch my shoulder blades toward the wall behind me or is it the stone wall of the cave. There's something both ancient and remembered in this place.

Each time Renee traces the outline of a spiral on my body, another part of me awakes and remembers something old. It's a non-word place and my mind is unable to wrap around it, but it's real and tangible and I'm choosing once again.

Renee draws the spiral on a point above my belly button, then rubs both hands together and places them over my womb, hovering in the air above my vulva. We look at each other, and I don't feel any sexual intent. She lowers her hands onto my body and holds them absolutely still. I feel the trace of the spiral shape, as I surrender to another round of grief, pain, then finally joy. By the time Renee is on her knees tracing the familiar spiral on the tops of my feet, I have no idea how long I've been standing here naked in front of this dear friend, my sister, the shape shifter. I feel her nudging me to lay on the bed, and by the time she pulls the comforter around my shoulders I'm already asleep.

When I awake in the morning, the sun is streaming in through the filmy curtains and Renee's bed is empty. Water splashes in the bathroom.

I sit on the edge of the bed. Something between jet lag and exhilaration rushes through my body as I slowly walk to the bathroom. I push open the door, lean against the wall and see Renee, eyes closed, immersed in a steamy, musky scented bath. She opens her eyes and smiles dreamily as I step into the room. I notice the brown bottle on the edge of the white tiled tub and a large abalone shell. Its turquoise interior reflects off the bronze heat lamp in the ceiling. I'm drawn to the shell, the color of a Caribbean ocean, and I'm back in that no-word place again.

***

Kat looks mesmerized by the abalone shell that appears

out of nowhere, just like the container of essential oil with only the word, "Otter", written in tiny hand calligraphy across a label on the side of the bottle. It's one more mystery in an ever longer list of mysteries on this journey. The warm water, now suffused with the heavy musk scent, saturates my skin as I relax. I've never done anything close to what happened with Kat, yet there is an odd remembering like something I did on a regular basis a long time ago. Kat steps to me, stops at the edge of the tub, and picks up the abalone shell. She holds it with both hands, closes her eyes, then offers the shell to me in some kind of welcoming gesture. I look at her with surprise, yet no surprise at all.

She motions for me to sit up, I wiggle my torso out of the water and lean forward with my back at a slight angle. Kat dips the shell into the oily liquid, then pours the contents of the vessel over my shoulders. I let out a long exhalation and part of me that is still contracted, relaxes. She scoops more water, gently pouring it over my back, my head, my throat, and my breasts. When I can hold my tears no longer, I cry. Kat continues to pour water with one hand. With the other, she presses gently at the center of my spine.

Her voice is soft. "You can let go, Renee. It's safe now."

As soon as I hear the words, I break into another layer of tears. It's a sadness of something bigger and older and indefinable.

Water cascades against my body as I close my eyes and find myself inside a beautiful sculpted cavern. Deep melodic tones resonate throughout the stone chamber. I recognize the cavern. Splashed across the walls, paintings in red colored tint depict snakes, spirals and the outlines of bountiful feminine shapes. I blink my eyes and I'm back to Kat drenching my body with water, while singing a wordless chant.

Each time I close then open my eyes, I'm transported to, then back from the stone cave.

I don't know how long I'm in the bath or in the stone chamber, but when the water cools, Kat stops and kisses the top of my head. The abalone clinks against the edge of the tub when she sets it down. I want to stay here forever. I want to remember this soft place where I can feel both strong and safe. I want to explain this to Stewart, but I'm not sure I can explain it to myself.

Kat gives me one last squeeze, then chuckles. "Come on Renee, we'd better get you out of this tub and into some clothes."

She guides me out of the slippery bath, folds the thick robe around me, and we walk slowly arm in arm out of the bathroom. I'm not sure of anything, but I know I am choosing.

Kat and I lie next to the pool. The sky is overcast and dampens the normal Phoenix burner, even on this spring day. It feels good to enjoy the sun before I head back to Stewart and the kids.

I know I've changed, but I wonder if it will last. I turn my head toward Kat and push my sun glasses on my forehead. "So, what was that all about in the room with the bottle of oil and the abalone?"

She smiles. "Which promptly disappeared while we were getting dressed."

I shrug. "I have no idea where any of it came from, but it was an incredible gift. I feel like I recovered a part of my feminine self I had lost."

Kat adjusts the chaise lounge to a upright position. "I know what you mean. I've always had resistance to the whole Goddess shtick, but something magical happened, something that was bigger than either of us."

My eyes well up with tears. I give a long sigh. "I'm afraid I'll forget this place where my heart is open and incredibly nourished in some ancient, mysterious way."

Kat yawns, covering her mouth with her hand. When she speaks, it's with an air of resolve. "What happened was nothing I can ever explain, yet it resonates deep inside of me. I hope I'll be able to bring it up when I choose, and these days, I am choosing."

"Thanks for reminding me about the choosing. It's like the entire month, if it was truly twenty-eight days, was a vision quest, and though my brain wants to figure it out, there's a softer place that already knows the answer."

Kat smiles. "Yes." She grabs her glass of fresh squeezed lemonade and takes a big gulp. "God, I can't get enough of these. Aren't they great?"

I laugh. "Comforts of home. Definitely better than getting yelled at by Cherry."

I get up from my chaise and wander over under the canopy. Clouds or not, my fair skin can only handle so much sun.

Twenty minutes later, Kat joins me, and she orders another lemonade with a chaser of iced bottled water.

I sip on my ice tea, but neither of us talks, though I know we're both attempting to make sense of the past however many days.

When the bartender leaves the drinks, Kat turns to me. "For the life of me, I still can't figure out how we lost an entire month."

With a spoon, I pick out a cube of ice from my tea,

drop it in my hand and rub it along my forehead. "When it comes to Biker Bob, nothing ever is as it seems."

Kat squinches up her face. "Do you think he was behind the oil and the abalone shell? That would be too weird."

I shrug. "No way to know, but it's so feminine and ancient, I don't think even he'd have a clue about that. I mean he's a biker, and dead or not, he's a man."

She laughs. "Okay, so the oil and the abalone ritual is a total mystery, but how about the time thing. I mean we lost three weeks. How could that be?"

I take a deep breath and let it out. "The part I don't get is how Cherry did all of that stuff with us and just disappeared like that. When we're done here, I want to go back to the gas station and get some things cleared up. Cherry has some explaining to do."

Kat gulps her lemonade, then sets the glass on the counter. "I know what you mean. I've got to get back to work, anyhow. I hate that most of this journey went by and I don't even remember it."

"I wouldn't mind giving that Billy Black a piece of my mind too."

She smiles. "If it hadn't been for Billy, we'd have never gone to the secret spot and everything else that followed."

That evening, Kat and I go to an early dinner, then take in a movie, but the missing twenty-odd days is never far from my thoughts.

The next morning, dressed in our riding leathers, we settle with the hotel, get on our bikes, and retrace our route back into the foothills toward Ed and Cherry's.

Missing Days

As the sun rests on the western horizon, Kat and I pull up to the station, but it's closed. I thought I remembered a house behind the little store, but when we drive around back there's only open desert.

Kat unfurls the kickstand and gets off her bike. "I'm exhausted. I say we stay the night here behind the station and wait for Ed or Cherry to open in the morning. We'll be fresh, and I don't know about you, but I'll be in a better mood to ask questions."

"Sounds like a plan, but I'm hungry, and I haven't seen a store for a hundred miles."

Kat unsnaps her plastic saddlebag and pulls out a pouch of rice and some freeze-dried mixed vegetables. "I think we can cook up something from all of this that'll get us through."

"Much rather have that sexy waiter back at the hotel."

Kat snickers.

Before the sun drops behind the hills, we scavenge the area for pieces of wood, mostly discarded shipping pallets. I find a few scraps of an old mesquite that died years ago.

We make camp a hundred yards behind the station at the top of a rise on the gravel. We keep the fire small because of our limited wood, but it's plenty hot enough to cook food.

Once dinner is finished and things are put away, out of the blackness of the night, a truck with howling tires and a big thumping radio speaker careens over a distant rise and roars its way along the highway that runs in front of the station. It's the first vehicle in hours.

When it reaches the station, the pickup pulls over and the speakers go silent. The engine stops, and the headlights drop the night back into inky darkness.

259

The truck door slams. Kat and I look at one another. She knee walks over to her bike, digs into the right saddlebag, removes a small blue pistol, pulls the slide back, and a bullet slips into the chamber.

"Where'd you get that?"

"Saved for a rainy day," she whispers as a flashlight strikes an arc across our campsite and the sound of footsteps echoes across the noisy gravel.

Kat keeps the little pistol hidden in her palm. I throw in another piece of wood and sit back on my haunches. I glance at Kat, but she looks so self-assured, lying next to the fire on one elbow.

A masculine voice speaks softly as though he's used to the silence of the desert and understands how far sound will carry. "Hello, out there."

I tense.

Kat and I are silent.

"I'm lost," he says while his footfalls get ever closer. "Can I ask directions?"

I want to respond, but my throat constricts. I look at Kat and her face scrunches.

Ten or fifteen yards away from our fire, the footsteps stop. The flashlight turns off. A little more cautious, he says, "I won't bother you if you don't respond, but I really need some help. I'm almost out of gas, and I have no idea where I am."

His tone has a different quality to it than before. It's more inviting, but I've read newspaper articles about serial killers and roadside rapists. Both Kat and I say nothing.

After a minute of silence, he huffs, then mumbles to himself. He turns and traipses back across the gravel. I look at Kat, she at me, then she says aloud, "Come on over, stranger, but I want you to know I have a gun in my hand, and I'm not afraid to use it."

The crunching of gravel stops. It's silent for a moment, then he says, "I don't know if it's safe."

Kat speaks again. "You act like a gentleman, and everyone will be safe. You start getting stupid, and we all got problems. Is that clear?"

The guy turns, puts his hands up, and says, "Jesus, ladies, I'm just lost. I ain't going to hurt nobody."

"No one out here is going to get hurt but you, pal. You behave and everybody gets along."

He takes a step toward the fire. Kat, quick as lightning, points the gun out toward the desert behind us. The crack of the pistol startles me.

The guy jumps.

Involuntarily, I scream. "Jesus, Kat, what did you do that for?"

"Just to prove that I do have a gun and to keep this guy on his p's and q's."

"Shit, lady, I get your point. My intentions are purely honorable. I just need some directions."

Kat slides the gun back into its hiding place. "Come over to the fire so we can see you."

He slowly steps toward us, his cowboy hat kicked back, pointy-toed cowboy boots spit shined to a mirror finish. With the snap-down lacy cowboy shirt, he looks like a walking Marlboro advertisement.

When he gets to the fire, he doesn't look more than twenty-two. His nervous hazel eyes dart from me to Kat's gun hand. "You ain't going to shoot me, are you?"

Kat gives him a mysterious, wry smile. "As long as you don't step out of line."

The kid pulls out a map and unfolds it. He points back toward the highway. "I musta taken a wrong turn somewhere, because as far as I can figure, I keep expecting Phoenix to be over the next hill."

I point the way he came. "Phoenix is back that way two hundred miles or so."

"Oh shit," he says. "I knew it. I'm not very good at directions. Jennifer kept saying it was back, but I wouldn't listen. I'm in big trouble now."

"Jennifer?" I ask.

He gets a sheepish grin. "I guess I'm in a jam with Jen, too, but more so with my band." He looks at his wrist. "I'm supposed to be in Phoenix in an hour, and I'm out of gas."

"Either way," I say, "you're not getting back to Phoenix in an hour."

"Is there another gas station around?"

I point west. "Not for another eighty miles."

He says. "We passed the last one an hour ago and it was closed."

"Is Jennifer in your truck?"

He gets an embarrassed look. "Yeah, she is."

I say, "It doesn't look like you're going anywhere else tonight, so you may as well go get her and come sit by the fire. The gas station will open in the morning."

He looks at Kat. "You ain't going to fire off your gun any more, are you?"

Kat grins, licks her finger, and crosses her heart. "You go get your girlfriend, and I'll put the gun away. That a deal?"

"Okay." The kid turns and trots back across the gravel, gets twenty yards out into the darkness, and stops. "Can I bring my guitar, too?" He pronounces it gee-tar.

Kat laughs. "Hell yes, boy, you shoulda brought the damn thing in the first place. You woulda got a whole different reception." Her inflection changes from the Kat that I know to a shit-kicking cowgirl, ready to rope a couple dozen head of cattle.

"Ya-hoo," the kid yelps and trots off into the dark.

"Where'd you learn to talk like that?"

"I lived in Joshua Tree most of my life. At least half the population is made up of cowboys or wannabees. A girl growing up around all of that testosterone has to learn to fit in, you know."

I snicker. Two doors slam and footsteps crunch across the gravel.

When the couple gets close enough, he's hand-in-hand with her, guitar and two folding chairs in his left hand. "This here's Jennifer."

I look at a petite girl in her late teens with a worn felt coat. She looks native American.

"I'm Renee." I point at Kat. "This is Katherine."

The young woman gives a small curtsy, unfolds her aluminum camp chair, and sets it close to the fire. On her right hand a stone too large to be a real diamond sparkles in the firelight. It looks like real gold, but I doubt it.

"What your name?" Kat asks.

"I'm sorry, I forgot to introduce myself," the kid says as he sits and unsnaps the first clip on his gray guitar case. "I'm Jason Raintree. You remember that name, because someday it'll be posted everywhere." The second snap is loosened, and he looks up. "I'm going to be a household name like Johnny Cash." He takes his cowboy hat off and bows his head. "He was my hero."

"Is that right?" Kat says as Jason pulls out a large, red guitar. He drops it across his lap like it lives there, pulls out a tuning fork. He strikes his knee, then tunes a string to match the hum of the fork. In a moment all the strings are adjusted to that one string, and he strums the guitar, which has a clear harmonic sound.

"Okay, we're taking requests tonight," Jason says, like he's standing on stage with a thousand people in the crowd. His chiseled face is alight, nose flared with excitement.

"You know any Randy Newman?" Kat asks.

"Why hell, yes. I cut my teeth on Randy Newman. What do you want to hear?"

Kat's face lights. "Baltimore?"

The kid lays his fingers across the fret board, pulls a fast strum to make sure everything is in tune and starts into the song, singing in a baritone gravely voice about seagulls and hookers and drunks on the streets of Baltimore. His fingers fly across the guitar, picking out obscure single notes high on the board, then dropping low for contrast while his voice follows suit.

When he finishes the song, I lean forward, grab another stick of wood, and drop it on the fire. "You know any Boz Skaggs?"

He gives me a big-toothed grin that reminds me of Biker Bob. "Give me the name of a song, and I'll pick it out for you."

"How about Ledo?"

"No problem." He lays into the soulful song and plays it better than Boz himself. Jason puts soul into the song, stretching the tempo in all of the right places, his tone reaching the high notes with little effort, dropping into the bluesy pits of the song leaving tears in my eyes. I've never heard it played so well. When he's finished, he ends the song with a suddenness that takes me by surprise, though I know each note of the song by heart.

I look at Jennifer. "Why don't you choose one?"

Jason looks at her. "She don't even have to say. I know what song she wants."

Jennifer smiles her small-toothed grin and looks at him with sparkly eyes.

He starts into a Charlie Rich song about trains, and pours his youthful soul into it. Although I usually hate country music, I can't help but admire the kids talent.

The evening continues without Jason missing one note. He plays jazz, blues, country, folk, a bit of Mexican polka, and a couple of sorrowful flamenco tunes.

I want him to play until dawn, but after a few hours, he puts the guitar back in its case and latches the steel clips. He looks up. "I could play so much more, but I'm tired, and I got a gig tomorrow afternoon at some park in Carefree."

He picks up his guitar and stands. "I guess me and Jennifer'll be going."

Kat speaks. "Where are you sleeping?"

"In my truck, I guess."

Kat looks at me, and I already know what she's going to say. "You two can sleep in my tent. Renee and I will double up in hers."

The kid gets a nervous grin. "Thank you, Ma'am, but I wouldn't want to—"

"It's no trouble," Kat says. "We'll just open up our bag and sleep under it instead of in it. You can have my bag and do the same."

"No, ma'am, I wouldn't want to put you out."

Kat stands to her full height of five-five and looks up at him. "Look, Jason, I insist. You just gave us a great performance." She glances at me and smiles, then back at him. "It's the least we can do."

Jason gets an ah-shucks grin on his face and says,

"Well, thank you ma'am. I surely do appreciate it, and I know Jenny here does, too." He reaches for her hand and she looks up at him.

Fifteen

Nick's Return

I take the long, ten hour drive from San Francisco, down the Imperial Valley, over the mountains east of Bakersfield and out the dry desert road of lower 395. I stop at Kramer's Corner to call Stewart at work. "Stew," I say after his secretary connects us. "Can you put me up for a few days?"

He hesitates. "Sure, Nick, but you've got to agree to not smoke pot anywhere around my house or my kids."

I grimace. "Look, Bob told me to quit a few weeks ago, so I did. I'm down here to get Carolyn back. She left because I was smoking too much."

"It's about time, Nick."

"Well, fuck you, too."

"Hey Nick, I didn't mean to insult you. I was just celebrating you getting clear-headed. Hey, man, that stuff's almost pickled your brain. You're an ace mechanic, but the rest of your life, you have to admit, leaves a little to be desired."

I don't know what to say to that, so I say nothing for

267

ten seconds. When I speak, it's to ask the question again. "Can you put me up for a few days while I figure out the Carolyn thing?"

"Sure, Nick. I'd be honored to have you as my guest. Renee is still on her adventure, so we'll have the house to ourselves."

"Us and your kids?"

"Yes, of course the kids, too. Where are you now?"

"Kramer's Corner on highway 395."

"Go on over. I'll call Mel and tell him you're coming. He's already home from school. Make yourself at home until I get there and set you up with a bedroom."

"Thanks Stew."

"No problem. It'll be good to have you back in the area. We've missed you at the fire circles."

"Me too," I say almost choking up. "Well, I'll see you at the house in a coupla hours."

"Nick, you going to join us for dinner?"

"No, I'll get—"

"Join us for dinner," Stew says as a demand.

Again, I'm choked up and can't answer for a moment. "Sure, okay, man. Is there anything I can bring?"

"We're having last night's leftovers. Lasagna is always better the second night, and I made plenty."

"Okay Stew." I can't imagine Stew knowing how to cook. As I hang up the phone, I'm thinking maybe I better get something in town just in case. I dial a second number, and two thoughts come back into my head almost at the same time. Maybe I'll insult Stew by bringing anything extra, and suddenly I want to ride my bike again.

"Hey, Donna, this is Nick. Is Carolyn around?"

Donna pauses. With a robotic response, she says, "She's not here right now. She'll be back later tonight."

"Oh." I feel a tinge of anger, because I know she's there. "Well, tell her I'm staying at Stew's. I'd like her to call me."

"Okay, Nick. I'll give her the message."

The line is silent for a moment. Lines are silent a lot these days with me. Donna finally speaks. "Hey, Nick?"

"Yeah?"

"Good to have you back. We missed you."

"Thanks, Donna."

I hang up by slamming the phone hard on its receiver. I don't know why I'm so angry, I just am.

I get back into my car, pull out onto the highway, and drive the half hour past Victorville, not tempting myself to stop at Tazz and Donna's to see if Carolyn is there or not. It's none of my business.

Much later, I turn left on Stewart's gravel road, then into his round driveway and up to the weird house of half moons and disk decks.

I knock on the front door, and Stew's boy opens one side of the big, round door. The kid says nothing, just stands there like I'm some sort of ghost or something.

"I'm Nick Brown. Did your dad call you?"

"Sure," he says and I think that's all I'll get out of him, but he continues after a pause. "You're the motorcycle guy who built my dad's Harley."

I smile. "I guess I am. Does he let you ride on it?"

"Sometimes, but screw the riding bullshit. I want to drive."

The kid hasn't made a move to let me in. He stands at the door blocking my entry. I nod. "Hey, it looks like you're getting old enough that he'll have to give you lessons someday soon."

"It's not soon enough," he says.

269

We stand in awkward silence until I say, "You going to let me in?"

"Oh sure, sorry. Guess I forgot my manners." He steps back, throws the door open, and motions for me to follow. I step inside and close the door behind me, then trail him into the kitchen. "My dad said to show you the fridge and make you a sandwich if you want one, but I got to get back to my computer." He points at the refrigerator. "Eat whatever."

He turns and walks out of the room, leaving me standing by the sink. I open the refrigerator and find a cold apple and a piece of cheese. I sit at the counter eating, when Stew's bike rolls up the driveway. In the few seconds it takes him to pull up, I hear one cylinder slightly out of tune. The chain is loose. A front shock is out of oil.

He pulls into his garage and kills the engine. I want to go out and meet him and tell him of his bike's problems, but I restrain myself. I'm no longer a mechanic. I'm an artist, though I have yet to make any money from my art, whatever that is, these days.

Stew comes in through a door from the garage and walks into the kitchen, his blue suit peeking out from under his leathers.

"Hey, Nick, good to see you." He opens the fridge and pulls out a wimpy non-alcoholic beer. He twists off the cap and tosses it in the garbage. "Hey, man, you really look great. Your face looks so clear."

"What do you mean?" I don't want to sound too demanding, but I do.

"Nick, you look great, is all."

I take another bite of my apple and nibble a piece of cheese at the same time. I've always liked the combination.

"Carolyn left a coupla weeks ago."

Stew gets a strange expression, like he knows something I don't. "I know. It got brought up at the men's group the other night."

My rage meter leaps off of the scale. I don't say anything or do anything about it, but I feel my face turn red.

"You okay, Nick?" Stew has genuine concern in his tone.

Just the question calms me enough that I can answer. "I'm all right, I guess." I realize it's Stew I'm talking to. He's one of my men. "No, I'm not all right, Stew. She left me, and when I quit smoking, I felt stuff I haven't since I was a kid." I've got tears in my eyes, and I feel like breaking down right here in the kitchen, but I hold back. I turn away from Stew and put my palms on my temples.

"It's okay, Nick." Stew speaks in a gentle tone. "It's okay to feel it here."

I turn to him with rage in my face. How quickly my tears turn to rage. "It's not okay, Stew," I scream. "There ain't nothing okay about it. That bitch left me, and she doesn't want to talk to me."

Stew steps three paces over to me and puts a hand on my shoulder. "Hey, man, I get it."

I flick his hand off. "You don't get shit, Stew. You don't have a clue."

He puts his hand back on my shoulder. "I get that the minute you need her, she decides to leave. Is that right?"

My rage turns back to tears. I put my hands over my face, lean down slightly and bawl. I feel Stew's hand on my shoulder. I feel his support, so I let it out, let the floods breach the banks. I cry for a few minutes into my hands, though I hardly make a sound.

Whenever my tears start, I'm afraid they will never end, but in five minutes, I wipe my eyes with the back of my hand and Stew gets me a paper towel to blow my nose.

"I don't know what's gotten into me lately," I say. "I can't control my emotions."

"You stopped smoking pot, man, and your emotions are free maybe for the first time in ten years."

"Fifteen years. It's been fifteen years since I took a clear breath of air."

Stew looks at me with compassion in his face. "Fifteen years? That's a lot of emotion bottled up inside that hull of yours. Personally, Nick, I'm glad to see you finally express any emotion at all. I don't think I've ever seen you feel anything since I've known you."

"That's not true," I say in my defense. "I got all teary that first day in the hospital, when I met you. You saved my folks from that fire."

Stew smiles. "Yes, and that was what, two or three years ago?"

I sniffle, put the paper towel up to my nose, and honk a wad of sinus crud. I put the towel in the garbage under the sink. "I guess."

"I'd say you got a lot of catching up, Nick."

I don't respond, but stand in a numb state.

"How about we go out by the pool and hang out."

"Sure, Stew." I follow him out the sliding glass door, down the first flight of steps, across the big middle deck, then down the second flight of steps and out to the semicircular pool. "Jesus, Stew, you got one hell of a view."

He sits on a lawn chair and gestures for me to sit.

I position myself across from him. "Hey, man, you've

got to get that engine of yours tuned up."

"I know. I'm taking it in to Twig next week."

"Don't drive it until you take it in. Air-cooled engines don't do well when they're out of tune. They tend to disintegrate."

"Well, heck, Nick, once you left, that bike has been nothing but trouble. I don't know, you had a way with bikes. Don't get me wrong, Twig knows what he's doing, but it's just that you always had some kind of magical spell over my bike. As long as you were around, Blue always ran great."

I kick my foot up on the little metal stool between us. "Twig's got a bike shop these days?"

"It sure makes him happy."

There is a bit of a silence, then Stew says, "Hey, you going to come to the couples meeting tomorrow night?"

"Shit, Stew, I don't know. I'm not exactly a couple these days."

"Carolyn came last week. Thought maybe you two could work out some of your stuff with us as support."

"I wouldn't want to screw up her good time. She'll have to be okay with it. I won't show up and surprise her."

Stew puts his elbows onto his knees and looks at me. "Why the fuck not? I think a good surprise might be just the ticket. I've heard from Tazz that she's not hooking back up with you. If that's the case, at the very least she and you need to face off one last time."

My face drops. "She's not coming back?"

Stew frowns. "That's what she told Tazz, but you know how women are when they're mad. They'll throw the whole thing out. I think you show up like you are, and she'll be forced to reconsider."

"What do you mean, like I am?"

"Hey, Nick, I don't know if you noticed, but you're all here. That pot deadened something inside you for all of those years, and now you're awake."

"Shit, Stew, I might be here, but I feel so raw inside that I can't even hold a conversation without tearing up or getting enraged. I yelled at the gas station attendant in Bakersfield earlier, and I still don't know why."

Stew smiles. "That may be true, but you're all here for the first time since I've known you, and I like what I see."

"Wait till I scream at you for some stupid nothing, and you might have a change of heart."

"Why would you scream at me?"

"Hell, man, don't you get it? I feel like screaming at everything. I feel like busting all the glass and kicking some ass. It's why I came back, mostly."

"Why's that?"

"To have someone around who understands me. I know you have trouble getting angry, but Twig'll understand."

Stew says, "I think Twig's got a handle on his anger. How come you didn't go see him?"

"Twig and Melinda live in that little cracker box. Man, I've been around a pregnant woman before. It ain't no picnic. I figure I'll catch him at his bike shop tomorrow by himself."

Stew smiles. "From what I hear from Twig, Melinda is an extra handful now that she's pregnant. She's one hell of a woman, though. She and Twig are a perfect match, don't you think?"

I smile. "She was way more woman than I could handle, that's for sure."

Both Stew and I giggle, but I think it's more out of nervousness than anything.

After a long silence, Stew asks, "So, you going to

be here at the house tomorrow night?"

"Let me think about it."

"Sure man. It'll be at seven."

"I'll let you know tomorrow."

"Hey, you don't have to check in with me. Just show up if you want or go to a movie or something. Unless you want, I won't say anything either way. If you show, it'll be a surprise for everyone, especially Carolyn."

***

The morning sun glows in through the tent like a light bulb. My eyes are forced open by the brilliance. I sit up and look out through the netting at Katherine's tent. It doesn't look like the kid and his girlfriend have stirred yet. I look at Kat and she's still asleep, so I slip out from under the sleeping bag, unzip the tent and climb out to a dead fire and a cold morning dew.

In ten minutes, I have the fire dancing and I warm my fingers and face in the heat of the blaze.

Kat makes some motions of being alive, climbs out of the tent, and stands next to the fire. She points at her tent. "Those two aren't up yet?"

"Pretty quiet so far."

She smiles. "He sure did play a great guitar."

I nod, but don't say anything.

Kat looks at her watch. "It's a little after eight. Maybe the store's open, and we can get some coffee."

"Good plan," I whisper, and the two of us crunch our way past our bikes, through a hundred yards of gravel to the little store. Once we're away from the tent and the sleeping beauties, I say in a regular voice. "I got so many questions to ask Cherry, I'm almost ready to burst."

"Me too, and the first is what happened to the extra days we're missing."

We step off the desert and onto blistered pavement so old that the original gravel driveway shows through in places. We walk around the building.

I say, "You know, Biker Bob did that losing-time thing to the whole group once. I heard about it from Stew, but no one could figure out what happened."

"Well, Cherry's going to give me some answers," Kat says.

We round the last corner and look at the closed store. Something hits me, but I can't figure out what it is. "What's wrong here?"

"No truck," Kat says with a catch to her speech.

I turn to her as my face drains. "No truck, and he was out of gas, wasn't he?"

"Out of gas, and no place to go."

We both turn and walk back around the edge of the building toward the tents. I feel another one of those chills as we retrace our steps. When we get to the tent, Kat grabs the zipper and pulls it up. She flips the flap open, and nothing but her sleeping bag is in the tent. "What happened to them?" She pulls a glossy black business card from the top of the sleeping bag. It has gold letters that reads, "One on One." Below, in smaller print, it says, "Biker Bob."

I flush. "Was that Bob all along?"

I look toward the little store as an old beat-up pickup truck rattles its way over the hill some two or three miles to the east. The truck, engine misfiring, one front fender gone, the raw workings of the suspension showing through, front tire exposed, hobbles along as it closes in on the little store. The side of the truck bed has been crushed, maybe by a falling tree, though there are no trees big enough to do that kind of damage for a hundred miles.

With no muffler, the truck comes to a noisy stop and parks along the side of the building, its one remaining headlight winking at us in a macabre gesture.

When the engine is off, it's so quiet, we hear only the sound of bugs circling above our heads.

A huge man with dirty blue bib overalls drops his legs out of the truck and pushes forward to a standing position. He puffs as he takes a step, pushes the tinny-sounding door closed, and makes his way around the back of the truck, using it as hand holds to support his enormous bulk. If he weighs four hundred pounds, I'm not surprised.

He gets to the far end of the truck and stops to rest, then notices us standing out here. I'm slack jawed.

He takes three hard-won breaths and pushes off the truck. After the second wobbly step, he disappears behind the building.

I look at Kat. "Maybe we give him a chance to open while we pack."

We break down the tents, fold our bags, scatter the fire, bury the ashes, then load everything in the saddlebags. I kick my bike to life after three tries. Kat touches her starter, and we drive across the gravel to the station and pull to the pumps. Once the engines are off, I click the handles and pump in a tank full of gas. Kat does the same using the second rusted pump with its broken glass and only three numbers, like some strange slot machine, clicking off the dollars and gallons in a clattery rhythm.

When we are both done, I walk to the rotting screen door with the Rainbow bread plate screwed to it. Maybe it's the only thing holding the door together. I open it and step inside.

The big guy sits looking at the same TV, positioned in the same place as the other day, or was it a month ago? Some morning talk show is on.

I walk over to him and drop a twenty on the counter.

"How much was it?" he asks, taking a short breath between each word.

"Seven fourteen for the both of us."

He pushes four keys hard on a rusted old cash register. The keys drop two inches, and three tabs pop up in the smoky glass window at the top of the register. He digs in the wooden tray and slowly counts the change aloud into my hand, taking a short breath between each word. "Fifteen, and a dime makes twenty-five, three quarters make eighteen, and here's two ones." Once the ancient ritual is finished, his attention returns to the television.

"Can I ask a question?" I say.

He raises one finger. "In a minute, at the commercial."

He and I watch the thirty remaining seconds, the burning interview about some mother's issues with her lesbian daughter, like I even care.

When a commercial for dish soap comes on, he turns to me. His lugubrious face cracks into a half-grin.

"Is Ed or Cherry around?"

His expression shifts to caution or maybe fear. There is a long moment before he speaks in his out-of-breath manner. "There is no Ed or Cherry, though you're not the first to ask."

I'm flabbergasted. When I finally get my voice, I say, "Ed and Cherry don't own this store?"

"There is no Ed or Cherry, and that I know, there never has been. I've owned this store for fifteen years, and I've never met an Ed or Cherry."

"I met Ed just the other day, right there behind your counter."

He gets a patient expression. "Two or three times a year, someone comes in here and asks the same thing, and I tell them the same answer. What is it with you people?"

He focuses back on the television as the program returns.

I look out the front door, then point. My mouth moves, but I can't speak. Eventually I say, "Thank you," and find my way to the front door, though I'm not sure how. I push the door open.

Kat gets off her bike fast. She runs over and grabs my right elbow, helps me over to my bike, and sits me on the saddle. "What happened? Where did the kid go?"

I'm taking in gulps of air as I try to catch my breath. I feel like I've run a hundred-yard dash in five seconds. "The kid is the least of our problems," I'm able to say.

Kat turns, puts one hand on her hip, and glares at me, the rising sun lighting her face. "What?"

I point back toward the little store. "He's never heard of Ed or Cherry."

"What do you mean?"

"They don't exist."

Her face goes pale, and she grips my handlebar for support. Her mouth moves, but no words come out.

It takes a minute or so before I tell her what the old guy said.

"How can that be?" she asks.

I shrug, pull my leg over the bike, lean down, and shift my distributor. I rotate the kick pedal.

"How are we going to find out what happened?"

I shrug again. "Maybe we go talk to Billy Black. He's

the one who brought us here."

On the third kick, the bike comes to life. I wish this thing had an electric starter.

With a push of her button, Kat starts her bike. We pull out onto the highway and head west, back toward Blythe and maybe some answers.

***

I drive across town to my beloved shop. Although I love Melinda, hanging out with her at times is exhausting, especially now that she's pregnant. I pull off the highway, up the driveway, and behind an industrial complex to an old barn-like structure under a large valley oak planted and cared for a hundred years ago. No self-respecting oak would ever be able to start by itself in this dry desert soil.

When I disengage the alarm and swing the door open, there it is, my dream, my bike shop. Three bikes I'm custom building for customers sit on big cedar rounds, two bikes left for repair sit on kickstands in the back corner, and myriad parts that need some kind of attention are scattered on three benches. The most wonderful part is that I have the choice of what I want to work on first and no boss or woman around to tell me what to do.

After I brew a small pot of coffee and sit for a while looking out the front door at the back of the modern tin buildings, I decide to install the transmission on the second bike, a 57' Panhead. I just got it back from the transmission guy in Los Angeles yesterday, and I've been thinking about taking that bike to the next step in the thousand incremental moves it takes to get it on the road and maybe to a bike show. This one is a beauty.

I've got the tranny bolted in, and I'm in the middle

of installing the primary chain, when a beat-up yellow Toyota pulls up. I recognize the car and smile as I grab a rag and clean my hands. "Hey, Nick," I say as he gets out of the car.

He walks to my big front door and we slap fingertips. "Twig, what the fuck?"

"Not much. You know, wrenching on bikes these days. What's up with you?"

Typical for Nick, he doesn't beat around the bush but gets right to the point. "You seen Carolyn?"

"I think she's staying at Tazz and Donna's. You'll probably hook up with her there."

He has a nervous look. "I guess I mean, you heard anything about her?"

I know what information he wants, but I don't want to be the bearer of bad news, so I skate the subject. "I think she's working with Melinda at the restaurant."

He gives me a pinched smile. "Restaurant?"

"You know, Maria's on Main Street. Maybe you could check her out there."

The conversation falls flat on the concrete of my shop floor and we stand in silence for a moment until I ask, "Hey, Nick, maybe you could help me a little with this Sportster. It's got electronic ignition, and I can't figure out what's wrong with it." I point toward the back of the shop at a yellow bike with black leather saddle bags.

I really don't need the help, but Nick needs a distraction, so I step toward the bike hoping he'll follow.

I'm five paces back into the cool of the building when I hear his car start. I turn in time to see him drive off. Damn, he's got it bad.

***

I'm back in my car in a second, and not because I don't want to help Twig. I'd love to get my hands greasy just for fun, but like a desert dust twister, my rage monster roars up from my belly and takes control. I barely make it to the car and race out of there, peeling dirt and gravel as I go. Like a coyote, I howl at the windshield and slam my fist on the back of the passenger seat, visualizing Carolyn sitting there.

I don't know why I'm doing what I'm doing. I never get angry. I never slam my fists or drive erratically, but I'm like a crazy man, screaming at everything.

Lucky for me, Twig's shop is at the southern edge of town. In a half mile, I'm driving on a straight-as-an-arrow deserted back road. My foot's to the floor, and I'm gaining speed every second.

The greasewood and star-thistle at the side of the road turn to a blur. The broken line of the center divider turns to a single line.

A voice goes off in my head. "Okay, my man, turn that killer-ape rage of yours into the emotion you're really feeling."

I look around, but no one is there. It's that fucking meddling-ass Bob.

"Hey, fuck you!" I scream to the windshield, but my foot loses some of its pressure on the gas. The tachometer, and it's the only thing that works to tell me how fast I'm going, drops from an engine-screaming fifty-five grand to fifty, to forty. Bob goes off once more in my head. "What are you really feeling, Nick? Because rage is a man's first response."

"What do you mean?" I ask as the tach drops to a more reasonable three grand, equal to seventy. The engine whine returns to the stupid hum of the little four-banger.

"Anger is some men's first response to everything," Bob says, "but go under the anger and touch the other emotion we men never look at."

My rage has subsided a little, at least enough to be reasonable. "I never get pissed."

"You never get pissed because you've been stoned for fifteen years. This is the first time you've allowed yourself to feel anything."

"That's not true, Bob, I've—"

"Stop your pathetic whining before the feeling goes away. Feel what's under the rage."

When Bob says something, I have little choice. I usually comply even if I don't want to. My fist-slamming, fast-driving, windshield-yelling anger takes a long leap off a ledge and dives into an abyss I've never known. My foot drops off of the gas pedal and the car coasts. My teeth-grinding rage turns to deep-seated fear, then a second feeling of abandonment, and finally into the pit of despair, feeling the deepest grief I've ever experienced.

My fist drops to the seat and relaxes. Tears well up in my eyes and spill down my cheek. My throat constricts. The car, now traveling less than thirty, slowly veers off the road, onto the shoulder, and farther out into the gravel of the raw desert floor. I don't give a shit as it bogs down in the loose gravel, slamming into mesquite bushes and small acacia trees until it comes to a halt.

My forehead rests on top of the steering wheel. My hands grip the wheel, and the tears flow.

"This is our true masculine feeling, Nick," Bob says in a soft tone. "This feeling is masked by our rage."

"But why?" I ask blubbering onto my steering wheel.

"There is no answer here, Nick. The job is to feel it

and not distract yourself with questions. Just feel it, my man."

"But there is so much," I whine. "It'll never stop."

I feel a hand on my shoulder, and I look over at the passenger seat. Bob, dressed in full black leathers, sits next to me with tears streaming down his face. He sniffs and says, "Don't be afraid that it'll never stop. Be afraid that it will never start again. For now, just feel the grief of Carolyn leaving you, of Melinda abusing you, of all of the women in your life who have left."

My bawling intensifies until I can't catch my breath. I'm one huge ball of sadness, expressing myself as much as I possibly can.

Bob says, "Remember how your mother walked out when you were eight?"

"Oh, my God." I scream and slam my forehead on the steering wheel. "Oh, my God."

I'm deep into my pit of grief, crying so hard that nothing else exists except Bob's hand on my shoulder, supporting me.

I've cried to the depth of my grief, and I feel myself begin to rise back to the surface. My tears lessen, then after a minute or two, dry up altogether. I look up at the morning sun, at the six-inch-thick greasewood tree that eventually stopped my car, at a small wren nervously leaping from branch to branch in search of breakfast. Everything is crystal-clear, perfect. I turn to Bob, but as I already know, he's gone.

His parting words go off inside of my head. "When you're angry, go under the anger and feel the grief."

I drop my head against the back of the seat, reach down to the side, twist the knob to rotate into a horizontal position and fall into a deep sleep for the first time in the nine or ten days since I quit smoking that crap.

I awake with something tapping on my side window. It feels like the clicking has been going on for a long time. I jerk up to a sitting position and look toward the source. A Highway Patrol officer dressed in a black uniform and wearing a gold helmet backs up a few paces and waits for me to roll down the window. His hand rests on the butt of his pistol, not in a threatening stance, but more of a protective one.

I roll down the window, but I'm too groggy to say anything.

"Are you okay?" he asks.

"Yes, Officer, I just fell asleep. I needed the rest."

He points at the greasewood tree that my car tangled with. "Looks like you fell asleep at the wheel."

I don't know how to explain what happened, so I just nod and say, "Nothing happened, though."

"You been drinking?" he asks.

I reach down and crank the seat back up to its sitting position. "No, sir, just the opposite."

He steps back two yards. "Mind explaining while you get out of the car?"

I open the door and climb out. "It's hard to explain."

"While you get your driver's license, maybe you could give it a try."

I fish my wallet out of my back pocket, drag the card from the windowed slot, and hand it to him. "The best I can say is my girlfriend left me two weeks ago, and I just realized that she may not ever come back. I was here, well. . . I mean. . . kinda crying about it."

The cop studies my license and says, "You're Nick

Brown, the Harley mechanic?"

"Not so much any more." I look at him for the first time.

His eyes are bright. "You worked on my bike a few years back."

"Not that one?" I point twenty yards to the highway where his police-issue Moto-Guzzi is parked.

"No, not that one, my bike. It was an older U-head, but I got a new fat boy these days."

"No kidding." I feign interest, though bikes are the last things in my thoughts. I guess I worked on them too many years. I'm glad he's not pursuing the crying issue. It's too embarrassing as it is.

He hands my license back. "I heard you quit bikes. Are you back working on Harleys again?"

"No, I pretty much gave that up a few months ago."

"What're you doing now?"

"I don't know. I'm kind of in transition. Trying to get my girlfriend back at the moment."

A call comes over his shoulder mike and he answers. It's something about an accident on 395 about ten miles to the west. He gives my car a nervous glance. "Maybe we better see if you can get your car out of this before I leave."

I get back into the car, start the engine, and with a lot of digging of the back tires, the car eventually pulls its way out to the highway.

The cop is already on his idling bike. He pulls up next to me. "Hey, if you ever start working on bikes again, let me know. I always got something that needs to be done to mine." He hands me a card, pulls off, makes a U-turn and races back toward town, his siren screaming.

I pull onto the highway, also make a U-turn toward

town, and drive at a sedate fifty miles an hour until I reach Maria's restaurant. I want to stop, but I have second thoughts and drive by slowly, trying to get a glimpse of Carolyn. The sun reflects off the front windows and I see nothing but my dirty car.

I drive to the end of the block and turn right toward Stewart's. It's probably best that I stay out of town for the day. Although I feel centered at the moment, my nerves are frayed, and I know I can go off the deep end at any second.

By the end of the hour, I pull into Stew's driveway and park. He's at work and the kids are at school, so I've got the place to myself until later this afternoon.

I make myself a sandwich, grab a few chips, and walk out to the pool.

Sixteen

Back to Blythe

We ride west toward Blythe. The desert is flat, open, and devoid of anything more interesting than an occasional creosote bush and a few deserted cars, rusted and decomposing into the desert. Kat's bike develops a miss in one cylinder, and we hobble to a shop in Blythe an hour before they close.

The mechanic, a muscular guy with a shaved head, wipes his hands on a red towel and follows us out to Kat's bike. "Okay, start it and let's see what you've got."

Kat touches the starter button, and the bike roars to life, then drops to a rough idle.

The mechanic waves his hand to kill the engine and it falls silent.

"Tell you what." He strokes his long beard, "I can change out the spark plugs right now. If that doesn't get it, you'll have to leave it here overnight, and I'll get on it first thing in the morning."

"You think it might just be spark plugs?" Kat asks, like she knows what she's talking about. I don't think she knows any more about these things than I do.

The name on his short sleeve work shirt says Sam, though I'm not sure it's his name. He steps back into his shop and grabs a set of spark plugs and a long socket wrench. When he comes out, he has a small wooden chair deeply stained with grease. In five minutes he has the plugs changed. Kat starts it up again.

The lumping sound is still hobbling the bike's idle. He looks at Kat with a sorrowful expression. "I guess it's tomorrow morning."

"It's okay," Kat says. "I was through riding for the day anyhow. I'm exhausted."

The big guy's muscles bulge as he leans the bike off the kickstand and up to a balanced position. He pushes the bike around the side of the building and into the work area. We follow and I ask, "You know where a good motel is?"

He parks the bike and points out the bay door. "Over one street is a nice place, but it's kind of close to the freeway. If you want more quiet, go out Highway 95 for a mile or so." He points left and north. "There's a coupla older ones without as much freeway."

We fill out the paperwork. Kat removes her personal things from both saddlebags and carefully places them into a canvas tote bag. We walk out of the shop, I kick my bike into life, and Kat climbs on back.

The mechanic standing at the opening of his bay door lights a cigarette and waves. We wave back and pull down his driveway, then out onto the street.

Over my shoulder, I yell, "Let's get a room, then look up Billy."

She leans forward. "Billy put us up once before. Let's go over first and see where it leads."

I make a left onto a side street and drive the mile to Maple. The bigger potholes force me to drive at an idle to dodge them. Up on the levy and looking down onto Billy's houseboat, I kill the engine.

Kat gets off. "I don't see Billy's bike."

I drop my motorcycle on the kickstand. "Maybe he's not here."

We walk fifty yards down the path, then step onto the small dock. I yell, "Hey, Billy, you around?"

No one answers, but I hear rustling in the houseboat and see the boat rock slightly from the shift in weight. It rubs the dock enough to squeak the rubber tires against the boat.

"Hey, Billy?" I yell.

No one answers, and there's no more movement.

I try once more, look at Kat and shrug.

"Maybe we'll come back later this evening," she says.

"Maybe." I turn and start back up the hill, when I hear the sliding glass door at the back of the boat scrape on its runner. A soft woman's voice breaks the silence. "What do you want?"

I stop and turn, but I can't see her. "Is Billy around?"

There is a long silence. When she speaks it's with a catch in her voice. "Billy's been dead five years."

Goose bumps climb my spine. "Billy Black?"

"I bought this houseboat from his daughter four years ago. Billy Black was his name."

"How could that be?"

The sliding glass door squeals again, and a slender woman in her fifties steps into view wearing a pale green housecoat. It looks like she hasn't brushed her hair in a few days and her face is drawn and jaundiced.

She pulls a wild strand of hair out of her face. "Ever

since I bought this place, people have been coming around looking for Billy. He must have had a lot of friends. Can I offer you a cup of tea?"

I look at Kat and she at me. She nods and we walk onto the boat.

"Have a seat, and I'll put some water on." The woman disappears into the boat.

We sit on the same chairs we sat on the other day, though it's beginning to look more like a month ago. It's definitely the same boat, but what happened?

When she comes out, she places a cup in front of each of us. She sits with a ledger in her hand and sets the book on the table, but doesn't open it.

I slide my cup toward me, dunk the tea bag four times, and glance at the fragile-looking woman. "We met Billy Black a month ago."

I expect her to turn pale or not believe me, but she does neither. She takes her tea bag out of her cup, carefully places it into a teaspoon, and wraps the string around the bag and spoon, wringing it out. She discards the tea bag in a saucer. "I know."

"What do you mean you know?" It takes every ounce of reserve I have not to yell.

Without a flinch or any indication of concern, she says, "I didn't want to scare you, because I was hoping you were really one of his friends from the past, but every person who comes here just met Billy Black a few weeks before. They have all been women, and they have the exact same wild story about being taken into the desert by a person named Cherry." She looks at me, and my face flushes.

"You're the first to ride in on a motorcycle, though."

Kat speaks, because my throat has constricted. "How

many people have you met?"

The woman answers without hesitation. "The first twenty or so I didn't count, so I'm not real accurate, but since then I've been keeping a journal." She opens the book to the second page and runs one finger down the list of handwritten entries. "One hundred fourteen, to be exact." She picks up a pen and points it at the next open line. "Can I ask your names?" She looks over her reading glasses.

"Renee Chance," I say absently.

"Katherine Burns."

The woman scribes in clear schoolteacher penmanship my name, then turns to Kat. "Is that Katherine with a 'C' or a 'K'?"

Kat responds, but without conviction, like she's distracted.

The woman writes the entry and closes the book. "You two make one hundred sixteen."

I look at her then at the book. "Doesn't this make you crazy?"

Her smile is unreadable. "It did at first, but it happens every winter. Sometimes I get five or ten visitors a month during the cool season. I don't know how it happens, I just know it does and I'm supposed to log in the names, so I do. I'm also supposed to offer you a place to stay for the night. Some stay, some don't."

I look at Kat and she says, "We have a place in town." She takes a last sip of tea and stands. I take her cue and stand, too. "We'll get going now," Kat says.

The woman stays seated. She doesn't hold out her hand. She doesn't move; she continues to sip her tea.

"Goodbye now." I turn and follow Kat off the undulating boat onto the solid deck and up the short rise to the top of the levee. Without saying a word, I start my bike, Kat gets on the back, and we drive down the far side of the levee, then out Maple Street to the pavement. I turn right and slowly idle my way toward town, shifting gears, but not giving the bike any gas.

"What do you think?" I ask over my shoulder.

"I don't know. I just knew we had to get out of that place."

We ride in silence to a small, quiet motel on the old highway. Its pink stucco exterior comes straight out of the 1950's. It may have been that long since it's seen a coat of paint. The sign over the entrance says Flamingo Hotel in tattered lettering from that era.

Along the sidewalk and next to the pool, plastic, pink flamingos dot the landscape in random groupings of five or six.

The trim and rain gutters long ago had been painted a desert-sky teal. The curved roof tiles are brick red, each a foot long.

I pull to the second door, which features a faded office sign. I turn off the bike, then lean it on its kickstand after Kat dismounts. The two of us enter the little room one door away from where the manager lives. He comes out in loud, tourist swim trunks hanging to his knees. A big tattoo of a palm tree has long ago faded and spread across the upper portion of his right arm. Under it reads the word "freedom." His pot belly sucks in. "Good afternoon." He speaks in a pick-you-up-in-a-bar kind of tone.

"A room with two doubles, if you have one?" I ask, not wanting to give him any indication that I might be the slightest bit interested in anything but his hotel room.

"Sure, we have one in the back. It's fifty-five." He

points through the wall to his right.

"Can we see it first?" Kat asks.

"The place is a little run down, but we keep the rooms clean." He pulls a key with a small brass tag and hands it to Kat.

"Thanks. We'll be back."

I follow and close the cheesy front door behind me.

We walk the length of the driveway in a U-shaped configuration of small apartments with single-car garages between each one. A large veranda roof extends over the sidewalk, and each room has three concrete steps leading to the front door. Kat unlocks the door to room twelve and we step into a cute little studio apartment, with a side room as a kitchen and small bathroom with all of the standard amenities.

The little kitchen has a 1950's chrome trim, red Formica table, and two small wooden folding chairs. "This isn't as nice as Phoenix, but it has character." I point to a small vase with a real red rose in full bloom between the glass salt and pepper shakers. The scent of the single rose fills the kitchen.

Kat nods but doesn't speak. She leans close to the rose and takes a long draw of its scent.

"Okay, we'll take the room," I say as we re-enter the office.

His smile is so slight I almost don't catch it.

After paying for a night and stowing our things, I turn to Kat. "I want to talk to that restaurant guy who sent us on this adventure.

"I think it was a breakfast and lunch-only place. Maybe we'll catch him for breakfast."

"Maybe we will."

***

After a movie, dinner at Denny's, and a long quiet night's rest, in the morning, Renee and I ride her bike to the restaurant.

We park in front of the big bay windows and walk inside. I ask the waitress if Mike is cooking.

She looks toward the kitchen, then turns back. She has an odd expression, like someone cut the cheese, and she's trying not to show her displeasure. "He's on today."

Renee says, "When he gets a break, we'd like to talk to him."

The woman looks toward the kitchen once again, then says, "He may not get a break for an hour or so. It's pretty busy this time of day. Maybe I can take your order while you wait." She poises her pencil on the tablet in her left hand.

Both Kat and I order, then I watch the waitress scurry to the order window, get Mike's attention, and talk to him in earnest over the counter. His big head peeks around the window, and we lock gazes. He slinks back into his kitchen. The waitress looks at me, then goes on about her chores, filling water glasses, delivering orders, bussing tables. It looks like she does it all.

We have long finished our breakfast and two cups of coffee before Mike steps to our table. He wears an embarrassed expression as he slides in next to Renee. "How are you doing?"

Renee scoots over to make room. Her next words are accusatory. "You sent us to Billy Black."

His smile drops to a frown. "I know; he's no longer alive, but he was there, wasn't he?"

He opens his big hands, palms up, spreads them wide, and shrugs his big shoulders. "All I know is when someone orders a Bob special, I'm supposed to tell them where Billy Black lives. . . lived."

"Who told you to do this?" I ask.

He looks at me as if I'm some kind of idiot. "Biker Bob, of course. I thought you knew."

Renee's doubled fist bangs the table, not loud, but with enough force to make the silverware dance. "Damn, I knew Bob had something to do with this." She looks at Mike with a glare. "How long has it been since we were here last?"

"About a month, give or take a few days."

"Damn that Bob," Renee says. "He had the whole thing planned."

We step out of the restaurant and I say, "I've got to get back to work, Renee. What do you have in mind?"

She looks at me as she puts her riding gloves on. "This adventure has reached its conclusion. I only wish I remembered half of it."

I put my hand on her shoulder. "However much I do remember, I'm sure it's the best part."

Renee smiles, steps over to her bike, lifts her right leg over the seat, and sits. She turns to me. "I'd like to ride back to Twenty-Nine Palms together. I want to finish this journey with you."

After she slams her foot into her starter pedal and the engine comes to life, I get on. In five minutes we pull in to the bike shop.

"One of your coils has gone sour," the mechanic says while wiping his hands on a shop towel. "I would have contacted you, to get your okay to change it out, but I had no idea where you two were."

"How long will it take to replace?" I ask.

"Fifteen minutes or so."

"Let's do it. Do you have the part on hand?"

"Oh sure. Coils are about the only thing that goes bad on these Yamahas. They aren't as classy as that road machine you got out there." He nods toward Renee. "But one thing you can say for them is they're dependable."

Renee gives him a condescending smile, but says nothing. "The waiting room is through there." He points at a side door next to a blue Honda Goldwing so dusty it looks as though it hasn't been driven in a decade.

We walk into the little room with its two dilapidated love seats, fake walnut paneling, and the biker magazines spread on a plywood table with peeling laminate.

I sit on one of the love seats and pick up the latest Thunder Press, thumb through until I come to a pictorial about last autumn's Street Vibrations Reno run, and there, big as life, is Twig in the largest picture on the page. I turn the magazine to Renee. "This guy lives in Victorville. You know him?"

"Oh, sure; it's Twig."

I turn the magazine back to face me. "He's my ex from six or seven years ago."

"No kidding," Renee says. "He and his girlfriend are going to have a baby."

***

In the mail, I get bills, two magazines for Melinda, and the latest copy of Thunder Press. I carefully step around that dangerous third step and continue up to our apartment. "Hi. Honey; I'm home," I say in an Ozzy Nelson dorky voice, but Melinda doesn't answer. She's somewhere out walking in the world, I know, because this apartment isn't big enough to get lost in, and her car is parked in the driveway.

I don't give it much thought. She's always taking walks.

I sit on the couch and thumb through my latest Thunder Press, mostly looking at the pictures, especially young women standing in front of exotic machines not built to drive, but to win awards. Cool machines, but completely useless.

On page twenty, I open the fold-out page, and there I am, big as life, posing on my bike next to Stewart on his Fatboy. I remember that picture.

I feel a twinge of fame flutter inside of my chest, or was that my heart doing flip-flops from the shock of seeing myself in a national magazine?

I read the caption under the photo. "Twig and the ever-famous Stewart Chance of the One on One club, riding in tandem just minutes before the big explosion that changed the course of events at the Street Vibrations."

Look at that, they even mentioned the name of our club.

I'm sure Stew is home, so I call his house. "Hey, Stew, check out the latest Thunder Press."

"Stew's not here, Twig, but we're expecting him home any minute."

"Nick, is that you?"

Never one for many words, he says, "Yup."

"Hey, what happened to you this morning at my shop?"

After a long silence, he says, "Couldn't stick around, Twig; I had things to do."

"You okay, man?"

Another long silent moment. When he speaks, he

sounds emotional. "Having trouble adjusting to my new life is all."

"You mean without Carolyn?"

"No, Carolyn can go take a flying fucking leap, as far as I'm concerned. I quit smoking pot ten days ago, and my life looks a little raw at the moment."

"Hey, Nick, you need me to come by?"

He takes a breath. "You'd do that?"

"Nick, you're one of my men. We stick together, right?"

In a quick response, Nick says, "I got to go."

"Nick?" I scream before he hangs up.

"Yeah?"

"You coming to the meeting with the men and women tomorrow night?"

After another long silence, he says, "Been thinking about it."

Knowing Nick and how non-committal he is, thinking about it is probably as much as I can expect from him. I say, "Hope to see you there."

He hangs up without saying another word. The phone simply goes dead. That's Nick for you.

Melinda opens the door with a small bag of groceries.

I say, "hey, Honey, how you doing?" She glares at me, but doesn't speak. She steps past me and drops the groceries on the table so hard I hope no eggs are in the bag.

I stand from the couch and step toward the kitchen. "Something wrong?"

She's still silent, but picks each thing out of the bag and slams it into place; peanut butter, can of olives, French bread, sliced ham. I'm trying not to get in her way as she fills the room with anger.

Without any warning, she takes the entire carton of

eggs and throws it across the room at me.

I raise an arm. The carton hits my elbow, careens off, and twelve eggs find their own way, spreading in flight making a wide pattern on the sink, the wall behind the sink, the cabinet below, and every dish in the dish rack.

"What did you do that for?"

She takes three quick steps across the room and closes the gap between us. Her little fist rises from nowhere and slams my jaw like a sledge hammer.

I'm knocked back on the slippery mess. One leg spreads and puts me off balance. I sit hard on the floor. She closes in.

My arm pulls back. My face contorts. She slugs me again, this time in the chest. It feels like the bullet that hit me while I was back on the force. Kevlar saved me, but the impact knocked the wind out of me.

I swing, but a voice goes off in my head like the noon whistle that shrieks in town every day. "Go under the anger, Twig."

"What?" I scream and turn, thinking someone walked in the house.

"What's under the rage?"

When I recognize Bob's voice, my entire conversation happens inside without making a sound. "What do you mean?"

"Feel the anger, my man, then go under it to what you're really feeling."

"I'm really feeling pissed that she, once again, decides she has the right to cold-cock me, just because she can't control her anger."

"That's right, but there is another feeling under that indignation."

I realize Melinda is standing, arms at her side, face

slightly turned toward the ceiling.

"What feeling?" I ask.

"I can't tell you, dickhead. You got to find it for yourself."

"I'm angry."

"Yes," he says, "and?"

A few seconds go by before my mind searches for any other possible feeling I might have, but I find nothing. "I'm pissed, Bob, and that's all there is."

"Come on, you wimp, you can do better than that."

"Jesus, Bob, not you, too. Don't I have enough bullshit from this she-lion to have to take shit from you too?"

"Stop whining you sniveling twerp, and go under the anger."

My rage monster, having already been awakened by Melinda's unprovoked attack, leaps to the forefront, but there is no place for it to land. There is no jaw to slam, no gut to punch, no arm to break. It's just that damn Bob in my head.

"Come on out, you chicken-shit bastard," I scream, but Bob's voice in my head is silent.

After thirty seconds, Bob says, "What's under the rage, Twig."

"Nothing," I yell aloud. "Nothing!"

Melinda looks down from the ceiling, and my killer ape takes another leap in intensity. Thanks to Bob, I'm beyond control. I feel myself move in her direction, but that fucking voice goes off in my head again. "What's under the rage?"

I can't move. Bob has frozen my limbs, and I'm in some kind of invisible straight jacket.

"Go under the anger, Twig. Go under it now."

I feel like I'm wrapped in duct tape. Nothing works,

but I'm struggling to pull free. My rage meter goes off the scale, and I let out a long wolf-like howl that reverberates off the egg-splattered walls.

"Yeeeeooouh." My scream lasts forever. My level of frustration is at an all time high. I'm pushing against my invisible bindings, and yet I can do nothing but make unintelligible sounds.

In a split second, I burst into tears. I howl again as I drop to the floor, but this time the howling is broken with deep sobs.

"I'm hurt," I say aloud. "I'm hurt."

"My man," Bob says inside my head. "That's the feeling under the rage. That's the feeling you want to find when you're angry."

Melinda, who was standing looking at me as if I was some kind of bug to squash, suddenly drops her fighting stance, leaps across the space between us, and throws her arms around my neck.

My tears roll down my cheek hard. I howl and choke with grief at the same time. My body is wracked with the pain of every violation I ever felt. It started with my dad and his insistence that I stand up and fight like a man. The kids in my class, my older cousin who lived around the corner, the young men at school when I got bigger, my Sunday school teacher who constantly ridiculed me. They all line up and take their turn at the grief I feel and hold inside, and I've been doing it my entire life. I cry for my mom who died and left me. I cry tears for many things, as Melinda holds me and strokes my balding head.

After ten minutes, with a bunch of starts and stops, then a calm feeling, I purge my hurt and pain.

Melinda sits on the floor cradling me like a baby, but

it feels good. Her soft talk says nothing I understand, but it soothes, and I feel like falling asleep. I close my eyes and bask in the love of my woman, who just minutes before was a freight train bent on destruction.

"It's your job to go under the rage, Twig," Bob says inside my head.

"What?"

"If you can get into your grief, your woman will have no choice but to follow. It's up to you to shift before fists fly, before someone gets hurt."

"But it took so long to find my feelings."

"You can do it, my man. You'll get better each time it happens. You'll catch it quicker the more you do it."

I open my eyes for a second to see Melinda in her angelic face, looking at me, stroking my beard, kissing my forehead.

"Look at what you have created," Bob says. "Find your hurt, and she will respond in kind. She has no choice."

***

I don't know why I do these things, but once again, I lose control and slug him. I know maybe it's the extra hormones flowing in my body that have me on edge, but hitting the man I love so much is ridiculous. I was pissed that he hadn't made it home in time to go to the grocery store with me like he usually does, but it's no reason to get violent. One second I'm putting groceries away. The next second I'm lunging across the room and slamming my fist into his jaw. The guy doesn't deserve it, but I can't help myself. Lucky he's so big.

After I slip my surprise fist onto his jaw and see his rage flare, I'm ready for action. I've already spotted the rolling pin and toaster to use as equalizers, but something happens. A voice goes off in my head. "Melinda, stop it!"

"What?" I turn and look, hoping someone has come into the house to stop this insanity before Twig or I get hurt again. No one is in the apartment.

I look at Twig, but with his deep tone, he couldn't possibly have spoken. He sits on the floor with his face blank and completely unprotected. His fist is clenched, but the arm is relaxed.

"Don't do it," the voice goes off again, and this time I know it's inside of my head.

"Bob?"

"Yes, it's Bob, and what do you think you're doing?"

I don't answer, because there is no answer. I committed to myself that I would never use violence again, yet here I am again, not only violating my promise, but putting our baby at risk.

Bob is above me. I know I can't see him, but I look up and search the ceiling.

In a sudden shift, Twig, as big as he is, bursts into a child-like cry and screams, "I'm hurt." After a few seconds, as if to confirm his statement, he says it again. I look down and see my man burst into tears, drop his face into his hands, and I can't help myself. He looks weak and vulnerable. I have to protect him.

I drop to my knees and put my arms around him. I'm kissing his forehead and stroking his long, coarse hair. I've got him cradled in my arms as he goes into a blubbering, body-wracking sob like I've never seen before. The guy is a little boy once again, and it is so sweet I can't help myself; I start crying.

I'm in my protective mode, holding him close, creating a cocoon for him to feel safe. We sit on the floor for five minutes before I feel him flinch for the first time. His sobbing stops and he attempts to untangle himself from my hold around one shoulder and his neck. I can't wrap my arms around his whole body.

I feel him struggle to get free, and I don't understand. Why does he want to ruin this perfect moment?

"That's enough," he says. "I can't take any more."

"Any more what?" I unravel my arms and give him a last sensitive kiss on the forehead.

"Too much mothering," he says.

My anger flares once again.

Bob goes off inside my head, this time so loud I think my eardrums are blown from the volume. "Don't do it."

"What, Bob? I'm not doing anything."

"Don't you get violent with this man just because he's rejecting you. Talk about it with him, yell if you must, but you made a promise to yourself and that baby of yours."

I look at Twig, who is backing up, scooting on his butt until he's against the refrigerator. "Too much mothering," he says again.

"What does that mean?" I ask, trying my hardest to hold the swinging bitch at bay.

"I don't know what it means, but I don't like too much nurturing."

"For heaven's sake, Twig, I was just being intimate while you were so vulnerable."

He reaches for my hand. "Yes, but it wasn't an equal intimacy. I felt smothered. My mom used to do it; my aunts; hell, even my school teacher, Mrs. Bunters. None of them could keep their hands off me, and I hated it."

"But I'm not them. I'm your soon-to-be wife and the mother of our child." I pat my belly.

Twig gives me one of his puppy dog looks. "It's too

much mothering, and I felt violated back when I was a kid. I would have felt violated just now, if you hadn't stopped. I love you, Melinda, but I don't want to be mothered by you. It's just not right. I'm a man, not a little boy."

I look at him. I see that he's serious, but I still don't understand. Why could he possibly not want to be nurtured? I soak up all of the nurturing I can get. It's good for my soul. Why is it not good for him? Men, I'll never figure them out.

***

An hour after the mechanic says it'll only be fifteen minutes, he steps into the waiting room and looks at Kat. "Your bike's ready."

She takes care of the bill, and in ten minutes we are riding out the little side road, then onto Highway 10 and west across the Colorado River and the long flat ride sixty miles toward Palm Springs. The desert is hot and dry by the time we turn off the freeway and climb the five miles into the hills to enter Joshua Tree National Park. When we pull next to the kiosk, an older woman dressed in her khaki ranger uniform looks out of her little window as Kat and I turn off our engines. "Well, I'll be damned. We weren't sure you were coming back."

"I love you, too," Kat says.

"No, I'm serious, we even have a pool going."

Still sitting on her ticking bike, Kat says, "You guys'll start a pool over anything."

The woman smiles and extends her hand through the window toward me. "I'm Mary."

I'm closest to the kiosk, so I reach for her hand and we shake. "Renee."

"We've heard a lot about you."

Kat gives her a slight glare. "How could you have heard about Renee?"

"When you didn't show up, Frank got worried. You know worry-wart Frank."

Kat turns to me. "Our supervisor."

"Oh."

"Anyhow, he would've sent out the National Guard if he could, but instead, he spent a day or two making a bunch of calls. Once he got a line on you," she nods toward me, "he kept the staff updated at every coffee break."

Kat laughs. "God, he's a pain, but it's sweet that he was worried."

One of those huge RV's pulls in behind our bikes. Mary steps out of the kiosk and collects the fee, then delivers the map and receipt. The RV pulls around us and disappears up the little two lane.

Mary says, "Where'd you go?"

"Spent most of our time in the desert north of Lake Alamo."

Mary crinkles her wrinkled face. "Never heard of it."

"About eighty miles northeast of Blythe."

"What the hell is out there?"

I know Kat will never be able to explain what we went through, mostly because neither of us understands what happened. I look at her to see what she's going to say.

"Desert," she says. "Lots of beautiful desert."

Mary looks at her. "You mean to tell me that you rode your bikes out into the desert?"

Kat smiles. "We walked."

The woman throws up her hands and shrugs.

Kat asks. "Is Frank in today?"

"Sure. When isn't he?"

Back to Blythe

Kat turns to me. "I want to stop and see him at the other end of the park."

"I'll tell him you're coming," Mary says.

Kat turns to her. "No, let me surprise him."

"Whatever."

We start our bikes and pull up the hill into a narrow canyon. It's more beautiful than I remember from last month.

We drive very slowly along the forty miles to the far end of the park. Kat points out landmarks and yells stories to me about kooky tourists and Joshua Tree folklore the whole way. We reach the far end and stop to meet Sammy, a pimple-faced kid who can't be eighteen. He's busy with incoming traffic, so we drive out of the pristine beauty of the park and into the starkness of a desert that's seen poachers, dune-buggy riders, dirt bikes, dead tires, McDonald's wrappers and broken beer bottles. The contrast is hard to get used to.

When we reach the bottom of the hill, Kat pulls into the visitor's center, and we park in an almost empty lot.

I stay with the bikes as she goes into the building. I really miss Stew and the kids. I'm ready to go home.

In fifteen minutes, while I walk the grounds and watch all of the different kinds of birds and desert rodents scampering around begging off the tourists, Kat returns and gets on her bike.

"You still got a job?"

She smiles. "Oh sure, Frank took me under his wing a few years ago. I'm the daughter he never had. He wouldn't dump me for being late back to work. He did dock my pay, though." She has tears in her eyes. "I love this job."

We ride the quarter mile to Highway 62 and turn left into Twentynine Palms, though I've never seen even one palm tree along the route. We roll through town, then sixteen miles to the town of Joshua Tree. A few miles north, we turn left onto a small side road, then up the hill. Kat pulls into the gravel driveway of an older cinder block flattop house. We park and turn off our engines.

The sound of the highway is in the far distance. A crow caws overhead as Kat leads me up the walkway to the turquoise front door. She gets out her key and unlocks the door, then leads me inside the coolness of the concrete-walled building.

"Have a seat," she says. "I'm going to the bathroom."

I sit on a small, leather couch that is so comfortable, my vibrating legs and feet immediately relax. I lean on the high back and rest my neck for the first time today. I look at a large painting of a sunset melting into the ocean.

"You like my couch?" she asks.

"It's great," I say. "Where did you get it?"

"Thrift store in Palm Springs. The story is that it was in Frank Sinatra's house, but who knows for sure? Paid a hundred bucks for it."

I point at the big canvas over the mantel. "Great painting."

She turns to it and puts one hand on her hip. "It's the only thing I got out of my divorce from Tommy. I stole it from him just before I moved out here."

"Where did you move from?"

"Florida."

"No kidding? Kind of a change of climates, don't you think?"

She turns back to me. "Most of us are from somewhere else where the climate is different. What about you?"

"Seattle."

"See what I mean? Talk about different climates."

I smile and stand. "Hey, as long as you're settled here, I'm heading back to Victorville."

She puts both hands up in a stop motion. "Let me check my messages and get some different clothes, and I'll come with you. I'd love to meet your family, and I want to be a part of your men's and women's group tonight. You did say it was Thursday nights?"

I'd completely forgotten about the meeting. "You really want to come?"

She nods.

"How about I call Stewart and see where they're meeting?"

She turns to her left and points at the phone on the bar between the kitchen and living room. I step over to an old-style dial phone and pick up the receiver, then turn the dial to slowly enter Stew's work number. "Hello, Sylvia," I say to his secretary. "Is Stewart around?"

When she transfers me to his line, I say, "Stew, how are you doing?"

After he gets over his shock at hearing my voice, he gives me the standard he's okay, then I ask about the group.

I hang up and I look at Kat. "You sure you want to be part of tonight's group? Maybe another week would be better."

"Why?" she asks.

"Nick and Carolyn are going to be squaring off tonight. The sparks might fly."

Kat smiles. "I deal with someone else's problems tonight or I deal with breaking up with my guy. Either way, I got drama to deal with. I'd rather make it your drama. It'll be much more interesting."

"What about work?"

"Frank told me to start on Saturday. I have to work weekends for a while, probably as some kind of penance."

I look over her shoulder at the clock on the wall of the kitchen. "It's three o'clock. If we get on the road now, we can be back in time for dinner. The meeting's at seven."

Kat steps to the answering machine. "Let me check my thirty-seven messages, then we can leave."

I sit back on the couch and lose myself in the painting. The clouds are peachy. The sky behind them is turquoise. The colors reflect through large breakers slamming against rocky crags.

By the time I return from my oceanic journey, Kat has deleted more than half the messages, most from her soon-to-be ex-boyfriend and her boss, Frank. Two messages were from her mother, and one from her brother in Florida.

When she's finished, she has written down three messages and dumped the rest. "Okay," she says as she disappears down the hall. "Let me grab a change of clothes for tonight, and we'll be off."

She returns with an armful of clothes and a pair of pumps. "Let's get out of here."

Once she has her stuff stowed, we're off. We turn left onto 247, crank our bikes up to seventy and float along the open two-lane, fighting gusts of wind from trucks coming the opposite way.

Forty miles later, I turn left and up our long windy road toward Big Bear Mountain. It feels good to be close to home.

Five miles into the hills, we turn onto my dirt road, and park in the driveway.

Mel is the first to greet me. "Hey, Mom, how was

the trip?" He speaks with his standard unenthusiastic teenager tone.

"Amazing," I say and scoop him into my arms while still sitting on the bike. I kiss him on the cheek and ask, "How have you been?"

Once he extricates himself from my grip, he rubs the place where I kissed him like it was poison, then says his normal one-word response, "Okay."

I point at Kat. "This is Katherine. Kat, my son, Mel."

"Pleased to meet you," she says while getting off the bike.

I dismount and we walk toward the big round front doors. "Where's your sister?"

"Oh, I don't know, some kind of after-school thing."

We step into the house, and I look at the clock in the kitchen. "It's only five," I say. "We made some good time. Hey, Kat, you want something to drink?" As I open the fridge, Nick Brown steps into the room. "Nick, what the hell are you doing here?"

He leans against the wall separating the kitchen from the dining room. "Couldn't stay away."

"Kat, Nick," I say. "She and I rode together this last month."

When I look at Kat, she stands with a nervous smile, holds out her hand, and takes three tentative steps toward him. He meets her in the middle of the kitchen.

"Pleased to meet you. . . Nick." She says the words with an awkward pause before speaking his name.

Nick mumbles something, but I don't hear what it is. I look at him, then at her, and I see it. There's an attraction.

They shake and retreat to their original positions. Nick doesn't lean against the wall, but stands in an awkward pose, completely out of character, hands stuffed in his two Levi's front pockets.

"Want some juice, Nick?" I reach for the container.

"No, thanks," he says. I've never seen him be so formal, but I don't say anything, because Kat is also twisting and turning in her corner. She finally pulls out a barstool and sits.

"Mel, how about you?"

"I'm going back to my computer game." He turns and disappears.

I pour two glasses and hand one to Kat. Instead of gulping it like I'd seen her do so many times, she takes some kind of ridiculous ladylike sip and puts the glass on the counter, then, I can't believe it, she blushes.

"Where'd you go?" Nick asks.

I down half of my glass, step over to the second barstool and sit. "Most of the time we spent out in the desert about eighty miles northeast of Blythe close to a place called Lake Alamo."

"I know that lake. It's out in the middle of nowhere."

"You got that right," I say.

"What did you do out there?"

"A guy named Billy Black," Kat chimes in.

There is a moment of silence, then Nick says, "Billy Black, the Viet Nam Vet ?"

"You know him?" I ask as I lift my glass and take another drink.

Nick steps over and sits on the third barstool on the far side of the bar. "I knew him. He's supposed to be dead; might be five years now."

"That's the one," I say. "We found out after he led us out into the desert to meet Cherry and Ed."

"Holy shit, you mean you rode with Billy?"

"That we did," I say, waiting for Kat to add something,

but, unlike her usual chatter, she doesn't.

At that second, a horn honks. I step over to the window as the UPS driver stops the truck at the front walk. I hurry down the hall and open the door as a small dark-haired woman jumps from the back of her van. She smiles.

"What happened to Jason?" I ask.

"Vacation." She hands the electronic pad to me. "Sign there." She points at the small rectangle at the top of the screen.

I pick up the stylus and scribble my name, then hand it back. The woman sets the pad on the bumper and jumps into the truck. "Hang on a second," she says from inside the van. "This one's pretty big."

She wrestles a flat cardboard box out the doors, jumps to the ground, and maneuvers it to the gravel.

She scans the tracking label, then hands the box over. It stands a few inches taller than me and is wider than I can reach, but since it's only three or four inches thick and weighs almost nothing, I get a grip on one edge and slide it through the front doors, across the floor, and into the kitchen where Nick and Kat sit in awkward silence.

"What the hell?" Nick asks.

There is no return address, so I have no idea who it came from.

I lay it flat on the floor, get a serrated steak knife from the kitchen drawer, and slice the only end of the box that has tape instead of heavy duty staples.

Nick and Kat stand behind me, looking over my shoulder while I pull the first cardboard flap back and unfurl the second flap. I look inside and see a handmade picture frame. The wood is rough, like it's made of old barn siding. I slip the frame out, but it catches on something inside of the box before I can see what is inside. I tug, but the contents won't budge. Nick kneels and grabs the far end of the cardboard box. He gives the box a hard pull, but the contents won't move.

Kat gets on her knees and grabs the far end of the frame with me and wiggles it three times before something inside breaks free and the frame slides out to reveal a canvas, but the thing is facing the floor. Once the canvas is halfway out, I read some scribbled message in heavy felt-tip pen, in a long scrawl, one line over the top of the other in the middle of the huge canvas.

"This one is for you,
though I don't know who,
nor do I have a clue
of what I can do."

There is no signature, no hint as to who wrote it or when.

Nick tugs on the cardboard, and the canvas slides out until it's free of the box. I study the inscription, but still have no idea who might have sent this.

"Turn it over, God damn it," Nick says. "The suspense is driving me crazy."

I grab one corner and lift the huge painting up on end and turn it. I have yet to see it, but Nick and Kat, as a single unit, gasp and turn pale. Kat sits on the floor putting her arms out to support her.

I look from her to Nick, then finish flipping the painting flat on the floor and let out my own gasp.

Seventeen

Desert Winds

"Unless he gets mad, the guy's not emotionally available," I say to Donna after she tells me that Nick is in town. "Why would I want to go back with him?"

"I know what you mean, Carolyn," Donna says. "Tazz's response to everything is anger. I don't get it; don't these guys have any other emotion?"

We turn left and walk across Main Street with its full load of traffic, then to the railroad tracks and north toward Barstow, as we have done every day for the past week and a half.

On the far side of the tracks a small path leads parallel with the rails. We walk fast while breathing hard, and I say, "The second he gets mad, I freeze. I can't help myself; I turn into an eight-year-old when my dad came unglued on my mother and beat her."

Donna looks at me. "No kidding."

"He only did it once, but his anger permeated the house for as far back as I can remember. What is it with men? Every man I know is a ball of rage."

We turn away from the tracks, down a blackberry-
infested trail toward the river. The trail is so narrow, we
have to go single file through ten-foot-high vines. Donna
huffs. "Not all guys."

"You tell me one."

She stops at the top of a small bluff overlooking the
trickle of water and turns to me. "Stewart Chance."

"What are you talking about? He's the worst kind."

"What do you mean?"

"Stewart can't show his anger, so all of his rage is
below the surface. He looks great on the outside, but
don't turn your back on him, because he'll stab you and
not even know he did it."

Donna turns, takes her first step down the ten-foot
drop to the meandering creek. She speaks as she slides
on the loose dirt. "Okay, maybe you've got a point.
Although he's much better these days, Stew used to be
the one man I never trusted, and I never could figure out
why. It was like he had some trick up his sleeve waiting
for me to relax."

When we reach the small stream, what is left of last
winters rains, what rains there were, we turn south
toward town and walk along the center of the almost-
dry drainage. We leap over the winding puddle of water
that snakes its way down the center.

I turn to Donna, now that we're walking shoulder to
shoulder again. "So, all of them are angry, and if that's
the case, I want nothing to do with men."

"I don't know," Donna says as we pick up speed and
almost break into a run. "Tazz is angry, but his men's
group siphons off some of that rage. When he comes
back from his Thursday night stuff, he's always Mister
Mellow. I didn't really like it at first, but pretty quickly

I saw the advantage in having him do his wild-man-in-the-woods thing with his buddies."

"You know, maybe that's what happened. Nick and I moved to San Francisco, and he stopped going to his meetings. He didn't get angry, because he doesn't do anger overtly, but instead, he smoked dope like a steam engine. God, when he got into that stuff, he disappeared. No one was home."

Donna leaps over a three-foot patch of water and I follow. It's an easy leap, because we're walking fast, but I catch the heel of my right foot in the water and splash my following foot, soaking my sock. I pay no attention as we keep moving. I'd missed and splashed in this particular patch of open water a few times in the last week, but I never soaked my sock.

"That must have been hard." Donna's breathing is fast and deep.

"It's why I left and came back here. There was no one around, and I need someone to talk to."

"I know what you mean."

We pace along in silence for a hundred yards and cross under the huge steel railroad trestle, then under the highway with its steady flow of traffic.

She turns to me. "Stew says Nick quit smoking."

We stop at the bottom of the highway overpass. Before we climb the concrete wall, I look at Donna. "I'll believe that when I see it. I wasn't with Nick for long, but he always had a damn joint in his hand."

"Twig says he's different without the pot. Maybe you want to come to the men's and women's meeting tonight and see for yourself. He's supposed to be there."

"I don't think so. I'm not ready to see him. He's nothing but trouble."

319

Donna laughs and puts one hand on my shoulder. "Girl, they're all nothing but trouble."

I smile, but inside a tourniquet twists my stomach. "They can't all be trouble. There must be one or two out there."

Donna looks me in the eyes as she puts her other hand on my shoulder. "I think they're all trouble. The question is, are they worth it? I got a man that's more pain in the ass than I can believe at times, but is he worth it? I say without hesitation that he is worth it."

I look at my soaked sock wicking down my ankle to my heel. "Is a guy like Nick worth it?"

Donna takes a deep breath. Her hands slide down my arms, and she takes my hands. "Carolyn, only you know if he's worth it or not. Only you can tell if he makes you happy, if being with him satisfies your soul. Only you know what kind of lover he is and if that love sustains you throughout the day. Only you can possibly know if he has the capacity to love you."

I break down and cry. My tears flow down my cheeks as Donna takes me in her arms and holds me close. "I don't know if he's worth it or not."

Donna, while patting my back and holding me close, says, "I don't think you two have been together long enough to know. If you want to find out, you've got to spend more time together."

We stand with traffic rushing overhead, a train whistles to the north coming our way, the gurgling water dribbles over a two-foot drop in the concrete. Donna holds me until my tears dry and I'm left with a few sniffles. She releases me and touches her index finger under my chin, then lifts my head to look directly into her hazel eyes. "If you think this guy might be worth it, and I think he is, you've got to give this relationship a chance."

"I don't know," I say, wiping my nose on my blue sweatshirt. "I don't know."

Donna points up the embankment, and I nod. She takes a step back, runs at the concrete wall and scrambles up its rough surface. I take two steps back and race up after her. As I get almost to the top, I run out of momentum, and Donna grabs my hand, helping me the last few steps to the side of the bridge. I look under the bridge, as I have for the last ten days in a row. Two people have taken up residence. They nod, and we return the gesture, then we climb the five or six steps to the highway. A train's whistle sounds, and I look toward Barstow and see the train chugging its way along the section of rail we crossed earlier.

Donna and I walk fast along the highway for a few hundred yards, then turn left into a quiet older neighborhood, with its huge elm trees and small front lawns, each with a waist-high wire fence and mail box at the gate. It's the same route we've taken the entire ten days. It might be the same route Donna has taken for years.

"I'm too nice," I say once far enough away from traffic that I can talk without yelling. "I've been told I need to find my anger, but it's not that easy."

"I know what you mean," Donna says. "I can only find mine during those certain days of the month."

I stop walking. Donna stops and looks at me as I say, "Even during those days, I can't find mine. I can feel it, but it doesn't come to the surface."

The neighborhood golden retriever, who has greeted us every day, trots up. Donna scratches behind its ears.

"I held it in for years before I met Tazz, but he brings it out in me. I don't know, though I love him dearly, he just naturally pisses me off almost every minute of the day."

"Really?" I stroke the dog's fur.

"I think it's a good thing to be bothered by your mate. I mean for God's sakes, he's a man, and don't men just piss you off?"

"Piss me off, no, but they are so weird they do irritate me a little."

Donna starts walking again, and I fall into place next to her. "Trust me, Carolyn, as you get older, they will piss you off."

I giggle. "Maybe everyone doesn't react the same way you do."

Donna shrugs. "Maybe, but every woman I've talked to that's gotten to my age feels the same way."

"No kidding?"

Donna doesn't answer, and we walk along in silence. We reach the top of the small hill, and turn down Randal Street on the last leg of our loop.

After walking for a minute in silence, I say, "If men feel they have the right to get angry whenever they want, we should be able to, also."

"Men don't have the right to get angry, but since they do, I agree."

"It's too scary."

"To get angry?"

"Yes. I freeze up thinking about it." I tuck my shirt in as if to keep out a winter breeze.

"I just want to gently work out issues with the man I live with. It's all I ask. I'd make a deal; I won't get angry if he doesn't get angry."

Donna tucks in her sweatshirt and looks around.

"The whole thing doesn't work that way."

"What do you mean?"

"If a man holds his anger in, something's gotta blow sometime."

"What are you talking about? I can hold my anger in, why can't he?"

"Because women never get angry as a first response. It's easy for us, because we want to be nice."

"Isn't nice a good thing?"

"Yes, when things are going well, but as a steady diet, we can't be nice all of the time."

"Why not?"

"Because two people, especially a man and woman who are trying to be equal, can't agree on everything for long. When a disagreement comes up, either they deal with it or they stuff the feeling and hide out from the other person. Sometimes hiding out is the only safe alternative, but most of the time hiding is out of convenience."

"What do you mean?"

"I catch myself using the 'it's not worth it,' statement, but even the littlest thing that keeps Tazz and me equal is worth staying current with one another."

A breeze tosses dried leaves from the elm trees.

I tuck my arms around my waist and reduce my eyes to little slits. "A dust storm is coming," I yell.

Donna turns to me, eyes closed. "Let's run for it."

Down the middle of the street, with a wild desert wind in our face, we go into a full run for the last half block, then down the small hill to Tazz and Donna's. The moment we turn, with the wind on our left, its intensity triples. Garbage can lids and broken branches bounce along the ground slamming cars. The wind pushes Donna and me to our hands and knees.

I want to call out. Although she's only three paces away, I know my voice will never be heard. I'm almost lying on the pavement. Desert rubble is stabbing and sticking to me.

I balance, then turn and grab her sleeve. I leap to my feet, pull her along, and crab walk across the street behind a beat-up yellow pickup truck.

The truck adds protection as the howling wind whips the wires overhead.

"You okay?" I yell while hunched behind the truck.

Donna sits on a small platform behind the passenger door and nods vigorously. "That was a surprise."

"All the big ones are."

She reaches up and opens the door like she expects it to be unlocked. I follow her into the truck and when the door closes, the air settles, though the truck is being buffeted like it's rolling down a pothole-infested country road.

"Holy smoke," Donna says. "This one's the mother of all wind storms. I hope no one gets hurt."

The driver's door opens and a man with a cowboy hat held close to his head with one hand looks at us, motions for Donna to scoot over, and leaps into the truck, though she's only begun to move over.

When the door closes, he speaks in a jovial Texas drawl. "What the hell are you two doing here?"

I put up one finger, but never get to say a thing before he tells his first joke, which makes me laugh.

After his third joke, and they're getting more stupid as we go, he starts the engine. "Where you ladies going?"

"End of the street," Donna says, barely able to get the words in before the next joke leaps out of his mouth.

He shifts into first gear, lets the clutch out and the old junker chatters as it picks up speed. At fifteen miles an hour and it seems like fifty with the wind and the condition of the truck, the shudder lessens and the vehicle tracks down the street, even with the crosswind.

"Right there," Donna says, pointing at her house, three in from the corner.

As our new companion steps on the brakes and they squeal all the way to a stop, he launches into a fifth joke, or is it a sixth? I've lost count.

I don't dare open the door until he's finished because we'll be blown to smithereens. So, we sit through the wee Irishman and his three-inch-wide-grand-piano-in-the-bar joke. I've heard it a dozen times, but his version is excruciatingly long.

Finally, he hits the punch line, and before he can say another word, I open the door and yank Donna's sweatshirt. When she is out, I look back in at the sad-faced man and his stupid jokes. "Thanks for the ride, Mister."

"You're welcome."

The door slams, and we're running for the house. I leap the two concrete steps onto the porch behind Donna.

Once the door is closed behind us and the air settles, we start the long process of getting cactus spurs off before going into the house.

Donna picks a tuft of debris from my hair. "That guy was too much."

"He seemed really lonely."

"Repressed anger," Donna says.

"What?"

"Think about it. The guy's a ball of nervous reactions. All he can do to let some of the steam out by telling jokes. If you really get him, then it's easy to see the rage under the surface. They've all got it. He simply isn't able to conceal it as much as someone like Stewart."

I lean forward, look at the floor, and shake my head to release any clinging particles. While Donna dusts my back, I say, "I guess I don't get this rage thing."

"Neither do I, but at least we're asking questions."

I dust off her shoulders and the back of her legs, then we go into the house. The neighbor girl, Miriam, sits with Donna's two boys mesmerized by television. Not one of the three looks up until the commercial, then Miriam asks, "You have a good walk?"

Donna digs into her pocket, pulls out a five, and hands it to her. "Great walk, except for the wind. We had to get a ride the last half block."

Miriam looks out the plate glass window. "It's pretty windy out there."

I sit in the chair at the dining room table. "It'd be nice if some rain came with that wind to settle the dust a little."

Miriam pockets the five and steps toward the door.

Donna says, "Maybe I better give you a ride home. That wind is nothing to mess with."

"That's okay. I brought a bandana. I'll tie my hair and make a run for it."

"You sure?"

"Thanks, anyhow; it's only three houses. I've got to go so I can get back before the commercial is over." She pulls on her bandana, buttons up her leather coat, opens the door, nods at Donna, then disappears into the howling gale.

Donna and I step to the window and watch as she fights the wind across the street and down two houses, then disappears through the front door.

Donna turns to me. "Want a cup of coffee?"

I nod, and we walk past her two boys who are

completely engrossed in a Chevy truck commercial.

In the kitchen, Donna puts on a kettle and digs the coffee beans from the freezer.

I sit at the table and pick up the salt shaker. While studying it for the hundredth time, I ask, "If they all have rage, what can we do to protect ourselves from them?"

"If I only knew the answer to that question. All I know is when Tazz goes into a fit, I can't get away from him fast enough. The guy's a walking time bomb."

***

Melinda and I are on our way to Stewart and Renee's for our weekly men's and women's meeting. The sun has set, but the sky is still desert blue. Cars have yet to turn on their headlights. Continuing the conversation we had at home before we left, I say, "I just wish there was a way for me to get angry and get support from you rather than have you match my intensity."

"Soon as you get pissed, it sparks my anger. I don't put up with any man getting angry around me. That's what your men's group is for."

"I guess it is." I shift the car into high gear, and we slowly plug our way up to fifty-five miles an hour. This certainly ain't no Harley. "But you're always complaining about me holding back my emotions."

She turns to me with the look of a cat who swallowed a canary. "Sure, Twig, but what does that have to do with this?"

"I'm not sure, but isn't anger an emotion?"

"It is, but it's not appropriate. Your anger is too big for me to handle."

I look at her as we come to the only stop sign along

the road. I look both ways and make a slow roll through the stop, shift back into first, then tromp on the gas and build speed. I shift into second and look at her. "You handle my anger just fine."

"I guess, Twig, but you know what I mean."

"I don't know what you mean."

She wiggles sideways in her safety belt and looks at my face. "It's just the way I respond to that particular situation. Some women cower, some get even, some call the cops, and some simply leave, but we all are frightened to death of male anger."

She nails it. Georgina disappeared in her own way. Katherine left after the first episode, and I only raised my voice. I think back at all of the women who've experienced my anger and realize that they all disappeared in some way or another. Even Melinda disappears by matching my rage, then bettering me. It's her way of protecting herself.

I slow, click on my turn signal, then make a right toward Big Bear and Stew's house. I look at her. "What if we need to express our anger, too, and we need to do it in a safe place where no one will get hurt."

"Who's we?"

I look at her as we begin the long pull up the hill. "We men, of course."

She smiles. "I wasn't sure if you were talking about you and me."

"Men." I say with an irritated snap.

"Hey, pal, you don't have to get pissy with me."

I take a deep breath, let it out, and say in a calmer tone, "Why is it that I have to always be the one who must calm any situation down by becoming friendly? Why do you always have to match me?"

She sits quiet for a moment as I take the first in many turns to get up the hill. I downshift into third, and the little engine picks up speed.

She speaks with an air of finality. "I always thought it was you who was matching me."

Once I'm through the turn, I look at her. "Come on Melinda, I know you really don't believe that."

She takes a deep breath and lets it out. "I not only believe it, but you just proved it."

I can see that we're at the threshold of another argument and with my stubborn woman, the only way we are going to nip this one in the bud is for me to shut up, so I do.

We drive in silence for five minutes until she says, "I didn't match you there."

"I can't believe it, Melinda; you matched me perfectly. I was the one who had to go silent, and you matched my silence."

"I was the one who broke the silence."

"Okay, I'll give you that one, but it still doesn't change the fact that I was the one who had to go silent first before the discussion got out of hand."

We spend the next ten minutes, all the way up to Stew's driveway, discussing who went silent first to disarm the situation. Along Stew's gravel road, a dirt bike blasts past us. I recognize Stew's boy on the bike with a big grin. I pull into the driveway and see Nick standing on the front porch as Melinda and I leap headlong into a full-blown argument. I give him a nod. He smiles, shakes his head, turns away, and walks in the house.

She's yelling at me, and I'm trying my hardest to slow the drama by not responding. She comes at me like a rapid-fire pistol, and all I can do is dodge the bullets.

"You bastard, you got me all fired up, and now you get to sit back with that stupid-assed smirk on your face and point your finger at me."

I don't say a word, because I know that even one syllable will worsen the situation, and besides, I'll never complete my statement anyhow. As usual, she'll cut me off before I finish my thought.

Finally, out of frustration, I reach to the little cubby above a radio that hasn't worked since I met Melinda and grab my reading glasses. I lift them between us and say, "This is the talking stick. You can use it first if you want." I set the glasses down on the emergency brake.

She snatches them up and points them at me. "You fucking bastard, you. . ."

I blur my eyes, and though I'm looking at her, I close my hearing to letting in one word in ten as she rants for almost ten minutes. I know, because I glance at the clock throughout the ordeal. As Bob told me, I'm supposed to listen for the emotion, but all I hear is her anger.

When she finally says all that she has to say, leaping upon and expanding her base of subjects to at least ten, she calms and sets the glasses back on the emergency brake handle.

I pick up the glasses quickly before she can think of another dozen issues to bombard me with. I used to try to write down all of her issues so I could, in my very male systematic, logical manner, answer each of her concerns and try to fix them, but I've learned that she doesn't want me to fix anything. She only wants me to listen. So, I listen. I only wish she'd do the same for me.

When I speak, Bob is right, my issue has nothing to do with what she said.

"The reason why we men think out our issues and

don't share them openly as they come up is because all of our lives we've been shamed into believing that what we feel is inappropriate and wrong. If we think them out first, we can come up with a package that looks to us like there are no holes. The problem is that we reach these conclusions by thinking about them instead of feeling. If we are dealing with other men, no problem, but in dealing with women, whatever I say is linear and inappropriate, either way."

I put the talking stick down, because I said exactly what I had to say. I don't need to say any more.

Eighteen

The Painting

I turn the canvas from its back with the short poem written directly on the cloth, to the front, with the dark scene of the Vietnam war zone. The skyline is dotted with palms backlit by the peach color of dusk. In the foreground three men stand sentinel on the forward deck of a gunship, each with an expression of awe. Of all the paintings that Billy Black showed us that balmy afternoon on his houseboat, though I never said a word, this was my favorite.

Katherine points at the lower right corner of the painting. With a hoarse whisper, she says, "It's Billy Black." Below the scrawled signature, in bold contrast to the dark jungle flora, is the date 1979.

"Yes, I know," I say as I stand the painting against the fireplace, take a deep breath and step back to admire it.

"How did he get it here?"

I shrug as I back up to my barstool and sit.

"That bastard," Nick's face is dark with a scowl.

I turn to him. "What do you mean, Nick?"

He shakes his head and repeats his "bastard" statement so quiet that I feel like a bomb is about to go off. "Nick, are you okay?" I reach out and touch his forearm. The moment I make contact, he jiggles his arm as if to shake off a mosquito. "Don't touch me," he yells.

I pull back and look at his enraged face. He's about to blow.

"Nick," I say, but he's nowhere around mentally.

Katherine retreats a step or two as his face goes a shade darker and his breathing stops altogether.

"That fucking bastard," Nick says as he paces the room; three steps out and three back toward me. With each step, his anger rises.

I know I'll have to talk him down before he blows. I've never seen Nick like this. He's usually so mellow.

I don't know what to do. He's certainly no Milquetoast like Stewart. This guy has always looked dangerous, like if he goes over the edge, he might break everything in the house before he comes around.

His color darkens more, and I take a step back. I'm not about to get in the middle of whatever he's going through and become another domestic violence statistic.

His focus is on the painting, and I'm afraid he's going to destroy it before this is over.

Of all things that could happen, Kat moves forward, grabs him by one arm, and spins him around to face her. "Nick," she yells, but he is not in this room. His muttering is of a drooling monster unaware of his surroundings, unwilling to look at what is about to happen.

Nick's back is to me, so I sprint from the room and do the only thing I know to do to disarm the situation. In the saddlebags that I brought with me to clean out later, I grab a small canister of pepper spray.

The Painting

With it hidden in my hand, I run back into the room to protect Kat if needed. I won't use it unless I have to.

"Nick?" Kat says to his face, but gets no response.

I have the can ready, with my finger on the button.

"Nick." Kat speaks louder. She grabs both his arms and shakes him.

Something in him clicks his body into action. He spins back toward the canvas. I lift the can of spray. If he takes one step toward the painting, I'm giving it to him.

He's about to attack the canvas. I aim the can. Kat grabs his shirt and spins him around. She throws him off balance. She is only an inch taller than my own five-foot frame, but I watch in awe as she screams. She uses a tone I have never heard come from a woman as she lunges for the glass of water on the bar. With a sweep of her hand, she empties the contents of the glass in Nick's face. He stumbles across the room and falls on the slick hardwood floor. I have my can of spray pointed at his face. Kat takes a kung-fu stance. He looks at both of us. The old Nick, the one I know, mister mellow, has returned. He puts his hand up to his face and wipes his eyes. "What did you do that for?"

Kat moves from her stance, opens both arms and shrugs, but doesn't speak.

His eyes are glazed. "I was okay, why did you do that?"

I drop my pepper spray arm to my side, hiding the can behind my right thigh.

Nick sits up, still rubbing his face. "I wasn't going to do anything."

Kat relaxes. "It looked like you were."

Nick turns to me. "You know me, Renee. I wasn't going to do anything."

"I never saw you like that, Nick."

He looks at me with a hurt expression. "I was pissed because that fucking Billy Black promised to sell that painting to me."

"What?" I ask.

"I knew him the last year before he died, and he told me the painting was mine once he was ready to let it go, but he died, and I always assumed that one of his relatives got it. I tried to hunt it down, but no one knew where it had gone. Hell, that was five years ago. After a year or so, I finally gave up." Nick gets to his feet and points at the canvas. "Here it is in your house."

"You wanted to buy this painting from Billy?" I ask. "It doesn't seem like you. I mean, hell, Nick, where would you put it? Your living situations were always so meager and temporary."

"I don't know where, all I know is I wanted this painting, and now that fucking traitor Billy Black has given it to you."

Although he is no longer in his raving maniac mode, I still don't trust him. I hold the spray ready for whatever he might do.

He gets a hurt look on his face. "I was just pissed. I wasn't going to do anything."

I shift positions. "Your being pissed looked pretty dangerous to me."

"It was pissed is all." Nick walks past Kat and me, out the sliding glass door, down the stairs to the lower deck. He leans against the rail, looking out on the desert.

I turn to Kat and whisper, "How did you know water would bring him out of it?"

She smiles. "My ex was a pot smoker. When he quit, he went into violent moods. There were only two things that would bring him out of it; a glass of water or sex. Although I'd have sex with Nick at the drop of a hat, I didn't think it was appropriate, for our first time, to be rolling around on your floor, especially with you watching."

I snicker. "Good call, but how did you know that he wasn't going to come unglued on you?"

"I didn't, but I figured that water was going to be much less harmful than your pepper spray. I want Nick in one piece tonight, because if he's willing, I'm jumping his bones."

"No kidding?"

She smiles. "Hell, if we've been gone over a month, then I'm horny as hell, and he looks like male pate' to me."

"He's chasing his ex-girlfriend," I say.

"All the better. If she dumps him tonight for good, he'll be more than willing."

"We'll have to wait and see."

She walks over to the sink and grabs a paper towel. "I'll clean up the water before someone slips on it."

***

"You have to understand, Donna," Tazz says as he drives us toward Stewart's. "Working out issues with you is not my favorite method of building intimacy."

"But look what happens after we work it out."

"What happens? All I feel is harassed, and you think we're closer."

"We are closer," Donna says as Tazz pulls away from the last stoplight in town and picks up speed.

I'm sitting in the back and thinking how Nick never engaged me in that kind of conflict even once. He always retreated into his smoke and disappeared into making pottery. At least Donna and Tazz have some contact.

Tazz shifts into high gear. "If your way of building intimacy is to work through conflict and I feel harassed by it, then I'm forever preparing myself for some kind of fight with you. If I'm constantly preparing, I never let down and relax around you."

Donna glares at him. "That is so much bullshit, even I can't believe you're saying it."

A big truck passes us going the other way, and its wind tosses the car around like an autumn leaf. Tazz fights the steering. "It's true, Donna. Lately, I've been feeling it more and more. I almost never let my guard down around you. I never know when you're going to come at me."

"Tazz, you're so full of it."

He turns to her, ignoring the fact that I'm also in the car, but in the few weeks that I've been living at their house, they go at it a lot, not caring who is around.

"It's true. Even this morning while I was shaving. I'm calmly getting ready for work, and you start in on me about the toothpaste. By the time I leave the house, the toothpaste has become an unsatisfied monster. The only way for me to successfully deal with you is to leave for work."

"What, you're too much of a wimp to deal with me about the toothpaste?"

I watch in silence in the back seat as the discussion escalates into a full-blown argument. Finally, Donna cuts him to the quick with some demeaning statement about his manhood, and I see his face redden in the mirror. He's breathing hard as his anger turns to rage. Three loud, angry words come out of his mouth, a weak response to her cutting statement, and she cuts him off. "You've got an anger problem, Tazz. Take your anger to your men's group where it belongs."

Tazz gulps twice. He grips the wheel, faces forward, and races down the highway, not saying another word until we get to Stewart's.

Twig and Melinda are sitting in their car with the windows up, obviously in a heated argument. What, is Mercury retrograde or something? It's like everyone's in conflict.

I open the back door and get out to leave Tazz and Donna to boil in their inverted rage. Why do men find it so necessary to shut down or get angry at every turn? Either way, they close themselves off to the possibilities of working things out.

I walk across the driveway, feeling lighter with every step. I knock on the front door and wait for Stewart.

When Renee opens the door, I'm surprised. "Renee, you're home."

She swings the door wide and steps aside for me to enter. "Got home a few hours ago." She looks out at the two cars. "Is everyone having a hard day?"

"Looks like it." In a whisper, I ask, "I heard that Nick was staying with you."

Renee turns to me with an odd look. "He's on the lower deck."

"Good, because I really don't want to talk to him without everyone around."

"You've got something to say to him?"

I smile and walk with her into the kitchen. "If you only knew."

A small blonde sits on the barstool with a glass of something tipped to her lips. She finishes her sip and puts the glass down.

Renee introduces us. "Carolyn, this is Katherine."

I step over to her and hold out my hand. "Pleased to meet you."

"Katherine and I spent the last month together in the desert."

"Really?" I say. "We were wondering where you were."

Renee looks at Katherine, then says something odd. "Us, too."

The blonde lets out a husky laugh.

***

It's five o'clock and my workday is finished. Today was particularly hard because there wasn't a whole lot to do and time moved slow as molasses. When Renee called and told me she was home, time dragged even more. What's it been since she left, maybe a month?

The kids and I worked out all the kinks in a few days, but I missed her after the first week, especially because she didn't call even once.

I shut down my computer and say good night to Sylvia, change into my leathers, then race for the back door and Blue. When I start the engine and hear the deep-throated sound of my two cylinders, all the boring hours behind my desk, the stupid telephone calls I was forced to field, the petty inner-office dramas, float away into the clear desert sky.

I kick the bike into gear, let the clutch out, and bullet for the front gate, past Ted, the new security guard, and out onto the street. As I drive through town, I'm forced to keep my speed at twenty-five, but the second I turn onto the open highway headed for Victorville, I crank her up and feel the wind go from a gentle breeze to a howling gale whipping past my face and ears, pushing me back on my seat, cooling my overheated office mentality. I'm in Harley heaven.

I bank deep into each turn feeling the bike bite the pavement.

Too quickly, I'm forced to slow as I enter the speed zone of Victorville. I cruise through town in thundering motorcycle bliss.

Another Harley pulls beside me at the junction and turns right with me as the light changes. Although I don't know him, the rider looks as though he also just got out of some office and escaped his workday. His trim goatee reminds me of Bob, but that's where the similarities stop. He's big and overweight. He and I ride in tandem for three miles through town, stopping at two lights, never saying a word, but feeling the two engines harmonize.

When he turns onto a small road at the last stoplight in town, we both wave, and I crank up my engine, reaching seventy in a few seconds. I feel free and unencumbered again.

The next twenty miles to my turnoff is eventless. It's the most boring part of my ride, because the road is straight as an arrow. Once I turn right and climb the familiar twists and turns of the hill, I have something interesting to do with my bike.

When I pull into my driveway, Nick's car sits off to one side in the shade. I'm anticipating my reunion with Renee. There is her bike, a little road weary with muddy tires, sitting in the garage. A big Yamaha sits next to it. I pull close to hers, shut down my engine, glance at the two bikes, and dismount Blue. I pat the tank as I do each time I leave my favorite pastime and give Blue a small salutation, then walk into the house through the garage door. "Renee," I say in a loud voice, excited to see her. I get no answer.

I step into the kitchen and grab a beer from the fridge and notice, leaning against the fireplace, a huge, dark painting of a jungle scene with three soldiers sitting on the forward deck of a steel ship. I walk to the big bay windows overlooking the lower decks and the swimming pool.

Renee waves to me from the lounge chair at the pool. A blonde woman sits next to her in a two-piece swim suit that looks like she painted on her body.

I make myself a quick baloney sandwich with a plate of chips and walk down the two flights of deck stairs to pool level, then the thirty paces across the deck to my wayward wife.

"Hi, Honey," she says, not even lifting forward from her reclined position to meet me.

Although I'm a bit put off, I swing with the punches. I put down my beer and plate on the round metal and glass picnic table we bought when we moved in.

Renee points at the woman. "This is Katherine."

The blonde rises, meets my outstretched hand, and shakes it with a vise-like grip. "I've heard so much about you, Stewart."

"I hope it wasn't all bad," I say in my standard greeting.

"Quite the contrary; this woman couldn't stop talking about you the whole time we were together."

I look at Renee. She shades the afternoon sun from her eyes with one hand.

"I'm happy to hear that," I say as I lean down to give her a kiss, but she turns and I'm left pecking her cheek. She's always a little distant after we've been apart. I'm used to it. "I'm glad the two of you made it home safe. Did you have a good time?"

Renee says, "Good time isn't exactly what I would call it, but it was pretty amazing."

I sit on one of the metal chairs at the table and grab my sandwich while Renee hits a few highlights of her journey, though I feel like she's not telling me the important part. She talks about Joshua Tree and the synchronicity of meeting Katherine and spending the first night in the park campground.

"Where did the painting come from?" I ask when there is a short lull in the monologue.

"Stewart Chance," she says with an aggravated tone. "It's part of the whole story. You're just going to have to wait until I get there."

I'm curious as hell as to how she was able to get that canvas on the back of her bike, but it's her story, so I take another bite of sandwich, munch on a few chips, and a draw from my beer before I ask again.

"One story at a time," she says with a prune face. "Don't you want to know what happened in sequence? It's such a great story."

"I just need to know how it got here. You couldn't have carried it on your bike."

"UPS, silly. It arrived this afternoon."

"Oh," I say and take another bite of sandwich. I wave my hand as I chew the bite, bidding her to continue. Renee launches into the strangest tale I've ever heard. By the time she gets to the part about meeting Billy Black on the houseboat, the sun has eased over the backside of the mountain and the temperature drops enough for Renee to pause the story as we go inside so Katherine can put on some warm clothes.

"Where's Nick?" I ask as we step into the dining room. Katherine goes to the second guest room to change.

Renee sits on a barstool. "Oh, he's sulking up in his room."

"Sulking?"

"You know what I mean."

I don't exactly know what she means, but I'm not that interested. I step over to her and try to put my arms around her to give her a proper greeting, but she slips from my grip and puts her hands up in a halt gesture. "You know I have a hard time reconnecting once I've been gone a while. Just give me some time."

"I missed you," I say as I hear the front door open and slam. I know only two people who could possibly slam doors as hard as that, and only one person could stomp across the foyer with such determination. I say, "Mel?"

"Yeah, Dad?" he says from the other room.

"Your mom's back."

"No kidding."

"You want to come in and say hello?"

"In a minute, Dad. Hi, Mom."

Renee looks at me, then responds with a raised voice, "Hi, Mel."

"I'll be there in a second."

Her face has a deeply hurt expression.

"Teenagers," I whisper.

"Where do you think he gets it?" she asks as she grabs the jar of rice from the counter and measures out two cups.

I know exactly where he gets his ability to distance, but I say nothing.

She grabs a pan and pours in four cups of water, turns the fire on and positions the pan over the flame.

The Painting

With nothing else to say, I ask, "What's for dinner?"

She turns to me, puts one hand on her hip, and says, "I don't know. What were you going to cook if I hadn't gotten home?"

"Hotdogs with macaroni and cheese."

She looks at me with a glare. "Is that what you've been feeding my children the whole time I've been gone?"

"No," I say. "Sometimes we go out."

"Stewart Chance," she says with a particular bent in her voice I know so well. It's the sound that kept me in line for all those years. It's the one that pisses me off to no end. It's the same tone that my mother used with my dad and me. I hate that voice, but I don't know what to do with it, so I do what I usually do; shut up and act like it's water off a duck's back, but I'm pissed.

Mel comes into the room to save the day. "Hi, Mom," he says as he opens the fridge.

"Hi, Kiddo," Renee says to his back. She still has a hurt expression on her face.

He grabs some bread, peanut butter, and a jar of blueberry jam and walks the load over to the kitchen table. He sets it down and says, "Hey, where did you get the picture?"

The peanut butter gets slathered on the bread as he looks at the painting. I'm also interested in the answer, so I say nothing.

"Dinner will be in an hour," Renee says, "So don't fill up on peanut butter."

"Sure, Mom." Mel takes his first bite and a squish of jelly drools out from the far edge of the bread and plops on the table. He stretches out one finger, swipes most of the blue glop up and puts it in his mouth.

"Mel, how many times have I told you not to—"

345

Channeling Biker Bob 3

"Oh, come on, Mom, what's the big deal. It ain't like I'm licking it off the floor."

Renee turns to me. "Is this how things have been while I've been gone?"

Her last sentence sends me over. "This is exactly how things have been since you left last month," I say with my voice raised a single decibel. "You want things to go different, then you stick around to oversee every move each of us makes."

"Don't you yell at me, Stewart Chance."

Katherine leaves the room.

"I'll yell at whoever I damn well please." Although I wasn't expecting it to, my voice raises another notch. It feels good. In fact, it feels great.

My son grabs his sandwich and heads for the living room, but Renee cuts him off at the door, pointing toward the back deck. "You know you're not allowed on the carpet with food. Go out on the deck."

He turns on his heels and bolts for the sliding glass door.

Renee rotates back to me with her disgusted glare. "Don't you ever speak to me like that in front of our kids."

I'm outside of my normal placating mode and I say in a softer tone, but with lots of force, "Fuck off, Renee." Oh, that feels extra good.

She lifts one hand to her right hip and cocks her shoulder like she does during high-stress times. "Stewart Chance, what the hell has gotten into you?"

I scream, "How about you taking off and never calling until two days ago? How about you coming home and immediately trying to lord your control over me and my son. How about just the fact that you are standing here

346

The Painting

with that look on your face." I stop, because I can't think of another thing to say, but I say just for effect, "You want me to go on?"

Renee raises both hands and drops them, like a road construction guy who wants you to slow down. Her face is red, like she's ready to rain all over me and anyone else who walks in her path, but she says in a whisper, "Calm down, Stewart. There's no reason to get abusive."

"Abusive," I say quieter, but with a sneer. "Abusive? Why you controlling bitch!"

She turns, runs from the room, and in a moment she's back with the fucking talking stick in her hand.

"You're scaring me, Stewart," she says as she waves the stick in front of my face.

I put my arms out and shrug, indicating that I don't give a shit. She has the stick, and I'm bound to not say a word.

She speaks in a quiet, composed, I'm-so-much-better-than-you tone. "You have no right to get abusive with me." She continues speaking for at least five minutes, but I hardly hear a word.

In the end when she puts the stick down, I grab it, but the juice that I felt minutes ago is dissipated and I speak in a rational tone. "I wasn't out of control. I knew exactly what I was doing, and if you want to talk about being abusive, let's have a conversation about how you talk to me at times."

"But Stewart—"

I raise the stick in anger and shake it at her. "You always want me to honor the stick agreement, but do I ever get to finish even one thought without being interrupted? Remember, Renee," and I put such a sarcastic tone on her name that it surprises even me, "this stick is for someone

347

else's benefit other than you."

Her face goes dark, but she shuts up. Unfortunately, with the dinky distraction of her interruption, I can't remember where I was going. I stand with my eyes looking up and to the right, trying to remember where I was, but it's gone. I don't know if she does it on purpose, or if it is a female intuitive ability to distract at the very moment that we men want to make our point. She does it with so much finesse that I'm left looking like an idiot.

Where's Bob when I need him?

Mel comes back in and looks at both of us; me with my stick held high in the air and Renee with her darkened face. Another unwritten female rule. Whenever someone comes into the room while we are arguing, then the argument is over, and we go back to being normal. God, I hate this one the most, but I shut up, turn away from her, drop the stick on the counter, walk into the living room, climb the stairs, and turn left into my den. It's the only place in the entire house, with all its rooms, that I can call my own. It's the only place where I can put whatever pictures I want on the walls without my so-called design-conscious wife intervening and telling me how little taste I have. It's the only place she can't enter without my expressed permission, though I know she violates that agreement whenever she wants while I'm at work.

I'm pissed about a lot of things, but I'll be damned if I can remember why I was pissed in the first place.

I sit on my favorite leather recliner sideways and leave one leg hanging over the arm. It's the one chair that wasn't allowed in the living room because it didn't match the walls or the carpet. Hey, fuck the walls and carpet. It's my house, too. When do I get to have some say in what goes where and what matches what?

In a few minutes, I've calmed enough to return to the kitchen, but the never-ending flow of letters catch my eye. I reach for the first in a stack of twenty or so that have shown up in the last week. Bob still answers them, but not so often as when the letters came in bags every day. It always calms me to read them and realize how universal the human condition is, especially in relationship with the opposite sex.

I look at the block script in dark felt-tip pen. The return address is Momence, Illinois. I open the letter. Inside, in the same careful hand printing, the letter says,

Bob/Stewart:

I'm writing this letter because I have no one else to speak to. People in my community tend to talk more about the weather and crops than concerns of the heart.

My wife of fifteen years, though I love her very much, complains that I do not show her my emotion, and when I do, the only emotion I come up with is anger. I've tried to tone down the grumpiness over the years, but as I get older, my rage raises its ugly head more often than ever. I wish there were some way I could be nicer to her more of the time, but the fact is that there are things that she does that irritate me, and the biggest of the lot is she is cranky to me whenever she feels like it, but just let one or two negative words come from my mouth in even a slightly raised voice, and she's not willing to listen. She forces me outside with my anger, even in the cold of winter.

I love my wife very much, but things are becoming intolerable.

Any ideas?

Thanks for your time.
Samuel Walker

I read the letter four times and each time it sinks in that, as usual, I'm suffering the same problem with Renee. She never lets me get angry. I set the letter aside and put a thick felt-tip line across the envelope to mark the letter, because I really want to see how Bob is going to answer him. I feel luckier than this guy, because I've got my men to go to once a week. They understand me.

I'm sitting askew in my leather chair contemplating my situation, calming down, when a knock comes at the door.

Maybe Renee has come to apologize. Fat chance, but I give her the benefit of the doubt and speak over my shoulder, "Come in."

The squeak of the door hinge makes me turn my head. I have yet to oil the hinge, and we have been here three or four months.

"Hey, Nick, what the fuck?"

"Just checking up on you, man." He points down toward the kitchen. "You did good down there holding your own with your wife."

"You liked my performance? Too bad I can never follow through and get really angry."

Nick steps into the room, backs up to my desk, and leans his butt on the edge. He crosses his arms in a typical Nick way and looks at me. "I don't think women can handle our anger."

"You certainly got that right." I turn toward him, drop my one leg into the seat of the chair and push the back to a half recline. "Renee is getting used to me standing up to her, but heaven forbid that I raise my voice one bit. All along, I thought it was me that was afraid to get angry, but the reality of it is that she doesn't want to see my anger."

"Hey, man, it's just the way it goes. It's what the men's group is all about."

I smile and nod. "Now that you're back, are you going to come to the Thursday nights around the campfire?"

"I don't know how long I'm back for, but every Thursday I'm here, I'll definitely be there. It's the one thing I miss in San Francisco."

We sit in comfortable male silence for a minute, then I ask, "You heard anything more about Carolyn?"

"All I heard is she's going to be here tonight. There's a big part of me that doesn't want to stick around. I'm almost sure she's dumping my ass, and I'm not so sure I want to be humiliated in front of all of those people."

"Hell, Nick, these aren't just people. They're your people. What better place to be dumped, then where you've got lots of support?"

"Maybe, but you watch, the women will side with her about what a jerk I am, and I'm so much on edge these days I might blow in front of her and them, proving once again just how much of a jerk I am after all."

"Look, you're no jerk in my eyes, and I know at least three other men who will be here tonight who feel the same way. If the shit hits the fan, hey, we'll be there for you, and I'll personally not allow those women to gang up on you."

"Really?"

I look at him and see that he's serious. Here's a guy who could whip most of the men in this county and he's really frightened of those women. "What is it?" I say. "Why do women scare us so much?"

Nick picks up one of Bob's letters and studies it absently. Without looking at me, he says, "I don't know, but maybe we were frightened as little boys by our mothers or our friends' mothers, or women teachers, and it stuck with us."

I smile. "You may have a point there, man. You just may have a point."

"Hey, Dad," Mel says as he bursts into the room, interrupting the moment.

"What's up, Mel?"

"Since I have to be out of the house tonight for your meeting, can I take my dirt bike over to Tom's now and have dinner at his house?"

"What'd your mom say?"

"I haven't asked her yet. I wanted to check with you first."

"Hey, it's okay with me, but now that she's home maybe she wants us to have a meal together."

"Oh, Dad."

I point downstairs toward the kitchen. "Check it out with her."

He turns, slams the door, sprints along the hall, then bounds down the stairs, shaking the house as he goes.

Nick looks at me with an embarrassed expression.

"What?" I say.

"Nothing." Nick stands to leave the room.

"Come on, Nick. I know when something is up with you, and that expression tells me something is definitely up. Spill it."

I'm expecting him to say something like I have a booger hanging from my nose or my breath stinks, but I'm glad I'm sitting, because what he says floors me.

"Your kid is smoking pot."

The Painting

"What?" I almost scream.

Nick stands with an awkward expression.

"How do you know?"

"Look, Stew, I smoked for fifteen years, since I was sixteen. I know what it looks like to be stoned, and your kid is stoned."

As Nick's last word comes out of his mouth, I hear the front door slam, and a second later the dirt bike starts up.

I look at Nick. "You're certain?"

"Without a doubt. He's covering it well with Murine, to keep the red eyes from showing, but I would bet ten tune-ups that he's whacked."

"Holy shit," I say. "What the hell do I do now?"

"You're probably not going to be able to find anything in his room, and you would piss him off tossing his room trying, but I'll bet you a dime to a dollar that you'll find a Murine bottle in his trash or in a desk drawer. It's a clear sign."

I push the chair into the up position and stand. "We'll just have to see about this." I leave the room with Nick in my wake.

I open the door of Mel's room and wade through strewn clothes, dirt bike magazines, school books, and scattered papers. I open the center drawer of his desk. In the middle of the slot deemed for pencils and pens, I pick up a small bottle of Visine. In the tag line, it says, "Gets the red out."

"Holy shit," I say and start to put the bottle in my pocket.

"Don't do it," Nick says.

"What?"

"Take the bottle. You have an opportunity to work

353

with him here. If you violate his space even a little, you will only succeed in pushing him away."

"How do you know all of this?" I ask.

Nick smiles. "Remember, I started when I was sixteen and still living with my dad. His tyrannical attempt to root out my every nook and cranny was the very thing that caused me to move out. You're not ready to lose your kid just yet, are you? I mean, he's going to be gone soon enough anyhow. How old is he?"

"Thirteen," is all I can say, because my head is reeling. I'm trying to figure out ways that I'm going to break the news to Renee and how she's going to blame me for it, because I was supposed to be keeping an eye on the kids while she was gone. I'm in deep shit.

I put the bottle back where it was and carefully close the drawer. "Okay, then I guess we'd better get out of here."

"Good move, Stew."

"But what do I do?"

Nick leads me out of Mel's disaster of a room. "If he's already smoking, he isn't going to want to stop. All you can do is help him regulate it a little so he can still mature and get through school with passable grades."

"Passable grades? The kid is barely passing now. Ever since puberty kicked in, he can't concentrate."

We walk to my den, and I drop back into my favorite chair. I point Nick to the small couch across from me.

"Maybe I'll say something to him tomorrow after school," Nick says. "It's not going to do much good, because he's already enamored by the smoke, but it will plant a seed he might use later, when smoking starts getting in his way."

I feel someone bounding up the stairs, and the way

he's taking two at a time, I know it's Mel. I turn to Nick. "Maybe your opportunity is now. I'll leave the room if you want."

Mel bursts into the room. Nick nods at me.

"Hey, Nick," Mel says without even glancing in my direction. "My bike took a dump about halfway up the street. Can you have a look at it?"

"No problem, Kid," Nick says as he gets off the couch and follows Mel back down the stairs. The front door doesn't slam, so I know Nick was the last one out.

I pick up the envelope from Samuel Walker, remove the letter, unfold it, and study the careful script once again.

Nineteen

Mel

I follow Stew's kid downstairs and out the front door.
The little yellow Yamaha sits on its kickstand in the
gravel slightly beyond the paved walkway. Dirt and mud
are caked under the front and back wheel fenders and
around the spokes of each rim.

"I don't know what happened," Mel says. "It was
running fine, then it sputtered three times and died."

I approach the bike and get down on my haunches,
eyeing the engine. "Was the sputter more like a quick
cough, or was it an extended engine losing power, then
catching back again?"

Mel hunkers down next to me. "More like a few
seconds of loss of power, then it would run fine for a
moment, then longer loss of power each time it sputtered.
Finally it died."

I know exactly what it is, but if I find the problem too
quickly, he and I won't have a chance to have our little
talk, so I stall by asking, "You got a spark plug wrench?"

"Yeah, sure," he says. "My dad has a bunch of tools."

He sprints toward the garage without another word.

"Get me a Phillips and slot screwdriver and a ten millimeter wrench, too, if you have them."

He's in the garage by the time I've finished my sentence and yells, "Gotcha."

I hear some rustling in a tool box, then he rushes back with a handful of tools.

He holds them out to me, and I take them. "Maybe get something for me to sit on," I say.

"What do you mean?"

"Something low like a milk crate or a wooden box, so I don't fuck up my knees in the gravel."

He turns and runs back to the garage, then yells, "How about a cat box?"

I'm thinking some kind of cardboard thing, so I say, "As long as it supports my weight."

He peeks around Stew's car and holds up a foot-tall, round, fully carpeted canister with an eight-inch hole on one side.

"That'll do," I say and he runs it over.

I drop it on the ground under me, sit, then assemble the spark plug socket and ratchet wrench. Mel leans in close and watches as I take the spark plug wire between my fingers and twist it. "You got to break the seal before you start yanking on the wire or you'll damage the filaments in the wire."

"How come it's sealed?"

"The heat from the engine kinda melts the plastic cable cover onto the spark plug. Some of them were designed that way to keep the water out."

"Oh," he says.

I pull the wire and slip the wrench over the spark plug, then tug on the handle and break the seal of the plug against the head. As I'm unscrewing the plug, he asks, "How do you know which way the thing turns to get it off?

I say, "With bolts all you got to remember is righty tighty, lefty loosey."

He laughs. "No shit?"

"Simple as that. There are times when bolts have left hand threads, but that's very rare."

I get the plug out and bring it up close between our faces. "Look at the firing surface of the plug. If it's a nice brown color and dry like you see here, the plug is doing its job. If it was black and sooty, there would be too much gas, and if it was wet with gas, you'd know the plug wasn't firing at all."

Mel takes the plug and looks close. "Hey, you can tell all that from this little spark plug?"

"It's the heartbeat of the engine. Fouled plugs are usually the problem with small engines that haven't been started for a while."

He hands the plug to me, but I don't take it. "You can put it back in. Use your fingers first to get the threads to start correctly."

He returns it to its position on the head and turns the wrong way.

"Remember," I say, "righty tighty,"

He finishes, "Lefty loosy," and turns the opposite direction.

As the plug is threading back into the head, I spring it on him.

"You smoking a little these days?"

He continues like I didn't say anything.

"Hey, man, I smoked fifteen years solid. I know when someone's stoned. It ain't no big deal to me."

He grabs the wrench and puts it on the spark plug then starts ratcheting, but it's going the wrong way.

"Flip this little lever to get it to tighten." I point at the back of the wrench.

He flips it and starts tightening. "You won't tell my parents?"

"I think they already know, but I'll soften the blow by calming them down as much as I can. You're going to get some kind of lecture in the next few days. All I can do is help shorten that lecture by fielding a bunch of the questions before they get to you."

"That's fair," he says.

"You got to listen to my lecture, though. It'll be short, I promise."

He doesn't say anything, but finishes reinstalling the plug, then cranks on the wrench.

"Spark plugs stay pretty loose," I say. "You want to tweak the plug instead of cranking on it."

He lets up and pulls slightly on the handle of the wrench.

"Here's a trick. Grab the wrench with one hand at the ratchet head. Crank as hard as you can with one hand, and it should be just right."

"How did you learn all of this shit?" Mel asks.

"I been working on bikes since I was your age, when I did a lot of dirtin' in New Mexico. Hey, if you got a dirt bike, you got to learn or forever put out cash to get the damn thing fixed."

"This one's been pretty good."

"These days bikes are much better, but when I was a kid, man, those things broke down at every turn."

He replaces the spark plug wire and looks at me.

"Okay," I say, "We've got a plug with a nice brown

Mel

color and it's dry. What's that tell you?"

Mel thinks for a moment, then says, "No gas?"

"You got it. Now, first thing we do is check the source of the gas."

"I checked the tank yesterday. It's full."

"Maybe so, but maybe something happened since yesterday. Let's check it now."

Mel unscrews the cap, and I launch into my speech. I've never done this before, so I have a bit of a rough start.

"Pot smoking is a hell of a good time, right?"

He's silent as he looks in the tank and shakes the bike a little. "It's got gas." He replaces the cap.

"You don't need to answer that question, because both you and I know how much fun it is. Hey, give me a joint and put me on a mound of dog shit, and I'm having a great time, right?"

Mel snickers.

"Let's work our way down from the tank to the carburetor." I lean down and point at the fuel line. Mel follows the line with his finger until he comes to what I already know is the culprit.

"What's that?" he asks.

"Fuel filter."

"What the hell's a fuel filter for?"

"There's all kinds of shit in gas, and you don't want that crap to end up in your carb, so the job is to filter it before it gets there."

He nods.

"Turn the petcock off first, then see these two clamps? You have to loosen them before you take the filter out to check it." I hand him the screwdriver, then continue my lecture. "Smoking pot is so much fun that I ended up smoking it all day every day for fifteen years."

"No kidding," Mel says, "How could you afford it?"

"It's one of the reasons I worked on other people's bikes. At first I would trade for bags of weed, but later I just charged a lot of money and bought my own."

He looks at me. "Tom came up with a coupla joints a few days ago. We're almost out."

"Now, pull the clamps back on the lines and tighten them so they hold onto the line and you won't lose them. It's no big deal right here, because I'm sure your dad has extras, but it's a good habit for when you're out in the wild. Hey, lose a clamp and you might have to walk your bike home, and that ain't no fun, stoned or not."

He slides the clamps back one at a time and snugs them, then looks at me.

"Shut your gas petcock off and go get a rag. There's going to be a little gas, and you don't want to get it on you. The shit stinks and it's hard to get off."

Mel stands, runs for the garage, and returns in a moment with two shop towels.

"Hold the rag to protect your hands, and crack the line by twisting it, then pull it away from the filter."

As he's struggling with the line, I say, "The biggest problem with the little smoke is, you want more. It really never ends. The more you smoke, the more you want."

"Yeah," he says, "It's just way too much fun."

"It's fun, all right, but there is a catch."

Mel looks at me. "A catch?"

The line loosens, and the filter comes free in his hand. He holds it out and looks at it. "This thing looks new."

"It looks new because the crap is on the inside. Shake all of the gas out of it first, then use the other rag and dry off the outside really good."

While he shakes the filter, I say, "The catch is that

the more you smoke, the less certain parts of your brain function. It's like the smoke blocks those parts."

As he finishes drying the filter, he holds it up.

"Try blowing through the end to see how plugged it is. There'll be a little resistance, but you should be able to blow through easily."

He lifts it to his lips.

"Point it down so any gas goes away from your lips."

He points down and blows.

"Nothing," he says, laughing. "It's totally clogged."

"There's your problem," I say. "Your dad's probably got a spare. I told him to keep extras. Let's go look."

I walk with Mel into the garage and over to the tool bench. As we dig around, I say, "You know pot smoke stays with you for a month."

"A month?" Mel says. "I stop feeling it after a few hours."

"That's the problem. The fun part is over after a few hours, but the after-effects continue for weeks."

"I never feel any after-effects."

I dig in the three wooden drawers and he roots the red, stand-up metal toolbox. I say, "It's subtle, but give it a test sometime. Watch a really sad movie while you're stoned, or even the next day, and see if you can feel the sadness."

"Why would I watch a really sad movie? Girls like those kind of movies."

"I don't know, *Saving Private Ryan* was a pretty sad movie, and I don't think it was much of a girl movie."

"Is this it?" He holds up a filter.

"That's a filter all right, but look at the difference in size. This one's for a car. We need one for a bike."

He drops it back into the drawer and continues the

search. "I never saw Private Ryan."

"Well, hell, Mel, you got to check it out. It's the ultimate war movie. A guy flick if I ever saw one. The other thing you can do is try to write something while you're stoned, you know, like a school paper or something. Try writing that same paper two weeks later not stoned all that time, then two weeks after that. Or read something that takes some thought, like with some kind of new concept or something, then read it two weeks later and two weeks after that. You'll be amazed that the further you are away from the little smoke, the more you'll be able to comprehend."

"Who cares, anyhow?"

"Right now, for you, it's the difference between being someone like your dad, who has a great job that pays for all of this," I sweep my arm around the garage and point at the house, "or someone like me who never graduated high school because I was too stoned to even attend class. Now, I ain't got a pot to piss in. I got to stay with people like your dad until I can land my next shitty-assed job with just enough pay to get a cracker-box apartment in town next to the train tracks."

"But you're Nick Brown," he says. "You're famous."

In the back of the bottom drawer I spot a filter. It looks a little banged up, but I blow into it, and it's clear. "Here's one that'll do."

"Yes," Mel says and grabs the filter. He races back to his bike and begins to install it. When I catch up with him he's tightening the hose clamps in the dark.

"Fame and fortune don't always go hand in hand," I say. "Your dad got through college with flying colors, and now, though his job isn't as glamorous as being a Harley mechanic, the dude makes enough to keep you guys comfortable. I couldn't afford to have two cats and a garage."

"My dad's famous, too."

"Ain't no doubt about that, and it's because he was clear-headed enough to go on television."

Mel tightens the last clamp. "It's because of Biker Bob."

"You check it out, did Bob choose some stoner like me? I don't think so. He chose your dad because he was clear headed enough to be present. I've got a lot of respect for your dad."

Mel stops and looks at me. "You have respect for my dad?"

"Damn straight. He's our point man."

"Point man?" he says as he drops the screwdriver, stands, and swings a leg over the bike.

"Out of all of the men in the One on One group, your dad is our navigator."

"Come on." He puts his foot on the kick pedal, leaps in the air, and drops his weight on the starter. The engine spins three or four revolutions, then comes to a halt.

"Your dad," I say before he can try again, "With his clear-headed leadership, has not only taken us One on One guys to places we would have never thought of, but since he's been on television, he's taken a large portion of the male population up one step too."

Mel kicks again, and the bike doesn't start. I know I have only a few more seconds before he figures out that he forgot to turn the gas back on, so I come in for the home pitch. "You check out those letters that he gets from all over the world. They're from men who need help. Your dad answers those men and helps them out."

Mel stops and looks at me. "You're telling me that

men from all over the world ask my dad questions and he answers them?"

I nod. "Ask to read the letters sometimes. They're pretty interesting."

He gets a confused look. "We're talking about my dad, right? Mister wimp city."

"I don't think you can say that too much these days."

"No, he's getting better. What the fuck is wrong with my bike, Nick? It's not starting."

"Let me say one last thing. Unlike me and everyone else I know, everything that's happened to your dad is because he wasn't stoned."

I reach under the tank and turn the petcock. "Before you start the bike, you have to replace the tools."

"Aw, Nick,"

I point at the garage and hand him the handful of tools.

"Shit," he says and sprints for the garage. In a moment he returns, leaps on the bike and kicks the engine to life. He smiles. "Thanks, Nick." He holds out his palm and I smack fingertips with him.

The bike digs gravel as it pulls away, then disappears into the dark.

While I'm wondering if I said the right thing, if he was even listening, the headlights of a car come down the driveway. It's Twig and Melinda, and as usual, their faces are contorted into grimaces. They're at it again.

Twig nods.

I smile, shake my head, and remember how difficult it was with Melinda. I turn and walk into the house.

In the kitchen, Renee and the new woman who doused me with water finish the last of the dinner dishes.

"How'd it go with Mel?" Renee asks.

Mel

I give her a confused smile. "One can never tell."
She dries her hands and opens the oven. "We saved
some dinner for you."

"No kidding?"

"Hell, Nick, anyone willing to go down into the pits
with a teenager deserves a good meal." She takes the plate
and some silverware over to the table, positions it next
to a patterned cloth napkin.

The new woman brings me a glass of juice and comes
in a little too close while she sets it down. I smell her, and
she smells different from how she did earlier. She smells
available. I take in a deep breath of her through my nose,
quietly, though, so no one will notice.

Equal portions of a pork chop, brown rice, and mixed
vegetables sit expertly positioned on my plate.

"It looks good." I put my napkin on my lap, grab a
fork, and take a bite. With my mouth full, I say, "Umm,
tastes good too."

"You like it?" Renee asks. "Katherine cooked dinner."

I turn and look at the woman named Katherine. I'd
almost remembered her name. "Good job."

She gives me a shy smile. It's not the kind of smile
that says I'm shy, but one that is like a cat waiting to
pounce on the mouse. Women are mysterious and often
dangerous creatures.

I ignore the smile and turn back to my food.

Renee says from behind me, "It's getting close to seven,
Nick. Everybody's going to start showing up soon."

"I know, Twig and Melinda are out in the driveway,
arguing, as usual."

"Twig?" The Katherine woman asks. "It can't be the
same Twig I'm thinking of?"

"Thomas Goreman." I say. "The guy is big as a house."

367

She smiles. "It is the same Twig. He and I were an item seven or eight years ago in a small town south of Las Vegas."

She and Renee go into a dialogue about Twig as I eat fast to give myself time to shower and change clothes before everyone shows up.

"This is pretty good," I say as the Katherine woman pours me some more juice.

"You like it?" she asks in a much deeper, sultry voice than she used earlier when everyone was around.

I look up and see that Renee has left the room, leaving us alone.

For the first time in a long time, I feel nervous. Is it that she's stalking me, or is it that I find her stalking exciting?

I finish my meal without another word, then make a beeline for my room, then the bathroom and a fast shower. I want to look fresh for Carolyn, or maybe it's to look fresh for this new woman; I'm not sure. Either way, I spiff up and come down the stairs looking sharp; hair combed, beard trimmed. I even cleaned my nails.

When I step into the kitchen, that big lug Twig stands leaning on the counter with his arms folded. He's got a grin on his face, but there is some expression in his eyes that I don't get. Is it pain?

"What's up, Twig?"

"Not much," he says in his bear voice. "What about you?"

I shrug.

"Melinda's in the other room," he whispers.

"You two at it again?"

He nods, "The woman will not let up. With her, the pressure is steady, and I've got no room to maneuver.

Mel

Having Katherine around doesn't help. How'd she get here, anyhow?"

I shrug as Bill and Paula step into the room. "Hi, everybody," Paula says in her normal irritating tone.

Twig and I respond with our usual greeting, and she heads for the living room. I hear the squeaking sound of females greeting one another as Bill rakes fingertips with the two of us. "How's it going, Twig?" he asks.

"Melinda and I are into it again and one of my old girlfriends showed up."

"Paula and I, too," he says with a sardonic grin. "What's going on? I swear everyone's having trouble today. Must be that wind that came through this afternoon."

"Hey," Twig says, "Wasn't that a howler? I had my doors open, and it about blew the bikes over."

Bucky and his girlfriend walk in, and he introduces her. "Nick Brown, this is Alice Harrison."

She reaches out a porcelain hand and gives me a typical woman handshake, just fingers, no grip. She smiles. Her dark, almost violet lipstick contrasts with pale skin, making her doll-like. "Hello, Nick Brown," she says with a soft bedroom voice. "I've heard a lot about you."

I smile. "Some of it good, I hope."

"Much of it."

I release her hand and turn to Buck. "Have you been telling lies about me again?"

"Get outa here," Buck says, as Tazz and Donna step into the room. I spin to face them. I'm instantly on edge when Carolyn rounds the corner in their wake.

Tazz says, "Nick, it's been a while." He steps over and gives me a manly two-second chest-to-chest bear hug. "What've you been up to?"

"Ah, nothing," I say glancing over his shoulder at

Carolyn. She's not looking too friendly, so I give her room, but I want to at least say hello.

When Tazz and I have finished our greeting, I turn. "Hey, Carolyn." I know better than to approach her, but I wait for a return greeting. She mumbles some vague words. Her gaze darts around the room, checking the exits, but she doesn't move.

"Good to see you again." I get no answer. I see she's uncomfortable, so I turn to Donna and give her a hug, purposely looking away from Carolyn. "How's things, Donna?" I ask when the hug is over.

"So-so," she says. "I'm just glad I'm here."

I look at her, then at Tazz who has his back to us. "What, is everyone having trouble in paradise?"

"Kinda looks like it," Buck says as he hugs Donna. "It's good to be here."

Mike Bendelson and his wife step into the kitchen, and the entire greeting thing happens again. Max and his mate come in and the room is filled with greetings and guarded laughter.

The women fade into the living room, leaving us guys with our macho strutting thing. It's a good dance though, and I missed it while I was gone.

Stew shows up, and we spend our time telling jokes and razzing one another about various situations. It's great guy time.

After ten minutes, Renee steps into the room and speaks over the noise of a half dozen men, "You guys ready for this meeting?"

Someone cracks a wise answer, we all give a respectful laugh, then file into the living room with couches and chairs positioned into a circle.

The women have claimed the most comfortable

Mel

furniture, leaving us men with kitchen chairs and plastic lawn furniture. It's just the way things go.

Once we're seated, Renee begins the proceeding by lighting the single votive candle in the bowl on the center of the coffee table. "Let this candle represent our community fire, and let the lighting of this candle bring in helpful spirits to guide us through this evening."

She couldn't have said it better. I can't put my finger on it, but there is some kind of new inner strength in Renee.

Donna stands, picks up a piece of sage, and lights it with the candle. She waits for a moment for the sage to go into flame, picks up a big turkey feather, then walks around the silent circle wafting smoke into each person's face. When she's done, she douses the sage and returns the feather to its position on the coffee table.

When Donna sits, she picks up the stick. "As a reminder for everyone here, one of our tools for the evening is the talking stick. The agreement is that whoever holds this stick is the person who is talking, with no interruptions until the person puts the stick down." She returns the stick to its cradle on the bowl, then picks up the beads. "The silence beads are a safety tool for when a person is feeling threatened and needs to be alone without leaving the circle. If any person puts these beads on, the agreement is that no one is to look at that person, talk to him or her, or ask why he or she put the beads on, even after they are removed."

She picks up one of six corks. "The corks are to remind the person holding the talking stick, without interrupting, to look inside and see if he or she is telling a story or speaking truth. A person does not have to stop talking once a cork is presented, just consider it. The more corks

371

that are presented, the more a person has to consider."

When she picks up the feather, she does so with trepidation. "The feather is for being in emotion. This tool overrides every tool but the silence beads. When a person picks up this tool, everything must stop to witness the person's emotional outburst."

The Katherine woman asks, "If I pick up the feather, everyone must listen, even if someone is holding the talking stick?"

"Yes," Donna says, "but you better damn well be in emotion. You can't just talk about emotion."

"Which emotion?"

Donna responds with a demanding finality. "Anger, rage, jealousy, sadness, joy, any emotion, but not the story around the emotion, just expressing the feeling."

"Oh." She drops back into her comfortable position on the couch next to Carolyn.

I glance at Carolyn, but get no response.

Donna speaks. "This time is set aside for a three-minute check in. Whoever feels so inclined can go first, with no interruptions or questions. It's simply a time to bring the rest of the group up to speed about your week."

I'm always nervous about this part of the evening, and going first gets it over for me so I can relax. I start off by reaching over the coffee table and picking up the talking stick. "As of twelve days ago, for the first time in fifteen years, I quit smoking pot. My nerves are still raw, so if I fly off the handle during this evening, I hope you will give me a little slack."

I reposition myself on the cheap plastic chair, then continue. "What caused me to consider quitting was Carolyn leaving." I look over at her, trying not to glare, but her eyes are averted. She's looking at her folded hands.

"I think there's an opportunity here, if you are willing. My head is clearing, and I'm thinking a lot better these days. I'd really like to give this relationship another try."

I have yet to see her raise her eyes and meet mine. I set the stick down and return to my uncomfortable little chair.

Tazz picks up the stick and complains about Donna constantly ragging on him. When he reaches his point, I look at Donna, and she's about ready to leap to her feet and scratch his eyes out, but Renee grabs her forearm. Donna glares across the room at him.

When he sets the stick down, Donna snatches it and directs every stiletto word at him.

For the next thirty minutes the stick moves around the room and a trend emerges as the stories unfold. This has not been a good week for relationships. Each and every person has some kind of complaint about their mate. It's just the way things go, sometimes.

The Katherine woman finally picks the stick up and begins her check in. "A month or so ago, I dumped my boyfriend." She studies the stick, not looking up. "For two years I tried, but the only emotion I could get out of him was anger. The guy was a perpetual nice guy until he took on too much, then he directed his frustration and rage at me."

She looks up and around the room. I'm following her eyes as she catches the attention of each female, and I see recognition in their faces.

"All I wanted was a little love and compassion, but other than sex, he never found the place in his heart to love me back, or at least show love. It was very frustrating, because when his anger boiled over, he screamed or broke things. Sometimes he hit me. Afterward, when it was over, was the only time I felt any closeness from him. The problem was that I was so frightened, I could not return his feelings. The guy was a walking time bomb, and I never knew when he was going to go off."

She looks at Renee. "The night before Renee arrived, I had a dream about her and Biker Bob. Once she drove up on her bike, I knew I was leaving, and I needed to go with her. The days that followed were more fantastic than my wildest dreams, though I still have a sneaking suspicion that when we met Billy Black, I was dreaming."

When the words, "Billy Black" cross her sexy lips, a noticeable gasp echoes in the room. I guess more people than me have met ol' Billy.

Katherine says, "I left my boyfriend because he couldn't put a cap on his anger."

She carefully puts the stick back in its cradle and returns to her seat.

Paula is our final check in. She tells similar stories about Bill only being able to find anger as his emotion of choice and how tired she is of having to witness that mono-emotional response.

When everyone has spoken, the floor is open for more in-depth study. Renee, with her new found calmness says, "I've heard two trends this evening; one, how difficult it is to be in relationship, and the second being how men can only express anger and have their other emotions locked up somewhere so their wives and girlfriends can't find them."

"That's not true," Tazz growls. He's obviously upset, and what self-respecting man wouldn't be?

"See?" Donna points an accusing finger at him. "This

is what I have to deal with each and every day. I've got a raging bull."

Renee holds up her hand.

I'm thinking Tazz wasn't raging at all. He was simply raising his voice in expressive frustration. I look around the room and see each female nod in agreement with Donna.

"Wait a damn second," I say. "You women mean to tell me that you thought Tazz was raging?"

Donna says, "Him and you, Nick. Both of you are about to go over the edge and that frightens us."

I look around and see woman agree.

"Now, let me get this straight. You're trying to tell me that because both Tazz and I raised our voice, you think we're raging?"

In that sexy deep tone, the Katherine woman says, "Not only that, but I'm never sure what will happen next."

I turn to her. "What will happen next is nothing. I blew off a little frustration, that's all." I hold up my thumb and forefinger and open a small gap. "This much is all."

Carolyn speaks up. "Well, Mister I-Never-Get-Angry, if what you expressed is just that much," she copies my hand gesture, "I don't want anything to do with you."

I whip my head back around and glare at her. "Why is it that women can rag on a guy forever, and he's supposed to support her, but a guy begins to show a little emotion, and she shuts him down with that kind of bullshit?"

The room drops into silence.

Paula finally says, "Because men are so much more frightening than women."

"I don't think that's true." Stewart speaks with an

irritated tone. "I've got a woman who's scared me to death for the last eighteen years. I—"

Renee speaks with a quiet, but commanding voice, "You chose not to show up, Stewart. It had little to do with me."

The room leaps into chaos.

The arguing back and forth rises in intensity until everyone is yelling. Donna reaches out and picks up the stick. Everyone is paying so much attention to expressing themselves to their mates that at first they don't see the stick. Donna waves it in the air for ten or fifteen seconds until the room quiets. "This room has just proven my point. We've got a bunch of angry men on our hands, and it's the only emotion they can express."

I want to scream at the bitch for setting the stage, then shutting all of us men down with that damn talking stick. I'm so enraged, I leap to my feet and yank the feather out of the sand. I have my eyes shut, so I don't see what the rest of the room is doing. All I know is my world, the one I thought was calm and collected, has ripped open and dumped a surprising amount of uncensored rage. It must be another part of coming down from marijuana, because I've never felt like this.

When my voice is ruined and my rage has had its way with me and tears come to my eyes, I drop the feather, put my hands to my face, and bawl like a baby. I drop to my knees and put my forehead on the carpet. I can't stop.

Seconds go by and I feel a soft hand on my back. I open my eyes and see Carolyn's polka-dot dress next to me. I growl in a loud voice, "Get the fuck away from me."

"Oh, come on, Nick, you'll be—"

Mel

I repeat myself, this time in a much louder scream and feel her leap to her feet and disappear. Only a woman would want to mother me at a moment like this.

I try to recapture the moment, but of course her touch and words have distracted me, and I can't get back to the emotion.

After a minute or two, I finally scream, "Damn it," and look around the room. It's curious that the men have congratulatory expressions, while the women are petrified.

When I return to my seat, sniffing and wiping my eyes, Carolyn, the uncaring bitch that she is, starts in. "What just happened proves what we were talking about, that the only emotion men can find is anger, and that's dangerous for us women."

I'm too overwrought with emotion to attempt to defend myself. I lean forward, grab the silence beads, put them on, and close my eyes. The meeting goes on, but I don't hear a word. I'm too caught up in what just happened to be able to take in any outside input.

***

Nick screams at Carolyn for no apparent reason and goes into a display of anger that stands the hair on the back of my neck. No wonder she left him. The guy is a ball of fury. I sure as hell wouldn't put up with that kind of anger from my Stewart or any man.

When he puts the beads over his head, I breathe in relief, and the meeting goes on.

Donna points at Nick, but doesn't talk to him. She says to the rest of the group, "It's that kind of display that proves to me that men have only one emotion."

377

Channeling Biker Bob 3

Tazz says in his own defense, "But look where he went afterwards. I'd say there's more inside of us men than meets the eye."

Paula speaks. "I'm not sure I want to go there, because men are so much stronger and I'd end up on the floor with a broken jaw."

"Oh, get out of here," Buck says. "Nick never hurt any woman in his life."

"There's always a first time," Paula says. "How do we know now isn't going to be that first time?"

"Because, Paula," Tazz says, "He simply needs to get the anger out first to get to his other emotions."

She scoffs. "That is so much bullshit."

Kat steps in, "Why can't we live in alignment with one another? I just want a man who wants to be in his feelings."

"Those are his feelings," Stewart says.

The front door clicks closed. It's so soft that I'm positive it's not the kids.

The room goes silent, and everyone looks toward the entry. It isn't like anyone is late. I look around the room and count heads. No one is missing.

The sound of two sets of heavy boots echoes from the foyer.

378

Twenty

They're Back

I come out of my fear stupor after that bastard Nick chided me for giving him support. One more nail in the coffin of our relationship, and now I'm definitely not going back.

I look from the carpet and directly at Renee. "Who is it?" I whisper.

She shrugs and stands as the first person walks around the corner and comes into full view. He's extremely short, built like a tank, and it looks like if he stopped lifting weights, he would immediately turn into a butterball.

As he rounds the corner and comes into full view, a tall woman with long, black hair steps in behind him. Her shoulders are strong, and she stands with a presence I've seldom seen in a woman.

Renee speaks in a frightened squeaky tone, "Cherry, what are you doing here?"

The woman and her companion walk to the circle. She says, "Is someone going to get Ed and me a seat?"

Stewart scrambles to his feet and races out the sliding

glass door, leaving it open. In a second or two, he's carrying two metal folding chairs. All of us open the circle as Stew positions the chairs between Renee and the new woman, Katherine.

"What're you doing here?" Katherine, the new woman asks. Obviously, she's flummoxed, too.

"We heard so much about this men's and women's meeting, we thought we'd join in for a night." The Cherry woman turns to Renee. "That is if you don't mind."

"No. . . no, I don't mind a bit." Renee slides her feet under herself. "I'm honored to have you."

"That's very good," Cherry says, "because I've got something to say about men and their anger."

The room, which I thought was so quiet I could hear the traffic on the highway far below, gets more silent.

Ed sits, but Cherry continues to stand tall over us. Her muscular arms bulge through her skin-tight black leather shirt. She opens her mouth and sings a short, eerie, Native American chant. "Hey, ya, ya, ya. Hey, ya, ya, ya. Hey ya, ya."

When she's finished, she looks around the room at each woman, skipping over the men. "What I have to say is directed to you women."

In a loud, demanding, almost angry voice, she says, "I hear over and over that women want their men to show emotion." She looks around the room once more, this time slowly, meeting each woman's eyes. "To feel the full range of a man's emotion, you must first witness his rage. When he feels safe enough to express that emotion without being shut down by us, or without being overridden, only then will you begin to experience his other emotions."

"What do you mean?" I ask, almost enraged myself

at the mere suggestion that men need to feel safe. "Men are the aggressive gender. What do they need to feel safe from?"

Cherry turns to me with her sharp eagle gaze. "They need to feel safe from our razor tongues."

"What?" Renee yells.

Cherry glares at Renee and says in a familiar tone of demand that I've used on men in my life. "We can't do that honey, it's not appropriate. Why are you so silly? Can't you just act civil? You have an anger problem. Don't project your anger on me." She turns to me once again. "Do any of those statements sound familiar, Carolyn?"

In a mousy voice, I say, "I've said all of those things."

She spins her body and looks at each woman. "Those judgments are but a few of the thousands of ways that we are aggressive with our men and that is what men need to feel safe from."

The bulldog, Melinda speaks with her acid tongue. "Hold on a minute, Sister. Who the fuck are you to come in here and tell us how we are supposed to act?"

Cherry turns to Melinda. "I've heard about you."

"Oh, yeah, well fuck off."

"You and Twig are the closest out of everyone here to having a truly equal relationship, that is if you don't kill each other in the process of getting there."

Melinda's voice softens and she speaks with curiosity. "What do you mean by that?"

"You don't pull the standard female manipulation. You and Twig are equal in your rage." She turns to Twig, who sits quiet like the rest of the men in the room. "With Melinda, do you feel safe to say whatever you want whenever you want without judgment?"

"Yes, well, I guess I do."

Cherry turns to Stewart. "Do you?"

Stewart blushes. After a long wait, he says, "Not really."

Renee huffs.

Cherry turns to Bill. "How about you?"

"Paula is always trying to control—"

Cherry spins on her heals and focuses on Tazz. "What about you with Donna? Do you feel safe to speak about anything?"

In a small, little boy voice, he speaks. "Not ever."

Donna gasps and almost shouts. "Ever? You bastard, you say whatever you please."

Cherry turns to Donna. "The question was does he feel safe doing it."

"Well, he sure acts like he feels safe."

"The point is not whether they're able to stand on their own or not, but do they feel safe around us. The overwhelming answer is they do not and it is mostly because we voice our judgments about them. How they act, how they talk, how they sit, how they eat. Come on, girls, maybe you can't admit it out loud, but go inside and talk to yourself and see if what I say isn't true."

I've already gone inside and it is true, every word. I've tried to control every man in my life with my judgments about him, then I resent him for it later. Isn't that why I really left Nick, because I stopped respecting him. God, I'm so embarrassed and I feel like such a bad person.

Cherry turns to me. "We are not bad because we do this to our men. We were taught by our mothers and these things, now that we are aware of them can be untaught."

She turns to Stewart. It's up to you men to help us un-teach ourselves by not giving in to our demands. You,

Mr. Stewart are getting better, but you have a long way to go. Don't let this woman push you around. It's best for you, for your daughter and Mel. Our children learn from how we act, not what we say. You want your son to act like a man, you must model manhood for him."

I ask, "How do we support men's anger? They're so frightening when they do it."

Cherry gives Ed a secret smile, then turns to Melinda. "When he gets angry, you don't attempt to match his emotion. It's his emotion, let him have it all the way through without adding in your two cents." She's speaking to Melinda, but she's talking to all of us.

Cherry turns to Donna. "Don't shame your man for his fury. He doesn't have an anger problem. Anger is his emotion and you help him express it by witnessing it all the way through to the end. Unless he's breaking the furniture up or hitting you, he doesn't need anger management, he simply needs a safe place to express it. If you love him, and I know you do, be that safe place."

She turns to Paula and points at Bill. "You want this man to share his emotion with you, back off on the micro-managing harpy bullshit. He doesn't need the harassment and you will never experience his softness if he is constantly protecting himself from your nagging.

She turns to Renee, shrugs and gives her a soft smile. "You, dear Renee, already know what you must do, correct?"

Renee blushes. "Give Stewart room to make his own decisions. I have to be in the back seat and stop taking over."

She looks at me. "Carolyn, maybe Nick isn't the one, but you're going to have to give some man a break sometime. You just can't continue to walk away from every man the minute things get a little tough."

She's right, and I'm so embarrassed.

She turns and looks at Nick. "You men must find a way to express rage without harming anything or anyone. The rage feather is a good tool. Use it with your women present to get them used to your primary emotion. This is part of the work of men and women in relationship."

Stewart speaks. "Anger isn't my primary emotion."

She glares at him. "Maybe it should be, Mr. I-never-get-angry. It's the nice guys like you that frighten me most. Bring that rage to the surface once in a while to let the steam off and we will all be much better off."

Cherry closes her eyes, draws her head back to look at the ceiling, lifts her muscular arms high in the air and goes into a chant. "Hey, ya, ya, ya. Hey, ya, ya. Hey ya, ya."

In a flash, the lights blink, then go out, leaving only the dinky candle to illuminate the room.

By the time Renee stumbles into the kitchen and lights more candles, I look around, and our two new visitors have disappeared.

"What just happened?" Stewart asks.

Katherine speaks with a shaky voice. "Last month, Cherry took Renee and I deep into the desert and gave us back something we'd lost. I think she's just given us all a second gift."

She turns to Nick. "Although what you did in the kitchen earlier frightens me to death, in the future, I commit to trying to listen."

I can't believe it, she's hitting on my man.

Twenty-one

Epilogue

This is one of those times where I know I'm dreaming, yet everything seems so real it's hard to tell. I'm riding Blue along a smooth back country road and Bob is on his wild machine next to me. There is no traffic. It's dusk. The first star of the night shines in the darkening sky. The wind blowing past me is desert hot.

We drive up a long gentle grade until we reach the summit overlooking all of creation and I pull to the side of the road. Bob slides in next to me and while turning off his engine, drops the bike on its kickstand. Except for a gentle breeze, the desert is quiet. All I can hear is the ticking of our cooling engines.

As I drop Blue on the kickstand and step off the bike, Bob sits side saddle on his seat and breaks the silence. "How's things, Stew?"

I turn to him with a worried look. "I don't know what happened to Renee in the desert, but she really has changed."

"How's that?"

"I don't know for sure, but there is something more centered about her. Her normal ever-constant nagging has stopped."

Bob smiles as he strokes his little goatee. "That's a good thing."

"It's good, Bob, but it leaves an eerie vacuum in our conversations. I keep getting the feeling that she's saving things up and one day the dam will burst and the whole load will dump at one time."

Bob stretches his arms high. "Cherry took your wife through a profound experience. I don't think there is any saving going on. She's made a fundamental change. The only real question is can you keep up?"

"Shit, Bob, it seems like I've been trying to keep up with Renee most of my life."

His smile turns to a full-toothed grin. "Stew, you got to accept the fact that most of the time women are light years ahead of us. It's in their nature to explore the edges of existence, while many of us men are content with where we are. Without prodding or some catastrophic event, we would never take even one step toward growth. It's just how we're hardwired."

"Maybe you're right."

We both stand in silence as more stars present themselves in the inky sky. A meteor bounces off the atmosphere and slowly disintegrates as it plunges toward earth.

I turn to Bob, now hardly able to see him in the darkness. I say, "What about Nick. Did that guy come out smelling like a rose, or what?"

"I'm not sure. Having two women trying to get your attention, accept for the overabundance of sex, can be a little confusing, don't you think?"

Channeling Biker Bob Heart of a Warrior
Excerpt

I have a bunch of questions, but I don't want to spoil the moment. I sit on the back of his machine as we roll off the miles. Eventually, I see something at the bottom of what might be a fifty-mile wide valley. In the center of the massive bowl a single light flickers, the only sign of life in the expanse, and we're heading directly for it.

We take a wind-whipping, twenty minutes to approach the flicker. The wind caresses me. The sound of his twin cylinders roaring into the night air lulls me. A strong smell of desert sage sharpens my senses. I'm alive!

As we approach, I've already guessed that the light is another huge fire, and probably one for me to stoke.

When Bob lets off the gas and allows his engine to slow, I see a line of Harleys. Twenty people wildly move around the blaze. Are they dancing? I have never heard of bikers dancing as a group. The closer we get, the more I'm sure who they are. Big clunky guys, little skinny ones; everyone dances around the fire.

Not until Bob shifts into third gear do I realize the fire erupts in the middle of the asphalt. As we pull up, familiar faces look our way. Bob shifts to neutral, kills his engine, and coasts the last hundred yards to a stop.

This time there is a difference in the party. The same people are here: Beer, Bucky, Tazz, Max, Shorty, and others, but they act different. As we dismount, their dancing stops. We walk over to a solemn circle of men.

I want to ask where the women are, but things start to happen, and I don't have time.

"A superb men and women relationship book in disguise. . . life in its most realistic, rawest form with no holds barred. . . a tough, no nonsense combination of *Men are from Mars and Women are from Venus* and *Iron John*."

Heartland Review

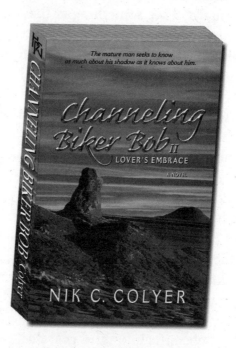

Channeling Biker Bob 2 Lover's Embrace
Second in a four part series by

Nik C. Colyer

Available through
Singing Reed Press
www.ChannelingBikerBob.com
($15.00 including tax and shipping)

Channeling Biker Bob Lover's Embrace
Excerpt

In a quick flash, one side of my hand-cuffs wrap around my thick wrist. With an effort, Tazz latches them. "Now Mr. I'm-a-Las-Vegas-police-officer, step over to the light pole, please."

"No, you wouldn't." He'll cuff me to the pole and pistol-whip me with my own gun. Now that the tables have turned, I'll be lucky to get out of this alive.

I wrap my arms around a rusted thirty-foot-tall steel pole and feel the second half of my cuffs bind around my other wrist. I prepare myself to be beaten when Tazz grabs my service revolver from Tubbo.

How many times will it take for me to learn I can't go off half-cocked and expect everything to turn out. I think of the reaming that I'll get from McKerney once I get out of the hospital. Hell, if I get out at all.

I wait for the first blow. Instead, Tazz steps in front of me. He opens the gun and drops six shells at my feet.

"I hate guns," he says and slams the pistol hard to the pavement.

The barrel digs a deep hole in the asphalt. He takes his heavy biker boot and smashes it. The open cylinder breaks away, rolls across the pavement and stops ten feet away. He continues to stomp his boot repeatedly into the body of my trashed pistol.

When he's done, he helps his little buddy to his truck and opens the door. Once Bucky is in the truck, Tazz turns to me. "We'll take Buck to the hospital now, because you ain't got a clue how to deal with your anger. Get a grip on your life, Twig and stop buggin' us."

". . . a very interesting metaphysical science fiction novel
structured around the soft science of psychology, sociology
and futurism. The plot is fast paced and shoots off in
unexpected directions."   Bob Spears 2004

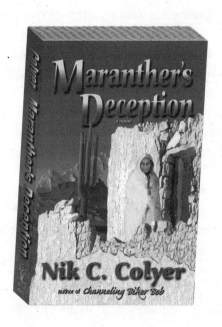

Maranther's Deception
The first in a two part series by

Nik C. Colyer

Maranther's Deception
Excerpt

When I search the other buildings, they all appear in better condition. Yesterday, only ours had passed as an enclosed shelter. The others were simply walls of crumbled adobe disintegrated from the weather; three sets of walls, each in its own stage of decomposition.

As I race between buildings to find scraps of wood I notice two with rotted, but serviceable roofs and count three more half-decomposed foundations, some with adjoining walls. Last night, three existed, but today six structures form a single line to the far end of the almost level boulder.

Blowing sand can make it hard to see. I must have missed the other adobe buildings, but it's odd; I've always had good night vision. I pass off the thought and search for a stick here, a scrap there, working my way back to our cozy bungalow.

I open the door, bend low, and pull it closed behind me. When I turn and look through the tent door, Leigha sits bolt upright in her sleeping bag. Her face is bone white.

I drop the arm load of wood and kneel. "Leigha, are you okay?"

Her colorless lips move as she tries to respond, but no sound emerges. Her terrified look runs gooseflesh up my back.

Her first sound is unintelligible, but eventually she forms the single word, "Ghost."

A SURPRISE MOON

Page 16
For the first time, in a predawn hour,
a full moon peeks through our dense forest
with only enough glow to spotlight my desk
in a ghostly brilliance.
I pick up a pen, seldom used these days,
a simple tool for the primitive moment.
Moonlight has centered on my paper,
from the one small piece of sky.
It hangs there for a fleeting moment,
allowing me to scribble these words,
to feel like a poet again,
after a long, dry spell.
The glow is so vague, I can't read the words,
only a formless knowledge
that the pen is still writing
chicken-scratch across a blank page.
Quickly, I write before the ghost light
disappears behind another branch.
Once the elusive sliver of radiance moves on,
I'm back in the blackness of my silent forest,
back to listening to deer crunch
through frostbitten autumn leaves.
Good-bye hoarfrost light, however uncertain,
and to you, poem,
who visits the poet so seldom these days.
11-99

Discussion Group Guide

1. When Renee left town, what were her intentions?
2. After she and Kat rode together, what town did they stop for lunch and what happened in the bathroom?
3. Billy Black's role with the two women was what?
4. What instantly shifted Nick's flu?
5. What is the significance of Nick making pottery?
6. How does the book title "Magician" connect to Nick.
7. When he quit smoking, what shift took place?
8. What emotion came up for him as his mind cleared?
9. What was Cherry's role?
10. What does the canyon represent for the women?
11. What hurdle did the cliff represent?
12. The Elk was what kind of animal for Renee?
13. Why the statement, "I'm choosing from now on."
14. Will Twig and Melinda ever work it out?
15. When the two women came out of the canyon, what changes took place in them?
16. Why the oil ritual between Kat and Renee?
17. How was Cherry different in Kat's eyes?
18. What happened to Ed and Cherry?
19. Why was Billy Black a painter?
20. Why was it important for Renee and Kat to connect with the ancient spirals?
21. What gift did Renee receive from Billy Black?
22. How did Nick respond to the painting and why were the women concerned?
23. If anger is a man's first emotion, what lies below?
24. If men can't express their primary emotion, can they ever get to the next level?
25. Why is this culture afraid of a man's anger?